of smokeless fire

# of smokeless fire

A.A. JAFRI

PENGUIN
VIKING

An imprint of Penguin Random House

VIKING

USA | Canada | UK | Ireland | Australia
New Zealand | India | South Africa | China

Viking is part of the Penguin Random House group of companies
whose addresses can be found at global.penguinrandomhouse.com

Published by Penguin Random House India Pvt. Ltd
7th Floor, Infinity Tower C, DLF Cyber City,
Gurgaon 122 002, Haryana, India

First published in Viking by Penguin Random House India 2021

10 9 8 7 6 5 4 3 2 1

ISBN 9780670093304

Typeset in Minion Pro by Manipal Technologies Limited, Manipal
Printed at Replika Press Pvt. Ltd, India

www.penguin.co.in

To my parents,
Athar and Tara

Part I

'He created man from dry clay like earthen vessels.
And He created the djinn of a flame of smokeless fire.'

—Qur'an

One

Djinns, the invisible beings made of smokeless fire, are Allah's creations. Human beings cannot create or beget them, but whether it was a djinn or not, a rumour took birth that day that a djinn had been born at the residence of Noor ul Haq, barrister-at-law.

Farhat Haq, the wife of barrister Noor ul Haq, almost died in labour that day. It had nothing to do with the delivery, wretched as it was, but had everything to do with that horrible midwife, Kaneez, and her piercing screams: 'Djinn, djinn! Oh Allah, he's a djinn! Take him away from me. Take him away from me; he will get inside me!'

What a thing to say after such excruciating labour and the relief of finally giving birth successfully after eleven miscarriages! True, propriety had never been Kaneez's strong suit, but a stupid outburst like that at such a critical hour was something that not even Farhat had expected from that ignorant one-eyed *churail*.

The well-established superstition is that churails are the most terrible creatures on this side of the Ganga. Born with inverted feet and an ingrained nail in their skulls, these one-eyed Medusas are believed to thrive on children's livers. Women who die in childbirth are sometimes reincarnated as churails who come back to seek revenge on other pregnant women. Everyone in Pakistan knows this even though the Qur'an doesn't mention churails.

Everyone in Pakistan also knows about djinns, the invisible beings made of smokeless fire; they exist because they are mentioned in the Qur'an. They are Allah's creation. Women can't carry them in their wombs for nine months, nor can they give birth to them. So how could Kaneez utter such nonsense with her loudspeaker-like mouth and broadcast that rubbish to the entire neighbourhood? How do you control a rumour once it leaves her blathering mouth? You can't! It grows wings and flies into every ear.

*

The malicious gossip that a hideous djinn had been born at Kashana-e-Haq, the sprawling residence of Noor ul Haq, on that fateful day in October 1951 acquired such currency that many people avoided going there for a long time. The day had begun as a scorcher, and no sooner had the sun come out from behind the eastern hills of Karachi than the city turned into a veritable tandoor, broiling everything in sight: buckling up roads, flaring tempers and wilting flowers. It was not even noon, and yet it felt like *dozakh*, or the sixth circle of Dante's hell. The chowkidar sat on a concrete bench under a neem tree just outside the front gate of the barrister's house, dozing off, his head falling forward on to his chest, jerking up now and again. The discarded front page of the *Morning Gazette* got picked up by the hot wind and caught against his leg, the picture of the first prime minister of Pakistan, with his fist raised, and his title, Leader of the Nation, prominently displayed on it. Suddenly, an ear-splitting horn from a black Hudson Commodore startled the chowkidar. He jumped up and instinctively saluted the car, as the *Gazette*'s front page peeled away from his leg, carried off by the warm breeze. From inside the vehicle, Noor ul Haq's driver, Sikander, craned his neck out and shouted at the chowkidar, 'Oye! Son of Genghis Khan, you are supposed to guard the house, not sleep.'

'Oye, Quaid-e-Azam, let a man sleep! How am I going to guard this Taj Mahal if I don't sleep well?' the chowkidar roared.

The servants shared a spirited relationship, always joking and pulling each other's leg. The guard's name was Changez Gul, but Sikander teasingly called him Genghis Khan's son. Changez returned the favour by calling Sikander Quaid-e-Azam, the Great Leader, the title given to the founder of Pakistan, Mohammad Ali Jinnah. It was not because Sikander was the founder's biggest fan or admired his politics; it was because he bore an uncanny resemblance to him. Tall, gaunt, with a triangular face and a slight gap between his front teeth that was noticeable only when he smiled broadly, Sikander could have passed for the founder's twin brother. However, that is where the similarities ended and the differences magnified. But to Changez, it was the similarities that mattered the most.

He opened the wrought-iron gate and let Sikander drive the car into the front porch. The driver had just returned home after bringing fresh naans for the luncheon that Noor had organized for his circle of intellectual friends. After closing the gate, Changez returned to his seat and twirled his thick black moustache. Then, leaning his head back against the brass nameplate set into the gatepost behind him, he closed his eyes again. The name, Kashana-e-Haq, meaning the House of Haq, or, in English, the Abode of Truth, had been carefully chosen by barrister Noor ul Haq. It was the only house on the street with a name instead of a number. No one knew if the name was a statement of sorts or if the barrister wanted to establish his aristocratic credentials in his adopted country. His house was in the Bihar Housing Society, a comparatively new and planned neighbourhood of Karachi. Uprooted from their homeland with the partition of India in 1947, the refugees brought pieces of their ancestral hearts to Karachi and built pockets of memory markers, giving them names like Delhi

Muslim Society, Hyderabad Colony, Bangalore Town, Rajputana Colony and Agra Taj Colony.

The streets of Bihar Housing Society, usually swarming with people, were deserted that morning. Most Sunday mornings were greeted by the discordant clamour of kids playing cricket in the park nearby, or the cacophony of snarled traffic and the competing calls of hustling pedlars. But that day, the heat muzzled the urban symphony; it swept away all memory of the floods of July and drove everyone away, except for a lone subzi-wallah, a vegetable hawker, who pushed his rickety cart to establish his monopoly in the neighbourhood.

Inside the Kashana, the ceiling fans recirculated hot air at full speed while the heavy silk curtains, drawn in every room, struggled to keep the house cool and dark. The mouth-watering aroma of tandoori meat, wafting out from the kitchen, was the only reminder that not everything had gone to hell. In the background, the radio blasted a hit song from a recently released Indian movie.

When the song ended, three loud beeps signalled the start of the midday news broadcast: 'This is Radio Pakistan: The news, read by Mukhbir Alam. We have just received information from our weather bureau that the temperature today has already reached a 110 degrees Fahrenheit and is expected to go up to 120 degrees later in the day. There is no relief in sight. The government has promised that it will leave no stone unturned to provide assistance to the heat-ravaged needy. In other news, the prime minister will be making an important speech today about . . .'

Barrister Noor had just finished a long, relaxing shower, but he felt like returning to the bathroom again when he heard about the temperature on the radio. He had come out into his bedroom wearing a white bathrobe, monogrammed distinctively with his initials, NUH, embroidered in navy blue, his greying chest hair visible above the robe's lapels. The room was too dark, so he turned on the bedroom light, only to be rebuked by his wife.

'Oh ho! Why did you turn on the light?' Farhat asked, still lying in bed in her nightclothes, her massive belly, her puffy face and the dark circles under her eyes all attesting to the full term of her difficult pregnancy. Letting out a loud sigh of irritation, she slowly turned over, carefully holding her lower abdomen as she did so.

Noor switched the light off and asked sheepishly, 'How are you feeling?'

There was no reply, so he asked her a different question, 'Do you want your lunch in bed?'

She snubbed him again, the silence in the bedroom shattered by the piercing call of the subzi-wallah outside: 'Very, very cheap! So many treats: potatoes, spinach, cauliflower, beets!'

'Don't you want to eat anything?' Noor persisted.

'I'll eat when I am hungry. I don't need your constant nagging.'

'I am just concerned about you, my *jaanum*, my life. You should be eating for two.'

'Leave me alone and go to your dear friends.'

'They are not here yet. Can I get you anything before I go?'

Farhat did not feel like answering such stupid questions, especially when she was so miserable. They seemed more like apologies-in-advance for the day-long neglect her husband planned to inflict on her. The mocking of the wall clock became louder as she watched Noor put on his silk kurta-pyjama.

He stooped a little to see his face in the mirrored dresser and began applying Brylcreem to his thinning salt-and-pepper hair. Then, methodically and with purpose, he combed his hair. Picking up the white bottle of Old Spice cologne, he slapped a few drops on his clean-shaven face and looked at himself in the mirror again. As he leaned towards the mirror, he noticed the bluish bump on the left side of his head—a mortifying reminder of the fall he had had at the Sindh Club two nights ago. It still hurt a little when he touched it. The memory, although a bit blurry, shamed him. He had drunk way too much that night, but then it was hard to resist a single malt Scotch whisky, especially when it was Balvenie and paid for by a client. Rumour had it that the founder of Pakistan used to drink the same expensive Scotch daily. The thought brought a proud smile to his face; he was in good company.

When he had tripped and fallen at the Sindh Club that night, it was his ever-so-loyal driver, Sikander, who had brought him home and helped him to bed. Farhat did not even want to be anywhere near him. A drunken Noor always became untouchable to her. She had left him all alone in their bedroom and moved to the zenana, the women's quarters, for the night. Ashamed and penitent, Noor had promised her the next day that he would never come home drunk again, but most promises are made to be broken, and deep down in his heart, he knew that.

That Sunday in October, Noor had invited his friends for some tandoori venison and a bottle of Johnnie Walker Black Label. The same industrialist client who had treated him to Balvenie at the Sindh Club had sent him another gift: a haunch of venison. Wild game meat, Johnnie Walker, and cerebral *gupshup*, or bullshit, with his intellectual friends were what Noor lived for. It gave him some respite from the tedium of droning on and on about corporate tax laws with his wealthy clients; it also provided him with an opportunity to lash out against the religious direction that Pakistan had started to take of late.

To Farhat, however, alcohol, deer meat and irreligious conversations were all satanic pleasures, and Noor's friends were, in her words, 'the Shaitan or the devil's comrades-in-arms'; she hated them with the same vengeance with which she hated his whisky breath. It repelled her whenever Noor tried to kiss or hug her after coming home drunk. Even a hint of that dreadful abomination would force her to rinse her mouth and perform the ritual ablution to purify herself again since alcohol was strictly forbidden in Islam. To Noor, however, these satanic pleasures were the best gifts that the British had given to their former subjects, not to mention their empiricism. He could fulminate against British colonialism and compliment them on their rationality in the same whisky breath. To him, religion and rationality did not go together. And so, as religion began to permeate the public sphere in Pakistan, Noor's hostility towards the country increased exponentially and whisky became his nightly ritual, his closing argument.

'I have asked Sikander to bring Sarwat over, to give you company...while my friends are here,' Noor offered apologetically.

Indignant, Farhat turned around and snapped at him tearfully, 'Should I thank you for arranging to have my sister over? Or should I thank you for being busy with your friends?'

Entertaining his friends was nothing new for Noor, but Farhat wished he would spend more time with her, especially during these last days of her pregnancy. According to her, the more care and attention she needed, the more insensitive he became.

'Sikander will be here all day, in case you need to call Dr Minwalla,' he said.

'For God's sake, just leave the room,' Farhat snapped.

Her tough pregnancy had given her the licence to mock him, to rebuke him and to kick him out of the room. Never before had she spoken to Noor in that tone.

'I promise that I'll keep the party under control this time.'

Noor was acutely aware that things would not stay under control once his friends arrived and the bottle of Johnnie Walker was opened, but he blamed his drinking on the stress of his 'rotten profession' and the agony of living in what he called an 'obscurantist country'. The partition of India and the consequent creation of Pakistan in 1947 had driven him out of his birthplace in India and turned him into a forced refugee and a reluctant exile. He had repeatedly declared to his wife that 'this mullah-land' was withering his soul, to which his wife would always reply, 'Those who don't have a soul can't complain about its withering.'

He remembered the last time his friends had come over to his house. Their discussions began with the sublimity and the scepticism in Mirza Ghalib's poetry and soon degenerated into jokes about the erotica in Wahi Wahanvi's writings. All his friends got so drunk that they passed out after dinner and spent the whole night at the Kashana. Farhat was so cross with him the next day that she gave him the silent treatment for three full days. To remain angry for more than three days was forbidden by Allah; it would make her a partner in sin, and of course, she did not want that. Three days of living with a taciturn wife would have typically been a welcome relief for Noor, but he couldn't take that chance now, not when he was so worried. Farhat's eleven failed pregnancies had left him hollow inside. This time around, Noor was particularly concerned. He had this haunting feeling that something was going to go wrong again. For a man who prided himself on his rationalism, these creeping absurdities were puzzling.

'Inshallah, soon we'll have a child, a healthy child,' he said, emphasizing the word 'inshallah' for her benefit.

Darting out of the bedroom, he wistfully stole one last glance at Farhat. This pregnancy had drained her spirit the most. Seeing her like this, he began regretting the invitation to his friends so close to her delivery date. But then the venison had to be eaten and the whisky had to be drunk. From the hallway, Noor called his servant, Budhoo, and instructed him to bring his friends to the mardana, the men's quarters, as soon as they arrived.

'And listen, Budhoo . . . bring me my cup of tea,' he ordered.

He ambled to his study to look for the wooden plaques that he had recently got custom-made for his friends as an inside joke. He remembered that he had put them in one of the drawers in his mahogany desk. He opened the drawer and found the four plaques with the inscription 'The Unholy Quartet' inside. This should make them chuckle, he thought, smiling. Thinking about irreverent titles had become a pastime for him. As he lifted the plaques out, he noticed at the bottom of the drawer a copy of the short-lived literary magazine that he used to edit back in India, *Taraqqi Pasand Aadmi, The Progressive Man.*

Life had not turned out for Noor as he had thought it would. In an ideal world, he would have been a scholar of either comparative literature or philosophy, who could move seamlessly from Ghalib to Milton and from Spinoza to Ibn Rushd. He kept Ghalib's book of poetry on his bedside table, imagining that someday he would write a bold reinterpretation of the master's poetry for an open-minded audience. But while he could fascinate his uninitiated friends with the originality and freshness of Ghalib, to write about poetry had become challenging. The only things he could write about with any fluency now were his legal briefs. The trauma of the forced migration from India during Partition and the manic urgency to succeed financially in a country he still considered foreign had deeply affected his psyche.

He picked up the plaques and went to the elegantly furnished mardana, which was almost dark except for that single rarefied beam of sunlight piercing through a slight opening in the middle of the curtains, highlighting the dust motes swirling in the air. The table, set with four whisky glasses, a silver ice bucket and the big bottle of Johnnie Walker, waited anxiously for Noor's friends, or so it seemed. On one end of the table lay a copy of the latest issue of *Time* magazine. The cover page had the picture of a burly Joseph McCarthy, his bright eyes searching for secret communists.

Noor picked up the magazine, slumped into a chair and began reading about the red-baiting senator from Wisconsin. American democracy, with all its imperfections, fascinated the recusant lawyer that he was. He thought about the nascent democracy in neighbouring India, and wondered why it eluded Pakistan. His reading was interrupted by Budhoo bringing in his tea. As he began sipping it, Noor noticed the smudges of dust on the framed picture of his late father on the wall.

'Budhoo, dust the frame, it has streaks all over.'

The servant pulled the dishcloth hanging from his shoulder and began cleaning the frame. He stopped and gazed at the picture for a while before continuing again. Budhoo had come to work for

Noor's family as a young man. Nobody knew his real name. The moniker, Budhoo, which in Urdu meant simpleton, stuck to him because of his childlike manners.

Noor was still thinking about Farhat. How badly they both wanted a child, and how ruthlessly nature had denied them. Eleven failed pregnancies. Why? All his friends had heirs, all except him. He had always wanted a family, sons and daughters. Twenty-three years ago, when he was only twenty, he had been notified by his parents that his marriage had been arranged with the daughter of Javed Sultan. No one even bothered to tell him the girl's name for a long time. But none of that had mattered on his wedding day. When Noor had lifted Farhat's veil, he was dazzled by her beauty, and when she raised her green almond-shaped eyes to look up at him, it was as if the whole room had lit up. Only seventeen then, she had retained her elegance and beauty throughout their married life, despite being pregnant almost always and now middle-aged.

The ringing of the doorbell broke his reverie. He stood up and drew the curtains that separated the men's quarters from the rest of the house. A few seconds later, Budhoo brought in Haider Rizvi and Sadiq Mirza, his closest friends from college. The loud-mouthed political editor of the *Morning Gazette*, Haider Rizvi was better known for his thick, black round glasses and his penchant for using tiresome cricket terms in his editorials than for his journalistic prowess. Sadiq Mirza, on the other hand, was his outright antithesis. A professor of comparative literature at the University of Karachi, he was soft-spoken, thoughtful and good at putting things into perspective. His trademark pipe mostly remained glued to the right corner of his mouth. Noor admired his erudition.

Haider sniffed the air, almost salivating as he savoured the delicious smell of the venison, 'Scotch and venison! Now that's what I call cricket!'

'My friends, that's what you get in my raj,' Noor replied.

'It would have been perfect, except for this bloody heat,' Sadiq remarked, lighting his pipe.

After they had settled down, Noor gave them their plaques and opened the bottle of Johnnie Walker. It was only during such meetings of the literati that he took out his Scotch; for his everyday needs, he quaffed the local whisky, which he called his *shahi tharra*, his royal hooch.

'I am going to hang this in my office,' Sadiq said, admiring the plaque.

'Me too, but before I forget, I have a message for you, Noor, from our publisher, Mr Azeem Shan. He would like you to represent the *Morning Gazette*.'

'Why? Did he forget to pay his protection money to the government?' Noor asked, pouring the whisky into the glasses.

'Very funny, but no. He paid his protection money. This has to do with something else.'

'Thanks, but no thanks. Tell Azeem Shan that I can't take any more cases. My workload has increased since Burmah-Shell retained me.' Noor handed one glass to Haider and the other to Sadiq.

'Well, at least speak to him.'

'Why should I? The thirsty go to the drinking well; the well doesn't go to the thirsty.'

'But what is this case about?' Sadiq asked, puffing out smoke from his pipe.

'Remember the corruption story we ran against that bloody-fool minister? He retaliated by slapping us with a lawsuit accusing us of libel,' Haider said.

Sadiq swigged down the Scotch and said, 'So that's why your editor wants the most sought-after attorney in Pakistan to represent them.'

'Frankly speaking, I don't want to get involved in these bloody political dramas. I have had enough of them in India,' Noor said. 'The English went away, but they left their poodles behind just to piss us off.'

'Come on, Noor, you'll become famous,' Haider said, and guzzled down the whisky.

'Fame doesn't inspire me, my friend,' Noor replied.

'So, what's this speech that the Leader of the Nation is going to deliver today?' Sadiq asked, as if Haider had an advance copy of the speech. 'I have heard that it's probably about a possible rapprochement with India,' he continued.

'Or it could be just another speech giving honorific titles to vacuous sycophants,' Noor replied.

'Everyone in this country has titles stuffed right up their asses!' Haider laughed as he stood up and began refilling his whisky glass.

'Titles in this country, my friends, are like haemorrhoids; sooner or later, every asshole politician gets them,' Noor interjected. The three friends burst into laughter.

'Okay, here is a deep mathematical question for you, Professor: What are the odds that we will have a Constitution ready in time to entertain us?' Haider asked Sadiq.

Before Sadiq could reply, Noor laughed and said, 'Between zero and naught! The Assembly has been on it since 1947; how much progress has it made in these last four years, huh?'

'The hard part is drawing a fine line between the secular and the religious,' Sadiq retorted.

'Well, I think the fault lies with the Great Leader. If he had not died so soon after the Partition, we would not only have a Constitution but a secular one at that,' said Haider.

'Instead, theocracy is now entering Pakistan through the back door,' Sadiq added.

'My friends, theocracy, in this country, is going to make a grand entrance, garlanded with flowers and wearing a turban. Just wait and watch,' Noor replied.

The bell rang again, and after a moment, Zakir Hassan made his entry, liberally doused in the most expensive cologne and looking his usual dapper self. A connoisseur of the bon vivant, he had recently joined the United Nations' Food and Agriculture

Organization (FAO). Based in Rome, he was back in Karachi on official business. After embracing all his friends, he accepted a glass of Scotch from Noor, and settling down, asked, 'What is this talk about theocracy in this great land of our geniuses?'

'Nietzsche once remarked that genius is the will to be stupid,' Noor quipped as he handed him the remaining plaque.

Zakir looked at the plaque and laughed. 'May we remain an unholy quartet forever!' he said, raising his glass in a toast.

Everyone raised their glasses and said, 'Cheers!' Sadiq raised his glass again and said, 'May God bless your whisky cabinet, Noor!' The revelry had begun.

The comrades discussed politics, poetry and philosophy; they ate venison and biryani; they laughed and glugged down their liquor. Sophisticated turned into silly, and silly became sordid. The partying went on until late in the evening when it was interrupted by an excited Budhoo.

'Sahib, Sahib! Farhat Bibi is going to be a mother,' he informed Noor, panting. 'She is screaming, Sahib. Sikander has gone to fetch Dr Minwalla.'

Budhoo couldn't have said that Farhat was going to have a baby; that was not the proper way to discuss childbirth, especially when it pertained to the mistress of the house. Saying that she was going to become a mother somehow made the whole affair more sacred, adding a veneer of respectability to it. After relaying this message to his sozzled master, he left in a hurry. The air in the mardana, already filled with tobacco smoke, now thickened with a surreal silence as Noor gathered his intoxicated thoughts. He saw Haider holding his glass of whisky on his head and starting to do a slow dance. His eyes dopey, his voice heavy, he broke the stillness in the room with a silly cricket rhyme: 'Twelfth Man . . . on the pitch . . . in he comes to serve; Zero gifts and zero knack; has a lot of . . . nerve!'

In the game of cricket, the twelfth man is a reserve player whose duty is to serve drinks to the other players and to be a substitute fielder for an injured player. Haider, in trying to be funny, had really infuriated the drunken Noor.

'What . . . do you mean . . . twelfth man?' Noor demanded. 'Are you saying . . . my firstborn is a . . . a twelfth man? The server of drinks and . . . lunches? Do you think . . . my wife . . . is giving birth to a . . . bloody servant?'

The veins on Noor's neck swelled menacingly as he staggered towards Haider, and had it not been for Sadiq and Zakir's intervention, Noor would have definitely punched him.

'I was just . . . joking, Noor. You know me. I am a cricket idiot,' Haider said apologetically as the other two sat Noor down.

'My child is never going to be a twelfth man!' Noor shot back.

The air in the room became suffocating as the stony silence grew loud. It was late evening, and the time for serious, thoughtful discussion was long over.

Two

Farhat had been feeling rotten since the night before. Earlier that morning, she was irritable not just because Noor was having his stupid party and had taken to continually nagging her, but also because of the intermittent contractions she was having. By the time her husband's party was in full swing, the contractions had started coming closer together. When she felt that the time had come, she told her elder sister, Sarwat Khan, to order Sikander to fetch Dr Zarina Minwalla, the only female doctor in the city at that time. Dr Minwalla, a Parsi doctor—a general practitioner to be exact—made house calls and delivered babies at home, but only for the affluent *purdahnashin* women of Karachi. She was not a trained obstetrician, but, by default, she became the doctor of choice for most of these women. While they waited for Dr Minwalla, Sarwat sat next to Farhat, wiping the sweat glistening on her forehead. The news of Farhat going into labour had spread like a contagion across the neighbourhood.

When Dr Minwalla entered the room a little while later, an entire retinue of anxious servants—Budhoo, Sikander, Changez and the gardener, Jumman, accompanied by his partner-slash-lover, Kaneez—tried to follow her in. The story around the neighbourhood was that Kaneez, the churail, had seduced

Jumman, the faithful dowered servant of Farhat, and had given birth to a daughter, Mehrun, out of wedlock.

Sarwat immediately ordered all of them out, but Kaneez stayed put.

'I said everybody out. Are you deaf?'

'Kaneez can stay. I have asked her to assist me,' Dr Minwalla said in a brisk tone.

A part-time servant at Farhat's house, Kaneez also moonlighted at Dr Minwalla's clinic as a midwife. She had this enormous gift of cultivating neurosis in the hearts of those around her, and so, at Dr Minwalla's response, Sarwat's mouth fell open and her eyebrows wrinkled with horror and anxiety. For Sarwat, Kaneez's presence in this makeshift birthing room was a bad omen. Annoyed and scared, she stammered, 'Sh-sh-she shouldn't be h-h-here, Doctor Sahiba.'

'Listen to me carefully, Sarwat Begum, she is my assistant; she will help me deliver the baby and you will keep quiet. Do you understand? If you don't want to see her face, you should leave the room,' Dr Minwalla minced no words. The threat silenced Sarwat.

With victory scribbled all over her dark, pockmarked face, Kaneez grinned and squinted her only good eye, while Sarwat scornfully catalogued her every churail-like feature. She blamed Kaneez for Farhat's eleven failed pregnancies, but the midwife, in turn, remained convinced that a djinn residing inside Farhat's womb was responsible for her misfortunes. Kaneez fully expected another disappointment for her mistress this time as well.

For both the sisters, Kaneez fitted the description of a churail perfectly. A severe bout of smallpox in her childhood had scarred her face, robbing her of one eye, and a congenital condition had given her a club foot. And as ultimate proof, someone somewhere swore that Kaneez had been either near or around Farhat every time she had a miscarriage: quod erat demonstrandum; she was a certified churail.

Sarwat prayed softly to Allah to protect her younger sister from this churail. She saw Kaneez in front of Farhat's open legs, simpering inanely, gloating over her victory, an authentic necromancer, their worst nightmare come true at that hour, but there was no time to challenge her presence, for Farhat was howling in pain.

'The baby is ready to come out. Now when I say push, you give a big push. Okay . . . PUSH!' the doctor instructed.

Farhat pushed, and her scream ripped through the muggy air in the room.

'Push again.'

Farhat pushed with all her strength and then lay back against the pillows behind her, moaning.

'Come on, Farhat Begum, push harder!' the doctor ordered.

'I can't. I'm going to die!'

'Doesn't matter, just push,' Dr Minwalla laughed at her own joke.

After half a dozen more pushes, Farhat finally delivered a healthy baby boy. Dr Minwalla, instead of putting the baby in Farhat's arms first, handed him to a shell-shocked Kaneez to clean him up. As she held the baby, Kaneez's face changed colour. Turning pale, she let out a loud piercing scream, 'Djinn, djinn! Oh Allah, he's a djinn! Take him away from me. Take him away from me; he will get inside me!' she blurted hysterically and almost threw the baby back at Dr Minwalla.

She must have been high on ganja, for she saw the baby boy vanish into thin air, out of her hands, only to then reappear in the arms of the doctor a split second later. But how could that happen? To Kaneez, it was unmistakable, no question about it. Instead of a boy, her mistress had given birth to a spirit—one of Allah's creatures made of smokeless fire and mentioned in the Qur'an, the ones she had heard about countless times from her mother, one that had once invaded her neighbour's body. Disguised as a baby boy, this djinn had now come out of Farhat's body to torment her after devouring the hearts of all her other eleven children.

In Kaneez's opinion, therefore, it was humanly impossible for Farhat to have a child. Then how could she have been proven wrong after all this time? A live birth! A crying and kicking baby! Well, there was only one explanation for this live birth: the djinn had come out of Farhat's womb in the form of an infant, in the guise of a boy! Ganja or no ganja, that fateful October in 1951, Kaneez stood in the birthing room in the Kashana, utterly convinced that this baby boy was a djinn.

The minute Sarwat heard Kaneez utter all this nonsense, she screamed in rage. 'I will kill you, churail! I will kill you!'

Dr Minwalla ordered both of them to be quiet.

'You clean the baby, now,' she told Sarwat.

Usually, that task fell to Kaneez, but the doctor couldn't take any more chances.

Cleaning the soft baby skin had a calming effect on Sarwat. When she was done, Sarwat reminded Farhat about the need for the azan, the religious custom of whispering the call for prayer in the baby's ear.

'Is Noor Bhai going to offer the azan in the baby's ear?' she asked her sister.

'No, he is not well enough.'

Sarwat knew what these coded words 'not well enough' meant: Noor was too drunk to perform this solemn ceremony.

'Why don't you do it?' Dr Minwalla suggested.

'No, Allah forbid . . . women are not allowed to do so.'

'What about Budhoo? He is a man,' Kaneez ventured hesitatingly.

'If you keep spitting filth, I'll hit you with my shoes,' said Sarwat.

The sisters began panicking, for nothing else was permissible without the azan being recited to the baby. Farhat wished her brother Zahid were there to perform the ceremony, but he was in Lahore, studying engineering. As for their father, Javed Sultan, he was out visiting friends.

'What's wrong with Budhoo doing the azan?' Kaneez persisted.

Sarwat turned and threw her shoe at the woman, but it missed her and hit the framed photograph of Noor and Farhat's wedding, kept on the side table. The picture frame fell and broke.

'Look, what you made me do!'

But there was no time to have another go at Kaneez; the azan had to be performed soon because the baby needed to be fed. Budhoo, a servant, was not the ideal solution to the crisis, but he was perfectly acceptable from the theological point of view. Farhat's head began spinning at the thought of Budhoo performing the azan for her child instead of her husband. She was furious. What would people say? Her only son and the first voice he hears is the voice of a servant!

Reluctantly, however, she agreed and told Kaneez to summon Budhoo, who completed this first rite of religion in his accented and garbled Arabic; and Sarwat Khan thought, this is not auspicious. May Allah have mercy on this child.

All this while, a radio had been playing somewhere in the house. Now, a mere second after Budhoo finished the azan, the song stopped abruptly and in a solemn voice, the broadcaster announced:

> We interrupt this programme to bring you news of a supreme tragedy. Our beloved prime minister, the Leader of the Nation, Liaquat Ali Khan, was mercilessly assassinated by a cowardly deranged man while he was speaking to a crowd in Rawalpindi's Company Bagh. We are God's creation, and unto Him, we return.

The evening darkened; the sky heaved as the sun plunged into the Arabian Sea. From a nearby mosque, the muezzin called the faithful for the evening prayers.

And Sarwat Khan muttered to herself, 'This is not auspicious. May Allah have mercy on this child!'

Three

Farhat did not forgive her husband for not performing the azan, but the joy of giving birth to a son made her forget his transgression. Noor named the baby Mansoor ul Haq.

'What does this name mean?' Farhat asked.

'It means the protector of truth. I have named him after Manṣūr al-Hallaj.'

'Who?'

'The great Sufi mystic who spent his life in search of the Truth,' he said.

Noor did not tell her the whole story, that when Manṣūr al-Hallaj thought he had found God, the Ultimate Truth, he concluded that since He was everywhere and in everything, he, Manṣūr al-Hallaj, had become a part of God. In his ecstasy, he said, 'Anā-al-Haq, I am the Truth,' and was executed for this heresy.

Farhat knew nothing about Sufism, but she liked the name. To her, giving the right name to a child was the most important thing. Two weeks before her delivery, she had heard an oft-repeated lecture from her father, Javed Sultan, on this very topic.

'It is important to give the *most* suitable name to a child, because a name affects the character, blesses the household, and protects the future generations. My daughter, the name of a

Muslim child should be distinctively Islamic and should have a good meaning,' he had said.

When Farhat told Javed Sultan that Noor had named their son Mansoor ul Haq, he too, liked it and responded, 'It is a very auspicious name.'

*

After finally having the child that they both had wanted so much, and a son at that, Noor slipped back into his regular work routine while Farhat devoted her full attention to the newborn. They began doting on him in their own ways.

Just before his friend Zakir was due to return to Rome, Noor gave a farewell dinner in his honour. Both Haider and Sadiq came as well, and the discussion turned to Pakistani politics once again.

'Your government is rotting, Zakir. It is suffering from gangrene.'

Whenever Noor referred to Pakistan or the Pakistani government in front of his friends, it was always preceded by the second person possessive pronoun, as if he himself were a detached resident, an alien who never embraced his citizenship. Deep in his heart, Noor felt embarrassed to be the citizen of a country defined by religion. To be religious, according to him, implied a step backward towards anti-intellectualism.

Circumstances had condemned Noor to become an unwilling resident in a country that he frowned upon. Nonetheless, it was his choice to remain an outsider. He proudly called himself a self-ostracized man. To him, it was this self-ostracism that gave some justification to his life in Pakistan. His friends, however, often challenged this dissonance.

The new country's Constitution was finally being written down by a few Pakistani lawyers, all trained in Britain. As someone who had studied law there, Noor had known and intensely disliked them.

'They were all self-righteous hypocrites,' he said, 'giving sanctimonious speeches about faith and country during the day and partying at night.'

'Now, how do *you* know that?' Zakir asked, crossing his arms, his eyebrows tightening.

'I was at Oxford, remember?'

'I was there, too, but I didn't hear anything.'

'No, you had already left for Harvard,' Noor reminded him.

'But we're all hypocrites. Aren't you one?' Zakir asked, finally ticked off.

'How am I a hypocrite?'

'You call yourself an agnostic, but you invoke God at every opportunity you get. Why do you say "inshallah" when you don't even believe in Him? In my book, that's hypocrisy.'

'My friend! That is a cultural phrase, a phrase of habit rather than of conviction. It has the same profoundness as the empty phrase "you know"!'

'But you have been proved wrong before, Noor,' Zakir replied, changing the subject back to politics. 'We will have a Constitution soon.'

'Well, only time will tell . . . inshallah.'

Sadiq noted the sarcasm, and Haider, seeing the vitriol in the air, tried to change the topic to cricket. It was a contrived attempt, and they all knew it. Noor, however, did not want Zakir to leave his house with a bitter taste in his mouth, so he apologized to him and the friends shook hands and made up. The next day, Haider and Sadiq went to see Zakir off at the airport, but Noor said his goodbye on the phone.

*

Work and the Sindh Club remained central to Noor's existence as his life lumbered over the potholes of Karachi, powerless to absorb the shocks and jolts of Pakistani politics. His drinking increased, and so did Farhat's daily vexations. His kisses became more intolerable for her; his attempts at lovemaking, more disgusting. Why did he have to drink every day, she wondered. He was not like this in the beginning. To her knowledge, his drinking began after they migrated to Pakistan and it intensified when his law practice started to flourish. The invitation to become a member of the elite Sindh Club had made matters worse. After that, whenever Farhat confronted him about his drinking, he would always have one reply.

'Your country stresses me out,' he would declare, 'and the whisky relaxes me; it helps my sanity. So leave me alone.'

In the beginning, he was discreet about his drinking, but later, when he became open about it, she began giving him paan, the betel leaves, to suppress the smell of whisky on his breath.

'At least eat one of these after you drink. I don't want people to catch a whiff of whisky on your breath.'

At times, she felt unloved. She felt as if fate had condemned her to be with a man whom she would never learn to love. At times, she longed for Israr, her first cousin, whom she had been engaged to be married to since she was twelve. Everything had been agreed upon between their parents even before she was born. She hardly knew him; she barely saw him. But everyone raved about Israr. They said that he was the most handsome man in town. That he was kind and gentle, and best of all, he was deeply religious. All her female cousins teased her and said that they would make the perfect couple, and they would have boys so handsome that everyone else would want to have their daughters marry them. Conditioned to accept Israr as her life partner, Farhat had begun developing feelings for him. However, kismet had other plans. While riding his horse to his farm one day, Israr was thrown several feet into the air; he broke his neck and died on the spot. They told Farhat that some evil churail had cast her ugly shadow on Israr. She felt cheated and crushed. She felt that without Israr, life would end. It did not; instead, she became part of an exigency plot; her marriage was arranged with Noor, who, on their wedding night, recited meaningless poems, some of them in Farsi! In the early years of their marriage, she felt disconnected, later she felt neglected, and after Noor started drinking, she felt downright disgusted. She hardly felt any warmth for him; now it was just contempt, while he grew more indifferent towards her.

'*Khuda ke wastey*, please stop drinking; it is haram in our religion,' she had pleaded one day when he came home tipsy.

'For God's sake?' Noor had turned around and replied. 'Farhat Begum, I don't believe in your God, so keep quiet.'

When life appeared unjust to Farhat, she buried herself in religion and its occupying rituals. Their separate attempts at preserving their own sanity caused Farhat and Noor to drift apart. They could wander away from each other's existence, as far as possible, but they couldn't separate. The word 'divorce' had not entered their cultural vocabulary yet; although permitted by religion, their traditional society did not condone it. Handcuffed by circumstances, Noor thirsted for an intellectual outlet that Farhat couldn't provide, while Farhat searched for a spirituality that Noor couldn't offer. They stayed lonely and alone in their togetherness.

*

That Pakistan was created by secular leaders like Mohammad Ali Jinnah and Liaquat Ali Khan as a homeland for the Muslims of India, had initially made Noor hopeful about the country's temporal path. After all, these were men steeped in the lofty traditions of Western education. But soon after their deaths, when their secular agenda was first challenged and later expunged by the reactionary right, Noor became increasingly disillusioned. Ironically, many of the same conservative leaders who had vigorously opposed the idea of Pakistan, migrated to the country when it became a reality. And upon arrival, they began sowing the seeds of their parochiality. As sectarianism deepened its roots in Pakistan, Noor felt more deracinated. He felt as if he had been transplanted into a country where normality meant heeding to the language of exclusion and bearing witness to the politics of hate.

During Noor's college years, alcohol had been his preferred symbol of rebellion, but in Pakistan, it had hardened into a daily ritual. In whisky, he found release, and he rationalized his increasing intake by calling it his 'defence mechanism' against the 'suffocating anti-intellectualism of this country'. Unable to speak his mind in public, he ranted privately at home about the political and religious situation in Pakistan. And so, when he wanted to lash out, it was Farhat at the receiving end. But Farhat was too smart to listen to these silly tirades. She also had her coping rituals. Every night, when she felt that a lecture was coming, she would pop two Optalidon pills from the orange bottle, take out a cotton ball (which she had ripped into two), stuff it in both ears and go to sleep.

*

On Mansoor's first birthday, Noor remained missing from the festivities at home, choosing to spend the evening at the Sindh Club. Farhat had invited all their close relatives for an elaborate dinner, and Noor's absence made people talk. Embarrassed and angry, she moved from one relative to another to avoid the wicked whisperings, until Nawab Khan Namaqul, Sarwat's ne'er-do-well husband, finally caught up with her. Noor had a private nickname for Nawab Khan: Nawab Khan Namaqul, or Lord Khan Idiot. An ageing Lothario, Namaqul's chief interests lay in erotic poetry, lascivious banter and patronizing Karachi's crumbling brothels. To embarrass Farhat, he recited what seemed like an extempore Urdu couplet about Noor, loud enough for everyone to hear:

Koi roshni nahi baqi baghair-e-Noor
Aaj shub chiraghan karain andhere me

(There is no light here without Noor,
Tonight, we will rejoice in darkness)

'Where is our Noor?'

'He . . . He . . . he is extremely busy these days with a very important case. He . . . usually w-works till la-late night,' Farhat replied.

Everyone knew she was covering up for him. The rising colour of her face revealed her anguish; her words betrayed her emotions. When all the guests had left, she put Mansoor in his crib and sank into her bed without changing her clothes. A deluge of emotions swept over her and she cried bitterly. Much later at night, Noor returned home, drunk as usual, and fell on the bed without changing his clothes or taking off his shoes. Farhat got up, covered him with a blanket and went to sleep in the women's quarters, taking her son with her.

She had a restless night, her dreams transmuting from one nightmare into another. Noor, Israr, Mansoor and Nawab Khan, all jumbled together as her brain created grotesque imageries. It was a dream about death, about her sobbing incessantly and about a horse. She woke up perspiring. Where had that horse come from? Had she suppressed her emotions and her pain for so long that they were coming back now in her dreams? Every night when Noor came home drunk, she felt that something inside her had died. Glancing at her son, she caressed his tiny hands and gently kissed his forehead. It was still dark and quiet outside, but then the muezzin's call for prayers shattered the night's serenity. Farhat got up, went to the bathroom and performed her ablutions. Spreading the prayer rug, she prayed to God, almost hysterically so, begging His forgiveness, pleading with Him to make her husband change into a better man, to show him the light, to put him on the righteous path. She prayed to Him to make Noor give up alcohol, and then, finally, she prayed for her son.

Outside, the vermilion sun began spreading its light over the dust-covered city. Farhat's heart ached and a dull pain throbbed in the back of her head. The soft call of a mynah bird lured her out to their dew-covered backyard. The crisp morning air mesmerized Farhat, softening the memory of the nightmare.

Four

Mansoor had a normal childhood, and much to Kaneez's amazement, he had no visible markers of a djinn. The boy's eyes seemed ordinary: the iris a bright brown, and the sclera as white as Tibet Snow's skin-whitening cream. Although, when Kaneez had touched his forehead a few times, much to his annoyance, it did feel hot to her.

A shy, quiet boy, Mansoor studied at the prestigious Karachi Grammar School. His early life had been so ordinary that the rumour about his djinn-hood began to dissipate as the years passed. Even Kaneez had started to doubt herself. But for Farhat, the very word 'rumour' was infuriating, not to mention that horrible churail Kaneez. She couldn't even make herself say the word 'djinn'. She couldn't risk any evil befalling her son.

'Why don't you send Mansoor to the Madrassa-e-Ifrit? They teach you how to control the evil djinns,' Sarwat had advised. To which Farhat had replied, 'Do you want my husband to divorce me?'

But now Mansoor had reached that age when formal learning about religion and its rituals became obligatory. Of course, Noor, the godless barrister that he was, did not believe in any of this and vehemently opposed the idea of a traditional religious education when Farhat broached the topic one night.

It was terrible timing, too, since he had just poured himself a glass of whisky.

'What nonsense! I don't want my son to become a mullah,' he replied as he dropped a couple of ice cubes into the crystal glass.

'Who is saying he has to become a mullah? I just want him to learn to read the Qur'an and to offer the namaz,' Farhat protested.

Ever since Mansoor's birth, she had become more disciplined about offering the five daily prayers, and she wanted to instil the same sense of religiosity in her son. To her, Mansoor was a miracle baby, and she had promised Allah that she would thank Him in her prayers every day. Sometimes, she even woke up at night to offer the special prayers of *tahajjud*.

'I don't want a mullah to drill the Qur'an into Mansoor's head in Arabic, without teaching him its deeper meanings. What will he learn from a mullah? Rocking back and forth? When he is slightly older, I will teach him about religion.'

'You and religion! May Allah shield my son,' Farhat laughed.

'Farhat Begum, I am the son of a religious scholar,' Noor replied and took a gulp of the whisky.

The fact was that despite his secular bend, Noor was well-versed in Islamic theology. His father, Mashood ul Haq, a well-regarded Islamic scholar and author of *The Philosophical Traditions in Islam,* had schooled him personally. By the age of fourteen, Noor had memorized the entire Qur'an and was on his way to following in his father's footsteps. But then he went to Aligarh Muslim University. There he met a few left-leaning intellectuals and Marxists, got exposed to the Muslim heretics— the *Zindiques*—learned about Western philosophers of the Enlightenment, studied the British empiricists, and his entire perspective changed.

'Aligarh was where I had my baptism, and Oxford was where I had my awakening.'

'Aligarh university was your *bhool-bhulaiyan*, your labyrinth. You never got out of it,' Farhat shot back.

'In Aligarh, the light of my being became a pest to all my darkness,' Noor replied, blurting out a well-known Farsi saying. He then continued, 'Once the seed of doubt gets sown, Farhat Begum, dogma withers. And then, what they did to Abba Jaan . . .'

Farhat firmly believed that it was this unburied memory of his father's murder during the Partition riots that gnawed at Noor's entrails. She had suspected all along that whatever lingering faith he had in a higher deity died on that ghastly day. She was there when strangers had brought Mashood ul Haq's bloodied body to their house.

'Abba Jaan's death was a shocking tragedy, but maybe God was testing you . . . He puts everyone to test,' Farhat replied. She noticed then that the whisky bottle by Noor's side was half-empty.

'My jaanum, I put your god to test and he flunked miserably. Don't talk about religion or god or his tests to me again.'

Realizing that the discussion had slowly veered towards blasphemy, Farhat changed the subject. She could tolerate his harangues against the politics of Pakistan, but she did not like his diatribe against God. As his rants became more regular, more impassioned, Farhat grew more resolute. She would give her son the religious education that she herself had received from her father, even if she had to do it covertly. Farhat did not want her son to follow in Noor's deviant footsteps. So, to keep off the infidel influence of her husband, she secretly hired a maulvi and set his visitation hours for well after Noor had left home for work following his lunch break. This was her first act of defiance, her first rebellion. In all these years of marriage, neither Noor nor Farhat had declared their love for each other; and now she did not need to assert her defiance.

To keep it a secret, she warned Mansoor as well, 'Don't ever mention Maulvi Nazir in front of your father, otherwise he will be very angry with both of us.'

Although they both showered their love on him, Mansoor remained afraid of both his parents. He was terrified of their relationship. Their usual iciness, their frequent sarcasm, their constant bickering, everything frightened him. Early on in his life, he witnessed his father's resentment of his mother's lack of formal education; he saw his mother's revulsion towards his father's drinking and his heretical bent. The word *sharab* was never mentioned in their house, and while nobody dared to tell Mansoor that his Muslim father drank the forbidden drink, he guessed it, realizing that his father was unlike the other fathers of his cousins and friends, devout men who he knew did not drink or berate their god and country every night.

Mansoor received doses of religious indoctrination not just from Maulvi Nazir, but also from his mother, and sometimes even from his English tutor, S.M. Zaidi, whom Noor had hired to refine his son's skills in the English language and to teach him literature. He had been highly recommended by Sadiq, who had told Noor about his erudition.

'Despite his religious bent, he knows his Dickens and flaunts his Shakespeare.'

'Where does he teach?' Noor had asked.

'Well, that is the problem . . . the young man teaches in one of those yellow schools,' Sadiq had replied.

The term 'yellow school' was a pejorative label that the snobbish elite of Karachi used for the government schools that dotted the city map with their crumbling yellow buildings. These schools and their poorly paid teachers were eschewed by everyone except the poor dwellers of this city. After all, you don't make the 'right contacts' with the 'right people' at a yellow school.

'If he is so good, why is he teaching at a yellow school and not at a private school or college?'

'Well, he used to teach at Karachi Grammar School, but he'd rather teach poor kids than rich kids.'

'Then why would he agree to teach Mansoor, a rich kid?'

'Well, I guess you have to make compromises somewhere . . . but to allay your fears, he was highly recommended by the principal, Mrs D'Souza, whom you know well.'

Noor wanted to select a tutor who came highly recommended, who could expose his son to the treasures of literature, and who could teach him to use the English language, the lingua franca of the educated class, not just correctly but also aesthetically. And so, after much deliberation, Noor hired Zaidi, who also became an afternoon fixture at the Kashana.

*

No one handed them any books about the rules of parenting, so Noor and Farhat made up routines for Mansoor. He would wake up at 5.30 a.m., eat his breakfast at 6.15 a.m., leave for school at 7 a.m., ride back home with his father at 1 p.m., have lunch with the family at 1:45 p.m., and have his siesta till 3 p.m. At that time, Noor went back to work and Zaidi came to tutor Mansoor. Maulvi Nazir followed discreetly around 4.30 p.m. and stayed for about an hour, filling the young boy's head with things he didn't really understand. By 8 p.m., Mansoor had to be in bed. And then there were all the infuriating don'ts without any dos that controlled all his hours: Don't play with the servants; you will learn bad words from them. Don't play in the blazing sun; you will become as dark as Kaneez. Don't fly a kite or play marbles; these are the games of the *lafangas*, the scoundrels. Don't play *latoo*, the spinning top; you might end up injuring your eyes. Don't eat kulfi sold by the kulfi-wallah; he buys the milk discarded by patients in hospitals across the city. Don't go out bareheaded in the afternoon; the Shaitan (Satan) will hit you on the head so hard that you will get a splitting headache. Don't yawn without covering your mouth; the Shaitan will pee in your mouth. Don't say *salaam alaikum* in the bathroom; evil djinns live there. If they reply, you die.

But these routines grew tiresome and Mansoor began stealing time from his siesta hour to get some respite. Of course, it wasn't any inner rebel coercing him to break the smothering rules, it was Mehrun, the daughter of Kaneez, the churail. She enticed him to do the don'ts. Mehrun was the temptress, the siren, whom Mansoor could see from his bedroom window, cartwheeling and cavorting in the backyard near the guava tree, displaying her simian skills.

*

With Jumman's persistent pleading and a solemn promise from Kaneez to never spread any more rumours about the family again, Farhat allowed her to get back into the folds of the Kashana some five years after Mansoor's birth. There was a shortage of domestic help, and Farhat needed someone to do her laundry. Kaneez's transgressions at Mansoor's birth were neither forgiven nor forgotten; they were simply cast away in favour of expediency. And so, Kaneez started coming to the Kashana three times a week, while Jumman came every day to tend to the garden and for other errands. Mehrun turned up every day after attending school. Sometimes, she helped her mother with a job that needed to be finished or invented work for herself. Occasionally, she also helped her father. Mostly though, she felt free to spend her afternoons at her favourite hideout—the guava tree in the back garden. The idea of playing under the guava tree in the afternoon, with the mischievous Mehrun, had a seductive influence on Mansoor.

One day, while his parents were napping, Mansoor sneaked out of the house and ran towards Mehrun, who was playing in the back garden. She seemed to be having an expansive conversation with her crude dolls, all of them made from strips of rags. Two shoeboxes haphazardly painted and glued together to look like a two-storey house, complete with cut-out windows and doors, stood under the guava tree.

'What are you doing?' Mansoor asked Mehrun.

'Playing.'

'What are you playing?'

'With my dolls.'

'But what are you playing?'

'Why should I tell you?'

When Mansoor persisted, she said, 'This is *my* house. I have invited some guests to my house, and my servants will make tasty chicken tikkas and kebabs, and I can do anything I want to in my house. Do you understand?'

Mansoor laughed and then said, 'Your servants are ugly, aren't they?'

'Your bottom is ugly. If you call my servants ugly again, I'll slap you so hard, it will make you pee.'

A few years older than Mansoor, Mehrun had inherited none of her mother's deformities, but she definitely had her sharp tongue. And although she was a beauty by no standards, the girl had striking features. She played games in which she was always the begum, the lady of the house, who issued orders to her imaginary servants, each time in broken English. She had picked up a smattering of this alien language at her Urdu-medium yellow school and also from eavesdropping on Mansoor's lessons with Zaidi, who preferred teaching him out in the verandah, making it easier for Mehrun to listen and absorb the lessons. Even when they were inside, she would find an excuse to stay nearby, within earshot. Every afternoon, when she saw Zaidi approaching the Kashana, she would casually drift towards the verandah, pretending to be busy with her work, while her ears stayed glued to Zaidi's diction and delivery.

Joseph Solomon also joined them sometimes. A tall, muscular, dark-complexioned boy, he came to the Kashana to help his mother, Pyaro, the sweeper, clean the toilets and collect the rotting garbage. But mostly he got distracted by Mehrun and Mansoor. Always dressed in a bright-coloured dhoti and a contrasting kurta, he would announce his entry into the back garden either with a bhangra dance or a bawdy Punjabi song. Whenever he saw Mehrun, he would raise his eyebrows, wink at her and smile impishly. If he found her listening attentively to Mansoor's tutor, he would make kissing gestures with his fingers or offer her a bidi to smoke. His antics always made Mehrun smile and Mansoor blush. To Mansoor, he was forever the most welcoming disruption.

Joseph belonged to the sweeper community in Karachi, which was entirely Christian. Originally untouchable Hindus, they were converted to Christianity by the missionaries from Europe. The change of religion, however, did not expunge their pariah status. The Hindus of the city still regarded them as untouchable because they originally came from the lowest of castes, while the Muslims avoided physical contact with them because they considered them unclean. Discrimination against them continued unabated and they remained social outcasts, languishing at the bottom of the social ladder. Joseph was fortunate to get some education at The School, run by British nuns in Bhangi Para, where he lived with his mother.

*

At first, Mansoor took extra caution to ensure that his interactions with these 'undesirable elements' remained hidden from his parents, but as their games in the Kashana's back garden became more amusing, more engaging, he became careless. To him, Mehrun and Joseph were far more exciting playmates than his wealthy classmates or his ornery cousins, Khaleel and Jaleel—Sarwat's sons. Joseph always had something new to tell: a cheap joke, a vulgar song, or a crude story, and Mehrun kept up a steady supply of her ever-ready *tuk-bandi*, her concocted Urdu doggerels.

'Mehrun, do you want to see a *filim* with me?' Joseph asked Mehrun one afternoon when the three of them were sitting under the guava tree in the back garden, whiling away the hours.

'Get lost! You're crazy.'

'The hero in the filim looks like me.'

'Have you seen your face in the mirror?'

'I see it in your eyes; I don't need a mirror. One day, when I become a hero in my filim, you will beg me to marry you.'

'I'd rather marry an idiot millionaire.'

'Just for you, I will become a millionaire first, and then I will change into an idiot.'

'Okay, so what filim are you going to see?'

'*Chummi Dey.*'

'Give Me a Kiss' was a made-up movie title, and Mehrun knew it. Mansoor blushed, and she convulsed into laughter.

*

While Joseph's flirtatious games were fraught with delicious anticipations, Mehrun's coquetry and her reciprocity to his lewd banter always had the element of the unexpected. Mansoor never knew what the next surprise would be. And that was the allure.

That day, Mansoor had been outside with his friends for longer than usual. Realizing that his parents would get up from their siesta any time, he decided to return to his ridiculous routine. But just as he was about to leave his forbidden friends, he saw Khaleel and Jaleel saunter in his direction. He despised them, especially Khaleel, the shifty blackmailer. Khaleel knew that Mansoor enjoyed the company of Mehrun and Joseph, 'the scumbags', and so, to keep quiet and not tell his aunt about what was going on, it was only fair that Mansoor paid him something.

Khaleel's usual cut, eight annas for himself and four annas for his younger brother, were wrested from Mansoor's weekly allowance of five rupees, and although it was not much, it still upset Mansoor. Both Joseph and Mehrun knew about the brothers' nasty habit. So they nicknamed them after the most commonly used Pakistani coins: the older one became Athanni, meaning eight annas or half a rupee, and the younger one, Chowwani, meaning four annas or a quarter rupee. The fact that Joseph and Mehrun had nicknames for them enraged Khaleel and he became more brazen in extorting money from Mansoor whenever he had the opportunity.

'Mansoor, what are you doing playing with these lowlifes?'
Mansoor kept quiet.
'Where is our money?' Khaleel asked.
Mehrun came and stood between them and started singing her made-to-order Urdu doggerel:

Athanni ney yeh gaana gaya:
Mein paisa churaney aya,
Chowwani ney mara panja,
Athanni Babu ganja

(Athanni sang this song:
I came to steal the money,
Chowwani hit and clawed,
And now Athanni Babu is bald)

'Get away from me, *kutiya*!' Khaleel pushed Mehrun aside.

The word 'kutiya' or 'bitch' was used so frequently at Mehrun's house that it did not sound like an insult to her. But as Khaleel moved closer to Mansoor, it was Joseph who now became a wall between them.

'Get out of my way, you *bhangi*'s litter,' Khaleel tried to slap him, but he missed.

Although the word 'bhangi' literally means one who is addicted to the narcotic drug bhang, it is used as a racially offensive term. Calling a sweeper 'bhangi' was a grave mistake. It was the ultimate insult. It was something that made even the pachydermatous Joseph bristle with anger. Scream the worst profanity at him, and he would laugh with you, but call him a bhangi, and you are dead. As the word stung his ears, Joseph grabbed Khaleel by his balls and snarled, 'Listen, you son of a . . . first of all, don't ever call me a bhangi. And second, if you ever take money from Mansoor Sahib, I'll cut these balls off and feed them to my kutiya.'

Khaleel wasn't sure if Joseph had just called Mehrun a bitch, or if he actually had a bitch and was serious about his threat. He pushed him away and ran towards the house, shouting, 'That's it! I'll tell Farhat khaala that you play with the bhangi and the churail.'

Both Joseph and Mehrun couldn't stop laughing as they watched the brothers run, but Mansoor smiled awkwardly, not knowing if what had just happened was a flash of victory or a loss of his freedom. Should he run back to his room, or should he try to hide behind the banana tree? If Farhat found out about his afternoon escapades, it would be the end of everything. But it was too late to do anything, for the ratty Khaleel was walking back towards them with a fuming Farhat right behind him, ready to have all of them thrashed.

'Mansoor!' Farhat shouted the minute she saw her son. 'What am I hearing? How dare you play with these two? Don't you have anyone else to play with besides servants and sweepers? Don't you have any concern about what people will say? If I catch you playing with them again, I will break your legs.'

She twisted Mansoor's ear so hard that he squealed. Then she pushed him towards the house and ordered, 'Now go to your room! And the next time I see you play, it better be with your cousins.'

Finally, Farhat turned her wrath towards the two 'lowlifes', berating them until she heard Noor calling her from inside. Throughout, Khaleel and Jaleel stood there, smirking and making faces, feeling triumphant.

Five

Although Mansoor remained a prisoner to his vexing routines, the punishment for his defiance did not last long. It wasn't that Farhat Begum suddenly became relaxed about class structures or social mores. It was merely that she became more gregarious and left the house more often to visit friends and relatives. Mansoor's flashes of freedom became more recurrent as his parents became lax in their supervision.

An unusually grey afternoon greeted the inhabitants of the Kashana that March. The clouds toned down the heat a little and made the indoors muggy. Farhat had darkened the rooms of the house by drawing the silk curtains together. Soon after devouring a heavy lunch, Noor and she fell into their usual, deep afternoon sleep. Outside, the fresh smell of moist earth permeated the backyard until one came to where Joseph sat under the guava tree, a bidi sticking out from the corner of his mouth, blowing a thick trickle of circles, the acrid smell filling the air. He seemed engrossed, whittling the stalk of a leaf from a coconut tree with his knife; Mehrun hung upside down from the guava tree, attentive to Joseph's artistry. The verandah in the backyard, packed with gardenia and rose shrubs in terracotta flowerpots, publicized the start of spring, a season perpetually scarce in Karachi. A cool breeze blew across the neatly manicured lawn. Butterflies played hide-and-seek, and somewhere in a jamun tree, a koel sang a mournful note. Across the verandah, near the boundary wall, a batch of fruit trees, all planted in a straight line, provided thick vegetation. The adjacent wall, blanketed with bougainvillea, was testimony to the care that Mehrun's father, Jumman, had given this garden. He had lovingly planted banana, mango, guava and coconut trees, and had made himself vital to the garden and to Farhat. By transforming the Kashana into an oasis in the middle of this desert city, he seemed to have gained permanent employment not only for himself, but also for Kaneez. He had convinced Farhat that he would turn the garden into a piece of heaven, and there was no question that he had done this.

As Mansoor's parents snored, he bounded out of the house, straight towards Joseph, slapping the flowers on his way out.

Mehrun dropped down from the guava tree when she saw him coming.

'What are you two doing?' Mansoor asked.

'Shush,' said Joseph. He pointed towards a lizard that sat brooding on the boundary wall near the jasmine vine next to them, its head raised up towards the sky and its tongue sticking out.

'Wait and watch,' Joseph whispered. His lips tightened and his murderous eyes narrowed into slits. A shiver ran down Mansoor's spine as he saw Joseph make a slip-knot noose from the coconut tree leaf in his hands and tie it carefully to a dead branch from the guava tree.

'Why?' asked Mansoor.

Mehrun answered him with another of her Urdu tuk-bandis:

Aadhi roti, aadha kebab,
Girgit ko marna bara sawab

(One-half roti, one-half kebab,
Killing a lizard is the highest reward)

'It is our religious duty to kill these *girgit*s, these lizards, because they are always mocking Allah by sticking their tongue out,' she explained, as if reading out aloud from a textbook.

Joseph, like an expert lizard hunter, practiced tightening and loosening the noose to make sure that it worked perfectly. Then, getting up quietly, he tiptoed towards the lizard, the other two following him. The creature remained motionless, its basilisk-like glare freezing the moment. Joseph carefully lowered the noose in front of it and patiently brought it around the lizard's neck. As if hypnotized by the knot, the lizard remained catatonic. And then with a sudden jerk, Joseph pulled the loop. The lizard struggled and wriggled and tried to escape as the noose tightened around it, suffocating it. Once it stopped struggling and all movement stopped, Joseph yelled at Mehrun, 'Go! Quickly!' Awed and excited, Mehrun scampered towards the kitchen, which was on the other side of the house, and within a few minutes, came back carrying a small kerosene lantern and a matchbox. Joseph handed over the dead branch with the comatose lizard to Mehrun and took the lamp and the matchbox from her. With his eyes still sealed on the limp vertebrate, he quickly removed the glass covering of the lantern and opened the kerosene container. He then took the lizard from Mehrun, doused it with kerosene and ignited the match. With a big poof, a flame leapt up and engulfed the poor lizard. Within seconds, the blazing glow had charred the hapless creature. The lizard was cremated alive, and Mansoor, paralysed by horror and fear, witnessed the raw power of fire. The child, rumoured to be a djinn, a being created of smokeless fire, now trembled at the sight of it. Seeing Mansoor frozen with fear, Mehrun approached him.

'Why, Mansoor Babu, you look as if you saw a djinn!' Laughing at her own joke, she continued mockingly, 'But why should you be afraid of yourself? You are a djinn yourself!'

'I am not a djinn! I am not a djinn . . . don't say that!'

Mansoor scurried back towards his house, whimpering, tears running down his cheeks. His divine duty done, Joseph danced with Mehrun, holding the partly burned branch with one hand and Mehrun's waist with the other. They both sang the bloody doggerel repeatedly. The odour of kerosene and the stench of the burnt lizard dangling from the branch subdued the combined fragrances of all the flowers in bloom at the Kashana.

*

Mehrun excitedly recounted the whole story to her mother that night after they returned to their ramshackle one-room home that had no electricity, no running water and no bathroom. Every wall displayed patches where the paint had peeled off, while the corners of the ceiling displayed a vine-like network of cracks. In one corner, on a charpoy, Jumman rested comfortably in his undershirt and lungi, his eyes closed, his left hand on the back of his head and his right hand listlessly twirling the curlicues of his oiled moustache. Two cotton sheets, draped over a clothesline strung across opposite walls, created a rough-and-ready second room. A couple of reedy bamboo mats lay on the other side of the clothesline. The flickering wick of the kerosene lantern made Mehrun and Kaneez's shadows dance as they squatted in front of the mud stove in one corner of their tiny home. Mehrun made chapatis while Kaneez stirred the potato curry. The deadly smoke from the burning coal and the smell of spices from the curry hung in the air in the stuffy room, making Mehrun cough as she embellished the events of the day.

'Amma, you should have seen Mansoor Babu's face,' she said.

'You should not play with him. I have told you hundreds of times not to. He has the shadow of a djinn on him,' Kaneez reprimanded her, stirring the curry.

'Shadow of a djinn? But you told me he *was* a djinn.'

Mehrun was disappointed that her mother's memory, which had remained consistent up until then, had suddenly become faulty. But it didn't really matter. She wanted to hear the original account again from someone who had actually been there at the scene.

'Amma. Please, will you tell me what you saw when he was born?'

'How many times do you want to hear it?'

'One more time! Please, Amma! What did you see?'

In Kaneez's mind, the retelling of what she had seen at Mansoor's birth to as many people as possible was vital to make her hallucination seem believable. So, despite her apparent resistance, she was actually more than willing to recap the story for her daughter. As far as she was concerned, it was an irrefutable fact to which she, Kaneez, was an eyewitness.

'Long before his birth, I had seen him in my dreams, and I kept hearing a voice that told me a djinn lived inside Farhat Begum's *kokh*, her womb, and that one day he would come out of there. I also went to Malang Baba, who said the same thing. That day, when Mansoor Babu came out of Farhat Begum's kokh, Dr Minwalla handed him to me to clean him. I held him in my arms, and I swear by God, he was hotter than this stove! He was there one minute and then he disappeared the next!' As Kaneez paused to lick the ladle for a taste of the curry, she was hit by Jumman's slipper.

'Oye, churail! Stop your babbling! You will have me kicked out of the Kashana. Don't talk bad about the Babu Sahib this way. He is not a djinn. He is a good boy and I like him!' Jumman hollered from his cot.

But Mehrun persisted. 'What happened to her other babies, Amma?'

'She had eleven before him. All died in her kokh. He ate all of them.'

'Who?'

'Your friend, the djinn you play with. He is the one who ate them alive in her disgusting kokh. That's why you shouldn't play with him. He will eat you up, too.'

Suddenly, with savage ferocity, Jumman picked up his other slipper and struck Kaneez hard. She howled in pain.

'Shut up, kutiya! One more word from your gutter mouth and I will strangle you!'

Jumman's violent reaction had a silencing effect on both mother and daughter. After making the chapatis, Mehrun spread a food-stained white tablecloth on the floor and put the food on it. Jumman joined them, and they all ate dinner quietly. Outside, it became dark as thick patches of threatening clouds covered the full moon.

*

At dinner time that night, Noor was, once again, absent. Farhat and Mansoor quietly munched on their food. Sarwat, a frequent and unbidden guest at the Kashana, was also there. She mostly escaped to her sister's house to be away from her miserable husband and wayward children.

It was Budhoo's day off, so Sikander was doubling up as a driver and an attendant-in-waiting. Farhat had dispatched him to buy chicken tikka and some greasy parathas from the famous Bundoo Khan's restaurant on Bunder Road. A sudden gust of strong wind slammed the gate outside, as if to protest Noor's absence. Farhat gazed at his empty chair and checked the time on her wristwatch, yearning for his presence at the dinner table. Why couldn't she have a regular relationship with her husband like everyone else? Why couldn't they have a normal conversation without blaming the government, without uttering blasphemies? Why couldn't they do normal family things?

She looked at her watch again. Where was Noor? Probably at the Sindh Club, binging on imported liquor either with his

Parsi clients or his good-for-nothing Shaitan friends. He never disclosed his plans to Farhat, and it was generally understood that if he did not come back home by eight at night, he could be found hanging out at the Sindh Club. Both Mansoor and Farhat dreaded those nights when he came home drunk, unable to walk without someone supporting him, mumbling incoherent sentences. But that night, Mansoor's mind was not on his father's whereabouts. Instead, it was the picture of that immolated lizard, the burnt smell afterwards, Joseph and Mehrun's victory song, and Mehrun calling him a djinn, that kept playing in his mind. As he slowly chewed on the chicken tikka, he asked his mother, 'Amma, what are djinns made of?'

His mother, still worried about her husband, snapped, 'Why for Allah's sake are you thinking about djinns at this godforsaken hour, and who told you about them? It was that churail Mehrun, wasn't it?'

'No, it wasn't Mehrun. I heard about them at school,' Mansoor lied.

'How many times have I told you to not play with those two?'

'You shouldn't talk about djinn *mamoo*, especially at night,' Sarwat interjected.

'Mamoo? Why did you call a djinn your mamoo? Djinns are not our uncles, are they?' Mansoor asked.

'No, silly. We call djinns our uncles out of respect, so that they don't harm us. Not all djinns are evil, son. Muslim djinns are good, but the kafir djinns who still haven't converted to Islam, they are evil.'

'But why can't we see them?'

'Because they are invisible, and that is why you can't even see their smoke!'

'But why are they invisible?'

'Okay, that's enough about djinns!' Sarwat became irritated. 'And one more thing, Khaleel told me that you call him names and take his money.'

'No, I don't. He—'

'Why would he take Khaleel's money? He is not poor,' Farhat interrupted, coming to her son's rescue.

That only poor people steal was something Mansoor was not going to think about at that moment. His mind was still on the mysteries surrounding djinns, their make-up, their invisibility.

After a long, distended pause, Farhat said, 'I don't know when he will return tonight.' Lowering her head, she gently massaged her temples to relieve the tension headache that was building up.

'Maybe he is still at work?' The elder sister tried to calm her fear.

Sarwat herself was no stranger to fear, having been physically abused by her husband repeatedly.

'Farhat, you are fortunate. At least he doesn't beat you up.'

But lately, the beatings had actually stopped. It was not that Nawab Khan had suddenly realized his errors and was making amends. It was just that he had found a new fascination. As Karachi's brothels began to be raided with increasing frequency, all on the orders of the newly installed military government, he switched to raising pigeons. They became his latest obsession. His days were now spent visiting his elaborate pigeon coop on the rooftop of his flat and flying them in flocks while he controlled their flight with high-pitched whistles and calls. His evenings were devoted to meeting with people who bred pigeons, and his nights to planning how to make a fortune selling them.

Nawab Khan had frittered away his modest inheritance, buying land and shops in the commercial area, only to eventually lose them to gambling and whoring. Now with no property or shops to his name, and with little money left, he often forced Sarwat to borrow from Farhat. Sarwat was a good seamstress and she made decent money from sewing children's clothes; that, however, was not enough to feed her five recalcitrant children and a demanding husband.

'It seems to me that your husband's you-know-what has increased,' Sarwat said, avoiding the word 'drinking'.

'I have tried to stop him, but what can I do? He . . .'

Realizing that Mansoor was listening, Farhat stopped and quickly changed the subject to their brother, Zahid; but Mansoor was no fool. He knew they had been talking about his father's drinking habit. He had heard Farhat's wailing supplications to Allah to bring Noor to the righteous path. He was aware of her frequent calls to his father's office to find out where he was, and he was familiar with her face that could not hide the shame when people inquired about him.

Dinner ended without Noor showing up. Sarwat went home, and Farhat took Mansoor to her bedroom. She felt guilty for snapping at him at the dinner table.

'Amma, why do you forbid me from playing with Mehrun and Joseph?' Mansoor asked matter-of-factly.

'It's complicated. It's like . . . you should play with children like you.'

'What do you mean?'

Farhat paused for a while and began explaining the complexities of class differences and the convolutions of social ranks, but when she saw Mansoor beginning to look increasingly confused, she changed her strategy.

'You should play with the boys.'

'Joseph is a boy.'

Exasperated by Mansoor's relentless questions, she thundered, 'Both Joseph and Mehrun are *kamzaat*. Should I say more?'

'What is kamzaat?'

'Low caste!'

'But Maulvi Sahib told me there is no caste in Islam, only Hindus have caste.'

'It has nothing to do with caste, Mansoor. You will understand when you're older. Now shut up and go to sleep.'

To Farhat, Mehrun was a bastard child born to a harlot—a stinking mishmash of *harami* and churail—the dirty whore who stole Jumman's seed and spawned this evil. The story that had endured all these years was that Kaneez and Jumman had never married. Nobody had witnessed it, and they couldn't provide any solid proof of their matrimony. Certificates never existed in their world, whether it was birth, marriage, or death.

Mansoor had heard the word 'harami' attached to Mehrun's name often enough, but he did not understand its exact meaning.

'Can we get a dog, Amma?' he asked as his mind wandered.

'No . . . angels don't come into houses with dogs.'

'Why? Are angels scared of dogs?'

'No, it's because dogs are unclean animals. The Prophet, peace be upon him, liked cats. Maybe you should get a cat.'

'No, I don't like cats; they make me sick. My friend Najeeb has one at his house, and whenever I go there, I start to cough.'

His mind digressed, and he started to think about djinns again. What if that lizard was a djinn? A twinge of fear leavened in his heart as he imagined hearing the rustling of approaching djinns. His face whitened and his forehead crinkled. Farhat, noticing his changed features, asked, 'Are you okay, Mansoor?'

'I am scared.'

'What are you scared of?'

'Djinns!'

'*Beta,* why are you still thinking about djinns? That vile Mehrun! Just recite the *kalimah*.'

'There is no God but God, and Mohammad is His prophet,' Mansoor recited the Qur'anic verse in Arabic, squeezed his eyes shut and buried his head in his mother's bosom. Farhat began to stroke the back of his hair. Mansoor felt better, but soon he started thinking about Mehrun again until sleep conquered him. Farhat called Sikander to put Mansoor in his bedroom. Noor came home quite late, but he was not drunk that night, much to Farhat's relief.

Six

That night, rain pounded the salt-rich earth of Karachi with all its anger. The sky rumbled endlessly and lightning zigzagged across it with a ferocity never seen before in this city of immigrants. All night long, it felt as if someone was pelting stones at the windows, while explosions rocked the rooftops. Rising water that had nowhere to go flooded the streets, the shops and the houses. The low-lying areas were the worst-hit, but even the elevated expanses of the metropolis couldn't escape its wrath. Less than ten inches of rain in a year was the norm for Karachi, but that night, fifteen inches fell in one go. Upheaval always accompanied the city even with modest rainfall, but fifteen inches choked up its sanitation system, and the primitive drains running all across the city vomited raw sewage non-stop. Every year the government set aside funds to build sewers, and every year, without fail, corruption sucked up the honest taxpayers' money. There was no one to question; there was no one to answer.

Mansoor slept restlessly. He twisted and turned; he moaned and cried and dreamt strange dreams, all of which had something to do with djinns—both Muslim djinns and kafir djinns, their hands clasped together, doing the *Jahanammi* nautch, the danse macabre, with Joseph and Mehrun flitting in and out of these nightmarish visions. All throughout, Mehrun's Urdu doggerel echoed in Mansoor's nocturnal brain:

Aadhi roti, aadha kebab
Girgit ko marna bara sawab

Hearing him moan, Farhat came to Mansoor's room and cradled his head in her arms. He woke up, a bit startled to see his mother.

'Is Abba back home?'

'Yes, he is. Recite the kalimah, beta, and try to sleep,' she kissed him on his forehead and left.'

But for the longest time after his mother left his room, Mansoor couldn't go back to sleep, and when he eventually did, the nightmares returned.

In his dream, he found himself in a room full of strangers. He saw his mother crying, and Sarwat comforting her. Strangers whispered in a bizarre language. He saw his father staggering along in a drunken stupor and ask no one in particular, 'Why is everyone after me?' Suddenly, he saw himself punching his father on the back and weeping uncontrollably.

And still dreaming, Mansoor felt an uncontrollable pressure on his bladder. He ran towards the bathroom, but there was none in the vicinity. Unable to control his urge, he began to urinate where he was, in the middle of an open field.

Wide awake now, he could hear his heart pounding and feel his pants clinging to his thighs. He had wet his bed. Feeling ashamed, he tried to focus. Where was he? Why was he sleeping in his pants and not in his pyjamas? The last thing he remembered was being in his mother's room, talking about Mehrun and Joseph. Who had brought him back to his room? But he was glad he was in his space, relieved it had happened in his bed. He touched the bed. It was only slightly wet, but his pants were all soaked. It was still dark outside, and the rain continued pounding on the roof and the windows. Wiping the sweat from his forehead, Mansoor got up, slipped out of

his pants and shirt, and put on his sleeping suit. Rolling up his wet
clothes into a bundle, he tiptoed towards his bathroom, dumped
the urine-drenched clothes into the wooden hamper and quietly
came back to his bed. He hoped that Kaneez wouldn't notice the
smell and tell Mehrun when she washed the clothes.

*

That same night after dinner, under the dim light of the lantern,
Mehrun opened her schoolbooks and started to memorize her
English lesson, mumbling softly.

'Is this the time to study?' Kaneez asked with a frown.

'Amma, I have to study. I have a test tomorrow,' she lied.

'A girl's hands are made by God to make rotis, not to hold a
book.'

Mehrun answered her with a ready-made Urdu doggerel:

Parho gey likho gey bano gey nawab
Khelo gey koodo gey bano gey kharab

(Reading and writing will make me a nawab
Playing and jumping will make me spoilt)

'Stop your poetry and go to sleep; we don't have kerosene to waste
on a girl's education.'

Reluctantly, Mehrun closed her books and went towards her
corner of the room, where a cold and tattered bamboo mattress
awaited her. The charpoy in the room was her father's sole
property. Her mother and she slept on thin bamboo mats. Mehrun
felt so tired that she went to sleep right away, but the non-stop
thundering and lightning woke her up in the middle of the night.
She saw the flickering of a candle through the slightly opened
drapes that hung from the clothesline. Without lifting her head,
she looked at her mother's mat. It was empty. Then she heard

her father's cot, shaking and squeaking. She saw the silhouetted naked body of her father crushing the equally naked body of her mother, both of them oblivious to the rampaging rain outside. Her mother's faint moaning petrified Mehrun. Jumman regularly took to beating Kaneez, but she had never seen anything like this. Shivering, she pulled the blanket over her face and curled up into the foetal position. Suddenly, Mehrun remembered her teacher's advice to recite the *Ayat-ul-kursi*, The Throne Verse, the most powerful of all Qur'anic verses, the warder of all evils, whenever she felt scared. She tried to recall it. But her memory failed her and all she could remember was that silly ditty:

> *Aadhi roti, aadha kebab*
> *Girgit ko marna bara sawab*

As her memory went blank, her mother's moaning grew louder and the charpoy rocked harder. Then, just as suddenly, it all ended, as if there was an unexpected power failure that shut everything down. All that Mehrun could hear now was the drumming of her own heart. She remained inert, trying not to breathe, suppressing her thoughts, restraining her movement. She wanted to melt away and disappear into the darkness. Then she heard her father mutter: 'Get the hell out of my bed.'

She heard her mother getting up, then the rustle of a shalwar being pulled up, the crunch of a bamboo mat, a dry cough—denouements of a play poorly produced. Mehrun squeezed her eyes tightly, yearning to sleep promptly. Beside her, she heard her mother lie down and snore loudly the minute her body hit the bamboo mat.

*

Jumman's hovel was mostly made of concrete, except for the tin roof. It escaped significant devastation from the flood, but

Joseph was not that lucky. His rat trap jhuggi, a mixture of mud, cardboard and corrugated metal, crumbled swiftly, just like his collapsed desires. The torrential rain flooded the open gutters and disgorged rancid sewage. Granted, Joseph had lived all his life amidst the stench of human and animal waste, but that night, the odour became more revolting, the air more putrid. Pyaro had woken him up when she heard the commotion outside. People were shouting and running to safety as everything around them began to crash. And when their shack began to crumble, Joseph and Pyaro quickly gathered their meagre belongings and ran out.

Joseph held on to his mother's hand tightly, pulling her up as they waded through the turgid water and made their way towards higher ground, the rain drenching them all over. Once they reached safety, Pyaro turned around to see what she had left behind—a hope, a promise—but all she saw was the raging flash flood. Then suddenly, Pyaro saw the body of what appeared to be a dead child floating right past them, arms spread out. 'Joseph!' she screamed, and Joseph pushed her face away from the horrific scene with his steady hand. Pyaro's eyes kept returning to the place where she had spotted the child's body, but now she only saw the dead branch of a tree, swept away by the strong current.

Joseph wanted to cross the railway line that lay up ahead of them, but then he saw a concrete shed nearby whose open door kept banging in the wind, as if inviting them to enter. They quickly went inside the shed and were knocked out by the musty metallic stench that hit them immediately. Bunged up with rusted iron bars, hooks and heavy chains, the dank railway shed was, nevertheless, a gift from heaven. Joseph examined the shelter and saw a narrow bench in the centre, laden with heavy paint cans. He cleared them one at a time and then asked his mother to sit there.

Pyaro, instead of sitting, kneeled on the floor, made a cross and prayed, 'Thank you, Jesus Christ, for providing us with this temporary abode. Please, Lord, don't abandon us. You did not abandon us when our cattle died, you did not abandon us when Joseph's Babuji died. Don't abandon us now.' Choking with sobs of anguish, she repeated the same prayer again and again even as Joseph clasped his strong arms around her shoulders and tried to comfort her.

They spent the whole night in that shed, shivering and huddling together, inhaling the noxious air. But at that moment, when their world had sunk deep underwater, the dank smell of rusted iron felt better than the fragrance of attar. Pyaro prayed all night, and in between remembered her dead husband, Samson.

She remembered the day when he had smoked his hookah for the last time. It had been his after-dinner routine ever since he earned his first rupee, cleaning other people's toilets. He had asked her to prepare the hookah, and Pyaro remembered filling the tube with water and the container with cheap tobacco. She had almost burnt her hand, putting the red-hot charcoal on the bowl above it. When the hookah was ready to be used, she had taken it to Samson. The water inside the pipe had gurgled as he took that first deep drag, but when the smoke began to fill his lungs, he started to hack uncontrollably. He continued to cough while pounding his chest and fighting to breathe. It was probably hours before his coughing subsided. And all this time, Pyaro and Joseph sat there, feeling helpless and petrified. The next day, Samson contracted a cold. After that, his condition got worse with each passing day. And then he began vomiting blood. Samson coughed up so much blood that his shirt got soaked. Pyaro became concerned now. They took him to the local hospital, but the doctors there would not touch him, giving them every excuse they could think of to turn them away. Pyaro went from doctor to doctor, and every single one refused to even look at Samson.

At last, she found a young physician who was kind enough to examine him. But the prognosis was gloomy. Samson had advanced tuberculosis, and since he had received no treatment for a long time, it was highly unlikely that he would get better.

Samson died two days later when, in a fit of coughing, he fell and banged his head on the floor of their shack. He died of massive internal haemorrhaging.

In the days that followed his death, Pyaro felt that her world had crashed. How would she take care of her son all alone? How would she send money to her mother, who lived with her widowed sister in Sialkot, Punjab? Would Samson's ugly sister blame her for his early death? She had a job, no doubt, cleaning people's toilets, but one income alone would not sustain her and Joseph. The responsibility of caring for her young son and her mother seemed all too oppressive to Pyaro. But as the gods took her husband away, they also provided her with a break—something that would change her son's life.

Her friend Mavis, who worked as a sweeper at the Kashana, suddenly decided to go back home permanently to take care of her elderly mother in Punjab, who had fallen seriously ill. Farhat had asked her if she could find a replacement. Mavis recommended Pyaro. When Farhat heard about Pyaro's predicament, she pitied the woman and hired her as Mavis's replacement; and when Noor heard Pyaro's story, he quietly gave her five hundred rupees.

'Maybe things would have been different if he were alive. Your Babuji had talked about building us a concrete house just past the railway line, closer to the city,' Pyaro said, recovering from the memory of her husband's death.

'Babuji was all talk; he did not do anything for us,' Joseph said.

Hearing him mock her husband, Pyaro stood up and slapped him so hard that he staggered.

'What was that for?' he asked, stunned.

'Never disrespect your father. He was a good man.'

Cupping her face with her trembling hands, she began to cry uncontrollably.

'Ma, calm down. I am sorry. I'll take care of you.' Joseph hugged her tightly in an attempt to comfort her. It took a long while before

Pyaro calmed down. Wiping her nose with her sleeves, she said, 'I'll visit Father Youhana tomorrow, maybe he'll help us.'

'Good luck, Ma . . .'

'What do you mean by "good luck"?'

'Ma, did he help you when Babuji died?'

'Well, we didn't really ask him to.'

'So? We didn't ask Barrister Sahib or Farhat Begum either, but she hired you and Barrister Sahib gave you five hundred rupees, that too without asking you any questions. Ma, leave it to me, I have a plan.'

'What is your plan? What are you going to do? Rob?'

'Trust me, Ma.'

'Tell me, Joseph, what are you going to do?'

'Tomorrow, we will visit Barrister Sahib and you will tell him about our plight. I know he'll help us.'

'I don't know, son . . . I don't think Barrister Sahib is going to help us again.'

'Well, if he doesn't help us, then you go to Father Youhana and beg.'

Pyaro began thinking about what she should tell the Barrister Sahib while Joseph started fantasizing about playing the lead role in a Punjabi film. The rain, meanwhile, continued to wreak havoc outside.

Seven

Mansoor saw his father at the breakfast table the next day. Dressed in a starched white shirt and the lawyer's band tied around his collar, Noor sat absorbed in the inside pages of the *Morning Gazette*. His wearing the lawyer's band indicated that a critical case was to be argued at the high court. And whenever that happened, he stayed back late in his office and prepared for it. Mansoor was relieved that his fear from the night before was baseless, but the thunderstorm and the nightmare still shook him.

The headlines of the *Gazette* screamed at Mansoor:

Flood kills thousands. Hundreds of homes destroyed. President closes schools.

Farhat had already told Mansoor about the school's closure, which was why he had not put on his school uniform and was wearing his kurta-pyjama instead. But as he read the glaring headline, Mansoor gasped and asked his father: 'Do you think Mehrun and Joseph are okay, Abba?'

Noor lowered the newspaper and replied, 'I hope so, beta, but I'm not sure if their houses can withstand such heavy rains. The paper says that many houses have been destroyed.'

'I am glad that they have closed all schools,' and after a pause Mansoor continued, 'how come your office is open today, Abba?'

'I have an important case at the high court, and they haven't closed the courts today. So, I have to make my appearance,' Noor replied, and as an afterthought asked his son, 'So, what are your plans for today, mister, now that your school is closed?'

Mansoor noted the sarcasm in the word 'mister', it was as if the school's closing was his fault.

'I don't know,' he replied, shrugging his shoulders.

'I want you to read a book, rather than waste your time.'

Sikander came inside just then, took the lawyer's briefcase from his study, and exited without saying a word. Noor followed him out briskly. But an hour later, they both returned. Noor held the black coat over his shoulder while his soaking white trousers clung to his legs. Sikander, equally drenched, followed him obsequiously with the briefcase.

'Already back?' Farhat asked.

'The car got stuck in the standing waters outside, so we had to wade back home through that muddy river of filth that is flowing through the streets. A policeman told us that all the roads are closed. I guess they will have to wait for me at the high court until the water clears.'

Noor went to his bedroom to change into something dry, while Mansoor tiptoed to his father's library to quickly hunt for a book that he could pretend to be reading. The floods meant that Budhoo wouldn't return from his day off. Farhat did not expect Kaneez to show up either, but she knew that Jumman would definitely come, and so she decided that she would ask him to prepare their meals. Farhat knew how to cook, but she hadn't done so lately and was not in the mood to do so now, especially not on so miserable a day. When neither Jumman nor Kaneez showed up, she dragged herself to the kitchen and opened the big white Philips refrigerator that Noor had recently bought from London. Taking out a packet of frozen mutton, Farhat braced herself at the thought of cooking again, hoping that she still had her skills intact. But then the sobbing figure of Pyaro entered the kitchen, followed by Joseph.

'Begum Sahiba! We lost everything, we lost everything!' she bawled in her accented Urdu.

The rotting smell of sewage from their soaking clothes choked the kitchen air. Clamping her nose shut with her thumb and index finger, Farhat asked, 'What happened? You two stink like gobar, like cow dung.'

Pyaro stepped back and recounted the whole story in between sobs, while Joseph stood solemnly behind her, his hands in his pockets, his face hanging down, his drenched shirt revealing his hairy chest. Noor, who had just changed into dry clothes, heard the bawling and came to the kitchen. Mansoor also came running from the library. When she saw Noor, Pyaro turned towards him, prostrated, and started to wail again.

'Stand up, Pyaro, and tell me, slowly, what happened,' Noor said.

Pyaro got up and narrated the whole story again, and Farhat saw her husband listening attentively. After hearing her tale, Noor asked her to calm down and added, 'You can stay at the empty quarter near Budhoo's till you get back on your feet.'

'Thank you, Barrister Sahib . . . thank you. May Yesu Masih grant you a long life and happiness,' she said, drying her tears with her damp chador.

Noor left the kitchen abruptly, but Mansoor stayed on. A sudden chill fell over the room as Farhat saw the need to re-establish her authority. She did not appreciate her husband's hospitality. It was one thing to have given Pyaro a job as a sweeper, it was quite another to provide them with a place to stay in the servants' quarters. These were unclean people. How could Noor make such an offer without even consulting her, as if she weren't even there? And how dare these two impose themselves on her house, and that too without her permission? If she had her way, she would have told them to find shelter in their own community. Powerless to rescind her husband's orders, yet desiring to assert herself, she laid fresh conditions.

'This doesn't mean you can live here forever; do you understand?'

'Yes, Begum Sahiba, we are not going to stay one more day than is necessary,' Joseph interjected.

'I wasn't talking to you,' Farhat snapped back at him with the imperial air that she assumed whenever she was addressing the servants.

'No, Begum Sahiba, we understand perfectly,' Pyaro hastened to assure her.

'And keep your lafanga son in reins.'

'The lafanga will be reined,' Joseph replied under his breath.

'If you talk rubbish, I will pull your tongue out from your mouth,' Farhat threatened Joseph.

'Shut up, Joseph!' his mother scolded him.

As they turned to leave, Joseph winked at Mansoor, who smiled back. Farhat saw that little exchange and gave Mansoor a dirty look.

A light breeze dispersed the insufferable smell from Pyaro and Joseph's clothes that had lingered on in the kitchen.

*

Pyaro and Joseph became a permanent fixture at the Kashana, but to Farhat, they were more like a scandalous stain on her landscape than mere interlopers. She felt ashamed to see them living in her servants' quarters, these low-life people. As if that churail was not enough, now there were two more who had installed themselves in her home to bring bad luck and cast an evil shadow over the Kashana. She felt like screaming at her husband. Why do you always want to torment me? The regret of having hired Pyaro in the first place permeated her mind, as her anger turned into a painful acceptance of this new reality, this new arrangement.

*

The floodwaters receded and the hot October sun began fracturing the earth again. Life returned to its ordinariness. One significant change that happened at the Kashana, at least in Farhat's eyes, was that Noor cut down on his visits to the Sindh Club. Most nights, he returned home relatively early, and after a light supper, drank his whisky and lectured his son before going to sleep. To Farhat, this was a sign that her prayers were finally being answered, and it was only a matter of time before Noor would see the light, give up alcohol altogether and revert to piety. So, she began to pray more fervently for that auspicious day.

The reality, of course, was different. Noor had decided that he would shape his son's mind through his nightly lectures; he believed that he could provide a liberal education that no school in Pakistan could. He thought of himself not as a scholar, but as a scholar manqué. Well-read, eclectic and with a keen analytical mind, Noor could easily dissect his opponents' arguments in court and disarm his intellectual inferiors. Often, he would argue about contemporary literature with Sadiq and debate history with the Harvard-educated Zakir.

After asking Mansoor a few questions about the history of the subcontinent and getting woefully shocking answers, Noor decided to take his son's education as a personal challenge. He asked Mansoor to bring his history textbook. As he read through it, Noor realized that the book was nothing more than a handful of dogmas disguised as history. To him, it was all propaganda, interwoven into chapters of lies, a curriculum that propagated hatred, especially towards India, the putative enemy. According to Mansoor's textbook, Pakistan's history began with the Arab invasion, centred on the Mughals and ended with the creation of

Pakistan. The Hindus, whose presence in the region long predated that of the Arabs, were a mere footnote in this hagiographic narrative.

'Beta, when invaders are portrayed as liberators and when the looters of temples become our heroes, the past ceases to exist and history becomes a pack of lies. The surest way to destroy your culture and your history is to erase them from the memory of your children,' he fulminated at the country's educational system.

Why was he wasting hard-earned money sending his son to the most prestigious school in the city? So they could teach him mendacities? Mansoor needed a re-schooling, a liberal edification. Noor felt compelled to take him under his tutelage. And thus began his daily lectures in the humanities and liberal arts, carefully calibrated, judiciously deliberated. Noor started ordering books from Thomas & Thomas for Mansoor. Located in Saddar, the city's centre, it was Karachi's oldest bookshop which had survived the mayhem of the Partition. Sadiq and Noor often went there together. While the professor would buy Turgenev and Trollope, Noor would purchase Bertrand Russell's books. The first book he bought for Mansoor was an abridged edition of Gibbon's *History of the Decline and Fall of the Roman Empire*, which he forced his son to read. Once the boy was done reading a book, Noor would then discuss it with him. This became his practice.

Mansoor, on the other hand, noticed a sharp rise of vitriol in his father's nightly discourses. He lashed out against the country, relentlessly berated the military rule and cursed the religious establishment. And all this time, Noor used the English language, as if to irk Farhat. But it annoyed Mansoor more than it annoyed his mother, especially when Noor kept referring to Pakistan as 'your country', as if he himself was just a passing critic, an alien resident—someone inside, looking from the outside. Mansoor hated his father's attitude towards Pakistan.

'Abba, why do you keep saying that it's my country? Is this not your country, too?' Mansoor asked one night.

'*It is* your country! You were born here; I was not.' Then, after a slight pause, Noor continued, 'I can live here physically, but I don't have to accept it mentally.'

Noor's estrangement with the country had deepened in 1958, after a military coup overthrew the prime minister and the President and tossed out the country's first Constitution into the rotting trash bin of history.

'Why didn't you go back to India if you disliked Pakistan so much?' Mansoor sighed.

Noor pursed his lips, then sighed before continuing, 'Because, my son, the India I grew up in has also left me.'

'Isn't there any other country where you can live?'

'I am a man with no country; I am a man with no faith. I can live anywhere and nowhere at the same time.'

The irony of his father's statement whizzed past Mansoor, but he still nodded; and Farhat, knowing little English, remained frustrated. Occasionally, she protested; frequently, Noor reprimanded.

'Why can't you two talk in Urdu . . . after all, it is our mother tongue and the national language,' she said.

'Why didn't you learn English? It is an international language, after all,' Noor replied in a mocking tone.

Belching out a sardonic 'huh', she replied, 'Who would have taught me English? If I had insisted on it, my father would have kicked me out of the house.'

'Just keep quiet when you don't know anything,' Noor shot back, his choler rising as he heard the truth in her statement.

'You men are afraid of educated women.'

'Yes, many men are, but I am not. If you had really wanted an education, you would have got it yourself.'

'Are you saying it is my fault? It was men like you who didn't want women to be educated.'

'Men like me would have given their daughters the same education that they gave to their sons. You don't have to go far.

Look at my sister. I fought with my father to get her an education, and now look at her! She has a PhD in political science and is a respected professor in Australia.'

Noor did face his father's ire when, against his wishes, he got his sister, Rehana, admitted at Patna University and then later paid the tuition for her to study at Oxford. His father did not speak to him for three months. In contrast to Rehana, Farhat had received only a primary education, that too at home, and mostly imparted by her grandfather. She studied fifth-standard textbooks, but as was the case for many of her other female cousins, the doors to education were slammed shut on her after that. Obscurantist tradition put a damper on her dreams, and Farhat's schooling settled on religious education, reciting the Qur'an in Arabic and the Hadith in Urdu. Technically, she was not illiterate, for she knew how to read and write in Urdu. But that was all she could do. She was not exposed to literature; she was never introduced to the discipline of history, or ever had any encounters with the liberal arts.

Tears rolled down Farhat's eyes as she turned to the other side of the bed. Mansoor felt a rush of blood to the head. He resented his father for treating her so gruffly, and although Noor never abused her physically, he would lash out verbally whenever she challenged him. After a temporary pause, Noor recollected his scattered thoughts and continued with his diatribe, 'Son, the ruin that ignorance has brought on this nation, especially on women, is unforgivable.'

Mansoor didn't know who to blame or what to do. Clearly, his mother regretted the fact that she had not received an education, and it was also clear that she had wanted it. He wished he could teach her everything he learned at school. But now, it was too late.

Eight

Haider Rizvi had learned from one of his 'anonymous sources' that the coup of 1958 had the backing of Dwight D. Eisenhower, the American President who knew about the overthrow of the government even before the Pakistani prime minister did. Haider's sources also informed him that Zakir had returned to Pakistan to move permanently to Islamabad, the new capital of the country, where he would head a new university rumoured to be funded by the American government. When Noor heard this, he yelled, 'Mashallah, this is Zakir's clever way of ingratiating himself with the new dictator. He wants to be the *gilli* to the military dictator's *dundda*,' he had replied to Haider.

Gilli-dundda is a popular subcontinent game that only needs a big stick, the dundda, and a small stick, the gilli. The objective of the game is to hit the gilli with the dundda as far as possible.

Suspicious of the dictator's intentions, the barrister had nicknamed him General Dundda Khan, because he was often pictured with a stick in his hand, especially when he donned his grandiose military uniform, the warrior image demanding to be seen in all its sinister glory in order to demoralize his democratic enemies.

*

It had been a while since The Unholy Quartet had had a proper gathering. So, this time around, Haider invited all of them for dinner at his house to celebrate Zakir's return and his new career as a would-be academic. He wanted to find out from the man himself whether what he had heard from his source was true or not. Haider lived in the north Nazimabad area of Karachi, a newly built enclave originally designed for federal government employees. When the capital shifted to Islamabad, many middle-class families were also allowed to move to this residential area. Since it was one of the best-planned areas in Karachi at the time, designed by Italian architects, Haider had decided to build his house there. It was a modest bungalow without a name—unlike the Kashana-e-Haq—and with a fractional address: 33/8, Block C.

Having no separate men's quarters, Haider had his friends ushered in by a Bengali servant to his working library. Cluttered with books, some opened, many piled precariously over each other, and with papers strewn all over his writing desk, his library accentuated its value in use. Four large bookshelves covered two adjacent walls. A twenty-four-volume set of *Encyclopaedia Britannica* and a fifty-four-volume set of *The Great Books of the Western World*, bookended by a brass horse, occupied much of the space. There were other smaller bookshelves in the room as well, containing an array of books on politics, a *Roget's Thesaurus* and two volumes of the *Oxford English Dictionary*. In one corner, an old sitar stood alone, surrounded by two chairs, a dusty reminder that someone fiddled with music in this household.

'Are you working on a story, Haider?' Sadiq asked, noticing all the handwritten notes that lay scattered over the writing desk.

'Actually, I am working on a book on the representatives of Muslims in the partition of India.'

'Oh, really? What are you going to call it?' Noor asked.

'*Representatives of Muslims and the Partition of India.*'

'A scholar amongst us?' Noor asked.

'We already have a scholar amongst us, and his name is Sadiq Mirza,' Haider clarified.

'Oh, yes. I forgot about your books, Sadiq. Sorry!'

'Don't worry, Noor; I am trying to forget about them, too,' Sadiq replied.

Although everyone laughed at his joke, one of Sadiq's books, *Poetry of Rebellion in the Urdu Tradition*, had already been hailed by the critics as path-breaking work.

After a few rounds of London Lager, the conversation turned to Pakistani politics, a requirement as usual. Two years into power, the field marshal, the first military dictator, had issued a public proclamation designating 27 October—the anniversary of his coup—a public holiday to commemorate the day as the 'day of revolution'. In one of his radio broadcasts, he declared: 'My beloved citizens, my ultimate aim is to restore democracy. I declare this to you, unequivocally, in the presence of God.'

'The man doesn't even know how to spell democracy,' Noor complained to his friends.

'Give the general a chance; don't be so quick to judge him,' Zakir defended the man.

'Give General Dundda a chance to do what? Ruin the country? Establish tyranny?'

'Is this the face of a tyrant?' Zakir asked.

'The face of a tyrant doesn't always resemble Stalin's, and the gulags are not always in Siberia.'

'You just need an excuse to criticize anything and everything about Pakistan. Show some patriotism, my good man!' Zakir got fed up with Noor.

'"Patriotism is the virtue of the vicious," said Oscar Wilde,' Noor replied. After a pause, he continued, 'If I criticize Pakistan, it is not out of hate, it is because of love, and if you don't criticize your country for its faults, you don't take your country seriously.'

A dead silence took over the room. It seemed that Zakir's confrontations with the barrister had begun to happen with greater frequency and with increasing zeal.

The call to dinner by Haider's servant came at a fitting moment, forcing the friends to move to a different room and shifting the conversation from the infuriating to the banal. During dinner, Zakir revealed that he had actually resigned from the FAO and was going to join the Planning Commission that Dundda Khan had set up. No wonder he was defending the government. Now that he has to wipe the field marshal's ass, he will not accept any criticism of the government, Noor thought.

Corruption in the country continued with reckless abandon as General Dundda promoted himself to become the Chief Martial Law Administrator (CMLA). To Noor, CMLA was really an acronym for 'Coordinate My Lies Accordingly'. After a slight hiatus, when the general appointed his cronies to write a new Constitution, Zakir hailed his decision as something wondrous, the outcome of which would usher 'real democracy in Pakistan'. Zakir's joining of the general's government created an uneasy distance between him and the rest of the group. From then on, the other three regarded him as a government mole.

*

Mansoor's education continued as planned by his parents, but Noor remained oblivious to the religious teacher's existence. Maulvi Nazir, a corpulent, grizzled-haired man, in the image of Sancho Panza, sans the donkey, his clothes smelling of spicy food, had endeared himself to Mansoor. His two-hundred pounds, sitting precariously on a five-foot, three-inch frame, shook with his deep rumbling laughter every time he told a joke. In between these jokes, Maulvi Nazir mostly scared Mansoor with threats of punishments of the grave. He told Mansoor that drinking alcohol was the root of all evil, and that the penalty for this sin was eighty lashes.

'You should never enter a place where alcohol is stored or served. If they ban sharab in this country, all evil will disappear like this,' the maulvi snapped his fingers.

The pronouncement made Mansoor so uncomfortable that he thought it best to change the subject.

'Maulvi Sahib, are djinns real?'

'Of course, they are real! What kind of a stupid question is that? Everyone knows they are real. If they weren't, would they be mentioned in the Qur'an?'

'Can you tell me more?'

'Well, djinns were Hazrat Suleman's slaves, who employed them to make his castles and buildings.'

'What do they look like?' Mansoor asked.

'How would I know? I haven't seen his castles!'

'No, I mean the djinns.'

The maulvi paused, closed his eyes and drew a deep breath before starting his sermon. 'God created men from earth, angels from light and djinns from smokeless fire. He created the djinns two thousand years before he created Adam. They are invisible creatures, but they can take the shape of animals and humans. Some djinns are Muslims, while others are infidels. The Muslim djinns pray five times a day, fast during Ramadan and perform the hajj.' He said all this as if it were a memorized lesson from his childhood.

'What do the infidel djinns do?'

'How would I know? I don't hang out with them.'

'Who was Hazrat Suleman?' Mansoor asked.

'Hazrat Suleman was a prophet of God, the master of the djinns, their king.'

The maulvi took out a red handkerchief and blew his nose.

'Do you remember that night last spring when it rained furiously?' the maulvi continued, his voice becoming dramatic now.

'Yes,' Mansoor replied.

'Do you remember the loud thunder we heard throughout the night?'

'Yes.'

'Well, all the evil djinns were having a farting competition. That's what it was.' He looked at Mansoor and then laughed so hard that his whole body started to shake. Just then, a muezzin called the faithful for prayers from a nearby mosque. Maulvi Nazir abruptly stopped laughing and hurriedly left for the mosque, leaving Mansoor wholly bewildered.

That night, before his father returned from work, he asked his mother, 'Amma, the thing that father drinks . . . is that sharab?'

'No! Absolutely not. Who told you that? Don't you *ever* use that word in our house! The thing that your father drinks . . . that's his medicine.'

But Mansoor was not stupid; he knew of his mother's attempts to cover up his father's addiction. And he knew that his father had no medical problem whatsoever. Mansoor couldn't remember ever seeing him sick. But even though his doubts didn't go away, he did not pursue this line of questioning any further. As it happened, Noor came home that night while Farhat was praying, and although it was a bit late, he was surprisingly sober. Farhat looked at the ceiling, smiled and thanked God. Her prayers were working. If you beseech Allah humbly and earnestly, He answers all prayers.

*

Weeks passed by. When winter came, it swiftly clipped the autumnal drag, and what remained of the year whizzed past. For Farhat, the new year brought no respite from what she called 'a donkey load of problems' for her. First, there were Pyaro and Joseph, who continued to live in her premises for what seemed to be forever now. When Farhat prodded Pyaro for the millionth time, the woman told her that the new hut that Joseph and his uncle were building was almost ready. After a long pause, she said, 'We will move back as soon as it is done, Begum Sahiba.'

'This constantly hearing the word "soon", it has infected my ears,' Farhat told her.

And then there was Mehrun, who became a little too visible around the Kashana for Farhat's comfort. Since schools were closed for the winter break and Kaneez was mostly occupied at Dr Minwalla's clinic (the doctor's business had suddenly boomed; rumours were rife that the general was going to launch a forced sterilization drive in the country as part of a family planning programme, so families had begun to try having as many children as possible before the men became *namard*, impotent), Mehrun showed up at the Kashana with Jumman every day, staying from morning till late evening and eating all her meals there. To make matters worse for Farhat, Noor conveniently left for the capital city to argue a case at the Supreme Court.

The presence of all these undesirable lodgers at the Kashana forced Farhat to visit her father on that frigid January day. Mansoor, feeling a little sick, had stayed back in his room and was whiling time away by fiddling with his Meccano set. He was always clumsy with all the nuts and bolts the set had. According to his mother, 'the boy has never successfully constructed anything from the set ever since his father bought it from England.' Getting frustrated now, Mansoor put all the green pieces back in the box and pushed it under his bed. He picked up *Gulliver's Travels* from his desk and began reading it, but soon got distracted by Mehrun, whom he could see from his bedroom window, sitting under the guava tree with a book in her hand. Usually, the girl's mere presence would have been enough of a gravitational pull to get him out of his bedroom. But with a book in her hand, it was simply too much to resist. So, despite being down in the dumps, Mansoor decided to go out and see what she was up to. With neither of his parents around, this was the perfect opportunity to fraternize with that 'lowly outcast' freely.

The dry, brownish grass of the lawn and the absence of any flowers made the backyard look dead. The only thing that coloured the landscape was Mehrun in her pink shalwar-kameez and a bright red sweater with a gaping hole at the elbow. Unperturbed by the bone-chilling wind and undisturbed by the dark winter cloud in the sky, she remained glued to her book.

'What are you doing?' Mansoor asked, walking up to her. 'It's so cold out here!'

'Are you a wimp? It's not cold.'

'What are you doing?'

'Can't you see I am reading?'

'What are you reading?'

With pursed lips and a frown on her face, she reluctantly showed him the book. *The English Reader: For Urdu-Medium Students.*

'Read to me what you were reading.'

'No!'

'I swear I'll not make fun of you.'

'No!'

'I promise.'

'No!'

'Please.'

'If you make fun of me, I'll kick your ass. Twice.'

When Mansoor persisted, she started to read one of the book's stories, 'Mrs Ahmad Goes on a Shopping Spree', haltingly.

'Mrs Ahmad told Mr Ahmad that she went to Bohri Bazaar in her motor car to shop for a *biloo* saree.'

'Blue saree,' Mansoor corrected her.

'Biloo saree,' she repeated.

Mansoor puckered his lips to sound the word 'blue'. As Mehrun imitated him, she began giggling. After a bit of merriment, she continued to read more, making more mistakes, feeling the traps of her mother tongue, unable to tackle the nuances of the foreign language, moving her lips, dancing her tongue under Mansoor's guidance. After she got the hang of the words, she beamed and said, 'Mansoor Babu, you are a good teacher. Why don't *you* teach me English?'

'I can if you want me to, but I have a better idea. After the vacation, when Zaidi Sahib comes back, why don't you ask him to teach you too? He can give us both English lessons.'

His eyes lit up when he proposed his grand idea, but Mehrun did not seem thrilled. In fact, she seemed bothered about that proposal, and after a pause, she said, 'Did you eat charas for breakfast? Where will I get the money to pay him for the lessons?'

'Oh, he is a nice man! He will teach you for free.'

Mansoor declared this with much confidence, as if being Zaidi Sahib's pupil had given him an insight into his teacher's complex mind. And Mehrun, though still not so sure about Zaidi's benevolence, started imagining about chattering away in English, watching English movies, reading English magazines, and best of all, giving orders to people in English. Dreams of becoming a high society begum started to percolate in her mind. Ah, the begums she had heard so much about, the begums who did nothing all day long but gave orders to servants like her, the begums who ate delicious chocolates and wore beautiful clothes and shopped at Elphinstone Street, or Elphi, as they so lovingly called it. She had heard about them from her mother, who was well acquainted with them from being on the rounds with Dr Minwalla to deliver their babies.

'They stay at home and smoke cigarettes and talk *git-pit git-pit* in English,' her mother had told her.

Kaneez had raved about their grand houses, their expensive furniture, their spoiled children and their servants, all in one breath. Yes, indeed, the first step was to learn their language; the rest would come later.

Joseph, however, shattered Mehrun's fantasies about these begums. He sauntered towards Mansoor and Mehrun from his new living quarter, singing the hit song from the Bollywood film *Awaara*:

Awaara hoon, awaara hoon
Ya gardish mein hoon aasman ka tara hoon

(I am a loafer, I am a loafer
Or perhaps an orbiting star in the sky)

Holding a bidi in his fist, he inhaled it with gusto, as though it was his last bidi before his execution. After exhaling, he continued with his song. He offered the bidi, ever so nonchalantly, to Mansoor, who declined it, and then to Mehrun, who accepted it as if it was the most natural thing to do. Mansoor was surprised at Mehrun's apparent ease in handling the bidi; he had never seen a girl smoking, let alone somebody who was only a few years older than him.

'Do you want to see my new house?' Joseph asked.

'That's not your house, you thief of Baghdad!'

'I am not talking about this house, but my house in Bhangi Para.'

'Is it finished?' Mehrun asked.

'Almost. I can take you both today, on my bicycle.'

'Where did you steal the bicycle from?' Mehrun continued.

Joseph laughed. 'I stole it from my uncle, who stole it from Pappu, the *dalla*.' Mehrun did not believe him, but she did not pursue the matter any further. Mansoor, however, squirmed on hearing Joseph use the word 'dalla', which was the Urdu word for a pimp, so easily, and that too in front of Mehrun, not that she seemed to mind it.

'So, what do you say, boss?' Joseph asked Mansoor.

Mansoor wanted to go, but he still wasn't feeling well. Besides, what if Amma discovered that he was hanging out with Mehrun and Joseph at Bhangi Para? What a scene she would create! He could see her standing there, grinding her teeth, flaring her nostrils and furrowing her eyebrows in anger, and he knew exactly what she would say: 'Not only did you play with *them*, but you also went to *his* house!'

'You two go ahead; I have a cold,' Mansoor said, sniffling.

But Mehrun saw that wimpy look, the look that he had whenever he heard his parents calling him back inside. Yep. She knew it all too well, the puckered face, the knitted brows and the bowed head.

'Nobody will know! And we will be back before Begum Sahiba returns,' Mehrun coaxed him.

'Come on, Mansoor Babu, I'll show you a world that you have never seen before. You will never want to go back to your house,' Joseph said, snickering.

'Okay,' Mansoor said weakly, giving in.

Joseph brought in the dilapidated bicycle that he had parked outside the Kashana and told Mansoor to sit on the crossbar, and Mehrun on the back rack. Once everyone was seated, Joseph pedalled the rusty bike without any exertion, singing a lewd Punjabi song as they went:

> *Main kasai nu bitya vikhia*
> *Usana mota keema liaia*
> *Usana kolhi nala maria*
> *Aur chhati nala dabaia*

> (I saw the butcher's daughter
> She brought the fatty minced meat
> Whacked me with her hips
> And minced me with her chest)

*

The way to Joseph's new house seemed to stretch on for an eternity, and throughout the journey, Mansoor's heart throbbed rapidly.

He had been up to the railway lines, but never had he ventured beyond that vast expanse of empty space that formed a cordon sanitaire between opulence and indigence, between touchable and untouchable. Joseph pedalled vigorously through the narrow, muddy path, dodging semi-naked children with bloated bellies. Mansoor saw little boys and girls in dirty rags, one of them pushing a spoke-less bicycle tyre. He saw two boys defecating in the open, engaged in an animated conversation, unmindful of their surroundings and undisturbed by the people around. The smell of faeces mixed with the odour of rotting garbage made Mansoor dizzy. He saw a woman, not unlike Pyaro, thrash her bawling child on his bare bottom. He spotted an old, dark-complexioned man in a turban urinate in front of a burnt half-demolished wall. Nearby, the rotting carcass of a dog attracted hungry crows that hovered above it in the air, waiting for their chance to feast. From every corner of Joseph's neighbourhood, poverty glared and screamed at the smartly dressed Mansoor. It was a frigid day, but little beads of salty sweat trickled from his brows, reaching his eyes and dripping to his lips. He felt as if someone had put a dagger in his heart. Suddenly, Joseph swerved into a blind alley and tried to stop the bike by dragging his feet along the ground. As it came to a halt in front of a hovel, Mansoor realized that the bicycle had no brakes.

'Welcome to Bhangi Para,' Joseph announced to his fellow riders with a flourish.

As Mansoor jumped off the crossbar, his feet landed in a pile of fresh cow dung. He felt something from his stomach move up and threaten to come out of his mouth.

'This, my friends, is my Taj Mahal,' Joseph announced, smiling proudly. He was pointing towards a little place that was a study in the architecture of absurdity. Hundreds of loosely compressed cement bricks formed a crudely built cabin, and in place of a door, hung a curtain made from patches of gunnysack.

'I feel like throwing up,' Mansoor said, trying really hard to clamp down on the vomit rising up his throat.

Joseph laughed and replied, 'Come on, Mansoor Babu! It's not that bad.'

But the smell and the sight of cow dung on his shoes had overtaxed Mansoor's ability to control his vomit. He took out his handkerchief from his pocket and whiffed the faint but clean smell of washing detergent. That seemed to have a settling effect on him.

Joseph, meanwhile, insisted on taking them to the back of the house, where the rusting front frame of a Volkswagen Beetle jutted out like the nose of a proboscis monkey. Two semi-naked boys chasing a squealing pig ran right past them as they stood staring at the house. Mansoor had never seen a pig before; he did not even know that there were pigs in Karachi, despite his father's frequent allusions to the ruling elite as such.

Mansoor had had enough; he could not take it any more. So, he told Joseph that he wanted to go home.

'But we just arrived! Have a sherbet, it will cool you down,' Joseph tried to pacify Mansoor.

'No, I want to go home.'

'Mansoor Babu, you are my guest. You should eat or drink something.'

'No, I am not hungry. I just want to go home!' Mansoor shouted.

'Don't worry, I'll give you the food in a Muslim plate.'

'No, it's not that. My mother will be back and if she doesn't find me at home, she will be very angry with me.'

'I think he is right, Joseph. If Begum Sahiba finds out that we kidnapped Mansoor Babu, we'll both get such a thrashing that we will remember our *nani*s, our grandmothers,' Mehrun intervened, noticing the crimson hue on Mansoor's face. Joseph's face changed, too, the hurt all too obvious to hide. Without another word, all three of them hopped back on the bike and prepared for their return trip, which seemed even longer now. This time, Joseph sang a mournful song:

Dil torney waley dekh ke chal
Hum bhi to parey hain rahon mein

(O heartbreaker, tread carefully
For I am also lying in the path)

*

When he returned home, Mansoor was glad to find that his mother was still at her father's house. He bolted straight to the bathroom, lifted the toilet seat, puked into the commode and immediately felt better. After flushing the toilet, Mansoor rinsed his mouth, washed his face and went into his room. As he collapsed on his bed, a baby lizard, glued to the ceiling, caught his eyes, its translucent glassy body more beautiful than anything he had seen at Bhangi Para. Mansoor closed his eyes and soon began dreaming.

In his dream, he felt light-headed and found himself falling down a pit, about to crash headfirst. Then, he noticed his feet. They were big.

'Oh, God! What is happening to me?' he roared.

'How are you, Djinn Sahib?' He saw Mehrun dressed in her tattered sweater.

'Have a Muslim plate, Sahib.' It was Joseph, holding the carcass of a cat in a deep plate.

'Mansoor, wake up! Wake up!'

Mansoor woke up with a start and saw his mother's worried face looming over him.

'Are you okay, beta? You were mumbling in your dream.' She felt his forehead. 'You are burning! You have a fever.'

Mansoor, shivering and delirious, remained like that until Sikander brought Dr Minwalla. After doing a detailed check-up, she told Farhat that Mansoor had double pneumonia and prescribed some antibiotics.

Was it the simple cold that he had from before that had turned into this acute illness? Or was it the sight of the unforgettable Bhangi Para that had caused it? Whatever it was, Mansoor remained confined to his bed for two weeks. It was the worst two weeks of his young life. The first week and a half, his fever disoriented him, bringing with it chills and delirium. At night, he hallucinated and whimpered and cried. Things improved dramatically after that, and by the time his father returned from the capital, Mansoor had almost recovered. It was as if he was waiting for his father's return so that he could get better.

Nine

Ramadan, the month of fasting, arrived with great anticipation. Everyone in Mansoor's class fasted, except him, but he pretended otherwise. It was not that his father had prohibited him from doing so, or that Mansoor did not want to fast; it was just his mother who had scared him. 'Your father will get angry if he learns about it, but if you really want to, you can fast one or two days without telling him. I will cover for you.'

Noor never forbade Mansoor or Farhat from fasting, but somehow, she had assumed that he would get angry with them if they did. As for Mansoor, he had once heard him argue with Haider on that matter.

'Forcing children to fast at such a tender age is a cruel and unusual punishment.'

That settled things for Mansoor.

After Mansoor recovered from his illness, his tutor came back to continue his lessons. Mansoor reminded Mehrun to ask Zaidi about tutoring her. At first, Mehrun remained steadfastly reluctant; she did not know how to approach Zaidi. Deep down, she felt that Zaidi would turn her down and it would all come to nothing. But when Mansoor kept prodding her, Mehrun finally agreed to do it. He convinced her that she was sharp and intelligent, and that with Zaidi's help, she could be transformed. Who knew just how many more opportunities might open up if she could read, write and speak even a bit of English? She could get a job as a full-time ayah, or she could perhaps be employed in some capacity in some school. At least she wouldn't have to wash dirty laundry at other people's houses like her mother.

When Zaidi came to the Kashana that day, Mehrun hesitantly came and sat near them. Since it was Mehrun's habit to flit around in the vicinity whenever their lessons where in progress, Zaidi did not even notice her at first. A poker-faced man in his late twenties, the young tutor had an air of inscrutability about him. His body appeared pulled down by the enormity of some unknown burden, but it could be that the fasting had sapped his energy. Whenever he sat on the wicker chair in the verandah, his posture stooped and his shoulders slumped; often, Mansoor found him looking into empty space. But when his attention returned to the lesson of the day, he became an engrossing teacher, expounding thoughtfully on how good literature was equivalent to a book of life that taught self-discovery.

That afternoon, as Zaidi prepared to start the day's lesson, Mansoor signalled Mehrun with his eyes to approach the tutor. Just then, a wasp flew by and landed on the arm of the chair next to Zaidi's, making him flinch. He picked up Mansoor's open textbook and tried to squash the wasp with it. But the wasp flew off towards the rose bush in the garden. The distraction gave Mehrun the perfect opportunity to come as close to Zaidi as possible. But when he noticed her right next to him, his expression changed. What was this lowly interloper doing standing in his face? His bushy eyebrows furrowed as he held his chin with his left hand, and then he looked Mehrun up and down. Mehrun recoiled a bit, wavering in her resolution. Then she looked at Mansoor, who moved his eyes quickly in code language, telling her to put her question to the tutor.

'Zaidi Sahib, um . . . can you . . . um . . . teach me . . . um . . . English?'

From deep inside his gut, Zaidi sucked up a glob of sputum and spat it out disgustingly into a potted plant behind his chair before he replied, 'I don't give lessons to haramis.'

The word impaled Mansoor's heart; he hoped that Mehrun had not heard the tutor, and that she would just go away, but there she stood firm, unfazed and undeterred, as if the man had said something routine, a fact, a run-of-the mill idiom. And then Mansoor heard her again.

'My father will pay you.'

'You filthy insect from a stinking gutter, I don't need your ill-begotten money!'

From the corner of his eyes, Mansoor saw Mehrun, her face now ignited by the dark flush of rage. She moved away from Zaidi and slowly started to walk back towards the servants' quarters, but then she stopped, turned back towards him and calmly said, 'You stupid shit-faced man, your mother is harami; your father is harami; your entire household is harami.'

Mansoor's face turned ashen. He saw his tutor kick his chair back and lunge towards Mehrun, his jaws snapping, his face trembling with anger. Anticipating the impending assault, Mehrun sprinted towards the servants' quarters where her father was taking a siesta. Zaidi chased her with full speed and within minutes, caught her shirt from the back, causing it to tear along the side seams. He then pushed her with all his strength. Mansoor saw Mehrun fall flat on the concrete surface and started screaming hysterically. Zaidi pulled her up, turned her around and began slapping and punching her mercilessly. The man was an absolute savage, overtaken by madness. Mansoor thought that he would kill Mehrun, so he started screaming as well. The commotion brought Jumman out of the servants' quarters. Shocked to see his daughter getting pummelled, he leapt at the tutor, pulled him away from her and began hammering him. The ruckus brought Noor and Farhat out.

'What's going on? What's going on here?' Noor yelled.

'Noor Sahib, she gave me a dirty *gaali*, a dirty swear word, for nothing,' Zaidi lied.

'No, Sahib, he called me harami first. Ask Mansoor Babu,' Mehrun replied, still sobbing, a trickle of blood flowing from her nose.

'All of you get out of my property and never come back,' Noor yelled. 'This is the house of decent people. Don't you ever use language like that!'

Mehrun got up, wiping her bloodied nose with the back of her hand, her face covered with tears and dirt. In between convulsive sobs, she begged her father to take her home. Jumman pleaded with Noor about her innocence, but to no effect. The order had been issued; the edict had been given. There was no backtracking.

*

When things settled down a little, Noor summoned Mansoor, who had gone into hiding in his room. He came and stood at the door of his father's study, his mouth drooping, his head bowed down, a confusing jumble of emotions. Noor asked him, 'Tell me exactly what happened.'

But the exact words betrayed Mansoor at that moment and he began to sob. Noor went towards him and hugged him. 'Take your time, beta. But I want you to slowly tell me what exactly happened this afternoon, all right?' he said gently.

Mansoor told him the entire story then, hesitatingly at first, but with great confidence gradually, and ended up amplifying Zaidi's offences and minimizing Mehrun's.

'All these obscenities hurled at the poor girl, just because she wanted to learn English?' Noor asked.

S.M. Zaidi was a graduate of the Aligarh university. He was a teacher of English language and literature, someone who was supposed to nurture civility in speech and promote the sanctity of the spoken word, especially in front of his pupils. How could he, a supposed idealist, have stooped to such vileness? His behaviour was absolutely unacceptable. His service must be terminated, and Jumman must be rehired.

So, the next day, Noor sent Sikander first to Zaidi's house with a letter of termination and one month's salary in an envelope, and then to Jumman's home to entreat him to come back; but Jumman had his pride too. He felt hurt and betrayed and sent Sikander back empty-handed. Mansoor blamed himself for the unfortunate fracas, but there was nothing he could do. The die was cast, and the lots were sealed. He resigned himself to the thought of never seeing Mehrun again. When Kaneez heard about the whole incident, she said, 'That djinn did this to my daughter,' and then she flogged Mehrun for associating with Mansoor in spite of her warnings.

*

Afternoons at the Kashana became too painful for Mansoor after the incident with Zaidi and Mehrun. The sense of estrangement with Mehrun, the blighted hope, the deep hurt, the utter guilt, all of it made him miserable. The precious time that he would have spent playing with Mehrun was now wasted in either sulking in his room or sitting under the guava tree, hoping to hear her voice, wishing to see her do her antics. To make matters worse, his favourite uncle, Zahid Mamoo, left for Germany for his studies soon after Eid. His week-long stay in Karachi had cheered Mansoor up a little, but what had truly lifted his spirits was the puppy his uncle had left behind as a parting gift. The Scottish terrier was nothing but a furry ball of utter mischief. Farhat was adamantly opposed to having an unclean animal in the house. But Mansoor manipulated her by insisting that Zahid Mamoo would be deeply hurt if he gave the puppy away. Farhat agreed to Mansoor keeping the puppy, but on one condition: the animal shall never enter the house. Mansoor promised. Because of the spirited nature of the puppy, he began calling him Chaos.

*

After Jumman was dismissed from the Kashana, his family's income came down by a third. But for him, it was a question of honour. His entire life had been devoted to the Haq family. He was not going to put up with slogging for any other *aira gaira nathoo khaira's* family; working for any Tom, Dick and Harry was entirely out of the question. So, Jumman withdrew from being part of the labour force altogether and ordered Kaneez to find extra work to supplement the lost income. She obeyed and began toiling at several other odd jobs. But with only twenty-four hours in a day, someone else had to pull her weight, too. Intense pressure was put on Mehrun to quit school and find work. But Mehrun shrewdly convinced her parents that she could do both. So, she stayed in school and began looking for a job.

However, as the days passed, Jumman began to sorely miss his garden at the Kashana, and so, he eventually found it expedient to forgive Noor, without insisting on an apology. He returned to the Kashana as if what had happened was just a horrible dream. With Jumman's return, Mansoor knew it was but a matter of time before he would find Mehrun sitting under the guava tree, singing some meaningless Urdu ditty or the other. But when days passed and Mansoor got tired of seeing Jumman at the Kashana without Mehrun, he finally went up to him and asked when she would return.

'Oh, she is working at Sadiq Sahib's house now.'

Mehrun had seen the professor at the Kashana and knew that Sadiq was very fond of Mansoor. She also knew that he was an English teacher.

The professor and his wife, Talat, a kind, petite woman in her fifties, lived in the newly built university housing complex. They had three daughters, who were all happily married. Lately, Talat had developed constant aches and pains in her joints, and when the doctor diagnosed her with arthritis, she began looking for hired help to assist her with all the work around the house. When Mehrun learned about it, she promptly offered her services.

At first, Talat had been reluctant to hire a young girl as a servant. But after hearing Mehrun dramatize her family's plight, she employed her to do the cooking and the dusting. Mehrun, however, had an ulterior motive in working there: she wanted to work at the professor's house to learn English from him. After all, he was a teacher of English literature and she was someone who was eager to learn this foreign language—a perfect match!

So, every day after school, Mehrun started taking the bus to go to work at the professor's house. Intelligent and industrious, she impressed Talat with her efficiency and her cooking skills. Talat also enjoyed Mehrun's company, especially her stories. Mehrun, too, liked her mistress and was touched by her kindness; Talat was so unlike Farhat, whom she found icy, aloof and insulting. One day, as they exchanged stories while she cooked, Mehrun casually mentioned her desire to learn the English language. As if it was the most ludicrous thing she had heard all day, Talat chuckled at the idea.

'You want to learn English?' she asked. 'What will you do with it? Make pickles?'

Mehrun shrugged. After a pause, Talat continued, 'My husband teaches English at the university.'

'Oh, really?' Mehrun feigned surprise. 'Do you think he will teach me a little?'

'I don't think he has the time.'

Mehrun devoted most of her time in the Mirza household to dusting the books in the professor's modest library. It was her downtime, caressing all those neatly bound titles that lined the bookshelves. It was there that she could leave behind her wretched world entirely and lose herself in the presence of books. All the writers on the shelves were strangers to her, and she could not even dare to look beyond the covers of the books, afraid that the professor might get angry and whip her, Zaidi-like, but one day, she finally succumbed to a tempting volume while dusting the room.

Pulling out the ornately bound copy of *Oliver Twist*, she wiped off the dirt, savouring the smell of old leather and buckram. Just sniffing these musty volumes made her giddy. Mehrun knew about *Oliver Twist* because the professor had gifted an illustrated edition of the book to Mansoor on his birthday. And Mansoor, after finishing the book, had recounted the tragic tale to Mehrun, reading bits and pieces from the book to her and showing her the illustrations. Now, with trembling fingers, she opened the book and started to go through the illustrations, searching for the sketch of Nancy's murder. There it was, in the end, with Bill Sykes, the cold-blooded murderer throttling her. How she had longed to learn how to read the story for herself, and then Mehrun's mind flashed back to that horrid day when Zaidi beat her ruthlessly—the pain still raw; the banishment still hurting. She dropped the book as her heart shuddered with fear. Tears rolled down her cheeks and trickled on to the hardcover. Why did Zaidi have to insult her? Why did Noor Sahib kick them out? And Mansoor, why did he not come to her defence? Lost in her thoughts, she brooded over that terrifying incident, and then she felt a heavy hand on her shoulder. She jumped.

'Sadiq Sahib, I'm sorry, I was just . . .' She shuddered, wondering if history was going to repeat itself, and braced herself for more indignities, more drubbing. But that did not happen. To her surprise, the professor seemed compassionate. He made her sit and then asked her why she was crying. And Mehrun found herself recounting the violent encounter with Zaidi, the ruthless beating she had received, the abuses she had heard, just for asking him to let her be there with Mansoor Babu during the tutoring session. The man had even called her harami, the worst profanity anyone could throw at a decent human being. Sadiq put his hand on her head to comfort her, as Mehrun dried her tears with the sleeve of her kurta.

After a moment, she turned to the professor and said, 'I know the story of *Oliver Twist*.'

'Oh? Have you read it?'

'No, somebody narrated it to me, but I would like to learn English so that I can read it myself. I want to speak the language fluently.'

'Don't they teach any English in government schools?' he asked.

'They do, but it is simple English. I would like to speak English fluently, like Mansoor Babu.'

'Then you must. I will not only teach you to speak and read English, but I will also teach you to see life through books.'

And with that, the professor left the room, leaving Mehrun puzzled about the last thing he had said. Not knowing what to make of either that or of Sadiq Mirza, she shrugged her shoulders and resumed her dusting.

*

Sadiq Mirza, a portly man in his late fifties, felt smothered by his family life. As was the case with most of his close friends, his marriage to Talat had been an intellectual disaster from the very beginning. It had been arranged by his parents when he was only twenty and she was sixteen. They were on a different plane when they started their married life, and with time and age, they had wandered further away from each other. Tethered together for thirty-seven years, they continued their life journey without any spark of love, without any bond of empathy between them. The longer they stayed together, the more detached they became. It wasn't a contentious marriage like Noor's by any means. Far from it, it was placid—their whole existence too unruffled for Sadiq's taste. He often reflected on a line from Virginia Woolf's

To the Lighthouse, which he had underlined: '. . . there was scarcely anything left of body or mind by which one could say, "This is he" or "This is she."' He felt bored in this togetherness, just like Mr and Mrs Ramsay did. Their only common link, the one that made them feel alive, were their daughters, but they too had got married and moved on. But Sadiq was not an egotist; he was not Mr Ramsay, for he did attend to Talat's needs; only, he did not love her. Like Noor, he too experienced solitude in marriage.

*

After she had finished her work for the day, Mehrun headed towards the bus stop. The thought of going home and making dinner for her parents made her feel exhausted. As she sat on the bench at the bus stop, she yawned and closed her eyes. To veer her mind away from all thoughts of the drudgery that awaited her at home, she began dreaming about her future again. Next year, she would be done with school. After that, college!

St Joseph's would be nice, she thought, but that was an impossibility. Maybe President's College, if she could get a first division.

Her mind meandered to her imaginary house—a house, not unlike the Kashana, where she, as the begum, would rule from her august divan, dressed in her expensive Banarsi saree, sipping imported coffee and talking mostly in English or refined Urdu. What a great life it would be! She imagined being taught by Sadiq Mirza in his nurturing tone. Was he her ticket to riches? No longer uneasy about him, she smiled. From a distance, she saw a packed bus, coughing out thick, noxious fumes, approaching her. As it stopped, a few passengers got down and Mehrun boarded it from the women's entrance. She paid for her ticket and stood sandwiched between two buxom women, both of them veiled. Summer stretched the daylight, and sparrows flew longer in search of food. The cloudless sky sighed as the cool evening breeze provided some relief from the heat.

Ten

When General Dundda gave the nation a brand-new second Constitution in March 1962, Noor declared to his son, 'Two Constitutions in fifteen years is no ordinary feat, *Sahibzadey*. By the time this country of *yours* is fifty years old, this version could very well become a collector's item!' His father's use of the word 'sahibzadey', which in Urdu means a sahib's son, was a sarcastic third-person syntactical way of telling Mansoor that he should have known all this. It was a word that always irritated him.

At first, Mansoor did not understand why his father lived in *his* country if he hated it so much. Why did he not move to the United States or Britain, the two countries he admired the most? But later, Noor's constant cynicism about *his* country and *his* leaders began to rankle his mind. In school, Mansoor was taught the binary lesson of '*My* country, right or wrong', that being patriotic meant never criticizing your country. At home, he was lectured about the perils of blind patriotism.

'If you just sweep the dirt under the carpet, you don't actually believe in cleanliness. And if you don't criticize what's wrong in your country, you are not serious about its future,' his father would say. And Mansoor, his shoulders slumped, his hands cupping his chin and his eyes cast down in a desolate gaze, began paying attention to his father's critique of *his* country.

*

General Dundda shed his stuffy military uniform for a sombre business suit and made himself the President. He banned public gatherings, prohibited political meetings and reined in the 'irresponsible' journalists. Haider Rizvi, a well-known *irresponsible* journalist, tried to play hide-and-seek with the government and often got into hot water with the censor board. When the progressive coalition, in tandem with the mullahs, took to the streets, Noor felt betrayed. It was as if he had rested all his hopes on the liberals. The mullahs and their left-wing foes were protesting together. The former were incensed that a country like Pakistan, formed on a religious identity, still had a secular Constitution, while the latter were enraged that there was still a dictatorship. Banding together, the opposition formed a new party, the Combined Opposition Party of Pakistan (C.O.P.) and protested in more cities.

To placate the vociferous religious parties, the general had amended the Constitution, and by the stroke of his Montblanc pen, inserted the word 'Islamic' in front of the word 'Republic'. When he heard the expected news, Noor exclaimed to Mansoor, 'A simple word, a simple insertion, and voilà, you are a grand theocracy!' The man who had repeatedly told Mansoor that nothing shocked him about this country was stunned by this cold official conversion.

One Sunday in August, Noor invited his friends to the Kashana, but only Zakir, who was in town visiting his family, and Haider came. As usual, they discussed politics and drank Scotch.

'So, the *brilliant* Oxford-slash-Berkeley educated lawyer is now our *brilliant* foreign minister. What do you have to say to that, Noor?' Haider asked, referring to the appointment of the new foreign minister.

Noor kept quiet, but Zakir answered, 'And he is a *brilliant* feudal lord, don't forget that.'

That Zakir's sarcasm was aimed at a government official did not go unnoticed. Had he started to see the reality of the government he served under?

'General Dundda has at least lifted the martial law. Maybe he is serious about democracy after all,' Haider said.

When no response came from Noor, the friends looked at each other. The barrister was not his usual self that day. He seemed weary and restrained, and his friends, unable to instigate him into making any bold predictions, left early.

*

On that cold day in November, when the dry wind scattered scraps of discarded newspapers everywhere, rubbishing every report that came in its path, the C.O.P.s held a massive protest rally in the city. Unaware of the protest call and feeling slightly ill, Kaneez had already left for Dr Minwalla's clinic to work her morning shift. But by early afternoon, she began complaining about dizziness, headache and nausea. When her condition became worse, she begged the doctor to let her go home early, but Minwalla refused. Kaneez pleaded several times, but the doctor remained steadfast in her refusal—the midwife had already used too many days off by 'pretending that she was sick'. Unable to take it any longer, Kaneez grabbed her tattered black burqa, picked her burlap bag and sneaked out of the clinic. Feeling fortunate to find a waiting bus at the nearby bus stop, she climbed on gingerly. Her entire body quivered as she sat down, the bus's violent lurching and jerky movements jarred her spine, as it picked up speed.

Kaneez had been dozing in her seat when the bus, virtually empty, suddenly stopped with a loud screech, jolting her awake. Kaneez heard a ruckus and, looking out of the window, saw an angry mob surrounding the bus. The protesters were yelling obscenities at General Dundda. One young man clambered inside the bus and ordered everyone out. As soon as the bus emptied, Kaneez saw someone splash kerosene on it from a canister and throw a burning rag. Within minutes, the entire bus was ablaze. Engulfed in a massive ball of fire, it looked like a fiery ogre. Kaneez felt a tremor under her club foot as she hurriedly limped away from the flaming bus, the smell of kerosene and the wafting black smoke making her feel even more queasy. Still quite a distance from her house, she decided to walk up to the next bus stop that was a few blocks away. The gusty wind continued to blow away discarded newspapers, plastic bottles and debris as she dragged herself towards the bus stop. Feeling cold, Kaneez tried wrapping herself tightly with her burqa. When she reached the bus stop, she found it deserted. She waited for a long time, but no bus came. It must be the cold weather that has driven people away, she thought. She was about to move again when she saw a turbaned man, tightly bundled in a thick blanket, coming towards her.

'Bhai, do you know when the next bus will come?' she asked him.

'There won't be any buses coming today, Mai. Everything in the city is shut down due to the strike,' he told her and quickly walked away.

Kaneez felt dizzy, her strength was slowly radiating out, her courage was gradually betraying her. But she had no choice; she could not give up. Not then, not there. She did not want to die on this deserted street. Taking a deep breath and bracing herself for the long walk ahead, poor Kaneez hobbled along. Even Farhat would have melted, had she seen Kaneez on that cold, empty street that day. As it became dark, Kaneez's condition grew worse. Two more blocks and she would be home. Her body was on the verge of collapse, but it was her stubborn spirit, the one she had also handed down to her daughter, that kept her pushing on. When she reached the men's clinic, which she crossed every day while riding the bus, she knew that her house was not too far away. She decided to rest for a few minutes before walking the last leg of her journey. Spotting a dilapidated bench in front of the clinic, she pulled herself towards it. As soon as she reached the wooden bench, she crashed on it. A giant billboard above her read 'Cure for Men's Weakness: Cure for Generative Organ.' A faded picture of a Western couple, embracing each other, appeared as irrelevant as Kaneez sitting in front of an erectile dysfunction clinic. From her burlap sack, she took out an elongated tin box and a bottle labelled 'pethidine', both pilfered from Dr Minwalla's dispensary. With some difficulty, she opened the tin box and took out a small syringe. Inserting its needle into the bottle, she extracted a small quantity from it and quickly stabbed the needle into her left arm. As the drug began to dance in her limp body, she felt better.

Suddenly the wind picked up speed, and from a distance, Kaneez heard a whirring sound, like a helicopter approaching. 'Allah has arrived!' she screamed, quickly dumping the entire paraphernalia back into her burlap sack. Lifting herself up, she staggered down the lonely path, her alley still nowhere in sight. After every few paces, the poor woman felt like collapsing, but Kaneez did not stop. She kept pulling her weight. And then, the familiar alley near her house suddenly appeared out of nowhere, veiling none of its ugliness. Her spirits brightened; her courage returned. But the very next instant, the whole alley lit up unexpectedly; it was as if somebody had turned on the floodlights. The whirring sound grew deafening and Kaneez froze. Her feet felt like boulders, her head like a ton of granite. She just could not move. Scared and trembling, she lifted her head and got the shock of her life. Standing in front of her was a gigantic apparition. His legs wide apart, his hands behind his back, his face familiar and his entire body engulfed in a bright blaze, he looked disdainfully at her. Without any doubt, it was a djinn.

'Ya Allah, it is a djinn,' she murmured. 'Mansoor Babu? Forgive me.'

She turned back and tried to flee but could not. Her legs remained heavy and motionless. She squeezed her eyes, scratched her arms and tried to recall the evil warding chant that she had heard Mehrun chant:

Jal tu Jalal tu;
Sahib-e- Kamal tu;
Aye bala ko taal tu

(You are Glorious; you are the Glory;
You are the bearer of miracles;
You are the warder of all that is evil)

'That won't work! That is in Urdu,' she heard the djinn say, his voice loud, as if it was coming through a loudspeaker.

She tried to remember something in Arabic, but her foggy memory failed her.

'Do you know who we are?'

'I don't know, Djinn Sahib. Please let me go.'

And then, as suddenly as it had appeared, it disappeared, without warning, without alerting. The whirring ceased. Kaneez, her feet liberated, raced through the darkened alley and kept running until she saw her house.

Upon reaching the door, she forced it open, screaming and panting all this time. Once inside the house, she bolted the entry, turned around, and grabbed the confused Mehrun. Howling hysterically, she started to hit her and then tore her kameez. A non-stop ream of gibberish gushed out of Kaneez's mouth, followed by unconnected profanities. Mehrun struggled to restrain her, but the more she tried, the more violent she became. And then she bit Mehrun and began frothing at the mouth. At the door, Mehrun heard Jumman yelling and banging. She pushed her mother aside and ran towards the door, holding on to her torn shirt.

As the door opened, Jumman rushed in and ran straight towards Kaneez, who was now twisting and writhing on the floor, becoming more frantic, more delirious. She had utterly cracked up. Between wails and laughter, she burbled out a litany of nonsense. The only word they could make out was Mansoor. Out of frustration, Jumman pulled Kaneez up and struck her on her cheek. The powerful blow staggered her and she tripped backward. But Jumman did not stop there. Bending down, he whacked her a few more times until she became senseless. Panting and recovering from the exertion of beating her, Jumman got up and stumbled towards his cot. He ordered Mehrun to bring a brown bag from the green steel trunk that lay next to Kaneez's mattress. She quietly followed his command, still holding her torn kameez together, and handed the bag to him. Jumman took out a large bottle of medicine from the paper bag, something that Dr Minwalla had given him in exchange for pulling out a dead tree from her backyard. His back had hurt from digging and pulling out the tree, and so she had given him this medicine. Not only had he felt better, but he had also felt happier after drinking some of it. 'This is better than money,' she had said. 'It is a miracle drug—*ikseer-e-zindagi*, the elixir of life.'

Jumman got up and went towards Kaneez. Squatting beside her, he pressed open her mouth and poured in the some of the medicine. She made a guttural sound but did not move. Jumman waited, as if expecting her to suddenly pop back into consciousness, but she didn't.

This entire racket had attracted a group of curious neighbours outside their door, including Naseebun, a frequent visitor to the house. She announced to the crowd that Kaneez was under the influence of an evil djinn.

'Jumman, you'll have to call Malang Miran Shah to cast the djinn out. If you want, I can bring him tomorrow,' she offered.

'We'll see about that tomorrow. Now go home,' Jumman replied and closed the door.

Throughout that night, as Mehrun kept a close watch on her mother, she heard the whirring sound of helicopters, and each time, the sound was followed by Kaneez's blood-curdling screams. It was the worst night of her life, far worse than when she had been thrashed by Zaidi.

*

The next morning, Kaneez woke up still delirious and incoherent. Jumman noticed that her body had begun to twitch, and that every now and again, she would have a fit of convulsions. He asked Mehrun to stay with her mother and make her sniff an old shoe after every convulsion, a traditional practice of dealing with epilepsy, popular in many parts of India and Pakistan. Jumman, in the meantime, went to fetch Dr Minwalla. The buses were still not running due to the general strike, so he took a cycle rickshaw. The rickshaw-wallah was a tattler. He talked non-stop and then asked Jumman if he had heard all those helicopters the night before.

'No!' Jumman said, still preoccupied with Kaneez's condition.

'It's the government snooping on us. Why are they wasting all these helicopters on us? Don't they know we are poor people who don't even have time to earn another rupee? Could you believe they would use helicopters on *us*?'

Jumman did not reply, and when they reached Dr Minwalla's clinic, he asked the rickshaw-wallah to wait for him. Although he had been to the doctor's house before, this was the first time he was entering her clinic. More like a dingy, back-alley teahouse, the clinic had a putrefying smell of raw sewage mixed with Dettol. In the small, dark waiting room, Jumman saw a horde of burqa-clad women, sickly children and a few old men with stubbles waiting to be treated. He bounded right past them and went straight into the doctor's office, where Dr Minwalla was busy with a patient.

'Doctor Sahiba, your servant Kaneez . . . I don't know . . . something bad has happened to her. Please, Doctor Sahiba, come with me or she will die,' he said, clasping his hand together as if begging.

'Get out! NOW!' Dr Minwalla yelled at him. 'Don't you see I am busy with a patient? How dare you invade my office like this?'

'Please, Doctor, I beg you, she is going to die,' Jumman persisted.

'She was the one who ran away yesterday when I strictly told her not to go. What do you want from me now?'

'Begum Sahiba, you are her *mai-baap*, her mother and father. You are her mistress; give her some medicine. Make her better.'

'Okay, okay. Stop babbling and don't make a scene. Go to my compounder and give him this.'

She handed him a hastily scribbled prescription. There were no questions asked about Kaneez's symptoms, no diagnostic queries made, no prognostic answers given, just a one-size-fits-all prescription ready to be handed to her compounder. Jumman took the order and went to the next room where he handed it to the compounder. Glowering at him over the rim of his glasses, the man behind the counter passed on the prescription to his assistant, who gave him a bottle containing a pink foamy mixture.

'Give this mixture to her every four hours,' the compounder said to Joseph. In the same breath, he added, 'And it will be three rupees and eight annas.'

'But she works here, Babu,' Joseph said, clutching his hands.

'So do I,' the compounder replied. 'This is not a free dispensary for all the wretched of the world. If you want free medicine, go to the beggars' hospital.'

Jumman shook his head in disbelief as he rummaged for money in his pocket. He took out some loose coins, counted three rupees and eight annas, paid the man and then raced back to the rickshaw. Kaneez's ear-splitting screams were still fresh in his mind.

*

It was true that Jumman had never married Kaneez and that he occasionally beat her up, but he also cared about her. Why else would he plead her case with Farhat Begum? Getting married was a luxury for them; neither had the money nor the inclination. And so, they went on living together, letting people draw their own damn conclusions. Jumman had stood by Kaneez all this time, despite the rumours and the innuendoes. He defied them when they called her a churail; he ignored them when they called her a fornicator; and he fought them when they named their child a harami. But now she lay there, possessed by a djinn, tenuously clinging to life.

When he reached home, he found Kaneez losing and regaining consciousness between bouts of epileptic seizures. He sat by her and carefully gave her the medicine every four hours, just as the compounder had prescribed. Her condition worsened with every passing day. Naseebun came daily, pressurizing Jumman to let the malang, the faith healer, see her. She had no doubt that Kaneez was possessed by a djinn, and the only one who could cure her was Malang Miran Shah. Jumman was not opposed to the idea; he had seen the malangs move things in the air without touching them, he had seen them levitate. The man believed in them, but he wanted the doctor to treat Kaneez first. So, the next day, he sent Mehrun to fetch Dr Minwalla, but she too came back empty-handed. Finally, Jumman relented and agreed to let the malang come and purge the djinn out from his woman's body. But no sooner did he accede to Naseebun's pleas than a black Morris Minor came to a stop two houses before Jumman's. Wearing sunglasses and a white doctor's coat over her saree, Dr Minwalla stepped out of the car with a black physician's bag in her hand. Naseebun came out to greet her.

'Which one is Kaneez's house?' the doctor asked.

'You must be the Doctor Sahiba. Kaneez is doing well now. You don't need to see her.'

'I am not asking for your opinion. If you don't tell me where Kaneez lives, I will call the police and put you in jail.'

The threat of police action worked, and Naseebun led the doctor to their house. As she entered the dilapidated house, Minwalla took off her dark glasses and put on her prescription glasses. When she saw Kaneez lying unconscious on a mattress on the floor and Jumman sitting on his cot, she reprimanded him for being thoughtless.

'Put her on the charpoy and fetch me that chair.'

Jumman lifted Kaneez, her hand dangling lifelessly, and slowly lowered her on to his charpoy, while Mehrun pulled the chair forward for the doctor. Dr Minwalla took out a stethoscope from her bag and began listening to Kaneez's breathing; she then checked her pulse.

'I am not sure what is wrong with her, but something is wrong. I want you to take her to the Civil Hospital first thing in the morning. Do you understand? And when she wakes up, give her the medicine I gave you.'

Jumman just nodded his head. Putting the stethoscope back in her physician's bag, the doctor got up and quickly walked out. Mehrun saw her driver reversing the car. After she had left, Naseebun, who had been watching intently from the entrance of the house all this while, came in and addressed Jumman, 'Don't listen to that witch. If you take Kaneez to the hospital, they will tear open her stomach and kill her. The malang is going to be here early in the morning. Let him work his power. He is a man of Allah. He can cure everything.'

*

The malang came early the next morning, but before entering the house, he chanted something at the door, not in Arabic or Urdu but in some strange language that no one understood, and he rolled his head at the same time. Dressed in a long, black cotton robe, his dirty black hair matted and tied in braids, and his thick black moustache blending with his bushy black beard, he seemed like a madman from the caves of Bela, Baluchistan. Three necklaces of turquoise beads and a shallow wooden bowl hung from his neck. In his right hand, he held a crooked wooden staff. He had instructed Naseebun to have ready for him seven *chattak* (an old unit of measurement) of uncooked rice, eight chattak of uncooked grams and six chattak of ghee, thus creating the number 786, the numerical representation of the phrase *Bismillah-ir-Rahman nir-Rahim*, 'in the name of Allah, the Most Beneficent and Merciful', which are the opening words of every chapter in the Qur'an. With the help of a few alarmed neighbours who were keen to drive the djinn out of their alley, the woman had obtained everything that the malang had requested.

Inside the house, the malang lit up seven joss sticks, their overpowering smell hanging stubbornly in the small space. With the groundwork done, he ordered everyone to leave the house, and once alone, he locked the door from inside. Mehrun ran to the back of the house and peeped in through the cracks in the wooden window. She saw the malang slowly approach the sleeping Kaneez, touching her forehead, caressing her face and then fondling her breasts. The very next instant, Kaneez woke up with a terrifying scream, as if ready to defend her honour. The malang jumped back, ran towards the door and unlocked it. He then motioned Jumman and Naseebun to come inside. In a hushed tone, he said to them, 'I have woken the djinn up, and now I will get him out of her body.'

Mehrun ran back to the front door. She saw the malang going for his staff, and then suddenly, without any warning, he began beating Kaneez violently with it. It was as though he had become possessed by the very same djinn he was trying to purge out of Kaneez's body. Jumman tried to intervene, but Naseebun stopped him. Mehrun hid her face with her hands and began weeping.

'Let the Malang Sahib do his work, child. He is a man of God. He is beating the djinn and not your mother. Believe me, she is not feeling a thing. You will see; she will get well,' she tried to mollify Mehrun.

By this time, Kaneez had succumbed to the beating and collapsed into a deep coma. Her breathing became difficult, her face became anaemic, but with every feeble breath in her body, she clung to life. The malang collected his money and the supply of food and left abruptly.

Eleven

Kaneez remained comatose for two more days and then died with a final hiccup, her life ending abruptly, bedevilled as it was by fear, superstition and sorcery. Only four mourners—Jumman, Mehrun, Joseph and Mansoor—attended the austere ceremony. Others were frightened away by the report of the exorcism. The sweeper's son took the barrister's son on his rickety bicycle, in utter silence. The death rites lasted no more than five minutes, witnessed by wilted trees and the cracked earth.

Noor heard the whole story of Kaneez's death from Jumman and gave him two hundred rupees to 'pay for any expense that he may have incurred'. And then, as if it was an act of sequential consequence, he took out his local whisky and resumed his nightly habit.

Mansoor came to his bedroom one night, wanting to converse with his father about death and dying. Kaneez's death had shaken the whole Kashana. Even Farhat appeared sombre.

'Abba, what happens after death?' He had asked Maulvi Nazir the same question a fortnight ago but hadn't received a satisfactory enough answer.

Noor thought for a while and then shouted for Budhoo, who came running. He ordered him to bring the burnt-out light bulb from the lamp in the men's quarter, which hadn't been changed for months, despite Noor's constant reminders. The servant ran towards the room and came back a few minutes later with the light bulb, nervous and quivering.

'You can go now,' Noor said, dismissing Budhoo.

Mansoor sat opposite his father, anxious and confused, with no clue about what was going on. Was his father deliberately avoiding a delicate question? Was he going to throw the light bulb at him for attending the servant's funeral without permission?

Noor did neither. Instead, he told Mansoor to take out the bulb from the lamp on his bedside table and bring it to him. Mansoor obediently followed his directive. Noor then held the two bulbs in both his hands and asked Mansoor to tell the difference between them.

'This one works and this one doesn't,' Mansoor replied.

'Look at them closely and tell me again.'

'The left one has the wire broken, but the right one is still intact.'

'This wire is called the tungsten filament. Do you know how it works?'

Mansoor shook his head.

'I don't know what they teach you in school, but here, let me explain the science behind it.'

Noor then proceeded to tell Mansoor that what he was holding in his hands was an incandescent bulb. 'It emits light due to heat. When the electric current passes through the tungsten filament, it gets so hot that it glows and emits light.' Here he paused, took a sip of whisky from his glass and continued, 'This tungsten filament is like our consciousness. When broken, it emits no light. When we die, the tungsten wire of our consciousness gets broken. This burnt-out bulb will be thrown in a dumpster, and when *we* die, our bodies will be thrown into a grave. This bulb will be crushed, it will become something else, but it will no longer be a bulb. Son, when we die, our body also changes into something else. We become part of nature. But when we die, that is *khatam-shud,* the end.'

'But Maulvi—' Mansoor stopped, realizing the man's name was unmentionable before his father, and then continued, 'But what about heaven and hell?'

Noor laughed and took another sip of the whisky before reciting a famous couplet:

Hum ko maloom hai janat ke haqiqat lekin
Dil ko khoosh rakhney ko Ghalib ye khayal acha hai.

He then asked his son if he understood the words, but Mansoor shrugged his shoulders.

'Son, this is a profound couplet from Mirza Ghalib, an Urdu poet without equal, not even in the West. It means: "I know the reality of heaven. If it makes your heart happier, Ghalib, then it's an excellent idea." Heaven and hell are human concoctions, Sahibzadey.'

*

Haider Rizvi's book, *Representatives of Muslims and the Partition of India*, received mixed reviews from the Pakistani critics. The pundits in the press, especially from the rival papers, excoriated him. He had walked a thin line between questioning the tactics of the Muslim leaders during the partition of India and criticizing their motives. His veiled critique of the founder of Pakistan and the first prime minister also did not sit well with sensitive journalists. The criticisms from the government-backed newspapers were even more spiteful, accusing him of treason and calling the government to arrest him.

The political climate continued to deteriorate as the C.O.P.s successfully paralysed the government with daily strikes and lockouts. To ambush the C.O.P.s effectively, General Dundda called for elections and declared his candidacy. Being in power for six years and ruling the country as the most powerful potentate in its brief history had made him confident enough to think that he would win the elections.

The call by his fellow journalists to arrest him made Haider fearful. So he, in turn, called Noor to get his legal opinion. Noor calmed him down and joked, 'There is no chance in hell that you will be arrested before 2 January 1965. After that, come to me.'

The elections were scheduled for 2 January 1965. Noor was right, the elections eclipsed Haider's book from the front pages of most dailies, except the *Daily Jadal*. It continued its campaign to have his book banned and demanded that Haider Rizvi, the traitor-in-chief, be arrested.

*

Just before the elections, Sadiq invited his three friends to his house for dinner. His wife, Talat, had made an elaborate Hyderabadi dinner that included biryani, korma and a few other delicacies before leaving with their daughter, Hannah, to spend the weekend with her grandchildren. Sadiq called his daughter Anna, as in Anna Karenina, and that is how he introduced her to everyone.

Haider came incognito with Zakir, hoping that the goons from the *Daily Jadal* would not dare attack a car that had the federal government's licence plate. Noor came with Sikander, who, after dropping him at Sadiq's house, went back to the Kashana.

The Unholy Quartet moved to Sadiq's unpretentious drawing room where the only item of decoration was a bookshelf filled with Western and Russian classics in dark buckram binding. A coffee table stood in the centre of the room with a sofa, bordered by two side tables, set against the wall and two wooden chairs across from it. The discussion invariably gravitated towards national politics. And how could they not talk about politics so close to one of the most hotly contested elections? Excitement and edginess permeated across the country. There was this faint hope of a true democracy, but there was also a fear of another martial law.

Despite too many noisy upstarts, the opposition parties had remained scattered and leaderless. Disarrayed and unprepared by this sudden call for elections, they fought each other. But as soon as they realized that their bickering helped General Dundda's cause, they reached a compromise.

To challenge the general (now affectionately known as the Saviour of the Nation, a title given to him by his brilliant foreign minister), the opposition parties had jointly nominated the sister of Pakistan's founder as their leader. A frail, silver-haired dental surgeon in her seventies, she had no political ambitions of her own but had been a close adviser to her brother and a supporter of civil rights. After her brother's death, she had devoted herself mostly to charity work. Drafted as a consensus candidate, she became a symbol of resistance and came to be known as *Madār-e-Millat*, the Mother of the Nation. Her candidacy appeared so formidable to the general that, to delegitimize her, he extracted a fatwa from a conservative cleric, declaring that a woman could not be the head of an Islamic republic.

'I think the Mother of the Nation will give General Sahib a good run for his money,' Zakir commented.

'Do you seriously think that Dundda Khan will let her win?' Haider asked.

'Noor, what do you think? Will the fatwa derail her candidacy?' Zakir asked.

'No, but the general will,' Noor replied.

The political discussion continued until after dinner, but then Zakir and Haider had to leave. The former had to catch a flight the next morning to Islamabad, while the latter had an editorial meeting to prepare for. Noor, too, was ready to leave, but Sadiq insisted that he stay back for a while.

After Zakir and Haider left, Sadiq opened the bottle of Rémy Martin that Noor had brought for him, and then tempted his friend with some chocolate cake, which Anna had brought for her father from his favourite Pereira Bakery earlier in the day.

Anything chocolate was Noor's weakness, so this enticement made the invitation to stay longer a tad more interesting. As Sadiq got up to get the cake from the refrigerator, Noor surveyed the drawing room. It was small but cozy. On the side table next to the sofa, he noticed the familiar orange and white cover of a Penguin book. He could not see the name of the book from where he sat, so he got up, put on his reading glasses and picked up the paperback. It was Nabokov's *Lolita*. Noor had read the novel some years ago, but he still felt uneasy about it. Throwing it back on the table, he subconsciously shrugged his shoulders and returned to where he was sitting. Sadiq came back with two slices of cake and gave one to Noor. As he sat down, he talked about Anna's love of baking and books, especially her interest in literature. After a while, Sadiq changed the subject to Kaneez's death.

'I didn't think that you knew Kaneez,' Noor remarked.

'Oh, didn't I tell you I hired her daughter, Mehrun, after you fired them?'

'No, I didn't know that, and in any case, I didn't really fire them.'

Sadiq told Noor how Talat had found out about the whole episode and had promptly offered Mehrun a job cleaning the house and cooking for them. He then praised Mehrun's intelligence and casually told his friend that he intended to teach her English language and literature.

'You know, your Mansoor introduced her to *Oliver Twist*.'

'Good for him.'

An uncomfortable silence overtook Sadiq, as he fidgeted with the cake on his plate. After a moment, he placed the plate on the narrow coffee table and turned towards his friend.

'Noor, what do you think of Mehrun?'

'What do you mean?'

'I love her, Noor,' he said in English. Uttering the words 'I love her' in Urdu somehow cheapened the sentiment, at least in his mind.

'I beg your pardon!'

'Don't be angry with me!'

But Noor was not angry with him; he was merely taken aback by this declaration of love. If Haider had said this, it would not have shocked him; if Zakir had uttered those four words, it would not have surprised him. But Sadiq Mirza, the distinguished scholar and literary critic, a married man with three married daughters? *That* shocked him. His eyes shifted between the copy of *Lolita* on the side table and Sadiq.

'Is that why you are reading this filth?' he asked, gesturing towards the book.

'It's not filth, and I am reading it to understand . . .' Sadiq paused and then completed his sentence, 'I don't know . . . I am trying to understand myself, I guess.'

'I think the cog-nac has affected your cog-nition, Sadiq,' Noor said sarcastically, emphasizing 'cog' the way his driver, Sikander, pronounced 'cognac'.

But it was not the cognac speaking. Ever since that day in his library, when Mehrun had talked about her love of the English language and her desire to read literature, it was as if she had guided Sadiq's heart towards the possibility of romantic love for the first time in his life. He knew it was stupid; Mehrun was not even twenty, but he had never felt like this before. He told Noor about that brief encounter in his library.

'You, my friend, are not in love with Mehrun; you are in love with language and literature, and with the idea of an intelligent young woman being enamoured with what you love—language and literature,' he paused and then asked, 'And what about Talat? Are you going to divorce her?'

'No, I don't have to divorce her. Islam allows for polygamy.'

'My God, Sadiq! I can't believe that I am hearing this from a liberal, educated and secular man like you! You have gone stark raving mad, my brother.'

'I don't know what to do. All day, I think about Mehrun. I know I can teach her English. I can be her Pygmalion, Noor.'

'Pygmalion, my foot! Pygmalion carved the statue and then fell in love with it. You, on the other hand . . .'

'I know what you are thinking, but I want your guidance.'

'You need to see a psychiatrist! Now, look . . . think about your family, think about your age difference, your intellectual difference and your distinct backgrounds.'

'Noor, you of all people are asking me to not fall in love because of our different social backgrounds?'

'I am talking about reality and your teenager-like behaviour at this age! Snap out of it, Sadiq. Stop reading *Lolita*. If your wife lets you live, you will regret everything.'

Right at that moment, Sikander rang the bell and informed Noor that he had come to pick him up. Worried that his friend had gone mad, Noor admonished him one more time to not be stupid and then left.

*

The elections came and the general won. The bigwigs of the C.O.P.s, charging the government with blatant rigging, promised massive protests. But internal party squabbling ended their lacklustre rallies, and the Mother of the Nation, demoralized by the election result, died a few months later.

Although the general assured the nation that he bore no malice and would exact no revenge as his election was nothing but 'the people's glory', his son had other ideas. Intoxicated by his father's victory, which the *Daily Jadal* called 'obviously rigged', he sent truckloads of thugs to beat up anyone who spoke out against his father. Sending his goons to Soldier Bazaar, the hub of the C.O.P.s in Karachi, he inflicted reprisal—burning property, firing at unarmed people and sowing the seeds of ethnic hatred. The city that had become the symbol of resistance against authoritarianism now became permanently labelled as the city of *muhajir*s, immigrants from India. The children of these immigrants, children like Mansoor, could never be the sons of the soil. Dictatorship got validated, and Western governments praised the new *civilian* President for bringing his nation into the family of democracies.

*

After the elections, among the many decisions that the government took, the one that shattered Joseph's heart and hopes the most was the banning of Indian films from Pakistani cinema halls. These Indian films had provided Joseph with a distraction from the dirty drudgery and the filth that summed up his life in Bhangi Para. But then Joseph realized that the ban might actually help fulfil his dream of becoming a movie star. Deprived of the Indian films, audiences thronged to see Pakistani films. Increased demand led to increased production. The ban thus became a blessing in disguise for the fledgling Pakistani film industry, and the 1960s became the golden era of films in Pakistan. It also coincided with the rise of the film star Waheed Murad, known as the Chocolate Hero, who dominated the industry until his premature death in 1983. Waheed captured Joseph's imagination in a way that Dilip Kumar, the Indian heart-throb of that era, never did. He began to talk like Waheed Murad, walk like Waheed Murad and even paid a full ten rupees to a barber to make him look like the actor. When he found out that the Chocolate Hero's bungalow was in the same neighbourhood as Noor's, he began to spend a great deal of his free time there, waiting to catch a glimpse of him. The stalking paid off, and Waheed Murad offered him a role as an extra in one of his hit movies. That offer, small no doubt, made Joseph feel big. And when he heard the news, he bought a pair of sunglasses, a cheap scarf and a pipe, and paid a visit to the Kashana. He found Mansoor and Mehrun in the backyard. When Mehrun saw him, she asked, 'Why are you dressed up like a cheap villain?'

'Meet Chocolate Hero Number 2,' he bowed, and then turning to Mehrun and pointing at her, said, 'Meet my Chocolate Heroine Number 1.'

Detailing his encounter with Waheed Murad, Joseph told them that he had been offered a key role in his up-and-coming movie *Heera aur Pathar*. He added, 'It can be translated as "Diamond and Stone", for the lovers of Angrezi language.'

'We will believe you when we actually see you in the movie,' Mehrun said.

Joseph did not care if Mehrun did not believe him. The proof of his stardom would be in that epic donkey-cart race, which, he was told, was one of the best scenes in the film. He did not have a donkey cart, so he just rented a donkey and a cart from a *dhoban*, a laundress, who lived outside his neighbourhood.

Unfortunately, on the day of the shooting, Joseph overslept, and that was the end of his chance to succeed Waheed Murad as the next chocolate hero. But now he was entirely obsessed with becoming a movie star. Cleaning 'people's shit holes' was no longer an option. He could not be a bhangi any more. That was history as far as he was concerned. But then his friend Anthony Masih, who did work in the film industry, told him, 'Once they find out that you are a bhangi, you will never work in the film industry here. I am going to go to Bombay, where they will never know anything about my past.'

Now the word 'Bombay' got stuck in Joseph's ears. It played inside his mind like a technicolour movie with no intermission. He wanted to leave his shack; he wanted to leave Bhangi Para; hell, he wanted to leave the country. There was no dignity in the scutwork that he did. For him, the only way to make a clean break from the bhangihood he was born into, was to make a clean break from Pakistan. His new fascination was Bombay, a city where no one would know about his life as a bhangi.

So one day, when his mother informed him that she had asked Farhat Begum to give her a raise, and that the begum had agreed without any arguments, Joseph dropped his bombshell: he was going to Bombay to work in the Indian film industry.

'Did you smoke bhang today? Or did you get bitten by a mad dog? Son of a lunatic! Where will you get the money to go to Bombay? From your father's inheritance?' his mother demanded.

'I don't know,' he said.

'And who is going to take care of me?'

'You should come with me. What is there for you in this damn country anyway? You are an *achoot*, an untouchable, and you will always remain an achoot here.'

'Do you think that you will not be an achoot in Bombay? Listen, *putter*, I left my home once when your father dragged me out of Amritsar. I don't want to leave my home again. And this *damn country* is my home.'

She burst into tears as she said that, and Joseph put his arms around her shoulders. But she quickly shrugged him off, saying, 'You are good for nothing. All day long, you just sit and cook imaginary pulao.'

Anger seared through his body as Joseph looked at his mother. Her flash of cynicism felt like a punch to his gut. Beaten down by life, she could never see herself as anything but a sweeper, nor could she imagine any other future for her son. His mind was now firmly made up. He wanted an escape, a permanent break from the work that generations of his family had done.

Unfortunately for him, his dreams of going to Bombay were shattered by the outbreak of hostilities between Pakistan and India. In their chequered history, the two impoverished nations went to war with frightening fervour, confident that they could casually bomb each other into oblivion. Blood was spilled, cities were shelled, children were orphaned, women were widowed and nothing was achieved—in the end, it was another meaningless war that wasted the lives of so many.

These useless motherfuckers; I will show them, Joseph thought, seething with anger as if he were the sole target of this insane, obscene war. That evening, he went out to unleash his rage even though people had been warned to stay inside their houses. But Joseph did not care. Death would be a better alternative compared to the shit he was living in. A scrawny dog trying to find some dinner in a reeking rubbish heap became the unlucky victim of Joseph's anger as he bent down, picked up a large stone and hurled it at the dog. Bullseye! It hit right on its head. The dog howled in pain, curled its tail between its legs and scudded like a bullet. 'Motherfucker, get out of this shithole!' Joseph yelled in Punjabi.

Darkness draped Karachi as the blackout snuffed out any remnants of nightlife. Every window was covered with dark-coloured papers: black, blue and green. Any gaps around the windows were sealed with black tapes. In the blacked-out city, artificial light underwent house arrest.

Joseph should have been going home, but instead, he kept walking, roaming aimlessly, his head bowed, his foot kicking anything it could find, his vacuous eyes lost in hopelessness. Suddenly, he heard the stabbing noise of warplanes approaching, followed by a flash of red and then the concussive sound of a bomb that had fallen. The blaring air raid sirens followed languidly, making a mockery of the early warning system. Suddenly, the starry sky was lit up by the fires of ack-ack guns. The loudspeakers of several neighbourhood mosques reverberated with the muezzins' calls for special prayers. Joseph stayed put, watching the lit-up sky. It was as if he was watching a dazzling display of fireworks, far removed from death and destruction. No one would bomb Bhangi Para, not in any war. It had no strategic value.

*

That night, it seemed as if the nation had a collective dream. It was a story repeated so many times by so many people that it became a fictive reality. The tabloids published it, the mosques relayed it and the people believed it as if the tale was solidly backed by undeniable evidence.

They said that an army of semi-invisible giants (now you see them, now you don't) made their divine intervention on behalf of the country. Dressed in flowing green robes, their effulgent faces dulling the blazing flames from the incendiary bombs, they shouted, 'God is great.'

So loud were their slogans that they muffled the noise of the enemy planes as they caught the bombs with their bare hands, blunting the attack and stunting the attackers. Then they drew their heavy swords from their scabbards and sliced the enemy planes, like cucumbers. The enemy planes that were piloted by Muslims were spared; the pilots were admonished to never kill their brothers again. An infidel air force pilot, who watched the miracles happening from the cockpit of his plane, converted to Islam instantly; his aircraft was safely escorted by these mysterious beings to the nearest Pakistan Air Force base.

People climbed on their rooftops and chanted:

Victory nears if God's help is included.
Victory nears if God's help is included.
The Greatest Slogan: God is great.
The Greatest Slogan: God is great.

The next day, people stuck bumper stickers on their cars: 'See you at Delhi's Jama Mosque next Friday!' and 'Crush India!' and 'Victory Celebrations in Delhi.'

The newspapers' headlines bellowed every day:

War till Victory!
Enemy Planes Destroyed!
Attack Repulsed. Heavy Enemy Casualties!

Houses shivered, heavens trembled, myths continued and delusions grew. People clasped on to these myths indiscriminately to repudiate the ugly reality that awaited them. But it was a short war, lasting only seventeen days and ending abruptly. Both countries agreed to a ceasefire. General Dundda went to the Soviet Union to meet the Indian prime minister. A picture of the general, holding hands with the Indian and Russian prime ministers, smiling at the press, appeared in the newspapers under the headline: 'Accord Reached!'

The nation was stunned! People came out on to the streets and shouted: 'How can he hold the enemy's hand?'

'Why did we have to stop when we were winning the war?'

'God was on our side. He sent an army of angels and djinns to protect us, to help us conquer the cowards who had attacked us in the middle of the night.'

*

The Indian prime minister died of a heart attack the day after the accord was signed. Some people said it was the overpowering presence of the general that killed him, while others declared confidently that 'it was the wrath of God.'

The newspapers blared again: 'Allah's Rod Is Noiseless.'

All this time, while the nation was led to imagine and believe that the enemy had suffered a heavy defeat, the sceptical Noor had never believed this. He told Mansoor the brutal truth, 'Sahibzadey, your country lost the war.' At that moment, Mansoor wanted to yell at him, 'No, you are wrong!' but instead, he kept quiet, ingesting his anger. Years later, when Mansoor read an interview of a chief of armed forces, in which the man confessed that the nation did not win the 1965 war, he remembered his father's sarcastic comment.

Part II

'When there was nothing, there was God.
If nothing had been there, there would be God.
What drowned me was my being,
If I had not been, what would matter then.'

—Mirza Ghalib

Twelve

Noor finally did learn about Maulvi Nazir's existence, when he unexpectedly returned home early one day, but, oddly enough, he remained calm. Farhat's plot did not upset him. His only complaint was that she did it behind his back.

'I wouldn't have kicked him out if you had told me. I am not heartless.'

Was he mellowing down? Was he having a change of heart? Mansoor had read somewhere that war changed people; it changed their self-perception. Had this short war changed Noor in a lasting way? Did it make him confront his own mortality? Was his inner tungsten filament about to snap? And what about those nightly lectures extolling Socrates' dictum that the 'unexamined life was not worth living' and Nietzsche's doctrine that 'there are no truths, only interpretations'? What about having the guts to doubt and puncture your most cherished beliefs? What about being secular?

Noor still drank every night and never prayed, but he often closed his eyes for the longest time, as if in a deep meditative state. Was his father, deep in his heart, a spiritual person despite being non-religious? Mansoor was now old enough to ask such questions. Indeed, his father had encouraged him to doubt and question things. He looked at his mother and heard her snoring.

War had affected her too. Every night during the war, when she heard the sirens go off, she would start trembling. When prayers did not cast out her fears, she would take a Valium. And now, as she slept soundly, Mansoor realized that it must be the Valium again, for she never snored so loudly and so soon after closing her eyes.

The 1965 war had matured Mansoor. There was no question about it. He felt it. But was it the war or the big lie about it that had transformed him into a doubter? He remembered his father telling him once, during one of his nightly lectures, that doubt is the seed that grows into a formidable intellect, like a banyan tree. When the government and the newspapers kept telling the citizens that Pakistan was winning the war, Mansoor had believed the lie. So who was he supposed to trust now? What was he supposed to feel now? What was the nature of truth? Did it begin with a capital T or a small t? Did it bring happiness or sadness? He had all these questions crowding his mind, clamouring for his attention. But one day, when he sat across from his father who clutched on to his empty whisky glass, his eyes closed, Mansoor could only ask this: 'Abba, do you believe in spirituality?'

He had asked the question in English, even though he knew the Urdu word, *roohaniyat*. It was a word that Maulvi Nazir used incessantly without explaining it. He wanted to see if his father could make it intelligible for him.

Noor opened his eyes, looking surprised at the question. He remembered when Mansoor had asked him about what happens when one dies, and he remembered the tungsten filament analogy he had used to explain death. This was his second tough question, at least for his age. Maybe his nightly lectures were paying off, Maulvi Nazir notwithstanding. He cleared his throat, took a sip of the whisky, and answered Mansoor's question with a question, 'Are you asking me if I am spiritual?'

'I guess what I am asking is, how do you find peace of mind? I heard you say once that whisky calms you . . .'

'I drink whisky to escape from the drudgery of my profession, but spirituality for me is listening to the songs of Saigal and Talat Mahmood, reading Ghalib and my friends Faiz's and Majaz's poetry. Son, I am a materialist to the core.'

'What about God?'

'What about Him?' Noor asked.

'Do you believe in God?'

'There is no evidence to back up such a belief. And all our knowledge is based on evidence, everything else is either a wish or a fear,' he paused, took a large gulp of whisky and continued, 'You know, son, with all their faults, the British gifted one good thing to humanity. Do you know what that is?'

'No.'

'It is the gift of empiricism. Hang on to it. It will stand you in good stead.'

As the lecture continued, Mansoor noticed his father's lips. They were thick and moved slowly as he spoke; their movement, he saw, but the sound, he didn't hear. Then suddenly, there was a bark, and Mansoor looked at his father. Had he done that?

'Look behind you, Mansoor,' his father said.

He turned around, and there was Chaos, his dog. And then he heard his mother's voice, 'Get that unclean animal out of the house! He should NOT enter my room!'

Mansoor quickly picked up the terrier.

'You should wash your hands seven times with soap and do your ablutions after you throw that creature out,' she continued her fulminations.

Mansoor took the terrier out of the house and put him back in his doghouse in the garden. He then retired to his room. Moonlight pierced through the curtains, making the room brighter and lovelier. Pulling the curtains to one side, Mansoor lay down on his bed and watched the magical moon. He found himself thinking about Joseph and Mehrun. She had lost her mother, and Joseph had lost his dream. Mansoor must have just fallen asleep when he realized that someone was trying to wake him up.

'Mansoor, it is time for morning prayers. Get up.' It was his mother.

He turned to look at the clock on his bedside table. It was 4.35 a.m., and the muezzin was calling for morning prayer.

'Prayer is better than sleep.'

'Prayer is better than sleep.'

Mansoor did not want to pray, but he also did not want to upset his mother. So he got up, went to the bathroom and closed the door softly behind him. After he wiped his face dry, he came back to his room and pulled out the prayer rug, a gift from his grandfather, from the almirah. He sat on the mat and looked at it vacuously, unable to genuflect, unable to prostrate, powerless to pray, every word of the Qur'an seemingly erased from his memory. He forgot all the forms, he forgot every ritual, his mind turned blank. Mansoor stared at the gracefully curved minaret pattern on the prayer rug. He stayed like that for some time, then he got up, folded the mat, kept it back in the almirah and returned to his bed to confront his unfilled thoughts. This became a habit, a routine for him every morning. His mother would wake him up just before the morning azan; he would do his ablutions quietly, come back, sit on the rug and stare at the minarets printed on it. Sometimes he would bury his face in his hands and lie prostrate on the prayer rug. He had prayed secretly in the past, but now he just could not bring himself to obey his mother.

*

The political turmoil in the aftermath of the war forced the shutdown of schools and the postponement of exams. For Mehrun, the delay was a welcome relief. It gave her the time to vent, to grieve and to reflect on her mother's death. It was

Dr Minwalla who told her that Kaneez need not have died. Her death was senseless. How was Mehrun supposed to process this bit of information? Aren't all deaths senseless? What about the family of eleven that had perished in Lasbela when the bomb fell on their house? Did that make sense? What about the worthiness of death when life is horrid? Did her neighbourhood matriarch, Bua Kareeman's death at the age of eighty-two make sense? Her mother's life was short and shitty, the unfairness of it didn't make any sense to Mehrun either. And what about the beating she took from that lecherous monster, the malang? According to Naseebun, Kaneez's death was Allah's will and had nothing to do with the malang. If you can't explain something, should you believe it blindly? Mehrun glanced at her father, lying on his charpoy and gazing at the ceiling.

Suddenly, a car's horn disrupted her ruminations. She wiped her eyes with her dupatta and went out to see who it was. It was Sadiq Mirza in his white Hillman.

'My wife sent me to see if you were doing okay,' he said when he saw her approaching the car. 'She sent some food for you and your father.'

From the front passenger seat, he picked up a brown bag, the spicy smell of food escaping from it.

'Thank you, Professor Sahib.' Mehrun took the bag from him and stood there motionless, the silence between them discomforting. She did not know whether to invite him into her shabby house or ask him to leave. Sensing her unease, Sadiq told her to put the food in the house and come back.

'My wife wants to see you.'

'This is too much food; it will go bad if I keep it in my house. Let me leave this food with my neighbour. She has a refrigerator.'

After leaving the food with the neighbour and telling her father that she had to go to work, she got into the back seat of the car.

Sadiq caught her reflection in the rear-view mirror as he reversed the car and drove away towards University Road.

Mehrun remembered the professor's words, when he had said that he would teach her to see life through books. Was that what was going on whenever she thought about her mother's death? Was she seeing life through the books she had been reading? She already knew how to read English before she met the professor, but with his help, she had quickly become more proficient. He was a great teacher, one who had the gift to not only make literature come alive but also to unearth its most submerged meanings, the hidden realities. Initially, she borrowed books from the professor, and then she began borrowing books from the 25-Paisa Library that had recently opened near her school. After her mother's death, she had the entire pigeonholed area in the house to herself. That space became her sanctuary, her private place to read and to reflect. The disruptions the war had caused gave her more time to study and think, and during the blackouts, she would study under the tiny flicker of the kerosene lantern and absorb more.

Sadiq kept glancing at Mehrun in the rear-view mirror. Dressed in a white shalwar-kameez, she looked like a model of simplicity and elegance. The young woman was transforming right in front of his eyes, not just physically but also intellectually. She asked smart questions, she replied thoughtfully and her English had improved considerably. If she were correctly educated, she could easily become well groomed and polished under his guidance, and then no one would believe that she was Kaneez's daughter. Sadiq smiled as he imagined the new and improved Mehrun. But then Noor's sarcastic comment from the last time they had met echoed in his mind: 'Is your Pygmalion *bhoot*, your obsession, under control or not?'

'How's your book coming?' he heard Mehrun's voice from the back seat.

'Slowly,' he replied.

During the shutdown following the war, Sadiq had spent most of his time at home, thinking and making notes about an idea for a book that he had. Both Noor and he would often talk at length about Ghalib's poetry, and it was his friend who had prodded him to write about the nineteenth-century Urdu poet. In fact, Noor had even suggested the title of the book—*Reinterpreting Ghalib in the Twentieth Century.*

'Why don't you write it yourself?' Sadiq had asked Noor.

But Noor had quickly shot that idea down. There were only two writers in their group: Haider and Sadiq. Besides, he was too old to write. The wistfulness in his answer was not lost on Sadiq.

As the car turned into the professor's street, Mehrun spotted Talat standing outside the gate. Sadiq pulled up the car near her and asked, 'What are you doing outside? Is everything okay? Where are you going?'

'Anna just called. Her boy fell from his bicycle and has broken his foot. She wants me to come over. Give me the car keys.'

As Sadiq and Mehrun hurriedly got out of the car, Talat said to her husband, 'I will try to call you from her house.' Then, turning towards Mehrun, she smiled apologetically and said, 'Sorry, Mehrun Beti!'

With that, she got into the car and drove off. Mehrun could not believe that she had called her beti, daughter. Even her parents had never called her that. She smiled wistfully.

'Well, I guess it's just you and me,' Sadiq said, walking through the front gate.

Mehrun, still glowing from Talat's unexpected sweetness, followed the professor as he went inside the house.

'Do you want me to dust the library?'

'You are not here to work. Today is your day off.'

Although he had seen her once after her mother's death, Sadiq had never had an opportunity to properly commiserate with Mehrun. Seeing her grief self-evident in her deep brown eyes, he now asked her about Jumman.

'Most of his days are bad.'

'And you? How are you?'

'I don't know . . .'

Sadiq wanted to reach out to her, but he did not quite know how to. To comfort a grieving person, let alone a servant, was something that even this professor of language and literature found hard. Should he just keep quiet and let her share whatever feelings she wanted to share, or should he say something trite like, 'I know what you are going through?' Luckily, he did not have to say anything at all because Mehrun felt comfortable confiding in her mentor.

'I was in shock at first,' she said. 'But now I am mostly angry. I can't shake it off, not after the way the malang beat her. He killed her, Sahib. He killed her!' She burst out crying and buried her face against his shoulder. More than a little taken aback, Sadiq tentatively put his arms around her, holding her awkwardly. Suddenly, he had this mad urge to kiss her, but he controlled it. The only appropriate thing for him to do at that moment was to comfort her. He searched for the right words, but all he could muster was, 'Let me know if there is anything I can do.' He felt incredibly stupid.

'Sahib, you have already done a lot for me,' Mehrun replied as she pulled back.

They were standing in the middle of the drawing room. Sadiq asked her to pull up a chair and sit. Since her first day in his house, Sadiq had broken all norms, all rules governing the master–servant relationship, and today, Talat had also joined him by calling her beti. Yet, Mehrun was uncomfortable about sitting next to her mentor as an equal; she hesitated and then reluctantly pulled a chair. Sadiq couldn't avoid noticing the unease on her face. He knew she was hurting badly and that he must practice caution. The professor could not let his emotions cloud his rationality. Noor's words about how he was confusing the love of an idea for his love for Mehrun were still fresh in his head. He needed to be sure before he professed anything in front of her.

'How's your preparation for the exam going?' he asked as he sat on the sofa.

'I haven't studied at all.'

'If you need my help in any subject other than science, let me know. I can help you prepare.'

'I may have a few questions on *The Great Expectations.*'

'Dickens is one of my favourite nineteenth-century writers.'

Their conversation hit an edgy pause, triggering beads of nervous sweat to gather on his forehead.

'Should I make tea for you?' Mehrun asked.

'That would be great, but make a cup for yourself also.'

'I'll make it for you.' Mehrun felt awkward drinking tea with her employer.

'I insist that you make two cups. I don't think of you as my servant. You are my student, my mentee.'

'Thank you, Sahib,' she said softly.

She wrung her hands, wavering a little, and then got up to go to the kitchen, leaving Sadiq alone to shuffle through his notes that lay scattered on the side table next to the sofa. As he began putting the documents neatly back in order, a few pages fell down on the carpet. He picked them up and thought of Noor. Sure, he was a professor, but he was no Humbert Humbert, and Mehrun was definitely not his Lolita. You couldn't be more wrong, Noor ul Haq. He raised both his hands in an imaginary defence against what the barrister had said that day. He remembered Noor's gaze alternating between the copy of *Lolita* and him.

Mehrun came back with the tea tray. She put it down on the coffee table and began putting sugar and milk in his tea. She did the same for herself and then sat back on the chair.

'Sahib, I was thinking . . . could you . . . I mean, could you get me admitted into President's College . . . I'll be forever grateful to you,' she said.

'President's is tough to get into,' Sadiq sat up and continued, 'Do you think you will have the marks?'

'I am trying for a first division. I have to, to get scholarships . . . otherwise I won't be able to pay the tuition,' she said.

'I know that,' he said. 'If you get a good first division, I'll do my best to get you admitted there on a scholarship. The current principal of the college is a former student of mine.'

He then asked her to come and sit near him. She chose the chair in front of him instead. Despite being somewhat at ease with him, the question of sitting right next to him still did not arise. She respected him, admired him, but she would always consider herself his servant. And even though his demeanour differed from Noor Sahib's, she still could not imagine him as her mentor. But then, while everyone else looked past her, Sadiq Sahib always looked into her eyes, that too with a smile. Was he attracted to her? Now it was *her* turn to smile.

'Why is education so important to you?' the professor asked.

'My English teacher once told me that while I was smart enough to get a good education, it would only matter if I went to an English-medium school. Ever since I was a little girl, my dream has been to learn English, but my mother never liked that. She did not even want me to go to school, but I went, and I always came first in my class. My parents never went to school, but I want to go to college and then teach like you.'

'You are still a little girl.'

'No, I am almost nineteen. I am practically a woman now.'

Sadiq sighed in relief when he heard her say she was nineteen. Mehrun was not a twelve-year-old Lolita. Noor was dead wrong. With his guilt somewhat abated, he asked her more questions about her dreams, about her interests and about her friends. And for the first time in her life, Mehrun felt that somebody was genuinely interested in her. The more questions he asked, the more comfortable she became. His lavish attention brought her to a happy place. In the excitement of this realization, she suddenly saw him searching her eyes. She blushed and lowered her head, and the next thing she knew, he was kissing her. Mehrun did not resist, succumbing utterly, allowing him a few moments of passion, the relational structure dismantling, the taboos breaking, but then she stood up.

'What are you doing, Sahib?' she asked, her voice trembling. 'Talat Begum, she just called me beti!'

Sadiq did not know what to do as he watched Mehrun run out of the house. It all happened suddenly. How did he lose control of his instincts? He felt embarrassed. What should he do? Should he run after her and apologize to her? But he stood there nervous and hesitant, long after Mehrun had gone.

*

The city lights returned with hurried normality, but the blackout in peoples' minds continued unabated. People wanted to block the memory of that inane war; so they avoided discussing it. But Haider Rizvi was not one of them. He wrote an impassioned editorial, entitled 'The Questions', in the *Morning Gazette*:

> There is a sense of loss, but what is utterly lost cannot be identified. There is a sense of ruin, but what is genuinely wrecked cannot be fathomed. Why did we fight this war? Was it indeed about self-defence? Was our territory really invaded? Was our honour actually slandered? Who will do the objective analysis? Who will be held accountable? Who will lead the way so that we do not waste our humanity in fighting unnecessary wars and devote it instead to solving the problems of hunger and illiteracy, and bettering the condition of 80 per cent of our people who wage a daily battle against grinding poverty?

The government issued a warrant for his arrest. The charge: incitement of public anger against the government. But the war had changed Haider, too. He was angry and he no longer feared the general. When the labour leader and their friend Hassan Nasir disappeared, it shook them all. Secretly arrested for being a communist, he was tortured and killed by the government. No, Haider Rizvi couldn't be silent any longer. He must fight the charges.

Noor gladly offered to take up Haider's case and began preparing a vigorous defence. Knowing fully well that he would be in a kangaroo court fighting bogus charges, he remained determined not to give the government a free pass. Noor was willing to risk arrest; staying on the sidelines was no longer an option. He couldn't let his friend languish in the Central Jail, not without putting up a good fight.

Thirteen

Joseph's quarrels with his mother turned into daily battles. He insulted her family and her profession, and hurled curses at Pakistan, where he thought his future was bleaker than hers. She, in turn, just bawled and called him an ungrateful traitor. Seduced by the dreams of becoming a movie star, he felt these dreams would become a nightmare if he remained in this morass that was Bhangi Para. Thoughts about faraway places like India, Dubai, England and even America obsessed him. Anywhere except Bhangi Para.

He stopped doing shit work altogether and found part-time employment at a decrepit restaurant called Café de Jamadar in his own neighbourhood. He could do a non-sweeping job only inside this enclave. Beyond it, cleaning toilets was the only fate of a bhangi. Society would not even allow him to enter a restaurant, let alone toil there. They were like lepers, ostracized and abandoned in their colony.

Joseph had also developed an addiction for American action movies, squandering all his earnings to satisfy this obsession. When his earnings ran out, or when he was a few paise short, he stole from his mother, borrowed from Mansoor, or begged Mehrun. Indian and Pakistani films were his first love, but American movies had more action and violence, and the censored sex scenes satisfied his sex-starved imagination.

It was a well-known fact in those days that some of the seedy movie theatres often inserted two-minute cuts from X-rated movies in between perfectly normal film scenes. Why those theatres were never shut down by the Censor Board remained a mystery to the aficionados. Known as *totay*, these X-rated clips popped up abruptly, and completely unannounced, in between a sequence. In *Ben-Hur*, for instance, the chariot race would suddenly be interrupted by a scene from what appeared to be a German porn flick. And when John Wayne snatched the gun from Mickey Kuhn's hand in *Red River* and said, 'Don't ever trust anybody until you know 'em,'— a naked, ageing Casanova would appear, uninvited, trying to seduce a half-naked English porn star. Joseph figured out the time and the day when these bits would suddenly appear. And so, he became a frequent patron of these movie theatres. One unintended effect of watching so many movies was that Joseph became a diehard fan of John Wayne. One day, he appeared at the Kashana wearing a cowboy hat and a plastic gun holster over his dhoti. When Mansoor saw him, he cracked up, to which John Wayne Joseph replied in a thick Punjabi accent: 'Howdee, *mainu* pardoner!'

Once, Premier Talkies, where the totays were shown with regular frequency, was screening Ronald Reagan's *Cattle Queen of Montana*. After the scene where Barbara Stanwyck is putting on her blouse behind a boulder and a young Ronald Reagan is watching her from his horse, the film projectionist introduced an erotic scene from a Greek movie, albeit one that had no nudity. When the scene was over and the feature film restarted, the people felt cheated. They began shouting and protesting, demanding their money back, for they had been denied a titillating sex scene. Joseph egged the audience on, complaining that the scene was not even in English, as if that would have made any difference. Suddenly, he saw a familiar face amongst all the men shouting in the hall. It was Khaleel Khan 'Athanni', sitting in the middle row. At first, Athanni did not see Joseph, but his continued stare made him conscious and he turned around. Joseph did not know if Athanni recognized him, but he saw him quickly exiting. He followed Athanni. Wearing dark glasses, Athanni tried to mix in with the pedestrians and began to walk fast, but Joseph walked faster. It was time to embarrass and humiliate him, to exact revenge for all the contempt Mansoor Babu, Mehrun and he had endured from that harami.

'Salaam, Athanni Sahib!' Joseph shouted as he caught up with him.

'What do you want?'

'Oh, nothing, Sahib. I just saw you watching the totay, so I thought I better convey my salaam.' Joseph smirked, scratching his neck.

'Are you mad? What totay? I . . . I . . . Get lost.'

Khaleel Khan quickly hailed a taxi and sped away, leaving the smiling Joseph in a fog of acrid exhaust fumes.

*

Joseph was fed up of everything. He felt tortured hearing the sound of the wind, breathing in the pungent smell of the food his mother was cooking, his mind was constantly venting rage, wanting to shatter the emptiness, to break things. He felt uprooted in his own neighbourhood. Nights of arguments with his mother turned into shouting matches—things thrown against the floor, meals dumped outside, abuses hurled. These were moments when Pyaro could hardly recognize her son and the person he had become. As for Joseph, he could not take it any longer. So one night, just to get away, he set off towards his newly discovered hang-out in the city's red-light district on Napier Road, fondly called Sona Mandi, or the Golden Market, by its diehard patrons.

The road was named after Sir Charles Napier, a general in the British Army, who brought Sindh under the rule of the British East India Company in 1843. Two years after the conquest,

Napier heard rumours that his troops were frequenting Karachi's
boy brothels. Becoming obsessed with the 'corrupting effect' the
brothels were having on his troops, he asked Sir Richard Burton,
a secret agent and the English translator of *The Arabian Nights*
and the *Kama Sutra*, to investigate the matter. If the rumours were
found to be true, Napier had declared, he would shut the brothels
down. After his investigation, Burton concluded that Napier's
hunch was correct and wrote a report that was so detailed and
graphic that many who read it came to believe that Burton was
a closeted homosexual. Napier got so incensed with what he read
in Burton's report that he gave orders to destroy all the brothels
and to rid them of the transsexuals, whom he called 'beasts'. In a
remarkably ironic twist of fate, the man who wanted to clean up the
brothels ended up having his name forever associated with them.

Napier Road had always been eclipsed by the famous Heera
Mandi, or Diamond Market, the red-light district of Lahore. So,
in an act of one-upmanship, the regulars of Napier Road began
calling it Sona Mandi and the prostitutes they visited, *dulhanain
ek raat ki*, brides for one night.

Sona Mandi was located in an old, decrepit part of the city
where cheap hookers were the leading merchandise. The more
expensive but anonymous call girls hung out comfortably in
small pockets within the newer settlements—invisible amidst
bungalows and mansions. Extreme poverty pockmarked Sona
Mandi at every twist and turn. Conspicuous by the absence of
light, it was a red-light district only in name. The only red colour
that one could find in Sona Mandi was the cheap lipsticks smeared
on the lips of its prostitutes, who subsisted without any of the
usual singing or dancing. Around here, life itself had become
a memento mori. The hookers of Sona Mandi were destitute,
pathetic and revolting. Existing only for the grubby green rupees
that their customers left behind, their squalid quarters cluttered
with sleaze, they offered unpretentious, mechanical sex and
cut-rate primordial thrills, day and night. In the sleepless alleys

of Sona Mandi, a putrid odour hung heavy in the air. A steady multitude of faceless, nameless poverty-stricken men sauntered in and out, ogling at the prostitutes through open windows and doors, exchanging vulgarity with them as they, in turn, tried to seduce them with their tired bodies and lewd gestures.

His eyes wide with excitement, Joseph followed a throng of men as they walked through Sona Mandi. Someone from the crowd made a crude remark about the whores and his companions guffawed; one man laughed so hard that he was overtaken by a fit of bronchial cough. A small boy, hardly ten years old, singing a hit Punjabi song, tried to sell jasmine garlands to the men. A little girl, probably his sister, her eyes hollow and her cheeks sunken, pushed her plastic begging bowl in front of the gang of sex-hungry men. One of them pushed her so hard that her begging bowl went flying as she fell to the ground, but she didn't cry. Life had impounded all her tears. Joseph lifted her up, found her begging bowl and gave her a few coins. Leading her down the narrow footpath, he admonished her to stay close to her brother.

Joseph wondered about these children, trying to earn a living at this godforsaken hour and in this hellish place. Was he better off than they were? Did he, Joseph Solomon, have a future brighter than these beggar children? He walked away from them, but then he came back to buy a jasmine bracelet from the little girl's brother. As he smelled the garland, he heard an enticing female voice singing a lewd parody of a Pakistani Punjabi song:

Apni biwi de ishq biyan kar kay
Aa seenay nal lug ja tha kar kay

(After declaring your love for your wife
Come cling to my breasts with a bang)

Joseph turned, and under the hiccupping fluorescent tube light, he saw the withered frame of a woman dressed in a cheap brocade shalwar-kameez, her jet-black hair cascading down her left breast. She looked tall, perhaps because of her thin frame. The grotesque make-up on her face that would have repulsed anyone else seduced Joseph. But what was precisely seductive about her was hard to say. Her dreamy kohl-lined eyes divulged tales of misery, her oversexed body chronicled stories of exploitation. Joseph sauntered towards her and handed her the jasmine bracelet, which she willingly accepted.

'How much?' he asked her the price of pleasure.

'Ten rupees for me and seven for the *batli*, the liquor bottle,' she replied casually.

'Five for you and five for the batli,' he haggled.

'The bottle's price is not fixed by me,' she replied.

The haggling continued until they settled upon a price of six rupees for her and seven rupees for the bottle. Even the crudely made liquor is more valuable than your trampled body, Joseph thought. He gave her thirteen rupees and smiled at his bargain. She motioned him to follow her, and they walked through a narrow, dimly lit corridor into a dull room that stank of sweat, stale cigarette smoke and cheap liquor. An unwashed rag of a curtain tried in vain to cover a grilled window, opposite the door. The only furniture that decked the room was a dirty charpoy that was wide enough for a single person to recline. Ordering Joseph to sit on it and wait for her for a moment, the woman went outside the room, leaving him alone to survey the bareness. A small lizard hugged the wall above the door, waiting for the show to begin, while a spider in the other corner slept soundly in its web. After a few moments, the woman came back to the room, carrying a green bottle and a plastic tumbler. Setting them down on the floor beside the bed, she raised her arms and set off tying her hair in a bun with her hennaed hands. The slit of her kameez rose up, revealing her bare waist. Joseph's heart started pounding like a tabla, a drum, and sweat beaded on his forehead from nowhere. Done tying her hair, the woman latched the door and then turned around to pass the tumbler to Joseph. She poured the liquor into the tumbler, then put the bottle to her mouth and finished the remaining alcohol in a single gulp. Joseph, on the other hand, had hardly taken a sip. The woman then took off her clothes, threw them in a corner and, after climbing on to the charpoy, waited for him to finish his drink. Joseph, however, was in no hurry, for at that moment, what interested him most was satisfying his voyeuristic itch. Plunging forward into coital ecstasy could wait a while. The woman destroyed both the burning itch as well as the anticipated thrill by ordering him to speed it up.

'The meter is running, hurry up. I don't have all night for you,' she said.

Joseph placed his drink on the floor and began undressing. Then he climbed over her, lusting with a frenzy while she lay there on the charpoy, cold as a fish, as if brooding over the ensuing transaction of feigned lovemaking. It was all over in a few minutes, a short burst of raw energy and the unadulterated performance of sexual oomph. As Joseph dropped to her side, she got up and quickly got dressed. She was just about to disappear from the room when Joseph caught her hand. He winked at her and asked, 'Marry me?'

She twisted her hand free from his and snapped, 'Get lost, *haramzada* bhangi.'

Joseph only heard the word 'bhangi', not 'haramzada', which meant bastard's son, but it seemed as if he did not care. Had the hateful word lost all its derisive character? Had it become impenetrable nonsense? But then suddenly, as if he was hit by the realization, Joseph got up and landed a stinging slap on the woman's cheek. She staggered back and howled and shouted, 'You motherfucker, get out of my house. I will call my dalla.'

Joseph reached for his shirt pocket and pulled out a crumpled bidi. He lit it up and inhaled its poison, slowly. He was not afraid of her threat to call her pimp. Sitting stark naked after a quickie, smoking a bidi, and hitting the prostitute for her insult made him feel liberated. But when the woman's pimp came in and saw Joseph—a big, naked guy—he politely asked him to cause no more trouble. Joseph gave him a dirty look, put on his clothes and came out, only to be accosted by another suspicious-looking man.

'You want pencil-in?' he asked Joseph in a hushed tone.

'What's that?'

'It's a drug for "bee dee",' he replied.

'What's "bee dee"?'

'"Bee Dee", *saala*! Bee Dee! Benereal Degeez!'

Scaring Joseph with horror stories of venereal diseases and the importance of penicillin after sex, the man took him to another dingy flat where he saw a long line of people waiting for a shot of penicillin. Joseph joined the line and waited for a tedious hour to get the injection, marvelling at the cottage industry that the sex trade created. An hour of post-sex-waiting, after six minutes of crappy pleasure, was not his idea of fun. His mind once again began planning escape strategies from his profession, his work and his country.

*

Haider Rizvi's trial in the august Sindh High Court building was short, swift and fair. Using several precedents and references, Noor destroyed the government's arguments. The rule of law had prevailed. In vindicating Haider, the judge not only defied the rule of force, but he also asserted the independence of the judiciary. In his ruling, he lectured that it is only in law-observing societies that human potential is achieved. After the verdict, a rather overwhelmed Haider hugged Noor and slumped back into his wooden chair. His head in his hands, he began to weep. Both Sadiq and Zakir, who were there for support, tried comforting him. The lead prosecutor later confided in Noor about the weakness of the case; but what could he do as a government prosecutor? He had to carry on with the sham. After the friends calmed Haider down, they all drove together in Noor's car to the Sindh Club to celebrate the victory. Noor wondered if General Dundda's grip on power had weakened, if the sycophants who flocked around him were finally abandoning him.

That night, Noor came home early, elated, and with an enormous, colourful box of sweetmeats. Mansoor was in his bed reading James Hilton's *Goodbye, Mr. Chips* when Budhoo knocked at his door.

'What is it, Budhoo?' he asked.

'Mansoor Babu, Sahib wants you.'

Budhoo's serious tone made Mansoor's face flush and then go pale. By now, he should have been used to those nightly lectures that metamorphosed into long discourses, but they still caused his stomach to churn.

'Why does he want me?' he asked Budhoo.

'I don't know, Babu, but he has brought a box of *mithai*, sweets, from Abdul Hannan's store.'

Abdul Hannan Sweetmeat Merchants, near Guru Mandir, was Mansoor's favourite store. Hearing the merchant's name, he jumped out of bed, straightened his crumpled shirt, put on his slippers and headed towards his parents' bedroom. Noor had changed into his kurta-pyjama and looked incredibly relaxed, while Farhat lay on their king-size bed, nibbling a sweet laddu.

'Come on, son, we are going to celebrate today. What do you feel like eating?' Noor shouted with exuberance.

'What are we celebrating, Abba?' Mansoor asked, sitting on the bed across from his father's tufted armchair.

Uncharacteristically, his father gave him a brief account of his legal victory. He seldom discussed the law or his practice with his son. In fact, he had forbidden Mansoor from even thinking about going into law. The only good thing about the profession, according to Noor, was that it exposed one to the Socratic method of arriving at conclusions.

'So, do you feel like eating Chinese or shall we order chicken tikka?' he asked.

'I don't know . . . what do you feel like Amma?'

'I asked *you,* not your mother.' Noor was slightly peeved.

They settled on Chinese, and Noor wrote down the names of a few dishes on a piece of paper and gave it to Budhoo along with a twenty-rupee note. Then he ambled to the liquor cabinet in the men's quarter, where he stashed his entire collection of expensive imported liquor. He came back with the navy-blue box of Royal Salute Scotch Whisky and two crystal whisky glasses.

'Tonight, we are going to have the best food, the best dessert and the best drink,' he announced, sitting down on his usual couch. He opened the box and pulled out the bottle from the navy-blue pouch within. Unscrewing the cap, he poured the Scotch into the two glasses and then added two cubes of ice and some water in both. He never drank his whisky neat. After taking a large swig from one glass, he offered the other glass to his son.

'How old are you?' he asked.

'Nearly seventeen,' Mansoor replied, trembling a bit and stealing a quick glance at his mother.

'I think you are eligible to have a celebratory glass with your father; you don't need your mother's permission, so stop looking at her.'

'You are corrupting my son,' Farhat remarked rather casually, picking another laddu from the box.

Mansoor was surprised by that mellow statement. A few years ago, she would have picked a raging fight with his father over this. But perhaps she had finally got used to his drinking. Noor fired back with a couplet from Ghalib:

Waiz na khood piyo, na kissee ko pila sako
Kya baat hai tumhare sharab tahoor key

He turned to Mansoor and asked if he had understood the meaning of the lines. When Mansoor hesitated, he said: 'This is another couplet from my favourite poet. What he is saying is: "What good is your liquor of piety, O'Preacher, that neither can you drink it, nor can you offer it to anyone."'

Noor seemed pleased with himself at coming up with an apropos couplet in reply to Farhat's mild protest. While telling Mansoor not to look at his mother for permission, he stole a guilty glance at his wife.

Mansoor had been introduced to the occasional sip of whisky from an early age. Noor called it a purging experience, a baptism of whisky. But Mansoor still felt uncomfortable drinking in front of his mother, who, he knew, disapproved of it sharply. He hesitatingly took a sip now. Satisfied that his son had defied his mother, Noor asked Mansoor a question, 'What are your plans after your Senior Cambridge exams?'

With Noor slightly inebriated, the conversation had switched to English.

'To go to college?' Mansoor replied, not sure why his father had asked that.

'Mashallah!' Noor exclaimed sarcastically. 'Mister, college is *the only* option for you. I am asking about your subject.'

'I haven't really thought about it, Abba. I still have a year to decide,' Mansoor answered.

'I want you to seriously think about economics.'

Never in his wildest imagination had Mansoor thought about economics.

'Will you get that third book from the second shelf of my bookcase?' Noor pointed at his precious bookcase standing in one corner of the bedroom.

Mansoor walked over to the bookcase and took out the book his father wanted. It was a book by a man called John Maynard Keynes and was titled *The General Theory of Employment, Interest and Money*.

'Do you know who this man was?' Noor asked, taking the book from him.

Mansoor shook his head and said, 'No.'

'He was the man who saved the world.'

Noor flipped through the pages until he came to a passage that he had underlined with a red pencil.

'Read the part that I have underlined.'

Mansoor took the book from his father and began reading:

The ideas of economists and political philosophers, both when they are right and when they are wrong, are more powerful than is commonly understood. Indeed, the world is ruled by little else. Practical men, who believe themselves to be quite exempt from any intellectual influences, are usually the slaves of some defunct economist. Madmen in authority, who hear voices in the air, are distilling their frenzy from some academic scribbler of a few years back.

Mansoor looked up at his father after he finished reading.

'That is why I want you to study economics.'

Noor's economic philosophy had undergone a series of transformations. During his early college years, he had been a communist sympathizer; he read *The Communist Manifesto* and fantasized about the proletarian revolution in post-colonial India. But Joseph Stalin's brutal repression and the Soviet invasion of Hungary turned him off entirely from it. In England, while studying for the Bar, he was influenced by the Fabian socialists. When he returned to India, like many other Western-educated men, he began supporting the secular politics and socialist economics of the Congress Party. After the Partition, when his law practice took off, he visited the United States and, impressed by the country's affluence, converted to capitalism. To him, the free enterprise system was *it*. The study of economics became his newest passion, and he pored over the tomes of Adam Smith, J.S. Mill, John Maynard Keynes and Milton Friedman. It was too late for him to become a practicing economist, so he started to think about living his dream through his son. At last, he had found a profession for Mansoor.

Mansoor's mind, however, would switch off whenever Noor talked about economics, so he only retained bits of the information that his father insisted on imparting. Seeing his father so successful in his chosen path, he had always thought that he would eventually take over Noor's practice, imagining an engraved gold-plated sign at the entrance of the Variawa Building where the office was: Haq and Haq, Advocates, Supreme Court. His admiration for his father's work had only intensified after he successfully defended Haider Rizvi.

'But I want to be a lawyer like you,' Mansoor said.

As soon as he had uttered these words, he noticed his father's complexion changing. The veins on his neck swelled; he took a deep breath and thundered: 'I FORBID YOU TO EVEN THINK ABOUT IT.' After pausing to clear his throat, Noor continued, 'Now look, son, I don't want to ever hear such rubbish from you again, understood? Don't even think about being a lawyer.'

He paused again, grabbed his glass and gulped down some Scotch. 'Do you know how much I hate this profession?' he asked. 'This is the most unproductive profession. It's a profession where you create tricks and loopholes and legerdemain. You defend your clients even though you know they are lying, and they have cheated.'

'But don't the cheats and liars have the right to be defended?'

'Yes, they do . . . but it weighs you down with a guilt which you will carry for the rest of your life.'

'But you defended Uncle Haider, and you had tried to help Uncle Hassan Nasir.'

Noor's face blanched at the name of his dear friend who had been dead for almost eight years. A shiver coursed through his being as the image of Nasir's tortured body appeared in his mind. Nasir had been regarded by the Dundda government as the most dangerous communist agitator in the country. When he went into hiding, his friends talked about him in code, never mentioning his name even in the privacy of their homes. Noor had bought a ticket for Nasir to flee the country, but the labour leader was apprehended before he could escape. It was only later that Mansoor learned about his father's involvement in the whole affair.

'Sahibzadey, things are going to become uglier and more corrupt in our legal system; you won't be able to survive. No, there is going to be no discussion about this topic again. Do you hear me?'

'Yes, Abba,' Mansoor replied.

Budhoo entered with boxes of Chinese takeaway just then, effectively ending the conversation. Relieved to see him, Mansoor got up and pretended to help him serve the food. After Budhoo left them, the three of them quietly slurped the shark fin soup and munched on the spring chicken.

After a while, Mansoor, out of nowhere, asked his father, 'Abba, can you tell me about djinns?'

'Djinns?' he echoed. 'Why do you ask?'

'Why are you always interested in djinns? Especially at night?' his mother interjected.

'No reason. Just curious,' Mansoor replied.

Noor had long ago heard about the rumour that Kaneez had spread regarding Mansoor, but he had forgotten all about it. Now when he heard the word 'djinn' from his son, he became a little worried and felt an urge to tell him what he thought. Reaching for his whisky, Noor took a sip and said, 'You know, son, your grandfather was a religious scholar and a firm believer, quite unlike me. But what I admired most about him were his impeccable character and his philosophical interpretations. He abhorred the literalists and fought battles with them.'

'But what did Dada Jaan think about djinns made of smokeless fire?' Mansoor asked.

'Well, let me tell you about his version of djinns.' Noor paused for a moment and took another sip from his almost-empty glass.

'The word "djinn" means "something hidden". A part of everyone's being is concealed, even from one's own self. That part is one's inner djinn. Find your hidden self, or your inner djinn, and you find your true self. The smokeless djinn is a metaphor for the rage that exists in everybody. You have a djinn; I have a djinn and your mother has a djinn. In fact, she has the biggest djinn!' Noor laughed even as Farhat glowered at him.

That night, as he closed his eyes to go to sleep, Mansoor couldn't stop thinking about what his father had said about djinns as one's hidden self. Is our concealed self our true reality? Why is it hidden? How do we discover it? Is the inner rage an ugly part of our reality that also needs to be discovered? That was a scary thought.

Fourteen

Even though Joseph lived in Karachi, he had never paid much attention to the *urs* or the birthday celebrations of Abdullah Shah Ghazi, the eighth-century Sufi saint. Regarded as Karachi's patron saint, his birthday was observed with great fanfare. His shrine, located on a hilltop overlooking Clifton Beach, attracted people of all faith, who came for supplication and spirituality. The tomb with its white and green striped dome, beautiful tile work and colourful bunting stood out from afar. Recently, tourists and hippies had also started visiting the shrine.

When Mansoor told Joseph about that year's celebrations, the first thought that came to his mind was the langar, the free 'consecrated meal' that would be served at the shrine. Rather than going home and eating the same daal and roti, he could have a feast there and all for the cost of a bus trip! The food at the shrine was believed to have miraculous power, and those who came to beseech Ghazi that day had their wishes granted by the dead Sufi saint. Who knows, Joseph might even get his heart's desire to become a movie star. He asked Mansoor to accompany him, but he declined. Feeling dejected, Joseph decided to go there by himself.

When Joseph arrived at the shrine, night had begun to fall. An interminable sea of pilgrims greeted him. He saw more people disembarking from buses, trucks, taxis and even donkey carts. Everyone ran towards the tomb as soon as they got out of their vehicles. Pedlars huckstered their wares, while beggars asked for alms. It was a chilly night, crisp and brittle, as men, women and children in tattered clothes, their faces garbled by wretched poverty, their hopes raised by vague promises moved towards the tomb. Joseph walked with them deliberately, as if he knew exactly what he would do once he got to his destination.

Suddenly, Joseph heard a loud firecracker. It sounded like the racket that the ack-ack guns made during the war. The next moment, he saw men, women and children falling even as others ran frantically in every direction. They were shrieking and screaming. It was a stampede. He stopped walking, and without thinking, he turned back and started to run in the reverse direction. He heard more shots as he ran. A haggard-looking man was running alongside him. 'Was that a firecracker?' Joseph asked him.

'No, I heard there was fighting between two groups; they must've fired at each other,' the man replied.

Joseph had seen policemen in their grey and khaki uniforms when he had got down from the bus, and he hoped they would bring order. But the police fired tear gas shells into the crowd, which caused even more panic. The cries of women and children could be heard everywhere. People were falling over each other, getting crushed in the process. A tear gas shell landed near Joseph, swishing thick smoke. As he ran past it, he felt a burning sensation in his eyes, and he began coughing as his chest tightened. But he kept on running.

After Joseph had cleared some distance, he stopped to rest for a while, and as he wiped his eyes with his sleeve, he saw a man on all fours on the ground, holding his side as blood oozed out. He looked confused when Joseph bent over to see him. He asked the man what happened to him, but the man had difficulty speaking. Without a second's hesitation, Joseph lifted him up in his arms and ran towards a slowly moving taxi. He waved at the driver, who stopped the instant he saw him—a big man carrying a limp body. Joseph gently lowered the man into the back seat and then ran to the other side. He opened the door and jumped in next to him, cradling his head on his lap.

'Civil Haspataal!' he shouted to the taxi driver.

The taxi swerved and accelerated convulsively as it headed towards the hospital, the rattling noise of the exhaust from the busted silencer annoying the wounded man. The man was having difficulty breathing. After a while, he whispered something to Joseph. It was then that Joseph realized that he was a foreigner.

'Where from?' Joseph asked in his broken English.

'Iran,' the man replied with difficulty.

'Don't talk,' Joseph said, 'we go haspataal.'

Throughout the journey, Joseph applied pressure on the man's wound, using his handkerchief to try and stem the bleeding. He kept comforting the injured man in his broken English, telling him, 'haspataal come soon.'

The man grimaced in pain as the taxi braked right in front of the hospital. Joseph gave the driver one rupee and pulled out the incapacitated Iranian effortlessly. He was a small man, so Joseph did not have any difficulty carrying him. He took him straight to the emergency, where the orderlies and the nurses whisked him away. One of the nurses came back and rudely ordered Joseph to wait. So Joseph went and sat on one of the wobbly chairs in the reception area. He stayed there for a couple of hours until a young doctor came out and told him that the patient needed blood. They asked him his blood type.

'It's red!' he replied.

'We need to take your blood to see if you're a match. It may save this man's life. He is in bad shape. Are you willing to give blood?'

'Yes,' Joseph replied.

They pulled him into a room and asked him to lie flat on the gurney. They drew vials of blood. Joseph did not know how many;

he had already fainted. When he regained consciousness, it was late. He went to the nurses' desk and asked about the Iranian. Relieved to hear that he was stable and had received his blood, Joseph headed home.

The next day, Joseph went to the hospital to visit the Iranian. One of the nurses had informed him that the police would be there to take his statement, but the police never came. The Iranian, Reza Dabiran, spoke little Urdu and no Punjabi, while Joseph spoke a smattering of English and no Farsi; they communicated in an odd mixture of sign language, Farsi, English, Punjabi and Urdu.

'Thank you for saving my life,' Reza said in English as he tried to sit up.

'Oh! No bother, Sahib,' Joseph replied.

Reza Dabiran, a man in his late thirties, was severely bruised and cut, but his face still displayed his handsome features. Although his injuries made it difficult for him to speak, he continued to chat with Joseph.

'I am a commercial attaché at the Iranian consulate,' Reza said.

'Shrine, Sahib?' Joseph asked and made a hand gesture asking why.

With a smile on his face, Reza said, 'I was on my way to the beach when I was suddenly hit by the mob, and then I don't exactly know what happened.'

Reza did not have any family or friends in the city, and his colleagues from the consulate visited him only once in that dingy Dettol-smelling hospital. So, to him, Joseph's company was a welcome respite. He stayed at the Civil Hospital for three days and was later moved to the Holy Family Hospital, which had better facilities. Reza stayed there for two more weeks, and Joseph visited him every day. One day, he even brought some fruits for him. Joseph had saved the man's life, and now he touched his heart with kindness. With a friendly, young doctor acting as Joseph's interpreter, Reza learned everything about his rescuer.

'You know, Joseph, I can help you find a job in Iran if you want, but not in films.'

'You can? Oh! Please, Sahib, I will be your servant!' Joseph replied.

'I can get you a job at one of the oil refineries.'

Joseph became ecstatic. He wanted to pack his bags the very next day and leave for Iran, but Reza laughed and told him to have patience. It would take time to get everything in order. But Joseph had found his miracle, and he called it hope.

*

After he returned from the hospital that night, Joseph wanted to broadcast his good news to the whole of Bhangi Para. He wanted to celebrate the offer of hope around those narrow pathways that always led to a dead-end. He wanted to tell his mother that her days of cleaning other people's shit were over. For at last, there was hope. But his mother was nowhere to be found. He saw the same dog that he had hit with a stone the other day in his frustration, but he did not hit him this time; instead, he threw him the sandwich that he had swiped from the hospital. The dog took a few steps towards it and began eating it.

From the sweltering oil refineries of Iran to the film studios of Bombay, Joseph could see his future stretch out in front of him like a long shimmering path, free of blind spots and dead-end alleys. He saw himself prancing around movie sets with Rajesh Khanna and doing a dance number with Sharmila Tagore. His fantasies, however, were rudely interrupted by the tired face of his mother as she entered their shack.

'Let me wash up. I'll get the chapattis ready,' Pyaro said.

'Ma, don't bother about dinner. I am going to get the food from the restaurant today.'

'Where did you steal the money from?'

'Ma, I didn't steal it. I have good news. I'll tell you all about it after I get the food.'

Joseph went to Café de Jamadar and bought kebabs, tandoori naans and some mint chutney, all of it wrapped in an old newspaper that prominently displayed a picture of General Dundda soaked in the oil from the kebabs. He wanted to celebrate in style. At home, he excitedly told his mother about Reza Dabiran as he served the food. Pyaro listened quietly. Once Joseph was done, she got up without finishing dinner, wiped her hands on a dirty towel and sank into her tattered mattress. Joseph felt a tightness in his throat as he swallowed the kebab in his mouth.

'I thought you would be happy to hear my good news.'

Pulling the blanket over her face, Pyaro turned towards the wall.

'I have told you a thousand times, I'm not like you or Babuji. I am not going to die in this pit like a dog,' Joseph said through gritted teeth.

*

The government finally ordered the schools to reopen for the first time after the war. The long, protracted period of political turmoil that followed the war had finally subsided, and people welcomed the news with a sigh of relief. The Education Board announced the dates for the school exams, which made Mehrun anxious. This was her final year in high school, and she was determined to achieve a good first division to get into President's College, the college of her dreams, her ticket to a good life, or so she thought. Because she needed the money, she kept working at Sadiq's house, both of them pretending that nothing had happened. Her satchel packed with books, Mehrun went to his house every afternoon after school and used every minute of her break to study for her exams. The professor helped her, polishing her English and making her memorize lines from Shakespeare.

But Mehrun's attention remained divided. She worried about her father, who was fast regressing towards insanity. Time, instead of healing his wounds, had created deep lesions in his soul. Kaneez's death made him look gaunt and prematurely grey. His existence atrophied right in front of Mehrun's eyes. And as his nightmares continued, his interest in life fizzled. No longer did he care about his garden at the Kashana; no longer did he care about going out, and no longer did he care about his own life. With stony eyes and a blank mind, he stared at vacant spaces, weighed down by grief. Mehrun, who had made her peace with Mansoor after her mother's death, finally convinced Jumman to visit the Kashana with her, for a change of scenery. He would spend some time there at her insistence, sharing his lunches with Chaos, who ate the food guiltily, as if somehow sensing his sorrow. But his attendance there, too, became sporadic, and Farhat, noticing his absence, started docking his salary. But Jumman never complained. Mansoor worried about Jumman as well, but he felt helpless. He tried to convince Mehrun about consulting a doctor, but she had lost faith in all healers—fake and real. At that point in her life, her only goal was to get a first division and a scholarship to President's College. Like Joseph, she was in a hurry to change her future.

Rain arrived early that year, but it did not drown the city, only sprinkling it gently, trying not to upset the already hard life of its inhabitants. On that misty Monday afternoon in June, Mehrun waited for the university bus outside her school. She was happy; she had done well in her preliminary exams. Nothing could make her sad. Not the wait for the bus, not the drizzle, not the denuding eyes of those odious men at the bus stop who looked at her as if they had never seen a woman in their miserable lives before. With a glow on her face and a romantic rain song on her lips, she waited for the bus.

How should I tell the professor about my preliminary exam results? she thought.

The professor, her mentor, her confidante; that mysterious scholar who had showed her great kindness but had also kissed her. After Mansoor, he was the one person she trusted the most. And Sadiq made her feel special. In those days, she rarely talked with Joseph, who remained lost in his secret fantasy.

At last, she saw the ugly British Leyland bus jolting and trundling towards the bus stop, emitting a toxic cloud of fumes. As it pulled over, a horde of young university students jumped out even before the bus had stopped completely, their angry impatience all too palpable. She got in and found an empty seat near the window.

'Double hai, double hai,' shouted the bus conductor, signalling the driver to drive on.

In half an hour, Mehrun was at the professor's doorstep. She rattled the door knocker. The drizzle had moistened her hair and clothes. After a few seconds, the professor, with his pipe in his mouth, opened the door.

'Areý, areý. Come, come. Come on in; you are drenched!' he said in a concerned tone and continued, 'Go and dry your hair with the bathroom towel.'

Mehrun dropped her satchel in the foyer and went towards the bathroom. After she had dried her hair and combed it with her fingers, she came back and excitedly began telling the professor the good news about her preliminary exams. He was genuinely happy for her. Mehrun reminded him of his promise about President's College. He nodded, as if without listening, his eyes distracted by her wet clothes that clung seductively to her body. Sadiq began to tremble, as if from the cold rain, and then suddenly overpowered by an uncontrollable urge, he caught her hands, pulled her towards him and kissed her. The warmth of his body melted her and she returned his desire with complete abandon. They kissed long and passionately, and Mehrun let his hands wander over her body of their own accord; the ecstasy, the joy, the rapture utterly mesmerized her. She would have given anything to remain captive to the embraces of this portly middle-aged man, but then a lightning bolt hit her back. It was Talat's hand that had slapped her backbone, inflicting a sharp pain on her shoulder blade. It was as if someone had stabbed her with a hot knife. When Mehrun turned around and saw Talat's livid face, it ripped her heart out. Talat pulled her away from the grips of her husband and continued with her beatings. She slapped her, hectically and hysterically. Covering her face with the back of her arms, Mehrun tried to counter the blows. Sadiq, who was shell-shocked at first, regained his composure when he heard his wife shouting: 'Get out of my house! You churail! You ungrateful whore! Never show your filthy face here; otherwise, I am going to break every bone in your body!'

Sadiq tried to intervene, meekly, but Talat pushed him aside. Mehrun took advantage of the momentary pause in Talat's attack and ran towards the front door, her eyes streaming with tears, her ears ringing with the slaps. She wanted to vanish from the house. Grabbing her satchel, she ran out in full speed, still hearing a salvo of imprecations behind her, only now they were directed towards Talat's husband.

Vilification had hunted her down once again. The cycle of beatings had returned. What was she going to do now? Without a job, where would she get the money for her exam fees? What was she going to tell her father? Haunted by these questions, she raced towards the bus stop. From a distance, she saw the same British Leyland bus that had brought her to her present misery now come back a full circle to fetch her again, as if playing a crude joke on her life. She did not climb into the bus. She was in no mood to let that contemptible means of transportation wreck her life again. The bus left her, belching noxious carbon monoxide fumes in her face. She held her breath, not wanting to inhale any more poison. The questions returned to torment her again. Sadiq Mirza had disrupted her life. He had pushed her back into darkness, making her feel forlorn, frightened and fatigued. Was she so worthless that everyone had to hit her? Was it her kismet to always be humiliated? The wait for the next bus became painful. When it finally came, it was one hour late. She waved at the driver to stop the bus. As it came to a halt, she climbed up and sank behind the driver's seat, near the window.

After she had settled, she was once again rattled, this time by her own weary reflection in the window. She tried to look outside, but she couldn't escape it. It became an image and then a picture, and then it transmogrified into her churail-like mother. Her mottled face, her hurtful cries were all too real. The word 'churail' echoed from the window, from the seat Mehrun was sitting on, from the metal bar she was holding, the very word Talat had uttered, the name conferred on her mother. The heir to the churail was now crowned—Mehrunnissa née churail née harami née whore—her list of humiliating nicknames growing long and weary. When the bus stopped near her alley, she stepped out with a heavy heart, her legs like soft vermicelli, and dawdled towards that gutter that her father called home.

*

That day, when she had panicked about not having the money to pay for her exam fee, it had been a moment of helplessness. But poverty often teaches the value of frugality; Mehrun had been religiously saving money from her job at the Mirzas. So, when the time came, she paid the exam fee on her own, and then for three whole months buried herself in her books, neglecting her shattered self and blocking out whispers of the scandal at the professor's house. On the day of the exam, she entered the hall poised and prepared. That year, all the examinations took place without any ugly incidents and disruptions. For the first time in many years, the students did not walk out of the examination halls to protest against difficult questions; they did not demonstrate when denied the opportunity to cheat, and they did not threaten the invigilators for being too vigilant. It was as if the students had finally become serious about education. The results were announced two months later, and Mehrun got the first division that she had hoped for. But getting admission into President's College was not on the cards any more. She even sent Mansoor, secretly, to Sadiq Mirza to remind him about the promise that he had made to her, but the professor made lame excuses. And without any *sifarish*, any recommendations or intercessions, getting admission to the prestigious college was unthinkable. She did not have a civil servant for a father or a rich uncle. She reminded herself that she was the daughter of a lowly gardener who was slowly surrendering to the madness of perception. Mehrun released her anger by burning the newspaper that had printed the exam result. She did not even try to get admitted into any of the other prestigious colleges in the city, but instead, got herself registered at the Government College for Women, merging her destiny with a 'yellow' institution once more. To feed herself and her father, she found a part-time job as a clerk at the newly formed High Finance Bank Limited, all on her own, without any pull or influence, and she was proud of that.

The chairman of the bank was the legendary Ameer Abbas Alvi, also known as Triple-A, a self-made man who overcame poverty, rose to the top and, in the process, amassed a considerable fortune in a short time. Despite his own new wealth, he despised the nouveau riche and the old moneyed class equally. But that is not to say he did not suck up to them when he needed to. In the age of puffery and pretence, he saw no contradiction in loathing and slavering in the same breath. He was a man possessed with an all-consuming drive to prosper in the emerging banking industry of Pakistan.

When Mehrun got this part-time job, she did not have to worry about finding work as a domestic servant any longer. The new fount of income made Jumman quit his job at the Kashana and become a full-time schizophrenic. The only annoyance that re-entered Mehrun's life was Khaleel Khan, alias Athanni, who, despite failing his school exams, also found a position in this new bank.

*

Reza Dabiran came through for Joseph, finding him work at the National Iranian Petroleum Company, and even sending him money for airfare and other expenses. Pyaro pleaded, cajoled and emotionally blackmailed Joseph, even threatening suicide, but nothing worked. Joseph's mind was made up. Anxious and ready to depart, he promised his mother that he would send her enough money so that she wouldn't need to do the 'shitty' job again. Feeling helpless, she hugged him and prayed to God for her son's health, all the while hoping he would not get his passport.

Her prayers went unanswered and Joseph got his first passport. It surprised him that the government had made it so easy that he was able to get it without paying any bribe and in good time. Was the reason for this to encourage its nationals to work overseas and send foreign exchange remittances to boost the country's dwindling reserves? After he bought his plane ticket, he went to the Kashana to bid the Haq family goodbye. Mansoor had mixed feelings when Joseph told him about his impending departure the following week. Happy that he had found a better-paying job, but sad that he may never see him again, he controlled his tears. Much to Joseph's surprise, Farhat gave him two hundred and fifty rupees and told him to buy some clothes. Noor asked him, 'What will your mother do?'

'Sahib, she says that she will go back to her family in Punjab.'

Noor asked him to wait and went to his bedroom. When he returned, he had an envelope in his hand. He gave it to Joseph and said, 'This has money for your mother; not for you. Give it to her.'

Joseph started to weep at the generosity of his employers. He wanted to hug them, but societal barriers prevented him from doing so. Mansoor followed him to the gate. As he was about to sit on his bicycle, Joseph said to his friend with a smile, 'Tell Mehrun, my marriage proposal is still valid.' Mansoor laughed and said, 'You will have to tell her that when you become an idiot millionaire.'

*

Meanwhile, Mansoor's imperious father forced him to study economics and political science in his senior year. Literature, philosophy and religion—Mansoor's newest passions—could wait until his career was established. When he had argued about this, his father had replied with his usual sarcasm, 'Sahibzadey, do you want to sell peanuts after you graduate, or do you want to teach in a mosque? Or maybe you can do both.'

Mansoor had slowly begun to feel that religion was that part of his culture which was sorely missing in his life. Except for Maulvi Sahib's wishy-washy, one-dimensional limited knowledge and his mother's odd chunks of dogma, he knew little else. At that juncture in Pakistan's history, for all practical purposes, religion remained a mostly private matter. But that cavity, a gift from his father, suddenly needed filling. Unable to explain to Noor his love of the liberal arts and his want of religion, Mansoor struggled within. With Joseph gone and Mehrun busy with her new job, he felt lonely. So, Mansoor immersed himself in books and read everything from the trashy to the transcendent, from James Hadley Chase to Albert Camus, from Harold Robbins to Bertrand Russell. He also pored over Urdu literature and read Faiz Ahmad Faiz, Saadat Hassan Manto and Qurratulain Hyder. Manto stirred his sexual consciousness, while Camus, Russell and Haider stoked his philosophical interest. And then there was Faiz, who made him fall in love with the poetry of dissent. The beliefs that had been hanging in his embrace, like dangling participles, came under fresh scrutiny. Vague religious convictions, which had been seeded here and there and had begun to take root, withered under reflection. Purveyors of religion, on his shortwave radio and the new television in the house, appeared as charlatans. And when the newly formed religious party, the Guardians of Divinity (G.O.D.) offered frayed certitudes wrapped in glossy packages, Mansoor's doubts hardened.

*

General Dundda sacked his brilliant foreign minister, who, with a blasted ego and a determination fed by anger, began plotting retaliation. He first tried to join different political parties, and when that failed, he formed his own—The Party of Oppressed People. Some people abbreviated it as P.O.P., while others went with P.O.O.P. Noor preferred the latter. And so, the P.O.O.P.s clashed with the G.O.D.s, and they both fought with the police. And when things did not calm down, the general imposed a curfew and arrested his brilliant foreign minister on trumped-up charges and made him a star. To divert the nation's attention, the general then ordered his sycophantic advisers to prepare for the 'Decade of Development', which was to be launched on the tenth anniversary of his coup d'état. Noor called it the 'Delusion of Development' and wrote an op-ed page for the *Morning Gazette*, but Haider vetoed it. It was too inflammatory.

Fifteen

The 'Decade of Development' was celebrated with pageantry and parades as General Dundda officially inaugurated the first television station in Karachi and gave his first and last televised speech. The cities shimmered with decorative lights, while the newspapers published special supplements paying glowing tributes to the President. Poets and writers wrote painful panegyrics, their barbarous expressions mocking human intelligence. And the flagrant contradiction of the last ten years stood there in all its nakedness as a farcical tragedy. Who prospered, who suffered, who won and who lost was no longer a mystery. A handful of the wealthiest families had amassed more wealth than the rest of the country put together. And when the news about the opulent lifestyles of these wealthy industrialists began to appear in the newspapers, patience started deserting the people of Pakistan. A fit of anarchic anger overtook them, and the time for violent action finally arrived; it was now or never. The day after the celebrations, the brilliant ex-foreign minister gave a stirring speech. Threatening to let the Russian bald cat out of the bag (a reference to the accord that the general had signed with the Indian prime minister in the Soviet Union), he suggested that his former benefactor was an American puppet. The nation rallied behind him as he called for demonstrations and strikes, his supporters clashing with the police, burning buses, destroying government buildings and torching cinemas, as well as the American and British consulates. Once again, the general retaliated by throwing the brilliant ex-foreign minister into jail and made him a bigger hero. Once again, schools and colleges were shut down. And with nothing better to do, the jaded students joined the protestors and the professional rabble-rousers, backing them in their chaotic protest marches and abetting them in arson, looting and killing. Then, in a strange twist of politics, General Dundda performed a volte-face and released all political leaders languishing in jail, calling for a 'reconciliation meeting' with them. When everything fails, you can always count on what the Pakistani public calls 'lota' politicians. These are turncoat politicians who are ready to wash the ass of anyone promising them power. But this time, nothing succeeded. And then, on the anniversary of *his* Constitution, demoralized and dejected, the general abruptly handed over power to the then commander-in-chief of the armed forces, making him the chief martial law administrator, and faded into obscurity. The people's agitation had finally succeeded in removing General Dundda.

According to the 'sources' of the lurid tabloid the *Daily Hulchul*, when the general had called the commander-in-chief, he was 'rumoured to be playing blind man's bluff with a bevy of beauties in a five-star hotel, utterly inebriated.' His bacchanalian temperament later earned him the epithet Rangeelay Shah, or the Colourful King. The scandalous story mentioned that the telephone call from the outgoing general had annoyed him as 'his frivolity' had been disrupted. His 'women' had to give him gallons of coffee to clear his head. With a semblance of sobriety restored, he gave a tiresome televised speech, promising a new constitution and fresh elections. At first, the people did not believe the Rangeelay Shah, but what option did they really have? The change of leadership and the promise of elections scattered the agitators and sent the students back to their schools and colleges. Much to everyone's surprise, Rangeelay Shah relaxed the emergency laws that General

Dundda had hurriedly passed and re-allowed political meetings, even as he continued the martial law.

*

During this whole political turmoil, the banks had remained defiantly open. Although many clerks and officers absented themselves, Mehrun diligently came to work every day. And since the colleges were closed, she could work full-time too. Her sedulous efforts and painstaking industry caught the attention of Ameer Abbas Alvi, who advised her to quit college and work for him full-time. Heeding his advice, Mehrun withdrew from college and buried herself in the affairs of this nascent bank. Success kissed her feet and she inched towards becoming the begum of her dreams. Mehrun now acted and attired like a successful professional. She was promoted to a loan officer and soon became a close confidante of Triple-A. In Mehrun, he saw his own past. He found affinities in her social background and the economic hardships they had both endured. Observing her working long hours, hearing her talk self-assuredly with her clients, and seeing her solve problems, he decided to take her under his wing. Alvi gave her the lift that he himself had got early in his career. Now, her career kicked into high gear and she was ready for the take-off to prosperity. Her personal life also returned to normal as her father suddenly snapped out of his melancholic state and went back to working at the Kashana. Life was suddenly a sweetheart, but not for too long.

One day, as Mehrun finished her afternoon meeting with her boss, a bank secretary came and whispered in her ear that a woman was waiting for her in her office. Mehrun quickly checked her diary to see if she had forgotten an appointment. But there was no entry for 2 p.m. Puzzled, she excused herself from the meeting that had almost ended and went to her drab office. Through the partially open door, she saw Talat Mirza sitting and waiting, twirling the loose end of her saree. Her stern face jaded the elegance of her beautiful saree. Suddenly, Mehrun had a sense of déjà vu: the face resembled the one she had seen on that fateful day, when Talat had found her with her husband and had hit her. She told herself that Talat was in *her* territory and could not resort to violence, but that did not calm her. Taking a deep breath, she pushed open her office door.

'Begum Sahiba?' she said.

At the sound of Mehrun's voice, Talat took out a wad of cash from her purse and threw it on her desk.

'I have sold my jewellery for all this. Take it and leave this city. Leave my husband alone, for God's sake,' she said.

Mehrun looked at the bundle of fifty-rupee notes and approached her desk. She picked up the money, looked at it with pursed lips and then, as an afterthought, threw it back into Talat's lap.

'Please leave my office,' she gritted her teeth, fighting hard to maintain her composure.

But Talat sat there defiantly, her choler rising, and said, 'I will never allow you to become his second wife! And if I ever see you with him, I will personally strangle you.'

Without saying anything else, Mehrun rang the bell on her desk. Within minutes, the security guard came in. He looked at Talat and then at the ashen-faced Mehrun, unsure as to why he had been summoned.

'Please show Begum Sahiba the exit door,' Mehrun instructed him.

Talat put the money back in her purse and left her office, but she issued another warning as she left: 'If I see you within twenty feet of my husband, I will kill you.'

The mild headache that had been lingering at the edges of her temple all day now began to pound Mehrun's head with full force. She rang the bell again and asked the guard to bring a couple of Aspro tablets and some water. As the guard left, her boss, Alvi, knocked on her door. He craned his neck through it and asked her if everything was okay. Mehrun just nodded and was relieved that her boss left without asking any other question.

The guard returned with the Aspro tablets and the water a few minutes later. Mehrun sat there at her desk, a little dazed, and swallowed the Aspro, washing it down with the cloudy water that the guard had brought, not even noticing when he left the room. Did she have any reason to feel guilty about anything? All she had wanted was to benefit from Sadiq's intellect. Why did her love of learning become a constant source of violence? Why did those written words, sources of serenity, become sources of sorrow? It was something she just could not comprehend. Why did Talat come to her office to humiliate her? And what was the second wife contention all about? As tears began to well up in her eyes, she buried her head in her hands. Was she losing her mind? She sat up and took out a handkerchief from her purse to wipe her eyes. Then she reached for the telephone and dialled Mansoor's number, but just as the phone rang, she put the handset down. What if Farhat or Noor picked up the phone? A second later, she picked up the handset again and redialled the number. If anyone else picked up the phone, she would say that it was a wrong number and just put it back down. But, after a few rings, it was Mansoor who picked up the phone at the other end. She asked him if he could come over to the bank.

'Is everything all right?' he asked.

'No, just come to the bank,' she replied.

'I'll be there in twenty minutes.'

Mehrun buried her face in her palms again and thought about calling Mansoor back to tell him not to bother, but it was probably too late. He must've already left the Kashana. She needed to unburden herself and the only person she could think of was her childhood friend.

*

There is an old saying that when the mind reaches for the stars, the soul yearns for the ordinary. While Mansoor's father was drilling into him esoteric ideas, he longed for simple teenage pleasures, such as being with friends, eating out and having a good time. Mansoor's edification by his demanding father had detached him from his friends. The few, who had found it difficult to relate to him in the past, now considered him downright tiresome. Noor's insistence on the value of doubt made Mansoor introspective and reflective, but it also deprived him of a healthy social life. Mehrun, on the other hand, had also grown intellectually under Sadiq's tutelage, and Mansoor found a kindred spirit in her. And although her presence at the Kashana had become irregular after her run-in with his English tutor, whenever Mansoor did manage to meet Mehrun, he cherished her company. The passage of time only brought the two of them closer. But until the day she called him and asked him to come over to the bank, Mehrun had kept Sadiq's pass a carefully guarded secret.

*

Mansoor had also taken his Senior Cambridge exam and done exceptionally well. He enrolled himself in the University of Karachi. The institution was no intellectual powerhouse, but he found a few teachers who excited his imagination and aroused his curiosity. His mind, however, remained agitated and his beliefs continued to collide. On the surface, he appeared tranquil, but inside he was bursting with uncertainties. The more profound metaphysical questions of life plagued him. He was a young man struggling with self-doubt. The sense of belonging to a family, to a tradition and to a geography began to elude him. Did belonging provide cultural comfort? Was an un-belonging self, a drifting self with no meaning, devoid of intent or purpose? Did a djinn reside inside his soul? Why did Haider Rizvi still call him the twelfth man?

These ontological questions tormented Mansoor regularly, and his utterly incompatible parents muddled things up every day. On the one hand was his father, a worldly man, well-read, thoughtful, secular in his politics, agnostic in his beliefs and resentfully living in a country where religion had gradually become a public face. On the other hand was his poor mother, an uneducated woman without opinions, faithful to her husband not out of love but out of loyalty to tradition, unwavering in her faith in God and deeply rooted in religion. And both wanted Mansoor to grow up with their beliefs, and in their likeness.

*

As a reward for doing well in the exams, Mansoor's father had bought him a new Datsun, which he now drove maniacally towards the High Finance Bank. He was trying to park near the curb when he saw Mehrun waiting for him at the bank's door, dressed professionally in a cream-coloured silk shalwar-kameez. She hurried over when she spotted him and opened the car's door, collapsing on to the front passenger seat.

'Are you okay? You look like you saw a bhoot, a ghost.'

'What? Yes, that's exactly what I saw,' she replied with a sigh, and then added, 'Could we go and have coffee at Chandni Lounge?'

Mansoor nodded and drove towards Hotel InterContinental, which lay in an exclusive part of central Karachi. The hotel's restaurant, Chandni Lounge, was the newest hang-out for the bohemians, the intelligentsia and the industrialists of the city alike. The dimly lit restaurant luxuriated in Mughal décor. The pistachio-green-coloured heavy silk drapes and the miniature Mughal paintings created an ambiance of warm elegance. In a corner, sitting on a slightly raised platform, a beautiful young woman, dressed like a courtesan from King Akbar's court, played the sitar.

Mansoor found an empty booth in the corner, and when the white-uniformed bearer came, he ordered coffee and jam tarts for both of them.

'So, what is bothering you?' he asked Mehrun.

With nervous trepidation and halting speech, she told him every detail: her job as a servant in Sadiq's house, his tutoring her, his flirtatious glances, his amorous embrace, his brusque kisses and then Talat's beating. She talked about how her job at the bank had restored her and her father's sanity. Then she spoke of Talat's visit an hour ago, the money she had offered, the reference she had made to Mehrun becoming a second wife and her departing threat about killing Mehrun. The stress apparent on her face, her voice quivering, she held nothing back. Mansoor did not quite know how to react. The sadness in Mehrun's voice jarred him. He could only shake his head slowly in utter disbelief.

'I could never have imagined Uncle Sadiq doing what he did to you, and then he did not even dare to come to your defence!'

'I can't understand, Mansoor Babu . . . why did she have to insult me like this, and that too in my office? She was practically shouting at me.'

She paused for a while and then continued, 'I tried to take good care of her house at less money than what your mother gave my mother. Sadiq Sahib taught me so much. And she too was good to me in the beginning. Why can't she understand that it was her husband who initiated all this?'

The bearer wheeled in their coffee and jam tarts on a squeaky tea trolley. A whiff of freshly baked scones brought out for another customer made Mansoor hungry. He poured the coffee from the pot for them and then asked Mehrun if she took sugar and milk in her coffee.

'One spoonful of sugar and plenty of milk, please,' she replied.

He added the sugar and milk to her coffee and passed the jam tart to her before adding some milk to his own coffee. While performing his gentlemanly duties, he saw Mehrun fidgeting with her pastry fork.

'Mansoor Babu, I am going to go crazy if this continues. Tell me, what should I do?'

'I don't know! I wish I could tell you.'

'Talat Begum wants me to leave Karachi.'

'Well, you don't have to do that. You belong here.'

'I don't know where I belong. My father . . .'

Her words dissolved in the delightful atmosphere of Chandni Lounge as Mansoor's mind focused on the word 'belong'.

'Mansoor Babu,' Mehrun whispered, bringing him out of his reverie.

'Do you remember that day when you and Joseph cremated the lizard, and then later you called me a djinn? I was so angry with you,' Mansoor changed the subject.

'Well, you are a djinn, and I am a churail. What difference does it make? Maybe we should team up and use our powers to destroy all those who hate us,' Mehrun said.

Mansoor did not reply. He kept drifting into his own nether world, far from the restaurant, far from the town, far from its people. But suddenly he noticed Mehrun's searching gaze.

'What? What are you looking at?' he asked her.

'Oh nothing!' She replied hurriedly. 'I just realized how much you have grown.'

'Not much, actually. I feel as if I stopped growing after I was ten.' And then Mansoor changed the subject again. 'You know, Mehrun, your mother was strange.'

'Huh!' She forced a smile, as if saying 'tell me about it.' And after a pause, she said, 'You know, when I was younger, she used to beat me up quite regularly and would blame me for all her problems. I know you know this, but I was the harami who brought innumerable miseries in her life.'

The word 'harami' slit his heart, just as it had some years ago when Zaidi had hurled that opprobrium at her. He still carried that oppressive guilt around.

'What did your mother say about me? My mother told me that she had spread the rumour about me being a djinn.' Mansoor didn't know why he asked that question.

Mehrun sighed deeply, then sipped her coffee and said, 'My mother was a superstitious woman. She lived superstitiously and she died because of it. I wouldn't worry about it.'

'I want to know what she told you about me,' Mansoor said.

'Your mother's eleven miscarriages sowed the seeds of this whole thing. My mother believed that there was a djinn inside your mother's womb and that the djinn killed every child that was conceived in there. When your mother was pregnant with you, Amma was convinced that you would end up with the same fate as the other eleven, but when you were born alive, she couldn't believe it. What could be the reason for such an anomaly? The only way for her to sustain her deep-rooted superstition was to believe that the djinn himself had come out. And so, Mansoor Babu, there you were; you were the djinn—'

'And so the rumour became a reality!' Mansoor interrupted her.

'She swore that she saw a djinn the day you were born,' she paused. And then she said, 'You know, she never really liked me playing with you. In fact, during her last days, before she went into a coma, my mother regained consciousness briefly, and the first and last words that came out of her mouth were your name and the word "djinn".'

'What? Are you serious? Why would she say my name?'

His heart began to race when he heard this. Was he, in some way, responsible for Kaneez's death? Why would she say his name on her deathbed? When Mehrun saw the change in his face, she tried to joke about it.

'But you are a good djinn,' she said, 'and my mother was an illiterate, gullible woman.'

Just then, Mansoor spotted Haider Rizvi entering the restaurant with Sadiq Mirza. Lowering his head, he whispered to Mehrun, 'What is the distance you have to keep from Uncle Sadiq to avoid getting killed by Auntie Talat?'

'What?'

Mansoor repeated his question.

'Don't joke, Mansoor Babu.'

'I am not joking. Don't look back, but guess who just walked into the restaurant?'

'No!'

'Yes. Finish your coffee, and we will try to sneak out without getting noticed. Here are my car keys. Go sit inside, in case they see me, and I am called.'

Mehrun had not finished her coffee, but she pushed it aside and got up. Mansoor left two hundred-rupee notes on the table and followed her. They tried to slip out of the restaurant quietly, but Haider noticed them.

'Mansoor!' he waved at him.

Mansoor tilted his head ever so slightly, signalling Mehrun to go to his car.

'How are you, Uncle Haider, Uncle Sadiq?' he asked the two men as he walked over to their table.

'Fine, fine! Who was that young lady, huh?' Haider demanded.

'No one; just a friend.'

'Uh-huh, uh-huh,' Haider winked conspiratorially at Mansoor as he said this.

Sadiq, however, appeared to be having the most awkward moment of his life as he shifted uncomfortably in his seat, his eyes trying to avoid looking at Mehrun when she passed them. He knew that Haider had recognized Mehrun and would try to tease him incessantly. He had regretted telling Haider about his feelings for Mehrun as soon as he had confided in him. Sadiq tried to change the subject swiftly, 'Congratulations on your exam, Mansoor.'

'Thanks, Uncle Sadiq. I would have stayed and chatted, but I have to go.'

As he sped out of the restaurant, he heard Haider yelling after him, 'Tell your abba we expect him at the club next Friday.'

Mansoor saw Mehrun inside the car, slumped against the seat, looking pale and scared. He started the engine and began driving back towards her bank on McLeod Road.

When Mansoor returned home after dropping Mehrun, he saw Athanni, who came running towards him.

'Did you hear about Nana Jaan? He is dead,' he said.

*

That night after his grandfather's funeral, Mansoor slept restlessly, with nightmares about Mehrun and Sadiq torturing his sleep, his heart pulsating with anxiety. At one point, he woke up thinking of Uncle Zahid. The next day, he asked his father about his uncle. Noor had telephoned him in Germany, but because Zahid was in the middle of his course, he wasn't able to come for the funeral.

Zahid, it seemed to Mansoor, had vanished entirely from the face of the planet. In the beginning, he wrote frequent letters to his father and to Farhat about the loneliness in a foreign country, a loneliness that he struggled to keep at bay by immersing himself in his studies and work. He also sent a couple of postcards to Mansoor. But with time, his letters became sporadic, and then they stopped altogether. And six months after the death of Javed Sultan, they received the terrible telegram informing them that Zahid Sultan had been killed in a fiery car crash. For the first time, Mansoor saw tears trickle down his father's cheeks.

*

Seasons rolled by without any fuss. The new general in charge of the country finally announced the date of the first election to be based on adult franchise. The people, however, didn't believe him. Demagoguery reached new heights as thuggery got enshrined in the body politic. The brilliant foreign minister granted himself the grand title of The People's Leader. Noor called him the Tippler. Holding one successful rally after the other, the man became genuinely popular. Sniffing victory, The People's Leader also became arrogant, not realizing that the ultranationalist leader of the eastern province, known as Bangabandhu, the Friend of Bengal, could rob him of the premiership. The eastern province, separated by India, was the largest, and if Bangabandhu took all the seats there, he was sure to become the next prime minister. A hung parliament would be good for the country, Noor had thought. It would weaken the dictatorial leanings of The People's Leader.

On the hustings, The People's Leader gave electrifying speeches to the poor farmers in the villages. In one such public address, he asked the villagers, 'How many of you have gone to those big cities of the exploiters?' A few in the crowd raised their hands.

'How many among you have seen these *kaloo,* black sahibs walking with their wives, holding their hands?' A few more raised their hands again.

'When I am elected, you will freely roam around in cities with your wives, holding their hands without shame. Are you in any way inferior to those bastards in the cities?'

And the farmers looked at each other, puzzled. Why would they want to roam around uselessly with their wives, that too holding their hands? Someone in the crowd yelled a new slogan: '*Surkh hai! Surkh hai! Asia surkh hai*! (Red! Red! Asia is Red!)'

The leader of the G.O.D.s gave a befitting reply, 'And to the socialists and the godless communists, I have a simple message: We will do unto you what was done unto them in the Islamic Republic of Indonesia!' This was a reference to the communist purge of 1965 in Indonesia that killed at least five hundred thousand people.

And his crowd chanted: '*Subz hai! Subz hai! Asia subz hai*! (Green! Green! Asia is Green!)'

And Noor, of course, would not be Noor, if he did not react to this. He chanted: '*Subz hai na surkh hai! Asia ko kabz hai!* (Neither green nor red! Asia is constipated!)'

And Bangabandhu said, 'This time, the struggle is for our freedom! This time, the struggle is for our independence! It has nothing to do with green or red!'

*

As the election day approached, people worked their enthusiasm up to a fever pitch. It was to be the dawn of democracy, as promised by Rangeelay Shah. Amid the chaos, they saw glimmers of order; amid anarchy, they noticed flashes of hope. Haider editorialized: 'From the cinders of dictatorship, the phoenix of democracy is rising.'

It seemed as if everyone except Noor was thrilled by the new politics. Ordinary men and women who had no political bones in their body now got drawn into the exhilaration of possibilities. It was as if the mere sight of a real ballot box was enough to bring deliverance from dictatorship and a relief to their tired lives. Zakir wrote an op-ed column concluding:

> Our democracy will succeed only if it has a Pakistani character. We cannot superimpose foreign institutions and foreign laws on domestic structures. Our democracy can only draw sustenance if it is indigenous, intrinsic and original. Otherwise, it will remain an illusion at best and a delusion at worst.

When Noor read his piece, he did not understand what exactly Zakir was talking about. Democracy was not like European food that needed to be spiced up to rid it of its bland taste. And what did he mean by the superimposition of foreign institutions over domestic structure? The country had appropriated and embraced colonial institutions for goodness' sake! Mansoor listened carefully to his father's criticism of Zakir's article. He, however, could not vote because he never registered, but that did not stop him from debating and arguing with the other students in his university.

All political leaders disgusted him. They represented the worst elements of society; they were all thieves—wicked and shameless as far as he was concerned. Athanni, however, found a new purpose in his life, a new self, something that excited his soul. He joined the Guardians of Divinity and began purveying their venom. Whether he genuinely believed in their cause or he found in them an outlet to feed his ignorance, Mansoor could not decide; but like a new cultist, Athanni spoke in tongues.

'When we come into power, our Faith will be our Code, and our Code will be our Faith. The thieves will have their hands chopped, the drunkards will have their buttocks flogged with eighty lashes and the haramis will have their heads severed. There will be no Christmas, no New Year's Eve and no cinemas. If you go to a brothel, you will be castrated; all the whores will be stoned to death.'

His orgiastic lectures about barbaric retributions sent chills down Mansoor's spine.

'How can you think of going backwards while the rest of the world progresses?' Mansoor challenged him.

'Our future is in the past. Our past is our present. You are slaves of the West; we are God's slaves. We are the true believers, and *you* are *jahannami,* you are hell-dwellers,' he replied, his face tense, spit flying out of his mouth when he shouted out the word 'you'. With animus, he added the English word 'hell-dweller' as if to deliberately make sure that Mansoor understood the meaning of the keyword 'jahannami'. It was also to warn his cousin that his English-medium education would not save him, the sinner, from the eternal flames of hell.

*

On the day of the election, Noor stayed home, but Athanni, along with his father and mother, dragged Farhat out and took her to the polling station. Noor told her, 'You can vote for anyone, but for God's sake, don't vote for the G.O.D.s.'

Once inside the voting booth, however, Farhat defied her husband and voted for the G.O.D. party. For the second time in her life, she went against her husband's wishes, the first being when she had hired Maulvi Nazir to impart religious education to Mansoor. In disobeying her husband, she not only denied his politics but also challenged his patriarchy. Democracy had emboldened her; the tiny ballot box emancipated her, and she cherished every microsecond of that moment, the fleeting excitement, the sweet liberation, thumbing her nose at her husband's belief. That the party she voted for would be the first one to trample on her self-esteem and treat her like a legal minor under the guardianship of a blood relative never entered her stream of consciousness. Noor had told Mansoor in front of Farhat that this was the party that would send the country crashing back to the Stone Age, when they literally used stones to kill non-believers, in a matter of minutes. And Farhat had replied, 'I long for those simple times; I crave for those happy days.'

The elections divided the population along linguistic lines. Bangabandhu's party won every seat in the eastern province, and the P.O.O.P.s won 80 per cent of the seats in the western province. The G.O.D.s, wholly routed, cried foul. Athanni was stunned, and Farhat wept bitterly. To the utter disbelief of The People's Leader, Rangeelay Shah announced that Bangabandhu would be the next prime minister of the country. But that was not to be. The idea that a Bengali could rule the entire country was deeply offensive to The People's Leader. Like a sore loser, he warned his party men that he would personally break the bones of anyone who joined the new assembly without his approval. Then, in an about-face, he offered a novel idea—although Noor called it a moronic idea—to share power in a system of dual prime ministership. The foolishness of a hydra-headed federal government was evident to everyone except to him.

Rangeelay Shah tried to placate The People's Leader, but his bullheadedness came in the way. In the process, he alienated the

Bangabandhu and his eastern brethren, who now openly called for secession from the west. The seeds of secession, truth be told, had been implanted back in 1948 when The Great Leader had declared that 'the state language of Pakistan is going to be Urdu, and no other language.' The relentless discrimination and the open disparagement could only be tolerated for so long, but what broke the camel's back was the ultimate humiliation of denying the Bengalis the right to govern when they had a clear victory. The east rebelled and used bullets and bayonets to take back what they had rightfully earned through the ballots. Rangeelay Shah sent his army to East Pakistan to crush the rebellion.

'He is treating the province like a giant slaughterhouse! And the government-controlled media keeps vomiting lies to the people,' Noor thundered.

'Stop listening to the BBC and the Voice of America. They are enemies of our country, of our religion; *they* are the real liars,' Farhat retorted.

Noor could not understand Farhat's inability to accept the truth. The context of her reality had an altered meaning, a different direction. The denial of reality, according to Noor, was the product of a chaotic mind.

'Shut your eyes, clog your ears and pretend that the genocide against your brothers and sisters is not happening!' Noor literally shouted.

Mansoor had never seen him so emotional. This was a different Noor, and that was a defiant Farhat.

Sixteen

War broke out again between India and Pakistan, in early December 1971, and like a broken record, they both accused each other of starting it. The Indian prime minister declared that she could not shake hands with a clenched fist. The barbaric lust for war and the urge to inflict sadistic cruelty on each other's people were seen as the best solutions. Following the Malthusian nostrum to periodically tackle overpopulation, they willingly sacrificed their people to Ares, the god of war.

While the propaganda machine played jingoistic war songs on the radio waves, the revolutionary poet Faiz Ahmad Faiz lamented:

> *Sajaey to kaisaey sajaey qatl-e-aam ka mela*
> *Kisey lubhai ga mere lahoo ka wa waila?*
> *Mere nizar badan mein lahoo hi kitna hai?*
> *Charaagh ho koi raushan na koi jam bharey*
> *Na is se aag hi bharkey na is sey pyas bujhey*
> *Mere figar badan mein lahoo hi kitna hai?*
> *Magar woh zehar-e-halahal bhara ha nas nas mein*

(How to adorn the carnival of this massacre
Who will be fascinated by my blood-curdling cries?

How much blood remains in my shrivelled body?
To light up the candles or fill up the wine glasses
To stoke the fire or quench the thirst
How much blood remains in my wounded body?
As the deadly poison streams across my veins)

*

The war in 1971 was much shorter than the previous war. Operation Chengiz Khan lasted a mere thirteen days, four days less than Operation Grand Slam of 1965. But the bombs were more destructive, the noise more deafening, the annihilation more pervasive and the humiliation more complete. The morning after, the nation was stunned. The people of Pakistan woke up to a truncated land. The eastern wing of the country became the independent nation of Bangladesh, and Bangabandhu became its first prime minister. As a parting gift to the people of a torn country, Rangeelay Shah handed over power quietly to The People's Leader. The *Daily Jadal* published an almost-blank front page with a single line from a couplet by the philosopher–poet Mohammad Iqbal:

Khamoshi guftugu hai, bezabani hai zubaan meri

(Silence is my speech, speechlessness is my tongue)

It was a Day of Silence, almost as though the entire nation had duct-taped its mouth. Sadiq published a poem in the *Morning Gazette*, entitled 'The Rape of the Nation', and asked, 'Who should she go to demand justice?/ Who is there to grant justice?/ Who is going to pass judgment?/ Who will be the hangman?'

Noor, the talkative barrister, became reticent, his tongue slashed by hysterical events. He had told his son that this war would destroy the country; he had argued with his wife about her naiveté; chastised Zakir about his blinders, but now he could say no more. Mansoor saw the pain writ large and clear on his father's face. He also mourned with the nation.

*

Several months after the war, Noor invited his highbrow friends for a late lunch to vent his muffled thoughts and to resurrect the life of pleasure that had died out in this defeated country. He had asked Mansoor to join them now that he had attained the level of intellectual sophistication that Noor had often demanded of him in the past.

When the friends arrived and settled down in the mardana, Mansoor joined them quietly. Opening a bottle of Johnnie Walker, he began pouring the whisky into the crystal glasses that had stood idly on the mahogany side table for a while. As he got ready to pour some for Zakir, he exclaimed, 'None for me, Mansoor! I will have chai. I have stopped drinking alcohol.'

The other three friends raised their eyebrows at the heresy, especially as it came from a devotee of fine liquor. Mansoor ordered Budhoo to bring two cups of chai, one for Zakir and one for himself.

The ex-diplomat had undergone quite a profound conversion— no to alcohol, no to any 'profane' discussions and yes to the 'true' faith—his brand-new personality was the most telling souvenir of another lost war. Noor was stunned. Zakir's new set of orthodox beliefs meant that from now on he had to regard Sadiq, who was Ahmadi, and Haider, who was Shia, as belonging to heretical faiths. The ultraconservative Sunni religious parties had been trying to declare the Ahmadis as non-Muslim since before the Partition. They also considered Shias as renegades.

'Can you tell me what is the true faith?' Noor asked Zakir. 'There are seventy-two different sects, each ready to call the others kafir, ready to slit their throats at the first chance.

Your true believers will be the first ones to declare our agnostic Ahmadi friend, Sadiq, a kafir.'

'Don't worry about me, Noor. I have already been declared a kafir by my Ahmadi co-religionists,' Sadiq replied.

Mansoor's eyes abruptly went to the professor's girth, which seemed to have doubled since the last time he had seen him at Chandni Lounge. Apparently, neither shame nor guilt had affected this man who wrote poetry about the rape of the nation while sitting oblivious to his dastardly role in Mehrun's humiliation.

That night, after his friends left, Noor drank more and spoke emotively with Mansoor about his friend's conversion. Zakir's oration about true believers had unbuttoned him entirely.

'Maybe he's just going through a phase,' Mansoor suggested.

'Grown men don't just go through a phase,' Noor replied. 'War twists us all, but a warped war coils us differently.' Noor looked at his son, who in his young life had already seen two wars, short as they were.

'My generation was distorted by the mayhem of Partition. Zakir should have gone through his conversion at that time, but he didn't. I, however, did . . . especially when I saw the murdered . . .' Noor did not complete his sentence, but Mansoor knew he was thinking about his father. The scars lay buried in his heart's alcove. Had Noor lost his faith when he saw his father's murdered body? Had he been killed by greedy relatives? The evidence was substantial that this was the case, but the story that got sold was that he had been assassinated by fanatic Hindus as part of a broader land dispute called Pakistan. That property would trump kinship was something Noor had never thought of. All property is theft, he had argued, echoing Pierre-Joseph Proudhon, until he migrated to this new country and built his precious Kashana. And as his adopted country became publicly religious, he became privately secular. His conversion was a long-drawn-out process that probably went through several revisions.

But what happened to Zakir? Although he was part of General Dundda's government in its dying days, he got recruited by Rangeelay Shah because of his foreign service experience. As an intrinsic member of his government, Zakir witnessed the slaughter of people, heard about the raping of girls and saw the looting of property, and yet he remained silent. Why? How could people who shared the same faith slaughter each other so quickly? But to Zakir, it was not the failure of religion; it was the bankruptcy of their inherited beliefs.

One of the members of The Unholy Quartet was now becoming holier than the rest. All these friends—well-read, profoundly intelligent, inversely affected—were now on a path that suddenly diverged, their friendship fissured by fervency.

*

Most bankers remained petrified by the rumours of nationalization, but not Ameer Abbas Alvi. For he was not a typical banker. When life gave him more than his share of tragedies, he accepted them with the stillness of a Stoic philosopher. Ready for a hostile takeover by the government, he sat calmly in his exquisitely decorated penthouse office, his feet crossed on top of the mahogany desk and his head tilted, resting against the black leather chair. The huge bay windows in the office were decked with a variety of plants, some brought by Mehrun. Two large leafy palms in red lacquer pots stood guard at each end of the windows. On the onyx ashtray on the table, a fat brown cigar lay burning, its smell, acrid and overpowering, permeating throughout the room. A picture of Alvi shaking hands with General Dundda hung defiantly on the wall across from his desk. On the adjacent wall, an enlarged photo of J.P. Morgan, the captain of the American banking industry, flaunted rugged capitalism. The fall of General Dundda and the election of a socialist prime minister had not convinced him to replace these precious pictures with the picture of the politician du jour.

Alvi never looked back at his life in India. When the madness of Partition claimed his entire family, fate spared his. Living in Bombay at the time, he worked as a lending officer at the Imperial Mercantile Bank of India. The financial hub of India, Bombay was one of the few lucky cities to have been spared the worst of the rioting. He received the news of his family's massacre with a resigned calmness. Losing the connection to his biological past made him rupture his relationship with his emotional self. He couldn't mourn their loss; he never went back to his ancestral home and he never bothered to find out what exactly happened. What was the point? Human beings are bastards, anyway. They will always find a reason to kill each other. Look at East Pakistan.

For another year, he remained in Bombay, worked hard, saved money and created fake short-term loans in fake names. When these loans came due, he converted them into long-term counterfeit investments and transferred the 'borrowed' money into foreign banks. Once all the money was in a safe haven, he fled to Turkey and from there to the newly created Pakistan, where he joined the nascent Muslim Trust Bank (MTB) and began his career as an accountant. Changing his identity from Sameer Lukhnavi to Ameer Abbas Alvi, he faked his place of birth from Lucknow to Rawalpindi. In his mind, it was all justifiable felony. To him, the Imperial Mercantile Bank of India was a British bank, and he had no compunction about 'looting the looters'. And changing his identity was just a tactical manoeuvre against the colonial enemy.

As an officer at MTB, he now put his prior banking knowledge to principled use. And it was his attention to detail, his disciplined work ethic and Atatürk-like self-confidence that thrust him up the hierarchy. Very soon, he rose to become one of the directors at the bank. Political intrigues and disputes with the managing director, however, led to his ouster. But it also provided a perfect opportunity to create a rival bank with the help of his former customers and wealthy acquaintances, all of whom he despised. As the managing director of the High Finance Bank, he made tremendous strides and put the new bank within striking distance of the MTB in terms of total deposits.

Triple-A worked hard and chased opportunities like an addict chasing hashish. He never forgot one lesson that his father taught him early on in his life: Don't become money's slave; make money your slave. Determined and ruthless, he expected the same single-minded tenacity from his subordinates, and in turn, rewarded the energetic and the efficient and punished the lazy and the laggard. Mehrun was one of the beneficiaries. She had the brains; and Sadiq Mirza, with his Pygmalion bhoot, had made her sophisticated enough to pass off as a modern begum.

While Alvi guarded his homosexuality ferociously, his enemies gossiped about it openly. He could compete with any bank, tear apart any opponent, but he could not risk any public humiliation. Pulling his feet down from the table, he reached for the intercom and asked his secretary, 'Mister Mehdi, please send Mehrunnissa to my room. And bring tea.'

He always called Mehrun by her full name. As he waited for her, he got up and went towards one of the bay windows. An ugly pastiche of vehicles and humanity called his attention to the chaos that was McLeod Road. Donkey and camel carts competed with rickshaws, trucks, cars and elderly ramblers for the scarce space. He saw a heavy-set woman in an orange shalwar-kameez balancing a rectangular wooden crate on her head. A skinny boy, his shirt torn, stood selling newspapers next to her. He saw beggars and pedlars fighting for their spots on the sidewalk—everyday scenes of a reiterated reality concealing the crush of human existence. Watching the people on the street, carrying on with their lives with a regularity and routine, was like seeing a *mujra* dance that you knew would end in a terrible tragedy. The world below dissolved into an indeterminate actuality as Alvi withdrew from the window and strolled back towards one of the large palm plants to appreciate the gentler side of life.

Ameer Abbas Alvi, a man in his mid-forties, of medium height and a dark brown complexion, his jet-black hair, slicked backwards, was an act of sartorial seriousness. Lately, his neurotic obsession was to be the Asian J.P. Morgan. The horizon never looked clearer.

Hearing a faint knock on the door, he returned to his seat and ordered the person to enter. It was Mehrun. She had changed her hairstyle recently and was wearing light make-up, the pale grey saree giving her an elegant look.

'Come in, Mehrunnissa, come in,' he said. It was not unusual for him to summon her to his office once or twice during the day.

'Please, sit down,' he said, gesturing to the chair across his table.

Mehrun sat down and waited for Alvi to open the conversation. But a long, painful moment of silence greeted her instead and she realized that Alvi had something important to say. He gathered his thoughts and forced himself to articulate them as clearly as he could.

'Mehrunnissa, what I am going to tell you is very confidential,' he said.

'Yes, sir,' she replied and became more attentive.

'I have not told anyone else about this, and I expect that you, too, will keep it to yourself.'

'You have my promise, sir,' Mehrun replied.

'I have decided to resign.'

'Sir?' she flinched, unsure about what she had just heard.

'Yes, Mehrunnissa, I am going to quit.'

There was another knock at the door, and Alvi's secretary entered the room, carrying a silver tray with a Royal Doulton tea set on it. The secretary placed the tray on the side table and got busy making two cups of tea. As soon as he was finished, Alvi signalled him to give the first cup to Mehrun, who accepted it with a thank you. Mehdi then gave the second cup to him.

'Anything else, sir?' he asked obsequiously.

'No, that will be all. And, Mr Mehdi, please hold all my calls.'

'Yes, sir,' he replied and left the room.

'Sir, may I ask why you are quitting?' Mehrun continued once they were alone.

'Mehrunnissa, I have been told point-blank by the new commerce minister that our bank will be the first one to be nationalized. I have slogged like a donkey for this bank, and I haven't done this so that some stupid bureaucrat or some illiterate son of a minister or a landlord may come and park his fat ass on this chair,' he paused. And then he continued, 'This is not acceptable to me. I have worked hard to be in the place where I am now, and I am not going to let this feudal landlord-turned-prime minister tell me how to run a bank. I hate to boast, but no banker in Pakistan has accomplished what I have, that too in such less time.'

'I agree with you, sir, and I would not be here without your kindness. But what will you do? Where will you go?' she asked.

'Well, I have been in touch with some foreign dignitaries in the Arab world. I have known them for years now, and they know me and my potential. They have asked me to set up an international bank in Dubai. It is a big challenge, but I have accepted their offer.'

He became quiet after that, and Mehrun, not knowing what to say either, started imagining her life without Alvi. In a male-dominated world, where positions were acquired through influence and promotions were gained through buttering, she and Ameer Abbas Alvi were a couple of rarae aves. Her confidence waned and she had this sinking feeling of being sent back to that hellhole of a house where she had grown up stifled. The image of working for a fat bureaucrat was hideous to say the least. Alvi noticed the tension on her face and tried to put her at ease.

'I don't know if your father will allow you to work in a foreign country, but you are welcome to join me if you want.'

Mehrun had never lied to him about her family background, but then, she had never really told him the truth either. She never discussed her personal life. At that point, however, she wanted to unload the facts on him, and unload she did. She told him everything: her struggles, the insults, her mother's estranged life and her tragic death. She told him about her father's schizophrenia. She told him about Mansoor and Noor ul Haq. Alvi knew Noor personally, as he had sought his legal opinion on many occasions.

When he heard her story, Alvi felt for Mehrun. The fact that she had been a domestic servant at one point made him admire her even more. His parents had also been domestic servants in India. He felt a peculiar but immediate affinity towards Mehrun, as if they both belonged to the same tribe; they both struggled for the same goal. He found himself thinking about her in a new light. He renewed his offer, and she told him that leaving her father alone would be impossible, but she would think about it. Mehrun left his office feeling cold and forsaken. In the elevator, she saw Athanni standing behind a group of people. She pretended not to see him, but he moved closer to her, and when Mehrun got off on the sixth floor, Athanni followed her out.

'Mehrun, stop! Mehrun!' he practically shouted at her.

'Oh, Khaleel Khan! I did not see you,' she said as she turned around.

'Can I talk to you, privately?'

'Sure, come to my office.'

The words 'my office' resounded deeply in Athanni's mind.

As they walked towards her office together, Mehrun noticed a gash on Athanni's face, extending from his left sideburn to his cheek. 'What happened? Did you get into a knife fight?'

'Wha . . . What? Oh. No, no. I fell and hit my face on something,' Athanni lied, covering up for the fight he had with his father trying to save his mother a few months ago.

Mehrun did not ask any more questions, and once they entered her office, she closed the door and motioned him to sit. It was difficult for Athanni to be in the office of someone who had once been a servant girl, but he knew that Mehrun could help him advance his career in the bank, and so he swallowed his pride. As he pulled up the chair, he said, shifting between Urdu and English, 'I have heard that Mister Hashem is going to start the Islamic banking section at our bank. I want to work there. Can you . . . um . . . ask him if he . . . I mean . . . could put me in that department?'

'I don't think anything concrete is going to happen soon, but if it does, I'll tell him.'

'Thank you, that is all I ask.'

After a few more moments of awkward silence, he got up and left her office.

*

Athanni's humiliations had piled upon him like the dirty laundry that piled up in the cavernous teak hamper outside his parents' bathroom. That hamper had been his childhood refuge from his father, an escape from his violent temper. For long stretches of time, he would lie hidden beneath the dirty clothes, unmindful of the stale smell, unflustered by his sisters dumping their undergarments. Lately, however, he began sensing that his life had stranded him on this strange island where all his acquaintances were spreading their wings. He had heard from his mother that Joseph had left for Iran, where he would probably make more money than he earned at the bank. And then there was Mehrun, ensconced in her air-conditioned office, she had become a close confidante of Alvi, her new success contradicting her preordained destiny. Mansoor had aced his exams and would soon be leaving for higher education in a foreign country. And all this while, what was he—a gofer for nameless people in unknown departments, running around doing meaningless errands? To make matters worse, the defeat of his party in the recent elections had robbed him of any chance at higher politics.

As he sat outside on the stairs of the bank, thinking about his brief conversation with Mehrun, Athanni's scar started to itch, but he resisted scratching it. His arms and face had received knife slashes when he had fought against his father with his bare hands, trying to protect his mother. The horrific memory still stunned him. When he was little, he remembered the shouting episodes and the continuous shoving and pushing. Later, the pummelling became more violent and came barbed with expletives and threats to kill. He was tired of his father, his constant yelling, the relentless beatings and then the attempt to kill his mother. Festering with hate towards his father, Athanni had promised his mother to always protect her. Tears rushed down his scar now, causing a burning sensation in the wound—the image of his mother crying and begging forgiveness still fresh in his memory. He thought about the G.O.D.s; he would leave the party as soon as he got into Islamic banking.

*

The shock of Pakistan's defeat in the war had been eclipsed by a new sensation, a new hero—Sher Khan, the son of the former cricket captain. By piling up a scintillating century and bundling out the visiting Australian cricket team cheaply with his fast bowling, he made a sensational debut in test cricket. He instilled terror in the hearts of the best batsmen in the world, with his accurate yorkers. His rugged, handsome looks and his Caucasian features made him an instant heart-throb not only in Pakistan, but in every other cricketing country. Wherever he went, his fans mobbed him; whatever he did, his devotees emulated him. Even those who knew nothing about cricket knew who Sher Khan was. He became the Lion Prince.

*

The new legislative assembly wanted all traces of General Dundda obliterated. So they repealed his Constitution and created the third Constitution of the Islamic Republic of Pakistan. Among many new features, it guaranteed 'the freedom of press'. Haider wrote an interesting editorial about it, asking the lawmakers to be explicit about what these words meant. To most journalists, the freedom of press was an alien concept. Obviously, it did not mean absolute freedom, for there is no country in the world where you have unqualified, unrestricted freedom of expression. Surely, you don't have the freedom to print anything or say anything; you don't have the freedom to publish scurrilous lies about others, and you don't have the right to come and piss on the boundary wall of someone's house. But of course, the right to free speech in a country that had just started to flirt with democracy was narrowly defined. You still did not have the right to condemn a bad law or criticize the dreadful government or complain about corrupt rulers.

The Ministry of Measurement under the new government began to codify what was *not* free speech. No one was allowed to use 'muddy language' or a 'mocking tone' or commit 'morphological errors', whatever that meant. They all came under the letter 'M'. Anyone found guilty would be subject to the following humane punishments: an unannounced tax audit, denial of foreign exchange and the rejection of an exit visa. Freedom of the press was, of course, guaranteed, but journalists had to use it 'wisely'.

As the new prime minister began to peddle his neurotic new utopia, called 'Faithian Socialism', the hyper-intellectuals became co-conspirators and keen collaborators. The latest recruit was the distinguished professor of English literature and humane letters, Sadiq Mirza, who was initially absolutely reluctant to write anything for the government, but persistent and rather graphic threats made him change his mind.

At his university, word had leaked out that Sadiq Mirza was an Ahmadi, the most heretical of all deviant Muslim groups. The smear campaign against his community that had gone on for years had finally reached his doorstep. It began when he noticed that some of his colleagues stopped using the traditional religious greeting when they met him. This was soon followed by them calling him Dr Mirzai, which was a spotting term for Ahmadis. But when the hate mail and the threats of extreme violence started appearing regularly in his mailbox, Sadiq contacted one of his students, who had become a top official in the new government, for help.

His student came back with a quid pro quo from his boss: if he desired protection, he must join the P.O.O.P. as its official 'writer'. Sadiq had no choice but to acquiesce. And so, he became their apologist—trading panegyrics for protection. Noor, who did not know anything about the threats and the hate mail, read his writings in disbelief. How could someone who was so steeped in erudition write such rubbish? It was nonsense, calculated and intentional. He could find no other adjectives to describe it. Had he lost all links with his intellectual past? Noor saw the inscription at the end of the article: 'The writer is Distinguished Professor of English at the University of Karachi.' He wondered if Sadiq now represented the new mindset of the intelligentsia that remembered little, retained nothing and wrote rubbish.

To prevent anyone from challenging his authority, The People's Leader created a paramilitary force, called the Security, Command, Action Brigade (SCAB), and gave it absolute powers. Noor, with his wry sense of humour, called it the Sinister, Coercive, Abusive Brigade, instead. The SCAB beat up the very people who had helped The People's Leader come to power. As the people's government turned despotic, Noor took Sadiq to task regarding his article.

Sadiq had known Noor since they were students at Aligarh Muslim University, and he knew him inside out. While his colleagues at the university lauded his articles, Sadiq knew well what Noor would say. So, to pre-empt him, he phoned his friend and invited his entire family for lunch the following Sunday. Mansoor felt awkward when Noor told him that Sadiq had invited him also. He made excuses, but his father wouldn't have it any other way.

When they reached Sadiq's home, Farhat went straight to Talat in the women's quarter, while the men sat in the austere drawing room. Noor noticed that the bookshelf filled with classics, which used to be a prominent feature of the drawing room, was now replaced by a glass cabinet filled with religious artefacts: an ornate Qur'an, a couple of verses from the Qur'an elegantly framed, a marble slab with the words 'Allah' and 'Muhammad' beautifully calligraphed. After the usual pleasantries, Noor turned to Sadiq's newspaper articles. But Sadiq quickly changed the subject, making some frantic gestures with his hands to indicate that his house was bugged. At first, Noor didn't understand his cryptic signs, but then he realized what could be going on and began talking about cricket.

A little later, Noor got up to use the toilet. With only Mansoor in the room, the air became a bit awkward. Sadiq's face blanched and he began fidgeting. After a painfully long minute, he smiled hesitantly and said, 'It was good to see you at Chandni Lounge that day.'

'Yes,' Mansoor replied.

'Do you go there often?'

'No.'

'I like the ambiance of the place more than the food.'

Mansoor just nodded. Giving up, Sadiq interlocked his fingers and leaned back into the chair, resting the back of his head on his hands, and surveyed the glass cabinet. Mansoor pretended to look at the scriptural hangings on the wall. His father was surely taking his time in the toilet. Eventually, Mansoor asked Sadiq about the courses he was teaching that term. Sadiq said he was teaching a new class called 'The Theatre of the Absurd'.

A delightful irony, Mansoor thought.

Seventeen

Mansoor was now in the final years of college. The political climate had worn him down, and the strikes and shutdowns had jaded him. He decided it was time to go abroad if he wanted to get a good education. Initially, his father wanted him to go to England for further studies, but it was the United States that attracted Mansoor more. It represented youth, vigour and dynamism, a place where the action was. Besides, most of his classmates had also gone to the United States. After convincing his father that the centre of economics had shifted from England to the United States, he began sending applications to as many American universities as he could. Noor insisted that he apply to all the Ivy League universities, but Mansoor did not and lied about it. He was not sure he'd get into any and he didn't want to waste time. Most of his life, he had studied at extraordinary institutions, now he wanted to try the ordinary. The idea of applying to the 'yellow schools of America' appealed to him.

*

It was Athanni's fourth ride on the elevator within the first hour of the day. Up and down, up and down, like Sisyphus, but pushing everyone else's meaningless weight. That is what he usually did

during the entire day, but on that particular morning he did more
in one hour than he did during the whole day. Everyone wanted
him to take something to someone or run some trivial errand for
them. If it was not the files, then it was the envelopes; if it was not the
envelopes, then it was the forms that needed someone's signature.
And then, as if he were their servant, he had to fetch tea for the clerks.
As he pressed the ground floor button on the elevator, he noticed
his reflection on the brass door. His new beard almost concealed the
scar on his face. His hand instinctively went to that area; the skin felt
stretched when he touched it. The elevator stopped on the second
floor and the assistant clerk from the Home Loans Department,
Javed Anwar, stepped in. As soon as he saw Athanni, he said: 'Arey,
Khaleel, where have you been? Mister Hashem was looking for you!'

'For me? Why?'

'I don't know.'

The elevator had already reached the ground floor. Athanni's
heart raced with excitement. He was sure that Mister Hashem would
talk to him about Islamic banking. As soon as Javed stepped out,
Athanni whispered, 'Thank you, Mehrun,' and pressed the button
for the second floor, where Mister Hashem's office was. Outside Syed
Hashem's office, his secretary sat screening everyone in quest of an
audience with her boss. The minute she saw him, she said, 'Where
were you? Mister Hashem was looking for you! Go in quickly.'

Inside, the burly Mister Hashem sat on his leather chair,
smoking a cigarette and going through a file, his handlebar
moustache covering his upper lip. As soon as he saw Athanni, he
gestured him to come in.

'I want you to take this box to Mister Kirmani at the Tariq Road
branch. Tell him I need him to act on all the files right away, and
tell him to return these to me by next Wednesday. Understood?'

'Yes, sir.'

Lifting the heavy box, Athanni made his way towards the
door. Suddenly, as if remembering something, he stopped, turned
around and said, 'Hashem Sir!'

'Yes, what is it?'

'Sir, did Mehrunnissa talk to you about me?'

'About you? No. What is this about?'

'Sir, I have heard that you are going to be in charge of Islamic banking here, and I want to work in that department.'

Hashem looked at him from head to toe, as if trying to figure out what exactly he had said. He then returned his stern eyes to Athanni's face.

'Areý, Mian Khaleel, growing a beard and having a prayer mark on your forehead doesn't qualify you to work in Islamic banking. Now, go take care of this business.' Athanni was furious at Hashem's insults and at Mehrun for not using her influence on his behalf. Carrying the box with heavy steps, he went towards the elevator and pushed the button. In the lobby, he saw Mehrun with Mansoor, laughing about something. As he struggled to hold on to the box, he felt a knot in his stomach. Concealing his face behind the carton, he walked past them without being noticed. Their laughter, like a hazing ritual, intensified his disgrace. 'You are not better than me, you bastards.' He took the box to the round tin dumpster at the corner of the parking lot, opened the lid and tossed it into its gaping mouth.

*

An unusually cold spell welcomed the first of April that year, veiling the city in a thick fog. It was as if nature was playing an April Fool's Day prank on the citizens of this tropical city. Before the muezzin's call for morning prayers, and before the crack of dawn, Athanni scaled the fenced wall of Kashana-e-Haq and entered its compound, staggering towards the backyard with an old satchel hanging diagonally around his neck. The bag bulged with what looked like a rectangular box with wires hanging out from it. Athanni's steps displayed a purpose as he hurried towards the doghouse that stood in one corner of the lawn. He saw Chaos,

Mansoor's dog, sleeping. Athanni whistled lightly. Chaos barked. He whispered the dog's name. Chaos whimpered. Turning around to make sure that the bark had not woken up Changez, the guard, he called Chaos again. The dog came out reluctantly, and recognizing Athanni, began sniffing him. The intruder stroked him with one hand, and with the other hand, he took out a piece of raw meat from the satchel and gave it to the terrier. The dog sniffed at the food and began eating it. Athanni then took out a black box from the bag and went inside the doghouse. After a few minutes, he came out with his satchel hanging loosely from his shoulder. He sat cross-legged on the grass and watched Chaos intently. Ten minutes later, the dog slumped on the grass. Athanni got up, lifted the unconscious canine in his arms and deposited him inside his kennel. He came out, wiped his hands on his clothes, walked hurriedly towards the boundary wall, climbed over it and disappeared into the darkness from which he had emerged.

*

As was his wont, Mansoor woke up precisely at 6.30 a.m. It was darker than usual. And as he pulled the curtains aside, he noticed the thick fog that had gloomed the landscape. He got ready to go to college. By the time he sat down for breakfast, the sun had cleared most of the fog away. Mansoor quietly finished his breakfast and went outside. He always played with Chaos for a few minutes before he left for university, but that day when he whistled, nothing happened. Usually, the dog would be out, sniffing the grass. When Mansoor didn't see Chaos, he called his name, but nothing happened again. That was unusual. He whistled again, called his name, clapped and whistled a third time, but still nothing. Chaos was getting old, yes, but he was still agile and never disobeyed his master's call. A sense of foreboding came over Mansoor.

What is wrong with him? he wondered.

He called Chaos again. When the dog did not come out, he decided to go and check for himself. Afraid of what he might find there, Mansoor approached the doghouse with trepidation. A disgusting smell of dog vomit permeated the yard. He stopped and sniffed the air. His heart pounded and his legs became weak, but he mustered the courage and went ahead. As he peered inside the doghouse, he got a massive shock. In a pool of blood, and what seemed like vomit, lay a moribund Chaos. Never in his life had Mansoor seen so much blood. The nauseating smell made it difficult for him to stay there any longer or do anything. He did not know if Chaos was alive, but there was no time to waste or panic. And with that thought, he sprinted back inside the house and headed straight to the drawing room where he picked up the bulky black telephone receiver and dialled the veterinarian's number. But as he was dialling, a piercing blast rattled the windows of the drawing room. Mansoor dropped the phone and ran out into the backyard, where a ghastly scene of destruction confronted him. Razed to the ground and strewn all across the lawn, like scattered matchsticks, lay the remains of the doghouse. And in the middle of the rubble, he saw the bloody remains of Chaos. Mansoor stood there, bewildered and benumbed, trying to make sense of this mayhem. The sound of the blast brought his parents out.

'What happened, beta? Are you okay? Where is Chaos?' his father asked, running up to him.

'Are you okay? Mansoor?' his mother asked him, shaking him when he didn't say anything.

Rattled and fazed, Mansoor stood there motionless, while his mother approached the disaster area. She stayed there for some time and then came back to stand with Noor and him. As if from a great distance away, Mansoor heard his mother say, 'Chaos is dead, but thank God you are alive. I am glad it was the dog that died.'

*

Mansoor wanted Chaos to be buried where his doghouse had stood, but Farhat did not wish to have a dog cemetery in her compound. She created such a big ruckus that Mansoor decided to have him buried at a pet cemetery.

The police came and interviewed the servants. They roughed up Budhoo, cuffed Changez and questioned Sikander, but they couldn't find the culprit. Traces of chemicals near the doghouse confirmed that a small bomb had destroyed it, and the autopsy of Chaos indicated that it was arsenic that had killed him. But the ultimate question was: who was the intended target? Chaos or Mansoor? And, more importantly, who was the killer? Mansoor had no clues and no suspects. That Athanni would undertake such a wanton act of brutality never entered his mind.

*

Two months after the senseless killing of Chaos, Mansoor got two letters in the mail, one from the University of Iowa and the other from Joseph. He opened the letter from the university first. He had been accepted into their master's programme in economics. Then he opened Joseph's missive, which was, much to his surprise, very neatly penned in Urdu.

Salaam Mansoor Babu,

You must be quite surprised to receive my letter. I must tell you at the outset that I am only dictating my thoughts to my good friend Salamat Masih. He is also a Pakistani Christian like me and works at the refinery. He used to teach Urdu at the school I went to, back in Bhangi Para. He has promised to teach me how to read and write in Urdu. So next time, maybe you will receive my letter in my own handwriting.

I wanted to write to you earlier, but I had been busy here. Living alone in a foreign country is hell, especially when you do not know the language. In the beginning, it was tough for me to understand Farsi, but now I have become reasonably fluent in it. You will be happy to know that I can now talk git-pit git-pit in English also, not as good as you or even Mehrun, but I can make myself understandable to some Amreeki and Angrez people here. Life in a foreign country teaches one about survival. For me, being in Iran has been busy and rewarding. I cannot thank my friend Reza Dabiran enough for giving me this opportunity to live and work here. I live in the city of Abadan, which is located in the south-western part of Iran, and I am currently working for an oil company. Many Americans live in this town. They are babus, like you, but they don't mind talking with me and shaking hands with me. You see, I haven't told them that I am a bhangi. I wonder how they would react if they knew. I have befriended some of them. One person has been very helpful. He is an old Amreeki, Peter Dawber, who says that he fought in the Second World War and visited Karachi in 1954. He loves Pakistani food. I often invite him for dinner at my flat. You know, when I was working at Café de Jamadar I learned how to cook. My friend Peter Sahib tells me I am so good that I should open a restaurant. Maybe someday, I will.

You know, my mother has gone back to Punjab and is now living with her sister. She is still angry with me for leaving her alone, but you tell me what could I have done? Kismet doesn't knock at your door every day. My mother doesn't understand that and begs me to come home in every letter she sends me. I am planning to visit her later this summer. I will get my vacation and guess what? They are not going to dock my salary! When I come, I would like to see you and, if possible, stay in your servants' quarters, if it is okay with Barrister Sahib and Begum Sahiba. Please send my salaam to them. How is Mehrun? She is a hot thing, isn't she? If I were not a bhangi, I would marry her in an instant. Too bad you can't marry her either. If you see her, tell her I still want her to be my heroine. I hope Athanni doesn't rob you

*any more. Did I tell you that some months before I left for Iran,
I saw Athanni in a cinema watching a nude filim? I confronted
him and he got angry at me and ran away in a taxi.*

*Please write to me and tell me about everything back home.
You will be surprised to learn that although I hated that country
of yours, I still miss it. My address is written at the back of the
envelope.*

*If you could send me Mehrun's address in your letter, I would
be grateful to you.*

*Your servant,
Joseph Solomon*

Joseph had signed his name in English. Glad to receive his letter,
Mansoor decided to reply to him soon, as he was not sure when
he would see his friend next. He called Mehrun at her office, keen
to tell her about Joseph's letter, but she was not there. So he left a
message and hung up.

*

Two weeks before his bank was nationalized, Alvi officially resigned
as the chairman and managing director of the High Finance Bank,
much to the dismay of his colleagues. They felt betrayed, and
made it sound as if Alvi, the captain, had abandoned a sinking
ship and used the only lifeboat available to flee alone, leaving his
fellow passengers to the sharks. Their reaction was to shun the
man. Avoiding him was their way of shaming him. Mehrun, of
course, knew about his planned resignation well before everyone
else, but she had still nurtured a hope that he would change his
mind. Without his protection, she was afraid to continue working
at the bank alone. Her meteoric rise had created enemies, and
her close ties with Alvi had made people whisper. But with Alvi
at the helm, she never had to worry about anything. The fear of

nationalization had made most people jittery; the tension levels were at an all-time high, but what flustered Mehrun more was the possibility of working amid angry wolves after Alvi left.

When Alvi finally announced his intention to resign, Mehrun busied herself in organizing a farewell party for him. But the party had to be discreet; the top bosses had to be kept in the dark since Alvi had already become a pariah. Throwing a farewell party for a deserter was tantamount to committing career suicide, nevertheless, Mehrun went ahead with the preparations.

A day before the party, however, she felt sick. But skipping it was out of the question. It would be a let-down for everyone, and she would never do that. She took four Aspro tablets before heading to work and psyched herself for the evening. Alvi had unfinished business to attend to, so he spent his last few days working till late, wrapping things up. On the day of the party, after the other bosses were gone, Mehrun tricked Alvi to come down to the basement of the bank. The surprise party touched him. Gratified that his staff still cared about him despite his lame-duck status, he thanked them in a cracked voice. He was deeply moved by Mehrun, who took the risk to organize the whole thing.

Compared to the farewell bashes of past eras, this one turned out to be a tame affair. Dancing, drinking and debauchery were obviously missing. The psychedelic index, a term coined by Alvi, did not rise above zero, but then he had never cared for frivolity. After giving a heartfelt speech, he came to Mehrun, thanked her and renewed his job offer. But how could she leave her real job for a pipe dream? How could she abandon her father alone in this behemoth of a city? Despite her emotional remoteness with her father, she wanted to stay close to him. They had no other relatives in the town, no family, and Jumman had no friends either. The Kashana was the only place where he functioned like a normal person, where he found purpose, meaning and happiness. Perhaps, if he shifted there and stayed as a live-in gardener, she could leave him without feeling guilty. Could she ask Mansoor to make that arrangement?

'Please think again about my offer.'

Mehrun smiled stingily.

'If you want, I can ask your father,' Alvi suggested.

'He will never allow his unmarried daughter to live alone in a foreign country.'

'Then get married!' Alvi suggested.

Mehrun laughed and said, 'Yes, it is that easy, especially for a girl of my background.'

'What is wrong with a girl of your background?'

Alvi knew everything about her background and the societal barriers erected like the reinforced steel around the bank's vault, but he still lingered on for an explanation, as if to keep the conversation running.

'Alvi Sahib, who do you think is going to marry me? For the men of my world, I am too liberated, too educated; I earn my own living; I am independent; I support my father. As for men from the other world, I do not even exist. Who is going to marry a daughter of a har . . . a gardener?'

She stopped to collect her thoughts, and after a split-second break continued, 'Besides, my father cannot provide any dowry for me.'

Alvi's persistent questions exasperated her, and her vigorous explanations caught people's attention. Realizing that people were eavesdropping on their conversation, she changed the subject.

Alvi stayed with her till the party ended, even helping her clean the place, which discomfited her more. With the cleaning done, he offered to take her home. It was too dangerous to use public transportation at that hour, so Mehrun accepted his offer. The night was starry and silent. They sat in Alvi's Mercedes convertible, which cruised smoothly on the dark, deserted road towards Clifton Beach. She knew that he was going in a direction that was diametrically opposite to where she lived, but she pretended ignorance. As they reached the oceanfront, she noticed a line of magnificent houses along the road, standing imperiously and looking down upon the rest of the city. He stopped his car in front of one of them.

'Why did you stop?' she asked, her heart beating faster, unsure about the next moment.

'Would you like to come inside my house?'

'No, please just take me home.'

But instead of taking her home, Alvi turned off the engine. Mehrun froze, conscious of her trembling legs. Alvi reached into his left coat pocket and took out a sterling silver cigarette box that had 'AAA' engraved on it. He took out a cigarette, pushed the car lighter and waited till it popped up. He pulled out the lighter from the socket and lit up his cigarette. Every passing second of silence stifled Mehrun's nerves. She gazed into the darkness. Alvi inhaled profoundly, holding on to the smoke for a moment, relishing it, and then exhaled.

'Would you come with me to the Middle East if I ask you to marry me?' he said as he tapped the ash from the cigarette into the car's ashtray.

Mehrun was stunned. Did he just ask her to marry him? Was that a marriage proposal or a job offer? She had always been a dreamer, but the idea of marriage had never entered her mind, not even when Talat Mirza warned her of Sadiq's foolish notion about making her his second wife. And here was her boss, a rich man, a man from the upper class no less, asking for her hand in marriage. Suddenly, the noise of cars swishing by and the wind ruffling through got amplified, and all she could say to him was, 'Please take me to my home.'

'Not before I hear an answer.'

Mehrun felt queasy, but then she mustered up enough courage to ask, 'Why do you want to marry me?'

'Why does anyone marry anyone?'

That was hardly an answer, and it intensified Mehrun's irritation. Alvi wondered if she had heard any rumours about his sexual orientation. But there was nothing in her demeanour that hinted at any awareness on her part of those constant, malicious gossips.

'So, what do you think?' he persisted.

'I don't know what to think. It's too sudden. I need time.'

'Mehrun, I will make you happy and very, very rich. Isn't that what you want?'

After a pause, she said, 'I don't feel well. Please take me home.'

'I will be leaving for the Middle East in a week, and I would like an answer before that.'

Was that an ultimatum? Mehrun remained quiet. He stubbed out what remained of the cigarette in the ashtray, turned on the ignition and pulled the car back on the road in tentative silence.

Eighteen

Alvi had done many favours for Mehrun: mentoring her, furthering her career, defending her promotions. He had even helped her financially, so that she and Jumman could move out of their old, rundown house and into the newer settlement of Baagh-e-Bahar, the Garden of Spring. Hardly a garden, this neighbourhood was still a significant improvement compared to the thickly populated slum they had lived in all their life. On more than one occasion, Alvi had stressed to Mehrun that success depended not only on hard work and connections, but also on having the correct residential address. So, to pursue success, Mehrun began renting an unassuming two-bedroom flat in one of those tall, tiresome buildings that stood restlessly like people waiting in queues to get their daily ration of sugar and flour. She had decorated the inside of the apartment with pride and love. This was her crowning achievement, and she showed off her new tenement to her few friends, but the one person she wanted to show her home the most to was Mansoor. Something, however, prevented her from doing this. Although she was still relatively hard-pressed for money, she had moved up a rung on the monetary ladder—the mischance of her birth had already ruled out the possibility of her climbing the social staircase. In a society where people have long memories of one's status in life and one's ancestry, she was destined to live and die a churail.

But she was happy in her new flat; it gave her a feeling of success. Her old hovel had begun to haunt her. Memories of the horror of her mother's last days filled every corner and gave her nightmares. She wanted to bury those memories, and her new flat helped her achieve this. This modern flat signified her rebirth, it was an abode free of past insults and ignominy.

That night, after she got home, she collapsed on her bed without changing her clothes. Jumman was nowhere to be found. It seemed that he had not come back from the Kashana. Mehrun's mind returned to the events of the day. What was Alvi's marriage proposal all about? Was she to take that as a compliment or as an insult? Could she afford to turn him down? He had said that he would make her happy and very, very rich. But words did not mean a damn thing. She did not know if more indignations awaited her. Torn by the events of that evening, she buried her face in her pillow and cried. She cried so much that she began hiccupping and finding it difficult to catch her breath. She cried until her tears dried out and she felt her energy vaporizing from her body. Even as her face radiated heat, she began shivering. She felt her forehead; it was burning hot. The proposal continued to lacerate her heart. She got up and went to the bathroom to splash cold water on her face. After washing her face, she lifted her head to look in the mirror and saw her mother's face instead—hideous and scarred. She shot out of the bathroom, screaming, her face still wet and soapy. Was that really her mother? Was she trying to say something? Mehrun ran towards the front door to get out of the house, but just then the door opened and Mansoor and her father entered the flat. As soon as she saw them, Mehrun became hysterical, clasping her father tightly around his waist and starting to hiccup again.

'Mehrun Beti, are you all right?' For the first time in her life, Mehrun heard her father call her 'beti', as if, at last, he was ready to reclaim her, willing to acknowledge his paternity. But Mehrun continued to shiver, and neither Mansoor nor Jumman understood what had taken over her.

*

Jumman had returned early that night and was waiting for Mehrun to warm up the food. But when Mehrun did not come back from work at her usual time, he got worried and went out to search for her. She had told him about the farewell party, but he had forgotten all about it. He took a taxi and went to the Kashana to see if she was there. When he did not find her there either, he asked Mansoor to help him look for her. Mansoor took his car and they looked for her at every possible place, but without any success. Disappointed, they decided to check back at the flat. And that was how, after a fruitless search, they saw the petrified Mehrun just as they entered the flat. Despite her irrepressible sobs, they were relieved to see her alive and well. When they asked her why she was crying so hard, she fibbed that she was afraid Jumman had gone missing.

It was well past midnight, so Mansoor said goodbye, but before departing, he told Mehrun about his admission at the University of Iowa. She had known that he had applied to American universities and would soon leave, but the news still depressed her. First, it was Alvi's proposal, and now it was Mansoor's news. She did not know how she was going to spend the night alone in her bed—afraid of that churail, confused about Alvi's proposal and desolate about Mansoor's impending departure.

Discussing the marriage proposal with her father was out of the question. Girls simply did not talk about such matters. The rules of marriage could not be transgressed; the power of taboo could not be broken. The most crucial decision in a girl's life was usually made without her consent. Mehrun's work might have liberated her, but cumbersome traditions and rusted customs still shackled her.

Mehrun's febrile state brought on delirium and nightmares. In her dream, she was transported to a surreal, inverted world, inhabited by bizarre creatures, a place where darkness ruled and emptiness prevailed. She felt alone, but suddenly, she became aware of someone's presence. She knew who that was. Sitting at some distance was that same withered churail she had seen in the mirror, laughing, and mocking and taunting her. For some reason, the churail stayed at a distance and never came near her, and then in the next moment, Mehrun heard a terrified shriek, like a cat crying during rutting time, and the churail evaporated into thin air. She saw Mansoor transform into a djinn. She saw Sadiq Mirza kissing a girl, and then he disappeared as well.

Mehrun woke up trembling, the nightmare had disoriented her sense of time and place, the churail, the djinn and the other demons all a vague blur in the dark cocoon of her memory. She remained in a state of delirium for three days, and then, after the third night, her fever broke, ending her phantasmagorical dreams. On the fourth morning, she woke up to the sound of the call to prayer from a nearby mosque. Having had enough of the spectral harassment, she got up and decided to tackle things head-on. The memories that she had successfully ejected from her conscious self must now be jettisoned from her unconscious being. With her eyes closed, she took three deep breaths and began reciting a verse from the Qur'an. As her mind began clearing, she deliberately turned her attention to Alvi. It seemed as if too much time had elapsed and too many events had happened since he proposed to her.

Realizing that her father was too incapacitated to make such a monumental decision on her behalf, she took matters into her own hands and began weighing the pros and cons of the marriage proposal. She had always liked Alvi, but could she imagine him as her husband? This would be her only chance to have a good life; perhaps this would be her ticket to becoming an authentic begum. Should she confide in someone? But who? The single name that came to her lips was Mansoor's. As daylight peeked in through the window, Mehrun realized that there were too many positives to decline the proposal. Marriage was not about love. Look at Noor ul Haq; look at Sadiq Mirza, both miserable in their marriages. Look at her own parents. Her mind finally made up, she readied herself to cross the Rubicon. She was prepared to say yes and transform the churail into a begum.

*

From her office, Mehrun made two phone calls. First, she called Alvi on his direct line, and when he picked up the phone, she said, 'My answer is yes.'

He replied, 'Good. I'll make the arrangements,' and hung up.

After taking a deep breath, she dialled the Kashana. Luckily, Mansoor picked up the phone.

'Hello, Mansoor Babu. How are you? I wanted to tell you something. Alvi Sahib has asked me to marry him, and I have said yes.' She said without stopping.

Mansoor tried to grasp what Mehrun had said. Then, after a pause, he replied, 'Oh.'

'Aren't you going to congratulate me?'

'Yes, yes, congratulations.'

'Is that all, Mansoor?'

'What do you want me to say, Mehrun? You have already said yes, and now you have informed me of your decision.'

'Thank you, Mansoor,' she said and put the phone down.

After a few minutes, the phone rang again, but she didn't pick it up. She knew it would be Mansoor, but at least for that moment, she wanted to have absolute power over her own life story. She typed up a brief resignation letter addressed to the personnel administration manager and asked one of the clerks to drop it off at his office.

*

Alvi made two conditions for the wedding ceremony. First, he wanted no guests, only two witnesses; and second, the nikah would be performed by a Shia maulvi. Mehrun accepted both. The first condition gave her an excuse to not invite Mansoor, and she had no objection to the second condition either. Although she was Sunni, or so she thought, she didn't care who performed the ceremony. The forceful, practical imperative to get married trumped everything.

In a service that mixed simplicity and speed, Mehrunnissa and Ameer Abbas Alvi were religiously and legally married. Their *mehr*, or dower, was set at a meagre one hundred and twenty rupees, of which sixty-two rupees and eight annas were to be paid promptly and the other half was to be deferred. The amount calculated by the maulvi was one-third of the median religious dower. But Mehrun could not dispute it since Alvi said nothing and the money was promptly paid to her. Was that bride money? she thought.

Hasan Ali, a banker friend of Alvi, and Jumman were the two official witnesses of the nikah. When Hasan Ali, at Mehrun's urging, had taken the formal marriage proposal to Jumman, he did not know what to do. That protocol had not existed in his family as far as he could remember. To him and his dead partner, marriage remained an extraterrestrial concept, and the idea of Mehrun's marriage had never come up when Kaneez was alive. So when the unexpected proposal came, he kept looking outside the window, busy in his distempered thoughts. Mehrun, listening to her father's continued silence, came out from her room and accepted the proposal on his behalf. Jumman asked no questions and got no answers. It did not matter to him that his daughter was twenty years younger than Alvi, and it was inconsequential that he was Shia.

*

Mehrun was not attracted to older men, but it seemed as if they gravitated towards her. To her, they were a source of wisdom and stability, and she could benefit from both. Her faith was essential only in the sense that it provided protection against churails and djinns. On the other hand, material culture and social status had always fascinated her. They were the real things. The time she spent at the Kashana, observing those high-society begums display their cultural capital, had made her hungry for the good life. And with Alvi as her husband, she had come one step closer to achieving it.

Two days after their wedding, Mehrunnissa and Ameer Abbas Alvi left for Dubai—she to start her new life and he to launch his new bank. Jumman vacated the apartment, sold all the furniture and moved into the servants' quarters at the Kashana.

*

Since the 1950s, the religious parties of Pakistan had tried to build a campaign against the minority Ahmadi sect to declare them non-Muslims. They finally succeeded in 1974, when the Pakistani Parliament passed the Second Amendment to the 1973 Constitution. Noor heard the news from Haider even before it became official. Haider's sources had told him that The People's Leader's wife, who belonged to the minority Shia community, vehemently opposed this. His sources said she feared that Shias would be the next to be declared heretics. The amendment deprived the Ahmadis of the right to bury their dead in a Muslim graveyard, to have any Qur'anic inscription on their tombstones, to use Islamic greetings, and to call their place of worship a mosque. Hell-bent on dividing the already divided nation, the so-called representatives of the people eviscerated a belief system with a simple vote. By stigmatizing their otherness, they had hoped to eradicate a group of people. For these brutal lawmakers, the process of cultural extermination started with constitutional extermination. And in this nefarious scheme, The People's Leader was the prime offender—a willing abettor and a cheerer in this crime against a weak minority, his wife's concerns notwithstanding. No one dared to question this injustice. There were no protests; there were no op-eds in even the most liberal of newspapers. People carried on as if this was no big deal.

'We are now the only Muslim country that has institutionalized discrimination,' Haider told Noor.

'The Second Amendment of America gave guns to the people; the Second Amendment of Pakistan stripped the Ahmadis of their right to call themselves Muslims. And I thought that was the sole prerogative of God,' replied Noor.

'No, the mullahs are the new gods.'

'Haider, you better watch out. You could be next.'

'Don't worry, I know how to play this game.'

*

Years before the passing of the constitutional amendment, Noor had warned Sadiq about this possibility. But Sadiq had been in denial about such a thing ever happening, believing that there were too many good people in the country who would rise up against such an injustice. In any case, the man was not really a believer, so why should he care? Noor tried to deflate the professor's optimism and even advised him to leave the country at the first opportunity he got. But Sadiq had migrated to Pakistan from India, believing that he would be safer here. Fleeing the country again, that too at his age, held no appeal to the professor. And where would he go? Going back to India was no longer a possibility. He never believed in organized religion; he never practiced his faith, but now, what was trivial to him would become deathly consequential. Noor knew that Sadiq would be stigmatized, harassed and hounded because his parents were practicing Ahmadis. When his fellow professors had first learned about his love of Scotch and secularism, they had dismissed him as an angrez *ashiq*, an anglophile. But now, with his Ahmadi roots exposed, they began shunning him as they would a contagion.

So, after Noor heard the news from Haider, the first thing he did was to phone Sadiq at his home, but no one answered. He called all the people who might know his whereabouts, but no one knew anything. Except for Anna, Sadiq's other daughters had already left for various parts of the world after they got married. So Noor called Anna, but she did not pick up the phone either.

It was as if the entire Mirza clan had vanished from the face of the country. Worried about his friend, Noor got into his car and asked Sikander to take him to all the possible places where Sadiq might go. But he came home empty-handed.

'These shameless lawmakers should all be lined up and shot by a firing squad,' he told Mansoor in a fit of escalating emotions.

Some of the lawmakers who had signed the death warrant of the Ahmadis were Noor's clients. He vowed to Mansoor that he would never represent them again. The *Daily Jadal*, in an editorial, commended the prime minister for doing something that should have been done twenty-seven years ago, when Pakistan became independent.

*

Intoxicated by power and distended by hubris, The People's Leader began tightening the noose around people's necks and cracking down on general dissidents. He then turned his wrath on the dissenters from his own party, stripping them from party ranks and personally ordering their beating by the SCAB. Those who remained defiant were labelled subversives, thrown into prisons without any charges and tortured physically and sexually. The few newspapermen who wrote against The People's Leader were routinely arrested and beaten.

Haider Rizvi was the only top editor who was spared arrest. He began playing the game that he had alluded to when he spoke to Noor a while ago. Under Haider's leadership, the *Morning Gazette* became the administration's mouthpiece, and in return, the government rewarded him generously with advertisements. Rizvi began enjoying the new limelight, hobnobbing with the powerful and the ruthless. Irreligious at heart, but steeped in slyness, he practiced his art of pretension to perfection. So shameless was his sycophancy at the time that his prickly friend Noor became uncomfortable in his company. Had he not been such an old friend, Noor would have dumped him altogether.

Part III

'Who holds the devil, let him hold him well,
He hardly will be caught a second time.'

—*Faust: Part 1*, Johann Wolfgang von Goethe

Nineteen

Mansoor completed his undergraduate degree in economics from the University of Karachi and was eager to study further in America. All his admission papers from the University of Iowa had arrived, but the prized American visa eluded him. The process was so labyrinthine that he almost gave up on it until Haider Rizvi offered his help.

'I know someone at the American consulate who can get you the visa, but there is one condition.'

'What is that?' Mansoor asked.

'You will let me call you the twelfth man!' Haider laughed so hard that he began to cough.

After he settled down, Mansoor replied, 'Uncle Haider, if you get me the visa, you can call me anything you want.'

'Okay, my twelfth man, come to my office tomorrow, and we will start the innings,' Haider said.

The next day, Mansoor drove his Datsun to Haider Rizvi's office. Located in an old colonial-style mansion, the fading yellow building grimly reminded Mansoor of the control the government had on it now. After parking his car inside the *Gazette*'s parking lot, a rarity in this densely populated, land-scarce city, he went straight to Haider's second-floor office. Sitting behind a sturdy table, a petite and well-groomed secretary in a light blue dress guarded Haider's office.

'I am here to see Mr Haider Rizvi.'

'Do you have an appointment?'

'No, but he asked me to come at any time.'

'You can't see him if you don't have an appointment . . . besides, he is with somebody right now.'

'I know him personally . . . could you just tell him that Mansoor ul Haq is here to see him?' he pleaded desperately.

'I am sorry, Mr Haq, no appointment, no meeting. I can get you an appointment for January.'

But January was two months away. Besides, he was supposed to be in America in January. Feeling thoroughly disgusted by the imperious, intransigent secretary, Mansoor turned around to leave, but Haider came out of his office just then and saw him.

'Oh, come on in, Mansoor! I am glad you came. Miss Davis, please hold all my calls.'

A sly smile on his face, Mansoor glanced at Miss Davis triumphantly and walked into Haider's office. Inside, he saw a man in a crumpled kurta-pyjama sitting comfortably across from the editor. Wearing a white prayer cap, his round moustache-less face concealed by a long salt-and-pepper beard, he looked familiar to Mansoor.

'*Assalam alai kum*,' Mansoor greeted him, raking his memory to identify the face.

'*Wa-alaikum assalam wa rahamatullahe wa barakatuh.*'

Greeting Mansoor with the additional benedictions of divine mercy and blessings, and squeezing out all the pietistic verbiage he could to assert his new self-image, was a man no other than Zakir Hassan.

Mansoor recognized that raspy voice. Gone was the man with the infectious smile, the dapper attire and the magnetic personality. In his place sat a shaggy mendicant with a stern face.

What a transformation! Mansoor thought. He knew that Zakir Hassan had gone through a period of exhaustive soul-searching, but such a drastic makeover he had never imagined.

Mansoor pulled an empty chair and asked, 'How are you doing, Uncle Zakir?'

'All praise is to Allah,' came the prompt reply. After a brief pause, Zakir continued, 'So you are going to America?' And before Mansoor could reply, he spoke again, 'Good! Very good! Our beloved Prophet Muhammad, peace be upon him, said seek education even if you have to go to China . . .'

Mansoor knew that there was a 'but' hidden somewhere and he waited for it to erupt.

'But, let me give you a piece of advice. You know I lived in America for many years, and I have seen its worst side and its best side. And as a person who cares about you, let me tell you— continue to pray five times a day, fast during Ramadan and read the holy Qur'an every day, and you will be saved from the worst side of America, inshallah.'

The confidence in Zakir's assumption that he would 'continue to pray', and the certainty of his conclusion that he needed to be 'saved', irritated Mansoor. But he was in no mood to hear a sermon, so he just nodded politely and turned his attention to Haider.

'Do you think you can get me an interview with the consul general?' Mansoor asked Haider.

'I certainly can! Not to worry, twelfth man,' Haider replied confidently and then changed the subject, 'Would you like something hot or cold to drink?'

'Tea would be great,' Mansoor answered.

'Well, I should be leaving; I have to go to four more places,' Zakir said and got up to leave. He shook hands with Haider, embraced Mansoor and kissed him on his forehead. As he was about to leave the room, he turned again and said, 'Mansoor, I would like to give you some advice about America, and perhaps even help you get the visa. I am on a first-name basis with the consul general. We were classmates at Harvard. Come to my house tomorrow after the midday prayer, or before it . . . perhaps we can go to the mosque together.'

'I will try.'

'That's all I ask.'

Zakir did not like Mansoor's answer. He knew that Noor's son couldn't be religious, and that was his challenge, but he was also confident in his abilities to persuade the boy. It was an art that he had used routinely as a diplomat. If only he could spend some time with the young man, he could save him from his father's beliefs. That was the plan.

After he had left, Haider told Mansoor that Zakir had joined a proselytizing group whose job was to convert the 'errant' Muslims first. He mockingly called them the Pyjama Dheela Topi Tight Party, a reference to the loose pyjamas and the tight caps that the members of the party wore.

'His life's mission now is to visit seven different Muslims every day and remind them about religion. It was a good thing you came, and just in time too, because he was throwing jerky googlies,' Haider said.

Mansoor stayed with him for another hour, but he just couldn't get a straight answer about the interview with the consul general. By the time he left, he knew that he had wasted his time.

*

The next day, Mansoor went to Zakir's house, which was located near the newly built Marine Drive, right next to the Arabian Sea. A beautiful exclave, with bricked bungalows overlooking the deep tantalizing waters of the Arabian Sea, the whole pristine development with its big, wide streets seemed at odds with the rest of the city that remained mainly unplanned and haphazard.

It was still a little before the midday prayer, so Mansoor whiled away his time by driving around aimlessly, enjoying the scenery. Palm and coconut trees lined the shoulders of the Drive, and a few seagulls majestically circled the blue sky. He saw a group of children on horses, smartly dressed in jodhpurs, partaking in what looked like their regular riding lessons. The sight of the blue water and the sandy beach invited him, but he decided against going in. After driving for about half an hour, Mansoor turned his Datsun around and headed towards Zakir's house.

As he pulled up near the iron gate of Zakir's bungalow, he saw him watering his flowers. Mansoor waved at him. Zakir came and embraced him warmly as he got out of his car. After exchanging pleasantries, he told Mansoor that he had some good news.

'Good news for me?' Mansoor asked.

'Yes, first come on in, and then I'll tell you.'

As they passed through the symmetrically landscaped front garden, Mansoor noticed a row of immaculately shaped hedges and rose bushes—red, pink and yellow. A large Italianate fountain misted the air and two marble pillars flanked the porch leading to the front door. Zakir might have traded his Saville Row suits for white kurta-pyjamas, but the grandeur of his property was non-negotiable. He led Mansoor straight to his library. Framed calligraphic verses from the Qur'an, painted by the Pakistani artist Sadequain, robed the otherwise naked walls. A desk cluttered with papers, manuscripts and a few open books stood in the centre of the room, suggesting some writing in progress. A Sony stereo cassette deck played a dulcet rendition of Qur'anic verses recited by a *qari*, a professional reciter. As he sat on the sofa opposite the desk, Mansoor asked impatiently, 'So, what is the good news, Uncle Zakir?'

'What are you doing tomorrow morning?'

'Nothing in particular . . . why do you ask?'

'I have arranged an interview for you with the consul general for tomorrow at 10 a.m. Can you make it?'

'Yes, I think so,' Mansoor replied. He couldn't believe what he had just heard. After a moment, he asked him, 'Thank you! But how did you arrange it?'

'Well, as I told you, the consul general is a friend of mine.'

Mansoor thanked him profusely. Zakir told him then that he did not think that Haider knew anybody in the American consulate; Mansoor agreed with his conclusion. Then, without any notice, Zakir changed the subject and asked Mansoor, 'Have you offered your midday prayers yet?'

Caught off guard by the question, Mansoor remembered, a little too late, the complaint Haider had of him yesterday. Had he anticipated that question, he would have lied, but not now. Not after the favour Zakir had done him. With a gnawing emptiness inside his stomach, Mansoor said, 'No.'

'Well, I haven't either . . . let's pray together then.'

Without waiting for a reply, Zakir led Mansoor to the bathroom to perform the ablutions. Feeling like a phoney who had just peddled away his authenticity, Mansoor wanted to scream and say, 'You have taken advantage of my weakness. I do not care about the damn interview!' But he could not. Too timid to stand up to Zakir and let this opportunity pass, he sold his soul and quietly prayed with him. After the prayers, a servant brought them tea and biscuits in a silver tray. Mansoor took the drink and thanked Zakir, but he knew that the worst was yet to come, and he was right. Zakir lectured him about the 'decadent West' and about the virtue of religion, liberally quoting the scripture from memory. And all this time, Mansoor sat quietly, nodding his head and pretending to listen.

'Prayer is the pillar of religion; fasting is the shield from sins. The good news is that you were born a Muslim. Allah did you a great favour by creating you in a Muslim household,' Zakir said.

A Muslim household? Mansoor thought. My father doesn't believe in any of these things, and my mother . . . well, she believes as a matter of habit, and me . . . I don't know what I believe in, he wondered.

Mansoor then heard Zakir say, 'Every day, after the early morning *Fajr* prayers, recite the ninety-nine names of Allah before you do anything else, and inshallah you will see that you will have a problem-free day.'

Mansoor's mind had begun drifting again, while his eyes conducted a grim survey of the re-invented Zakir Hassan. What earth-shaking event, what calamity in his life had made him give up his prestigious job in exchange for converting people to his beliefs? One must have a bucketload of certitude to believe that they possess the absolute truth, one that everyone should hear about. How could a man change so profoundly and in so abbreviated a period of time? How did Zakir support his family and pay for the upkeep of his elegant bungalow?' Mansoor knew he had four daughters, but he never saw them. They must be observing the purdah by now. Mansoor's ordeal lasted for another hour or so. When he finally managed to leave, he thanked Zakir once again for arranging the interview and bade him goodbye with the promise that he would keep him informed about his visa status.

*

With Zakir's help, Mansoor obtained the visa for America. As the date of his impending departure neared, Mansoor noticed a jump in his father's alcohol intake. Was he hurting? Didn't his father want him to go to America? He could drown his emotions in Chivas Regal; he could carry on a normal conversation, but he would never say no to higher education. So what was the matter? Then, two nights before his departure, his father summoned him. Mansoor felt flustered as he walked into his parents' bedroom.

'Come, sit with me. I have something important to talk about,' Noor said in English when he saw Mansoor.

Struggling with her own sadness, Farhat lay on the bed, cursing her husband, her eyes all red and puffy from continuous crying. While Noor drowned his sorrows in alcohol, Farhat submerged herself in her faith. Every day after Noor left for his office, she picked up the Qur'an, recited a few sections and cried her heart out on the prayer rug.

After Mansoor had seated himself on the chair, Noor poured him a glass of whisky. Mansoor accepted it reluctantly. Catching a quick glance of his mother's scowling face, he winced. So close to his departure, he did not want to antagonize his mother, but then he couldn't reject his father either. Noor raised his glass and said, 'Cheers.' Mansoor forced a smile and raised his glass as well.

'Son, now that you are almost ready to go to America, I thought that this would be an opportune time for me to give you some last-minute advice . . . not that you need any,' and with that, Noor laughed his familiar, inebriated laugh. Pausing for a while, he took a sip of the whisky before continuing. 'My first advice to you would be to get the highest education possible. Actually, nothing would give me greater satisfaction than you getting a PhD. I am going to support your education for as long as I have to, so don't worry about money. My other advice to you would be to try and settle in America if you can. Don't ever think about coming back to this wretched country.'

Mansoor felt sad when his father said that. This was *his* country, *his* place of birth. If he didn't belong here, he wouldn't belong anywhere.

'Why do you say that?' Mansoor asked.

'Why? Why? You ask why? Because, Sahibzadey, you have no future here. Even if you get a job here, you will not be able to live honestly. Corruption in this country of *YOURS* will eat you up like cancer, and no amount of radiotherapy will cure it. If you come back, you will do so without my blessings.'

'What are you two talking about? Can't you speak in Urdu?' Farhat interrupted. She jumped into the conversation because she thought Noor was berating Mansoor for something.

Noor had never liked her interruptions, especially not when he was talking with their son. Now, he rudely told her off, 'What we are talking about has nothing to do with you. So turn around and go to sleep.'

'How can anyone sleep with you talking so loudly?' Farhat remained defiant.

To diffuse the situation, Mansoor quickly intervened. In a soft tone, using the most polite Urdu words he could think of, he said, 'Amma, Abba is just giving me some advice about living in a foreign country . . . that's all.'

The answer did not satisfy her. Farhat turned to the other side, pulled up her blanket and began crying softly. Noor's insults had lacerated her feelings again. To upset her like that was nothing unusual for him, especially when he was boozed out. That night, however, she was more tearful than usual. Living with this man for all these years, watching him drink every night, listening to him talk in English, witnessing his impossible-to-understand lectures to their son, all of it still enraged her. And when father and son joined in this *sinful* act, it hurt her deeply. And that night again, hearing a conversation in that alien language made her feel like a foreigner in her own bedroom; she hated these legatees of British colonialism.

As Mansoor fiddled with his half-filled glass, Noor continued with his lecture, 'Now look, son, I hope you don't believe in patriotism. Remember, it is the last resort of scoundrels.'

Noor laughed awkwardly at his own words, and then, raising one of his eyebrows, he waited expectantly for an answer, but Mansoor kept quiet.

'Don't think that it is your patriotic duty to come back, okay?' Noor continued.

Pausing for a moment, he switched gears and railed against The People's Leader, cursing him for Pakistan's current mess. When he eventually realized that he had veered away from the task of advising Mansoor, he said, 'Son, excuse my candour, but I also want to give you advice of an intimate nature.' He paused to gather his thoughts, and then continued, 'I hope . . . that you will listen to me very carefully and not get embarrassed.'

Already turned off by the encore lecture, Mansoor quickly forced himself to tune back in when he heard the word 'embarrassed'.

'Sure,' he replied.

'I don't know if you have already, and I don't *want* to know . . .
ha ha ha . . . But in America, you will have temptations and . . .
ahem . . . in my books, there is nothing wrong with it, and I am not
forbidding you to have . . . before you get married, but I just want
to caution you about a few things. Number one: never . . . ever . . .
never coerce anyone.'

Is he trying to give me advice about sex? Mansoor thought.
Checking to make sure that his mother did not understand any
part of this awkward conversation, he replied in English, 'I am not
stupid, Abba.'

'I know you are not, but I am your father and I have a
responsibility to tell you these things.' Then he cleared his throat
and paused, trying to remember point number two. 'Ah, yes, what
number is that? Whatever, yes . . . always . . . take precautions; you
don't want to have a bast . . . ahem . . . unwanted . . . you know.'

As the conversation turned clumsier, Mansoor felt increasingly
embarrassed, his body heat rising to his ears. He wanted to think
of something else; Mehrun perhaps. He was hurt that she had
not invited him to the wedding. A day before she was to leave for
Dubai, she had made another brief call from her office to tell him
about it. The shock that she had gone ahead and married Alvi was
not as deep as the shock he'd received when she first informed him
of her intention. It had made him react in the most unnatural way
when he had congratulated her. And now Mansoor was saddened
that she, too, was leaving for another country.

He heard his father clear his throat again, louder than before,
and say, 'I don't mind if you marry a white woman, but . . . don't
marry before you finish your studies. Marriage is a responsibility,
and you should not take it lightly. However,' he paused here and
took a sip of the whisky, 'however, I can tell you this; your mother
would be deeply hurt if you do marry a white woman.'

Was his father hiding his prejudices behind his poor mother?
How would Noor feel if he married a black woman? And why

was he talking about sex and marriage at this late hour? Noor was about to give more advice to Mansoor when the telephone rang in the study. Mansoor looked at the clock. It was 11.25 p.m. Who could be calling at this hour? He ran to the study and picked up the telephone. It was a long-distance call from Anna, Sadiq's daughter. She was calling from Paris, and she was hysterical.

'Is everything all right, Anna Apa? Why are you in Paris?' he asked.

'No, Mansoor. Nothing's right. They killed Abba, and Ammi is missing. They murdered him, Mansoor. They . . .' Suddenly, the line got disconnected before Anna could say anything more.

Mansoor stood there, stunned, his heart thumping wildly, the black telephone handset still in his hand. He did not know what to do. He couldn't tell his father, not in his inebriated condition, not at this hour. Putting the phone in its cradle, he went back to his parents' bedroom and lied to Noor that it was a wrong number. Excusing himself, he returned to his room. This news will kill my father, he thought. He stayed awake for a long time that night, thinking about how he would break it to his father.

*

The next morning, Mansoor woke up with a headache. After gulping two Optalidon pills, he rushed to the bathroom, where he reflected on how to talk to his father. As Mansoor approached the men's quarter a few minutes later, he heard the sound of voices and sobs from within. Inside, he saw that his father, tears streaming down his cheeks, had his arms around Zakir's shoulders and was trying to comfort him. Zakir was weeping uncontrollably, while Haider sat on the sofa, looking visibly shaken. When he saw Mansoor, his father told him the news, which he already knew but pretended otherwise. Haider filled him in with the details.

He told him about the harassment and the death threats that Sadiq had been receiving, especially after the passage of the Second

Amendment declaring the Ahmadis non-Muslim. Scared of the intimidations, Sadiq, his wife and Anna's family went into hiding. Sadiq had withdrawn all his savings from the bank and bought tickets for Anna and her family and persuaded them to leave for Paris, where her younger sister Sarah lived. He and Talat then took the train to the city of Rabwah, in Punjab, where the majority of Ahmadis lived. Even though they were not Punjabis, they felt that this would be the only place where they would be safe. They had decided to stay there until the madness against their community calmed down. One station before Rabwah, when the train stopped, a group of madmen got in and dragged Sadiq off the train. They killed him on the platform of the railway station, right outside the train, in broad daylight. When Talat tried to intervene, they knocked her senseless. Anna had trunk-called Haider, who called her back using his office phone and got the details.

*

Noor, Haider and Zakir went to Rabwah and found Talat lying in a coma in a local hospital. They arranged to fly her back to Karachi, where the hospital facilities were much better, but a day after their arrival, she succumbed to her injuries. They could never find Sadiq Mirza's body.

The seekers of Paradise were determined to create hell for anyone who competed with their cartelized truth. Their image of heaven, paved with the blood of heretics, included only their narrower sects, rejecting the rest of humanity. The god of their inheritance demanded blood, exacted revenge and promoted hate. It was a weak god with a small heart and a shrill voice.

*

Mansoor delayed his departure by a week, and Noor, upon his return from Rabwah, came back angrier and full of hate. He would have liked to find the perpetrators of this crime and bring them to justice. But justice in a poor country is subservient to the rich and powerful, and Barrister Noor ul Haq was well aware of that. Although he had fought and won many battles in the court of law, he knew that the odds of getting justice for Sadiq were almost zero. Even if the murderers confessed, no judge who feared the fanatics more than he feared his gods, would allow a conviction to happen.

With his father's rage rising each day, Mansoor worried about how his mother would cope while he was away in America. How would his father muddle through? In Sadiq Mirza, Noor had found intellectual compatibility, despite his peccadilloes; it had always been a treat to hear him speak of Joyce and Woolf, Ghalib and Faiz. Away from the infuriating inanities of Pakistani politics, their discussions had always remained fascinating to Mansoor. Now his father's future without his friend seemed intellectually barren. How would he be diminished by Sadiq's death? Would he rage against his own survival? Would his death precipitate a crisis in him? Mansoor thought about all these questions with anxiety.

Just to be with his father for a little while longer, Mansoor delayed his departure by two more weeks. But that didn't really make much of a difference. Noor had become more detached from his country. His sense of dislocation grew. More than ever, Noor now felt like he was living in a parallel universe, estranged from everything and anything. There were so many wrongs in his father's life that a right could no longer be conceptualized. And then Mansoor began to feel sorry for both his parents. They were both alone in their disengaged worlds, fighting their lonely battles, clinging to their personal crutches. It was only recently that Farhat had found a soulmate in Talat. They shared their marital difficulties, revealed their hates and hurts and confided about their squabbles and sensitivities. Talat had, in a short time, become more of a sister to Farhat than Sarwat ever was. But now, her new friend was also dead.

*

Noor's denunciations of the politics of the corrupt did not bother
Mansoor as much as his inability to show his softer side. He
had been listening to these denunciations ever since he could
remember. It was as if his father's relentless resort to logic had
atrophied his heart muscles. Did he have his own emotional ethos
where rage and disgust were attached effortlessly but love and
empathy remained strenuously aloof?

On the day of Mansoor's departure, Noor was like that
fluorescent light in their garage which, when turned on, flickered
for a moment and then dimmed out. With a poker face and
stony eyes, he bade his son goodbye, and that was all. No hugs,
no handshakes, no tears. Farhat, on the other hand, was an
emotional wreck. She cried all day, hugging Mansoor tightly and
slobbering him with kisses, while Noor rebuked her for making a
scene. Neither came to see him off at the airport. It was Sikander
who dropped him off at the terminal, gave him a hug and cried
irrepressibly.

As Mansoor sat on the airplane, he bade farewell to a life that
had come to a close. Going on an epistemic journey of loneliness,
to a world different in age and temperament, where he knew not
a soul, his heart sank as the airplane ascended into the dark sky.
Mansoor remembered when the travel agent had asked him if he
wanted a one-way ticket or a return. Of course, he could not buy
his return ticket now since he did not know anything about his
return trip. He did not know when he would return home. But does
one ever return home? Aren't all of us on a one-way ticket, going
to a place of no return? What was the point of returning home,
anyway? To recondition our past? To complete the miserable
circle of our miserable lives? Odysseus returned to Ithaca after
ten years, but he never came home. Getting depressed, Mansoor
closed his eyes and thought about Mehrun.

Twenty

It was not until after Mehrun had arrived in Dubai that the reality of her sham marriage kicked in. The first week, they stayed at the Hotel InterContinental in a room with two double beds; she slept on one and he on the other. And the first night, when she tried to crawl into his bed, he rudely sent her back. His apathy towards intimacy had shocked her. She felt cheap and used. Was it her? Was she unappealing? Or was it him? Was he jet-lagged? Was he impotent? The whole night she racked her brain but couldn't come up with an answer. So, the next day, before he left for some meetings, she confronted him.

'I had always heard that the first night is the most romantic night,' she said.

Alvi remained silent, but his silence gave away his secret. He avoided any eye contact, but his unsettled eyes revealed the truth. After he left, Mehrun sat down and tried to read his unsaid messages. And then it finally dawned on her. All those veiled allusions at work, all those hints dropped here and there, the oblique and expressive snickers about him, all of which she had thought were childish, were really a reference to him being impotent. Was he really impotent? But then why did he marry her? Was there any sinister intent behind this arrangement? He seemed like a gentleman. Nothing made sense to her, nothing at all. So when he came back later that afternoon, she mustered more courage and asked him again, just for confirmation.

'Tell me, why don't we . . . I mean, we are husband and wife . . .'

Words betrayed her; thoughts frustrated her. She was scared, ashamed and tongue-tied. A woman just did not ask those sorts of questions. But Alvi knew what was on her mind, and so, to put her mind at ease, he said, 'Look, Mehrunnissa, if you are trying to ask me why we haven't consummated our marriage, I think you know the answer.'

'No . . . No, I don't.'

'Well, I am a bloody *hum-jins parast,* a homosexual. There! There, you have it. It's all in the open now,' he blurted out.

In the whispering corridors, she had overheard echoes of the word 'namard', non-man, meaning impotent, being repeated after Alvi's title. But never before had she heard this Urdu word, which also meant same-sex devotee. It sounded like an ersatz invented word.

'I don't even know what that word means.'

'It means that I like men.'

'Most men like men. What has that got to do with me?'

'I am a bloody homosexual, for god's sake,' Alvi shouted in English.

In one of her discussions with Sadiq about Oscar Wilde's trial, he had expounded the word to her. She hadn't paid much attention then. But now, when her husband confessed his homosexuality, it hit her like the punches she had received from Zaidi and Talat. A distressing stillness permeated the room as Mehrun turned into a catatonic wreck.

'Say something,' Alvi said. But Mehrun kept quiet. Over and over again, he repeated these two words, shaking her shoulders back and forth.

'You knew that it had to be a marriage for the advancement of our respective careers! I thought you knew that. God knows everyone else in the bank knew about it!'

'No! *I* did not know about it,' Mehrun shouted as tears began to roll down her cheeks. 'And how is this marriage going to advance *my* career? I gave up my career for you!'

'Don't start bawling. I needed to marry to accomplish what I want to accomplish. The rumours about me and my . . . preference kept growing and I had to silence my enemies; besides, I was sure that you knew about it.'

'I am sorry I wasn't that smart.'

At that moment, everything began to make sense. Mehrun realized that she was to be Alvi's front, his facade in the world of international banking and finance. To reach the position that he aspired to, he not only had to reveal his banking genius, but the financial wizard also had to show that he was a straight family man.

'What if I want to have children?'

'Don't be silly,' he said dismissively. But a few seconds later, he added, 'Well, if you do want children, you'll have to go somewhere else for that.' He collapsed on his bed, and then continued, 'Look, Mehrunnissa, you have a choice. You can stay with me and preserve my secret, and I promise to provide you with everything you want. I will make you a rich woman. I will make you acceptable in this wretched society . . . I have purchased respectability for myself, and I can do the same for you. You can do anything you want, enjoy life, be happy . . . you will have most of the freedoms that modern Pakistani women have, maybe more . . . But if you feel betrayed and you want a divorce, you can have that too. I can pay back your mehr right now and buy you a one-way ticket for the next flight home.'

With that, Alvi pulled out his chequebook and looked at her questioningly.

Mehrun snorted. She turned her face towards the window. So that *was* my bride price, a measly one hundred and twenty-five rupees, half paid at the time of marriage, half due at divorce. That is why you married me, because I could be bought dirt cheap, she thought.

Alvi got up from his bed and came towards Mehrun. Thrusting out a minatory forefinger, he said, 'But let me also warn you, if you ever reveal my secret to anyone, I will destroy you like I have destroyed those brilliant banking minds of Pakistan.'

What a man! So generous in the choices he gives me, she thought. He wanted her to make a decision about whether she wanted a divorce or not, then and there, without delay, just like he had wanted her to make the decision about their marriage, then and there. She could not understand how a man who was so meticulous in his professional career could be so reckless in his personal relationships. This sordid slant to his personality was new to her, and his matter-of-fact approach to their bogus marriage jolted her. Her lips still quivering and her heart still thumping, she felt vanquished by a sinking feeling. Without saying a word to him, she rushed into the bathroom, locked herself in and prostrated herself on the tiled bathroom floor in a violent paroxysm of sobbing.

Mehrun stayed in that position until she could cry no longer. She got up and looked in the mirror, expecting to see the churail, but the churail was nowhere in sight. Wouldn't this be a perfect time for that wretched creature to reappear and harass her? To taunt her and make fun of her life? And this time, Mehrun waited for her as if her arrival were a foregone conclusion. But the churail never came, and Mehrun felt forsaken entirely. In your time of need, she thought, it is not only your friends who betray you, but your tormentors abandon you as well. Frustrated and tired, she washed her face and dried it with the thick towel on the rack. When she came out of the bathroom. Alvi had left. She didn't know where he had gone, and she couldn't care less. She called the front desk and ordered a cup of tea. At that moment, she desired Mansoor's presence, the only friend whom she could trust, but then she had left him with only a quick good-bye phone call.

A bearer in a crisp white uniform and a red cummerbund brought her the tea tray. Pouring the tea from a silver teapot, the man ogled at her with his creepy, denuding glances, making her eyebrows twitch. After he left, she took her brew and sat on the wing chair near the window. The setting sun arched towards the horizon, bathing the earth in its glow and agonizing Mehrun. She turned off the air conditioner and opened the windows, letting in the desert air to freshen the room. With the windows open, the room became alive to the urban racket outside—horns blaring, brakes screeching, people talking and shouting. Way down below her fifth-floor window, she saw Arabs in their white flowing robes hobnobbing with Westerners in their dark suits, and people from India and Pakistan in their native dresses, roaming on the streets. The allure of oil money had mixed and matched people of all nationalities and social classes.

This nature-neglected country, now nourished by oil, had turned into a major hub of global finance. The town, inhabited by impoverished Bedouins who braved the desert heat on their camels' backs until a few years ago, was now populated by flamboyant sheikhs who subjugated the scorching desert heat in the backseats of their chauffeur-driven Bentleys and Jaguars. It was a town that bustled with activity, where power was brokered and deals were made. It was the perfect place for a man like Ameer Abbas Alvi to rearrange the monetary order.

As Mehrun glanced at life on the streets, she thought about her new life up here in the luxurious hotel room and how it had come to a screaming halt. She turned away from the window and returned to a rococo chair in one corner of the room. Darkness began to invade the room, but Mehrun did not feel like turning on the light. She had to get used to this new darkness, this obscure turn. And as she sat there all alone, Mehrun reached a decision. Remaining a victim was no longer an option for her. She was not going to take things lying down; she was ready to play this game on her own terms. She had no other alternative. Her life in Pakistan was finished. She could never get another job at another bank there. Going back to washing dishes and dusting rooms was

no longer part of her life plan either. Besides, what was the future
of a destitute divorced woman anywhere? No, she was not going to
let this 'opportunity' go by. She would swallow her pride, confront
her life and take this bull by the horns; she was going to accept
her homosexual husband on her terms and then . . . and then, she
did not know what her future would be beyond that. With her old
confidence back, she decided to leave the past, not worry about the
future and relish the present.

That night, Alvi came back to the room slightly drunk, and
Mehrun smelt the liquor on his breath. It reminded her of her
father's breath when he drank the crude, home-made spirits.
Mehrun only said two things to Alvi—she did not want a divorce
and that she hadn't had dinner. And he said, 'Good, I haven't had
any either.'

The silent agreement thus made, the unsigned contract thus
attested, he told Mehrun to change her clothes so that he could
take her out for a nice dinner. She obliged him and wore her pink
chiffon saree, the most beautiful one in her new wardrobe, and
then, like a shy bride, went downstairs with him. The charade had
begun, the curtains had been raised and Mehrun became a willing
performer in the dissolving drama of her marriage to Triple-A.

*

Joseph delayed his return to Pakistan by six months. And when
he eventually came, it was because he had been cashiered. But he
did not tell anyone about this. The signs of a revolution in Iran
had begun appearing early on, and the Shah of Iran dealt with the
agitators harshly—first it was the subversives and then it was the
foreigners, especially those with darker skins. And Joseph became
an unfortunate casualty to this reprisal. But before he departed, he
went to see his American friend, Peter Dawber, and dramatized
his sob story. Dawber, a senior executive at the oil company, felt
sorry for Joseph and promised to find him a job in the company

in Texas when he returned to America. Joseph gave him the Kashana's address, care of Mansoor ul Haq.

When he returned to Karachi, Joseph went straight to the Kashana and pleaded with Noor to let him stay there once again for a few months, till he got his call from America. Noor doubted his story but allowed him to stay for two months in the servants' quarters where Jumman had moved in. When Noor asked him why he did not go to his mother's house in Punjab, he replied, 'Sahib, my mother got married to my father's worst enemy. I have cut all ties with her.'

Jumman, however, was reluctant to share his quarters with a bhangi, albeit a *vilayat-palat*, a foreign-returned bhangi.

'But Jumman Chacha, I am not a bhangi any more!' Joseph protested.

Joseph had called him chacha many times before, and Jumman had never cared about it. After all, everyone else in his old neighbourhood had started calling him chacha after his beard turned prematurely white.

'*Abey* harami, bloody harami, even if you bathe in the Ganga a thousand and one times, you will still remain a bhangi. Your grandfather was a bhangi, your father was a bhangi and you are a bhangi. You will always remain a bhangi, saley,' replied Jumman.

'But, Chacha, I have become a Muslim,' Joseph deflected Jumman's insults and tried to hide the blot of his being a bhangi by lying about his conversion to Islam. But that did not work either. So Joseph tried the only fail-proof strategy he could think of: bribery. He offered to pay Jumman a rent of twenty-five rupees a month, which Jumman gladly accepted. And with the stigma of untouchability thus laundered by lucre, Joseph became a subtenant of Jumman, unbeknownst to Noor or Farhat.

Every day, Joseph waited impatiently for the postman, but the letter from Peter Dawber remained elusive. The money he had saved from working in the oil refinery would sustain him for a few months. He had faith that Dawber would eventually come through with his promise. And soon enough, just like old times, he began his weekly pilgrimage to Sona Mandi and the cinema halls. Jumman and Budhoo were puzzled about his sudden interest in English movies, but Joseph convinced them that it was purely educational.

'I want to talk like a motherfucking *firangi*, like a foreigner,' he declared.

Of course, it was not his love of the English language alone that drove him to those tantalizing cinema halls. His disorderly hormones shoved him equally hard. Deprived of sex and porn flicks since his return from Iran, Joseph checked out his former purlieu, Premier Talkies, where the movie *Samson and Delilah* was doing roaring business with a sell-out crowd. Before he left for Iran, he had become good friends with one of the ticket clerks, who, for two rupees, would reveal to Joseph the days when they were going to embed longer pornographic clips in the featured film.

Although he had seen the movie three times already, Joseph went again. The last two times, the management had inserted bits of hardcore pornography between the scenes, and Joseph was sure of scoring a hat-trick this time. But it did not happen. For some reason, the cinema hall bosses did not play any pornographic scenes that day, thus disappointing Joseph severely. Not only did they not include the totay, but as if to send Joseph's hormones into a complete tailspin, they also censored the kissing scenes that were there in the movie. Joseph seethed in anger.

'These haramis did not even show a single kiss!' he vented his rage to the guy next to him and continued, 'What do they expect me to do with this?' he pointed towards his crotch. 'Cut it off and throw it in the fucking gutter?' His neighbour was equally disappointed. 'I wasted five rupees on this motherfucking movie for nothing!' But he suggested another cinema hall to Joseph where they showed doctored movies with nude clips of a flop Pakistani actress. That seemed to pacify Joseph and he decided to try his luck there the next day.

As he came out of the cinema hall, he noticed a motley crowd demonstrating and yelling slogans outside. Within seconds, even as he stood there watching the scene, the angry mob began pelting stones at the theatre. The demonstrators shattered the newly installed windows of the cinema. At first, Joseph thought that they, too, were protesting against the management for not showing any pornographic bits, but he soon realized that they were inveighing against *Samson and Delilah*. With the possibility of a riot looming large, he quickly turned around and sneaked out of the back door, but his curiosity brought him back to the crowd. He came and stood next to a man with a placard that said, 'Don't Ensult Our Riligion! No Samsung No Dilaala!'

'What's going on?' Joseph asked.

'They have not only shown one of our prophets; they have also shown him kissing!'

'Which prophet is that?'

'Hazrat Shamoon, peace be upon him.'

'But there is no Hazrat Shamoon in the movie!'

'You idiot, Samsung *is* Hazrat Shamoon. I have seen the movie, but I didn't know it then,' the man said.

After hundreds of showings of the movie going unnoticed, somebody had informed the public that the hero of the story was not just a Judea-Christian prophet, but also an Islamic prophet mentioned in the Qur'an. And *that* incensed the public since it was a grave sin to show images of prophets, kissing prophets no less.

Having had his curiosity satisfied, Joseph left the scene in a hurry on a motor rickshaw, knowing that it would get ugly there, and he was right. A little after he left, the angry crowd beat up the staff and the manager and then torched the cinema hall. The G.O.D.s exploited the situation and tried to destabilize the government, which, in turn, promptly banned the movie.

The movie that had been shown hundreds of times was now declared insulting to religion.

*

Two and a half months passed by, but Joseph heard nothing from Dawber. Idleness and boredom made him a pest, and he began getting on everybody's nerves. In the meantime, Farhat made his life difficult by constantly encouraging him to move out of the servants' quarters. Just as Noor had done the last time, he had not consulted her again about letting Joseph stay, and she felt slighted.

'Why can't he stay with his relatives in Bhangi Para?' she asked Jumman.

'Begum Sahiba, he says all his relatives are dead and rotting in hell, and he doesn't want to go there.'

'He is a liar, and he is lazy. Tell him to find a job and move out of here by the end of this month.'

When Jumman announced this new deadline to Joseph, he became angry with Farhat and cursed her under his breath. He decided that if he did not get the letter soon, he would move to Lahore and try to find a job there, may be in the movies. But the long-awaited letter finally arrived, just five days before Farhat's deadline. Joseph was ecstatic. Dawber apologized for not writing sooner. He was waiting for everything to get confirmed before sending him the letter.

Along with the personal note, Dawber sent an official letter of employment not from the oil company, but from himself. It appeared that he had recently opened a Pakistani-Indian restaurant and he wanted to hire Joseph as his head chef for an annual salary of $10,000. This was news to Joseph, but then who was he to argue when so much money was at stake? Dawber had often suggested that he should open a Pakistani restaurant in Iran, but he had never hinted at his plans to open one himself, and that too in Houston, Texas. It did not matter to Joseph what the job was as long as he could go to America. After watching countless Hollywood flicks, America had become his latest fixation.

With the letter in his hand and a Rajesh Khanna song on his lips, he set off to the American consulate, where he was told that there was no possibility of an interview for at least another month. Disappointed, he went to see Noor, but Noor had no contacts at the consulate. He, however, directed Joseph to Zakir. While all of this was going on, Joseph got a telegram from Dawber, asking him to hold off on everything and not come to America till he sent another telegram. Joseph tore the telegram up and went to see Zakir anyway. He showed him Dawber's letter. At first, Zakir was reluctant to help him, not because of Joseph's lineage but because the authenticity of that piece of correspondence looked suspicious to him. But Joseph convinced him, and among many other canards, told him that he had converted to Islam, while in Iran.

'By the grace of Allah, I am a Muslim now and no longer a bhangi.'

'I don't believe you. Recite the kalimah for me.'

To pass off as a Muslim in Iran, Joseph had, in fact, memorized the kalimah, the two-line profession of faith. So without any hesitation, he recited it in his accented Punjabi.

'Praise to Allah. This is a momentous change, Joseph!'

Thoroughly impressed, Zakir promised to help him, but on one condition. 'My bhangi has run away and I want you to find me a reliable bhangi.'

'Sahib, I will send you a white bhangi from Umreeka; he will be more reliable than any kaloo bhangi, Sahib.'

'No, I want a kaloo bhangi, okay?'

Joseph nodded his head, happy that his odds of going to America had just multiplied. The next day, Zakir contacted his friends at the American embassy and arranged the interview for Joseph.

*

With his quick wit and flattery, Joseph regaled the interviewer and obtained the most sought-after visa. Now there was only one glitch: he was short of money. Having squandered most of his money on movies and brothels, and after paying rent to Jumman, Joseph had nothing left for the trip. He needed ten thousand rupees for the airfare alone. His only hope for a bailout was Noor. So, he called the barrister's secretary at his office and arranged a meeting. This would be his most important meeting with him. He spent the whole day enacting the scene, rehearsing the dialogues and anticipating the questions, for this was his chance to kill two birds with one stone: to give the performance of his life and to obtain the money. The next day, after eating a hearty breakfast, he went to see Noor at his office. The minute Joseph was summoned into the office, he began his act. But Noor interrupted him immediately.

'Don't start your acting. Just get to the point, Joseph,' he frowned impatiently.

'Sahib, I need ten thousand rupees. Please give it to me as a loan, Sahib. I will return it to you very soon. I have eaten your salt, Sahib; I have lived under your roof. Please don't disappoint me, Sahib.'

Noor pressed the button on his intercom and spoke into the machine in his clipped English, 'Mr Siddique, please come to my office at once.'

Convinced that he was about to be thrown out of the office, Joseph pleaded for mercy, 'Sahib, if you can't give me the money, I can try my luck somewhere else, but don't throw me out!' He began to walk back towards the door to leave the barrister's office.

'Stop, you donkey! Where do you think you are going?' Noor thundered.

Before Joseph could reply, the office door opened and a bespectacled man entered the room.

'Siddique Sahib, go to the bank with Joseph and give him twelve thousand rupees,' Noor told the man brusquely.

Joseph was dumbstruck. He was so moved by the barrister's generosity that he started to blubber and rushed to touch his feet, but Noor stopped him and said, 'Don't create a spectacle . . . just get the money and go.'

*

When he reached Houston, Joseph obviously did not expect Dawber to be at the airport, but he telephoned him nonetheless, feigning surprise at not finding him at the airport. Dawber, too, was surprised to hear Joseph calling him from the airport; he had assumed that Joseph had received his telegram.

'Didn't you get my telegram?' he asked.

'What telegram, Sahib?'

'Well, I had sent you a . . . never mind, just wait at the airport. I'll come and pick you up.'

It took Dawber forty-five minutes to reach the airport. On their way back to his house, he told Joseph that he *had been* planning to start a Pakistani-Indian restaurant in Houston in partnership with a colleague from Pakistan. But when the deal fell through at the last minute, he had rushed him another telegram asking him not to come, at least not for the time being. Dawber felt terrible that Joseph had ended up coming to America for nothing and he promised to help him find a job. Feeling guilty, Dawber also let him stay at his sprawling house in the suburbs of Houston.

Joseph hung around at Dawber's house for a week, trying to luxuriate in his stylish splendour, getting used to the comforts that never visited him. But the longer he stayed there, the more uncomfortable he became. Opulence did not suit him.

The American economy had fallen into a deep recession, and that made it difficult for Dawber to help his uninvited guest find a decent job. But Joseph, as it turned out, did not need his help since he found work flipping hamburgers at a Burger King restaurant. And once he learned the nuances of working at a fast-food place, he began searching for an apartment. Luckily, his manager owned a decrepit house, infested as it was with rats, in downtown Houston, just two blocks from his workplace. He rented it out to Joseph. But this dilapidated house—a luxury compared to his one-room mud shack in Pakistan—was all he needed. Determined to drag himself out of this situation, Joseph worked long, hard hours, reminding himself that this would be his temporary abode. When he found out that it took only a few days and little money to get a telephone, he immediately applied for one at the nearest AT&T office. After procuring the phone, the first thing he did was to call Mansoor, whose number he had acquired from Noor. His friend was pleasantly surprised to hear his loud Punjabi voice again. Talking to Mansoor regularly became Joseph's favourite pastime.

Twenty-One

Mansoor did not attune well to life in Iowa. The frigid winter, the hog reports on the radio and the narrow provinciality of the ordinary Iowans made him miserable. For the first two semesters, he stayed in university housing; after that, he rented a one-bedroom apartment, a short walk from the campus. The university attracted students from all over the world, including Pakistan and India, but Mansoor did not mix with them. An introvert by nature, he made several acquaintances but no friends. The rigours of the semester system made his academic load onerous, and so he made the university library his main hang-out. His goal was to complete his degree in the shortest possible time. Overloading himself with courses, he finished the requirements in a year and a half.

He invited his parents to his graduation ceremony, but only Noor came. Seeing his father come out of the arrivals hall of Chicago's O'Hare Airport all alone, Mansoor became upset. He had explicitly written to his father and asked him to bring his mother as well, especially since she had never ventured out of Pakistan. Had his father ignored his request or had his mother deliberately chosen not to come? As they exited the airport, Mansoor asked him, 'Why didn't you bring Amma?'

'She doesn't like to travel,' he replied.

That was surprising since Mansoor knew that Farhat had always wanted to visit places. Her only trip outside Karachi had been the one she had taken with her sister to the historical city of Lahore, when Zahid lived there as a student. Was Noor embarrassed to bring her with him? Did he think that she would be his excess baggage?

'How is she doing?' Mansoor asked.

'She is fine; she has become very religious since her illness.'

'What illness?'

The word 'illness' had inadvertently slipped out of Noor's mouth. He had not told Mansoor about Farhat's hysterectomy, and the news shocked him now. Distressed by his mother's surgery and angered at being kept in the dark, he raised his voice at his father for the first time in his life.

'Why did you hide it from me?'

'I didn't hide it from you; I just didn't want to upset your studies.'

His father did not say 'upset you' but 'upset your studies'. His choice of words was inhibiting, the most important word, *you*, was clearly besides the point. Mansoor felt hurt.

'I know that you didn't want to upset me, but I am an adult and I know how to handle worrying news. You should have written to me about Amma's surgery. She must be thinking how uncaring I am for not even writing to her about it.' For the first time in his life, Mansoor lectured his father and it felt good.

'Well, it was her wish as well . . . to not inform you.' Noor tried to deflect the blame on to his wife.

*

It rained during Mansoor's graduation ceremony. Noor sat alone, hunched and miserable, in the parents' gallery. He should have savoured his son's success, but the Pomp and Circumstance were not for him.

That night, Mansoor wanted to take his father out for a nice steak dinner, but Noor turned him down, using the tedious rain as an excuse. For someone who came from a rain-starved Karachi, a little rain should have been nothing to complain about. But Noor insisted that he did not want to go out in the rain. Just a simple omelette or scrambled eggs was what he wanted. So, they stayed home.

While Mansoor beat the eggs in his kitchen, his father looked at the rain hitting the living room window. In his right hand, he held a glass of whisky. He turned around, lowered his head and timidly apologized to Mansoor for keeping the news of Farhat's surgery from him. For a while, Noor stayed there in the living room, not knowing what to do. He then moved to the kitchen, lost in his thoughts, and stood watching his son prepare the eggs. He opened his mouth to say something, but then said nothing, as if the moment was not right.

'Abba, is everything okay?'

Noor shrugged his shoulders in response. Mansoor knew that his father wanted to talk about something, something important. Once dinner was over, Mansoor made a gin and tonic for himself and offered the same to his father. But Noor only drank whisky. Slowly, he eased his father into opening up about what was bothering him. Noor began complaining about Farhat's religiosity, her superstitions, her ignorance and her blaming him for everything wrong in her life. Although he did not spell it out, it was also about his self-isolation.

With Sadiq's horrific murder, Haider's betrayal of his principles and Zakir's regressive certitude in matters of faith, Noor's loneliness was complete. When Mansoor had been in Pakistan, he had felt his father's pain and had listened to his cynicism, but with him no longer there, Noor's social cord had been permanently cut off. In lampooning the grotesque politicians who ran the country, he found himself not only rejecting Pakistan, but also utterly abandoned.

Mansoor had never seriously reflected on his father's 'regrettable citizenship'. Was his Abba still grieving for the India that he had lost? For the home that he had to flee from, the dreams that had dissipated? And what could he say about his life with Farhat? Tradition had wedded them, but their conflicting natures had separated them. Love had little traction in their conventional marriage; it was merely a Plan B, one concocted by their respective parents.

Suddenly, Mansoor's ears perked up when he heard the name Khaleel Khan.

'What did you say?'

'I said your mother is turning into a zealot.'

'No, what did you say about Khaleel?'

'I said people like your nincompoop cousin Khaleel Khan and that troglodyte Zakir Hassan fan her extremism.'

'Extremism? What do you mean?' Mansoor asked.

'Well, your mother's life nowadays revolves around a very harsh belief system. She performs all the rituals, which I don't mind, but then she goes to that bloody fool Zakir's house for his weekly sermons. He has become her spiritual mentor. He incites her, and she criticizes my every habit and blames me for her past sins,' he said, making air quotes when he uttered the words 'past sins'.

'What past sins?' Mansoor asked.

'She says that I prevented her from performing her religious obligations in the past. She blames me for never taking her to perform hajj. She even blames me for all her miscarriages.'

'But why?'

'I don't know why she blames me for everything, but I have never ever imposed my beliefs on her or on anyone else. I never forbade her from practicing her faith. And if I had taken her for hajj, I would have felt like a total fraud. Why should I do something that I do not believe in? I told her that I would pay for her trip if she found someone to go with.' He stopped, gulped his drink and continued, 'She nags me about my drinking, she pesters me about my beliefs, and she accuses me of corrupting you . . . The other night, she asked me if I believed in the existence of God.'

'What did you say?'

'I got really angry and just told her off. I didn't want to have a theological discussion with a . . .' Noor's voiced trailed off.

Mansoor had heard his father's explanation about his non-belief. His father didn't believe in the supernatural. Human existence was just brain chemistry according to him—the firing of neurones and the synaptic connections. Take away the brain, and you take away the being. Religion, to him, was nothing but wishes and fears.

'So what's Athanni's role in all this?' Mansoor asked.

Noor laughed when he heard Khaleel's nickname. Mansoor had told him why Joseph had coined that sobriquet.

'Khaleel Khan has become Zakir's trusted lieutenant. You know he was fired from his job?'

'I knew that he was fired, but I didn't know that he works for Uncle Zakir now.'

'I don't think that's his full-time job. Haider told me that Khaleel has found work as a photographer for the *Daily Hulchul*,' Noor told him.

'That's a perfect fit, Maulvi Athanni, a tabloid journalist,' Mansoor said.

It was getting late, and Mansoor realized that his father's crapulous recollections were making him sentimental. He felt sorry for him. Sitting there across from him, Noor cut a figure of lonely irrelevance to his wife, to his friends and to his country—a grim relic of disconnection, stranded in his own time zone. The Unholy Quartet had collapsed; his wife of nearly fifty years had openly rebelled and there was nobody who could commiserate with him, nobody who could share his angst. That was the oppressive cruelty of his life in Pakistan.

*

Mansoor was in no mood to start his doctorate immediately; he wanted to take some time off to see the world, but his father tried his best to veto that.

'You will have plenty of opportunities to see the world, but I won't be there to support your studies for long. I can continue to support you for now, but if I retire, as I am planning to, I may not be able to support you later,' Mansoor's father told him.

'But, Abba, I'm not sure if I want to do a PhD, and even if I do go for it, I would like to do it on my own, without your financial help.'

A blank expression suddenly appeared on Noor's face. He sighed and turned his body sideways, as if avoiding his son.

'Abba, I didn't mean to hurt your feelings. I am sorry.'

Noor pursed his lips. He appeared deep in thought for a moment; then he turned his head towards Mansoor and said, 'Look, son, I am supporting you not because I have to, but because I want to. I am one of the highest-paid lawyers in Pakistan, and I can easily afford to support you. Everything that I have belongs to you and your mother. So even if you can support yourself, let me continue to send the money anyway. If you don't need it right away, you can save it for the future. In any case, the money will have more value here in America than it will back in your country.'

'Let's talk about it later. I just finished my master's degree. I need time to think.'

They didn't talk about it at all, and Noor, after staying for only ten days, left for Karachi. In his presence, Mansoor had felt stifled, but the day he left, he missed him sorely. Old age had finally defeated his father. His tall frame now slightly bent, his salt-and-pepper hair completely grey, his eyelids darkening and the sagging skin under his chin, all publicized the onset of his autumnal years.

*

It was Haider who had told Mansoor about Zakir's new mission: reminding people to become better Muslims. Like a true evangelist, he would wake up seven people every morning for the predawn Fajr prayers and would give fragmented sermons to them. But his mission expanded from waking up people for the predawn prayers to warning them about the menace of 'Faithian Socialism' and creeping secularism. As he extended his base from the mosques to the corporate offices of Karachi and Lahore, Zakir's fame spread and countless people became his devotees, including Farhat and Nawab Khan Namaqul's family. Prestige, power and glory grazed his feet, and he moved people with his rhapsodic speeches. As a diplomat, he had learnt several foreign languages, and his ability to fluently move from Urdu to Arabic to English and French made him a unique preacher—the likes of whom people had never seen before. He enjoyed the limelight and relished the attention; it fanned his ego and sustained his mission. For him, conviction demanded certainty; there could be no doubt in religion. Faith made us human; secularism made us animals. He had been both, so he knew what he was talking about. Zakir spoke to his followers with a forbidding rigidity; the sterner his sermons became, the more following he gained.

To Noor, Zakir had transformed into a dangerous demagogue, a charlatan who was probably on the payroll of a foreign government. The founding member of The Unholy Quartet, who regularly toasted Scotch and pledged to always remain unholy and secular, had now become sanctimonious.

To Farhat, however, Zakir was the quintessential true Muslim who had found the light, who had saved himself from eternal damnation, and maybe, just maybe, he could do the same for her wayward husband. And that was how Zakir's house became her new hang-out, and Athanni, his right-hand man, gladly drove Farhat there. It was here that *Bhabi* Farhat received special treatment. Zakir had always referred to her as bhabi, meaning sister-in-law, a term that is commonly used in Pakistan and India as a mark of respect for a friend's wife.

*

Every afternoon, men and women congregated in Zakir's
magnificent drawing room and offered the midday prayer,
the women behind the men, all prostrating synchronously, all
supplicating earnestly. After the prayer, the women went to
the zenana while the men stayed in the drawing room. From a
microphone that connected both the rooms, Zakir ladled out his
latest dollops of homilies with the delight of a new convert. And
after the pious dramaturgy, he answered questions. One day, he
talked about drinking.

'In the dark times, known as *Jahiliyyah*, there were many vices.
Two that were out of control were gambling and drinking. But our
faith gradually outlawed them. I have lived in decadent America,
my brothers and sisters, and I have survived corrupt Europe; they
are the dens of debauchery. Gambling, prostitution and alcohol
are their gods. I know that some of our brothers are involved in
those depravities; in fact, some of my best friends still indulge in
them.'

When Zakir said 'best friends', Farhat knew he was talking
about Noor; her head went down in shame and trickles of tears
coursed down her cheeks.

'I am ashamed to say that I, too, once strayed from the path,
brothers and sisters. I, too, lost my sense, my peace and my soul.
I, too, acquired a taste for that forbidden drink. My head spun
with pride and my heart throbbed with greed. I became the gravest
sinner of all, the most serious evildoer. But one day, I had an *ilham*;
in English, they call it an epiphany. God picked me up from that
street littered with offal and put me on the true path. I gave up
that life; I escaped the path of evil and left the company of sinners.
And by the grace of God, I am at that stage in my life when I am at
peace with myself and with God. My message to all of those who
drink is this: avoid it, give it up. Break that bottle of sin, for it is
the *mother* of all evil. Alcohol is the enemy of faith; they cannot be
mixed together; they cannot live in the same heart. If you know a
brother who drinks, beseech him to give it up. If you see a bottle

of alcohol, drain down the poison and shatter the bottle. A house where liquor is kept is a house of shame, a house of sin; it's a cursed house where Allah's blessings are absent.'

That day, Farhat came back home with a firm resolve. Taking the alcohol bottles out from her husband's liquor cabinet, she emptied them into the toilet—Royal Salute, Chivas Regal, Rémy Martin, all flushed down the gutter.

'It looks like urine, it smells like urine and now it goes down the toilet like urine,' she muttered to herself in her frenzy, her hands trembling, beads of sweat trickling down her cheeks.

The thought that her husband drank something that looked and stank like urine made her throw up, and with her vomit now mixed with it, she flushed thousands of rupees worth of whisky and brandy with apostolic zeal. It was as though she had drained all the family sins down the toilet.

After emptying the bottles, she ordered Budhoo to smash them to pieces and throw them away. She then went back to the bathroom, where the stench of alcohol and vomit still hung resolutely, and opened the window. She brought in a pedestal fan and turned it on, full speed, to force the smell out. Now she needed to cleanse her body because she had touched that uriniferous drink. In the bathroom in the zenana, Farhat took a long shower, performing her ablutions seven times, until her sins-by-association were wholly washed away. She put on a fresh pair of shalwar-kameez, offered the prayer of thanksgiving and asked for God's forgiveness.

That night, she slept restlessly. The house was cleansed of the 'bottles of wickedness', but her heart was filled with fear chewing her entrails. With Noor in Iowa, however, she had the luxury of time before his wrath descended on her head.

The next day, she went to Zakir's house early and confided in him about what she had done and about her fear of her husband.

'Bhabi, I know Noor. I know you are scared of his temper, but if you fill your heart with only one fear, the fear of God, believe me, you will liberate yourself of all other fears. You can withstand any scolding, you can buck any rebuke, any berating,' he said.

But Farhat remained apprehensive and her heart continued to pound nervously.

That day Zakir spoke about scepticism and faith in his sermon. Doubt should never reside in a faithful's heart. Belief requires certainty. Anyone doubting or rejecting the basic tenets of the faith, through words, deeds or thoughts, was an apostate. 'And that, my brothers and sisters, is no laughing matter because apostasy means death. An apostate must die and burn in the eternal fire of dozakh,' the preacher thundered.

By the time Farhat returned home, she was shivering, as if suffering from the contagion of impiety. She had never directly asked about her husband's beliefs and he had never clarified anything. However much he ridiculed the mullahs, he never blasphemed against religion, at least not in front of her. She had often heard him say that of all the human frailties that existed, convictions without evidence were the most perverse. Should she confront him or just leave it at that? Should she reason with him? She must seek help from her new sage.

So, the following day, she went to Zakir's house again, early enough to have a confidential audience with him. As she sat in the women's quarter, she asked Begum Hassan if she could talk privately with her husband. Farhat's discussions were becoming more like confessionals behind the curtain. Mrs Hassan willingly obliged her and went to get her husband. She knew Noor well; she knew about his habits and his beliefs. Not too long ago, her husband had also been a part of this ugly landscape, and so sympathy for Farhat came naturally to her. Zakir came as soon as he heard about Farhat waiting for him and announced himself from the other side of the curtain that divided the zenana.

'Bhabi, I have known Noor since our student days. I do not know what is in his heart now, but I know that not too long ago, his heart was filled with doubt and disbelief. But maybe he has changed. Ask him directly about all the elements of faith. Because, let me tell you candidly, if he does not believe in any of these, then he *is* an apostate. And then your nikah with him is null and void. As a matter of fact, if he openly disavows his faith, then your marriage is automatically annulled. You will be guilty of *zina*, and so will he.'

When Farhat heard the Urdu word for fornication, she clamped her hands over her ears and shook her head vigorously. Not long ago, Zakir would have concurred with Noor that this was the most minimalist definition of fornication. But not now. Now it was simply a matter-of-fact, no-nonsense explanation. The irritating sore that had festered for so long was now becoming a full-blown malady of the heart. In Zakir's freshly minted unencumbered mind, Noor epitomized all that was evil in the country. His other former friends, like Haider, were all lapsed Muslims who occasionally went off on a drinking spree, but not Noor. For quite some time now, Noor had become persona non grata in Zakir's books. How Zakir came to develop such a militant view of his ex-friend was something that even Haider could not fathom. The man who had cried uncontrollably at Sadiq's murder now believed that it 'could be a justifiable homicide'. When Haider heard this austere verdict, he too began shunning him like Noor.

That day, throughout the sermon, the word 'zina' kept reverberating in Farhat's ears. She did not know what to do or how to confront Noor. A sinister fear lurked in her heart: what if he actually did not believe in any of these things? What would she do? How would she live? When she began hyperventilating, Zakir's wife called Athanni and told him to immediately take her home. At home, Farhat spread the prayer rug in the zenana and earnestly begged God to show her husband the correct path. All night she prayed, and the next day she fasted. When she finally fell asleep the following night, she dreamt of her wedding day.

Noor had looked handsome in his white sherwani, and at the time of the nikah, when the maulvi had asked him if he was a Muslim, he had answered: '*Alhamdolillah*, praise be to Allah.' She woke up from her brief slumber, content and happy, for the dream was a clear sign from God that her husband had seen the enlightened path. She knew that her prayers had been answered, and why not? After all, the house was free of alcohol.

*

On the day of her husband's arrival from America, Farhat felt better, confident that he had changed. The message in her dream could not have been any clearer. She sent Sikander to pick him up from the airport. But when Noor arrived home, her hopes shattered to pieces. He was drunk again. She threw a fit so intense that Noor's blood alcohol level dropped quickly. Shocked and jolted, he was caught completely off guard. There in front of him was his wife, her head covered in a hijab, her mouth full of insults, her hands out of control; she pushed him so hard that he fell and hit his head on the edge of the bedside table. Blood trickled from his forehead. Was this a new sort of a welcome? Who *was* that woman? Had he somehow come to a different house? He took out his handkerchief. Pressed it against his forehead and surveyed his surroundings. But he found nothing bizarre, nothing odd. Before he could say anything, Farhat shoved him out of her bedroom and locked the door. Jet-lagged and confused, Noor staggered to the men's quarter and slept fitfully, still dressed in his travel clothes.

The next day when he woke up, it was high noon. His head throbbed with intense pain as he went to his bedroom to check on his wife. But Budhoo told him that she had already left for the sermon. Noor tried recalling the events of the previous night, but all he could remember were the incoherent curses of this woman who had stood gesticulating wildly in a hijab, and the banging of his head on the edge of his bedside table. He checked his forehead;

the blood had congealed, but his head still hurt. Ashamed and confused, Noor dragged himself to take a shower in an attempt to revive himself. It didn't help. Feeling hungry, he called Budhoo to bring his lunch. Noor had eaten alone in the past, but he had never felt so lonely and miserable. He thought about his increasingly frayed relationship with his wife. What had got him to this point?

Farhat came home that evening, her eyes red and swollen.

'What happened to you? Why were you shouting at me last night?' Noor asked her somewhat fearfully, but she remained silent.

'Won't you even ask me how your son is? What have I done to deserve this?'

'You were drunk last night, weren't you?' she asked at last.

'So what's new about that? It was a twenty-three-hour flight and I drank a little more than usual to fight the fatigue and the boredom.'

'Well, now you won't be able to drink at all because I have flushed all your bottles down the toilet.'

At first, Noor did not understand what she was talking about, but then as she went on and on about Satan's urine being flushed down the toilet, he went to check on her bluff. And the next thing Farhat saw was his red, contorted face bursting with anger. But Noor restrained himself. Calmly, he approached her and asked, 'Do you know the value of all the bottles that were in that liquor cabinet?'

'Yes, equal to an eternity in dozakh.'

'Don't you *dare* talk to me like that. Don't you dare talk to me like I am a child or a . . . I have been very patient with your nonsense,' Noor paused and took a long deep breath, and then he continued, 'and get rid of this . . . this . . . this thing off your head; you look like a bloody nun.'

His temper had returned, but Farhat remained defiant and said, 'I don't tell you what to do, and I don't want *you* to tell me what to do from now on.'

'You don't tell me what to do? You just broke all my bottles. Listen to me, and listen with your ears open: I am the master of this house, and you are going to do whatever I tell you to do,' he growled.

'I am not going to blindly jump into a well if you tell me to.'

'Do not talk like an illiterate woman. I have never put any undue pressures on you. You can do anything as long as it is within reason, but wearing a hijab is against everything I stand for.'

As Farhat stormed out of the bedroom, Noor felt that he was standing face-to-face with irrationality and bafflement. He did not know what had come over his wife. Was it a new-found fervency? Or was it that she was in love with Zakir? The first possibility seemed likely, and it made him anxious. The second possibility, no longer remote, seemed a little irrational to him. But then there was no love between Noor and his wife to lose, and that realization made him anxious.

*

That night, even though she did not want to confront him any more, Farhat's head swirled with uncertainty and her heart sank with fear. The word 'zina' and Zakir's explicit pronouncement echoed in her mind: 'Your nikah with him is null and void. Your nikah with him is null and void.' One of these days, she would have to put the question about Noor's true beliefs before him; she could not live the life of a fornicator.

Twenty-Two

Farhat rejoiced when The People's Leader, who relished his Royal Salute, banned alcohol to appease the religious parties. Earlier on, when he had stoked latent hostilities between the muhajirs and the Sindhis, the sons of the soil, she had called him *ullu ka patha*, literally the son of an owl, a mild imprecation. Unlike her husband, she called Pakistan her *watan*, her homeland. So why was religion no longer a binding force? Did Pakistan, as a metaphor for the greater religious community, suddenly lose its meaning? Why was she still called an immigrant after having lived almost half her life in Pakistan? And what about Mansoor, who was born in Sindh?

But now The People's Leader was in Farhat's good books again—the alcohol prohibition trumping the sectarian controversy. At last, her prayers were answered, or so she thought. Now the whole country would be free of the curse of alcohol. If the Shaitan's drink was banned from the country, it would automatically be removed from her house. But Farhat had seriously underestimated her husband's resourcefulness. A few days after the prohibition, Noor bought half a dozen bottles of Scotch to replenish his stock, from God knows where. Farhat's blood pressure shot up again and she threw another violent fit. Confident that the new lock he'd got installed would safely guard his precious liquor cabinet,

Noor coolly paraphrased Mark Twain, 'Begum Sahiba, too much of anything is bad, but too much good whisky is barely enough, especially when the Tippler prohibits it.'

*

For the next several months, although a facade of peace returned to the Kashana, it felt like the lull before a storm. The servants sensed the iciness between the barrister and his begum; the relatives detected the chill.

'Areý O, Quaid-e-Azam, this is like the Rani of Jhansi's rebellion against the Angrez,' Changez Gul whispered to Sikander.

'May God save these unhappy people,' Sikander replied, shaking his head.

As expected, the clashes between Farhat and Noor resumed. He saw Zakir's hands in their latest altercation, as his wife repeated the most virulent parts of Zakir's lecture, especially his damnations of sinners, using the most sophisticated Urdu words.

One day, Noor telephoned Zakir in utter desperation. The conversation started off in a civil tone but deteriorated quickly as Noor became frustrated by Zakir's sententious moralizing.

'Zakir, you and I go a long way back. As your old friend, I am requesting you . . . no, no, I am *pleading* with you to tell my wife to show moderation and respect.'

'What do you mean by showing moderation, Noor?'

'Well, she has become quite extreme in her views . . . almost fanatical.'

'Well, brother, one person's faith is another person's fanaticism.'

'Yes, but I have a feeling that her faith is directed more towards me, you fanatic. I don't have any problems with her faith. I have a problem when it trespasses on my lifestyle, and I have a bigger problem knowing that you are inciting her.'

'Well, Noor, I know what your beliefs are, and in my opinion, you are misguided. And it is my solemn duty to tell her that your beliefs are wrong when she asks me about them.'

'It is not *your* duty to talk about my personal beliefs, especially not with my wife. If you think I am wrong, convince me, not my wife. I dare you to debate with me, one-to-one.'

Because his argumentative prowess was legendary, and because Zakir had witnessed it himself, both on and off the court, Noor knew that he would never agree to such a debate.

'Well, Noor, I will do what I have to do and if you will excuse me now, I have better things to do.'

'You ought to be ashamed of yourself, Zakir Hassan, for sowing the seeds of discord between my wife and me. You have become more than a mischief-maker. Is it your religion to poison her mind against me?'

'I have not poisoned her mind, Brother Noor; your wife comes to my house of her own free will. If you don't want her to do that, tell her not to come,' he replied calmly, using his diplomatic skills.

'Don't lie to me, Zakir Hassan. I know that you have been inciting her about my drinking and my beliefs. I warn you, they are none of your business, and if you interfere in my personal life again, I will hold you personally responsible.'

'Let me also warn you, Brother Noor, drinking is illegal in this country now and I can have you lashed for this offence!' Zakir's voice quivered as he said this.

'You can go and get yourself fucked by an asshole!' And with that, Noor hung up the telephone.

That night, when he went home after work, Noor witnessed a new storm brewing. It so happened that when Farhat went to Zakir's *dars,* the sermon, that day, he asked her to leave his house. And when she asked him the reason, he detailed the fracas with her husband, stressing that Noor had used the most vulgar language— '*aisee gundi, gundi gaaliyan,* such dirty, dirty swear words'—he had ever heard in his life.

Farhat tried to apologize to him for her husband's behaviour, but to no avail. Too incensed to accept her apologies, he asked her to leave, and Farhat left Zakir's house in tears. When Noor arrived home after work, she greeted him with a new fusillade of recriminations and reproaches. And then she asked him the question that she had been dreading all this while, 'Tell me, do you consider yourself a Muslim or not?'

'Don't talk to me about subjects you know nothing about,' he shot back.

She pressed him for a direct answer, but he ducked the question. The more she pushed him, the more irate he became, until he finally ordered her to shut up. That was when all hell broke loose. Farhat announced that she was going to go and stay with her sister until Noor gave her the 'right' answer.

Noor spent two disturbed nights in his bedroom. Like a madman in a mental asylum, he paced from one end of the room to the other. What else could he do in this time of crisis? Read Ghalib for answers? Pull Boethius from his bookcase and seek solace in *The Consolation of Philosophy*? On the third day, realizing that he could neither raise the stakes any further nor jeopardize his marriage of fifty years, Noor sent Sikander for her. But Farhat remained resolutely defiant and sent Sikander back saying that she needed an answer from Noor. She had finally matched his intransigence with her tenacity. By this time, all the servants and the neighbours had heard about their quarrel, and all sorts of rumours took wings.

One whole week passed by and Farhat did not come back. Even though Noor felt as if his blood would clot in his veins, he could still not push himself to telephone his son in Iowa—at least not right away. He must cajole Farhat first, express regret and nourish her needs.

*

After Noor left for Karachi, Mansoor went back to spending his days at the library. The Special Collections section would have been the perfect getaway from his parents' escalating problems. But repressing his convoluted emotions turned out to be an impossible task. The guilt kept coming back, tearing him apart. He had been cold with his father, a bit stand-offish. Turning down his father's offer to finance his education must have shredded the man's heart. On more than one occasion, Noor had repeated that his only goal for the remaining years of his life was to earn money for him and his mother. He had lived in a mental wasteland for far too long to strive for anything else. Mansoor had no right to turn down his offer, and this realization now made him angry with himself. Despite all his failings, he knew that his father was a good man. How many people had he helped? How many lives had he improved? All their servants, his friends in The Unholy Quartet, his relatives and even total strangers had benefited from his magnanimity. When his father gave, he gave unconditionally; when he helped, he helped unreservedly.

Mansoor's mind wandered to his mother and her religious metamorphosis. Maybe it was a good thing. Perhaps she needed religion to fight loneliness; perhaps she required the retreat that faith provided. But what about his father? Who would be *his* companion in *his* solitude? What would be *his* crutch? Scotch and Pakistani tharra? As tears welled up in his eyes, Mansoor quickly took out his handkerchief and wiped them dry. He did not want anyone to see him crying. At that moment, he just wanted to go home, hug his parents and tell them to be kind to each other, to take care of themselves, but instead, he heard a pleasant voice ask him gently, 'Are you okay?'

'What? . . . Yeah, yeah,' Mansoor replied hurriedly and looked up to find a girl standing in front of him, gazing at him questioningly.

'I'm sorry, but you seemed to be crying. Are you all right?' she asked again.

'It's nothing, it's nothing. I'm just a little homesick,' he hastened to assure her.

The girl nodded her head. 'I'm Lisa,' she said after a moment and extended her slender brown hand towards him.

'I'm Mansoor.'

As Mansoor struggled with the conflicting need to be alone and the desire for some company, Lisa Reid came into his life at the perfect time. Her big, kind brown eyes and soft smiling features drew him instantly to her. Tall and slightly built, with shoulder-length hair, she was an attractive African-American woman of mixed heritage. Mansoor pulled a chair next to him at his table and asked her to sit down, and they went through the banality of a perfunctory chat.

*

Since their chance meeting at the library, Mansoor and Lisa met every day. There was something about Lisa that reminded Mansoor of Mehrun, something that lived in a deserted corner of his consciousness, but exactly what it was he just could not pin down. Not her face, not her voice, maybe it was the way she looked at him. The fact that she was writing her doctoral dissertation on the socio-economic causes of the partition of India and Pakistan made her even more attractive to him. Although Mansoor had read a fair bit about the Partition and had heard the personal stories of loss from his father and mother, he found the American perspective curious and refreshing.

'My father was involved in the freedom struggle, and he was actually in the Working Committee of the Congress Party. In the first Congress government, he was the political secretary to the education minister of Bihar.'

'Oh, I must meet him. I would give anything to interview him!'

'You just missed him. He was here just recently. Too bad I did not know you then; otherwise, I would have definitely introduced you to him.'

'Well, the next time he is here, be sure to introduce me.'

One night, as they sat on a bench near the university pond, under the starry sky, Lisa said to Mansoor, 'We have gone out a few times, but I still feel as if I don't know you . . . you are . . . you are . . . What is the word I am looking for . . . so inscrutable?'

'But I think I am an open book!' Mansoor protested. 'What do you want to know?' he asked rather casually.

'Like who are you, Mansoor ul Haq?'

In the beginning, she used to pronounce his name as 'Man-Sooer', and the way she said it, it sounded like a compound English–Urdu word meaning 'Man-Pig'. He told her about it, laughing as he tried correcting her pronunciation.

'It's Mun-Soor,' he told her.

'So, who are you, Mansoor ul Haq?' A twinkle appeared in her beautiful brown eyes as she pronounced his name correctly.

At that moment, Mansoor had this irresistible urge to kiss her and tell her that he may very well be in love with her, and the next second, he succumbed to that urge. He kissed her, savouring every moment of it, as if he would never get another chance to kiss her again. And then abruptly, he pulled back from her. 'I am a djinn,' he said, answering her question.

'What's a djinn?' Lisa asked, not missing a beat.

'A djinn is a being created by Allah, from smokeless fire; they are airy beings with transparent bodies, who can transform themselves into any form or shape.'

'Oh well, that explains everything!'

'Have you read *Aladdin and the Magic Lamp*?'

'Oh! You mean you are a genie, like a genie in the bottle?'

'Something like that! Except that I'm out of the bottle now.'

'Boy! Can I have my three wishes now?'

He kissed her again. A long, lingering kiss. Her lips, warm and sweet, tasted of mint. Mansoor felt drowned in her exuberant sensuality, but then, without any warning, a trembling fit seized him, a fit that shook his very being. It was early June, but he felt cold, terribly cold. Not knowing what exactly was happening,

Lisa wrapped her arms around his body and kissed him again. He had read about sensual kissing and had heard stories about it from Joseph, but what he experienced then, in that moment with Lisa, was an ineffable feeling, an out-of-body experience. Soothed by her tender embrace and encouraged by her warm reciprocity, Mansoor took her to his apartment, where he made love to her. As their bodies touched, they became fused; their hearts whispered sweet melodies. At that moment, Mansoor only had desire, that incandescent feeling, where reality blends with fantasy, where the humdrum of existence melts away. He kept wondering where she had been all this time during his stay in America.

Thinking about it afterwards, he realized that Mehrun had also aroused sexual feelings in him that he had forcefully and deliberately suppressed. Was it because she was a servant? Or was it because he was afraid of her? With Lisa, his awakening was complete, insensate to everything else. For the last two and a half years in this distant land of dreams, he felt as though he had walked like a sleepwalker; but now the touch of a woman had woken him—he wanted to dance. Oblivious to the loss of his virginity, he lay there, delirious, with this tender, beautiful woman in his arms.

At that moment, he kept hearing a chant inside his head: '*Haq, Anā al-ḥaqq*; *Haq, Anā al-ḥaqq* (Truth, you are the Truth; Truth, you are the Truth).' At that moment, the only certainty was the truth of love, the single act, the act of love. Was this the moment he had always waited for? Had he lost his head like his namesake, Manṣūr al-Hallaj? He lay there, pondering over these metaphysical questions, with Lisa in his embrace, snoring softly.

The sharp ringing of the telephone brought him back to earth. He turned around to look at the radium hands of the timepiece that his mother had given him and realized that it was 2 a.m. Who could it be at this hour? As he picked up the phone, he immediately realized that it was a long-distance call. On the other end, a female operator shouted in a shrill voice.

'Is this Mister Mansoor ul Haq?'

'Yes, this is he!'

'Hold on, sir, this is a trunk call from Pakistan. Mister Noor ul Haq wants to talk to you!'

His heart began pounding; he had this sinking feeling that at this late an hour, a call from home had to be bad news, and a few seconds later, he heard his father's hoarse voice on the other end.

'Hello, Mansoor . . . beta . . . Hello?' he was practically shouting because the connection seemed terrible.

'Yes, Abba, this is me! Is everything okay? Is everything okay?' he heard his echo on the line.

'Beta, I have been trying to call you for a few days now. Where have you been?'

'I have been here only, Abba . . . I have been here only, Abba.' The echo began to annoy him.

'I want you to buy a ticket for the next flight to Pakistan.'

'Why? What's wrong? What's wrong?' Mansoor became concerned now. By this time, Lisa was also partly awake.

'Your mother had a big fight with me, and she has gone to her sister's house. You are the only one who can—' Before Noor could finish the sentence, the line got disconnected.

Mansoor tried to call him back, but he could not get connected.

The telephone call had shaken him; he wanted to get up. But with Lisa still in his embrace, he couldn't, so he stayed still and looked at her face in the darkness.

'Is everything okay?' Lisa asked in a raspy voice, her eyes still heavy with sleep.

'My father wants me to come home immediately, my mother . . . my mother is . . . sick.'

Lisa raised her head and asked, 'Nothing serious, I hope?'

'I don't know; the line got disconnected.'

No sooner had he said this than the telephone rang again. He quickly picked up the receiver, thinking it was his father, but much to his surprise, it was Joseph, and he was drunk.

'Mansoor Babu, did you hoist the flag? Did you use your weapon?' Joseph had this habit of calling him at odd hours, but his uncanny, vulgar telepathy struck Mansoor now. How did he even know that he had just made love?

'Are you in an insane asylum?' Mansoor asked.

'Yes, I am in Houston!' Joseph replied, laughing convulsively.

Irritated with his friend, Mansoor hung up the phone. Lisa turned around and went back to sleep, snoring softly again. He got up and tried calling home but could not get a connection.

The next day, Mansoor called a Pakistani travel agent in Chicago and reserved a seat on the next Pakistan International Airlines (PIA) flight to Karachi. With his ticket confirmed, he sent a telegram to his father informing him about the day and time of his arrival in Karachi. On his day of departure, he received a five-page letter from his father, posted three weeks ago, pleading with him to come home immediately. It was a rambling, disturbing missive about the crisis in his family and Zakir Hassan's role in all of this. He read it hastily and put the letter in his jacket pocket, thinking that he would reread it on the airplane.

*

Mansoor was acutely aware of the dominance–dependence relationship between his father and mother. Though he never physically abused her, Noor was often rude to her, sometimes even in front of the servants. Most of the time, however, he ignored her. Farhat existed like a docile, permanent fixture in his bedroom setting. Her lack of formal education was a sore point for Noor. Many of his corporate clients, especially those from the younger generation, had wives who were all well-educated, who spoke fluent English and talked to men with confidence. Farhat had none of those 'qualities'. She, in turn, despised his 'over-education', his penchant to talk in English, especially with their son, his boozing and his 'grievous beliefs' about her country and religion. Where she found refuge in faith, he glued himself to his work. As the chasm between them widened, their relationship unravelled. But the breakdown, when it came, came rapidly after Mansoor left for America.

The patchy telephone conversation with his father and the long-winded letter had unsettled him. The night before he left, Mansoor tried calling home again, but the old-fangled telephone system made that impossible. So he dispatched another telegram to his father, confirming his arrival. He had too many things to do in too short a time, so he hastily packed a few items for his trip just a few hours before he was to leave for the airport. Lisa had introduced him to Herbert Marcuse and had given him a copy of *Eros and Civilization* for his birthday. He stuffed it into his hand luggage. Mansoor had lived in a culture whose mores had taught him to repress his sexual desire, but its gratification, of late, had made him a man who was sure of himself, who was confident in his own skin. Lisa showed him a reality that he never knew existed.

He was thinking about Lisa when she came to say goodbye and reminded him to send her a note as soon as he reached home. Mansoor kissed her and said thank you, much to her puzzlement. He told her that he would explain that thank you when he wrote to her from Pakistan.

'Aren't you coming back?' she asked.

'Yes, why?'

'The way you thanked me, it seemed as if you were going back home for good.'

'I shall return,' he promised.

'Mansoor, I . . . I think I . . .' she paused and then said, 'Never mind, it's not important.'

'What?'

'No, no, it's nothing. I will tell you when you return.'

Before he could press her more, he saw his airport shuttle approaching. He kissed Lisa again and quickly boarded it. As the shuttle pulled away from the apartment building, he turned around and saw Lisa wiping her tears.

The traffic on I-80 was sparse, so the shuttle reached the airport in good time. After Mansoor collected his boarding card, he headed straight to the departure lounge. He had a few hours to kill, so he decided to spend some time in the duty-free shops. He ended up buying a bottle of Chivas Regal for his father and a Chanel No. 5 for his mother. Feeling hungry, he then picked up a couple of slices of pizza to eat at the gate while waiting to board his flight.

A strange feeling of misgiving gripped Mansoor when he boarded the airplane. He took out his book, but his mind was on his parents. When the air hostess came with the refreshment cart, Mansoor asked her for a gin and tonic.

'Sir, we do not serve alcohol on our flights any more.'

Mansoor noticed that the word 'alcohol' made the passenger seated next to him frown and mutter something under his breath.

'Since when?' Mansoor persisted.

'Since about a few months ago. The government has passed a new regulation prohibiting the serving of alcohol on all PIA flights, sir.'

Mansoor was disappointed. But before he could say something, the passenger intervened.

'Young man, Pakistan is an Islamic country where there is no room for alcohol. You should be ashamed of drinking.'

'And you had to interfere! I wasn't talking to you, and what *I* do is none of your business,' Mansoor replied, becoming irritated.

'As your Muslim brother, I have the duty to tell you what is right and what is wrong.'

Why did everyone seem so duty-bound, so obligated to tell right from wrong? Mansoor wondered.

'Here are three things that you should know, old man. First of all, I am not your brother. Second, you have no right to tell me what is right and what is wrong. And third, what makes you think I am a Muslim?'

'Well, I am sorry, but you look like a Muslim,' the man replied.

Mansoor did not see the need to dignify his last comment with a reply, and when the passenger got out of his seat to go to the toilet, he quietly picked up his hand luggage and moved on to an empty seat a few rows away. After settling down, he took out his father's letter and began to read it again.

Noor wrote that in his absence, Farhat had started going regularly to the sermons at Zakir's house, dressed in her new hijab, which was her symbol of revolt, her flag of independence, according to him. About the hijab, he had written:

All of sudden, I see so many young women covering their faces, wearing the burqa, chador, hijab, niqab, and all sorts of veils. My own mother fought against the whole institution of purdah back when she was a young woman. She believed that it was all about controlling women. I think it is also about sexualizing them. They would deny it, but it is true. The mullahs believe that a veil's purpose is for women to cover themselves so they are no longer attractive. If that is not sexualization, then tell me what is? They justify it by saying that it is to prevent men from having sexual fantasies about them. These troglodyte mullahs believe that a man has nothing else on his mind except copulation. That's an insult to a decent man's decency. It is essentially sending the message to all good men that you are not to be trusted. You, too, are a potential sexual predator. And do you know that these people are also forcing hijab on girls as young as six or seven? By doing this, they also see these poor innocent girls as sexual objects. Do the women embracing hijab today not understand what struggles women in the past went through to free themselves of the purdah? To be able to leave the confines of the house and receive an education, have a career, don't they believe in that any longer? My mother gave up wearing the burqa, and now I cannot believe my wife is willingly wearing a hijab.

Your mother doesn't understand any of this, saying that it is only about modesty. I asked her, 'Before you veiled yourself, were you immodest?' Her answer was yes. Can you believe this? Here is a woman well past her prime, about to enter her seventh decade of life, and she feels that men will look at her with lust because she is sexually attractive.

In his letter, Noor described Zakir as a religious rock star. His fame had spread to even the most neglected areas of the country. Eminent people like the legendary cricketer Lion Prince, and failed movie stars, like Salome, came to his house to be blessed by what Noor called his religious nonsense.

I tell you, beta, his followers are a bunch of religious bargain hunters, his house a one-stop-religious mall, just like the mall you took me to in Iowa. He has started to sell his holier-than-thou-crap on cassette tapes to these gullible idiots. Zakir relishes every moment of it. You had said to me in Iowa that you couldn't understand how he could give up a career in foreign diplomacy for this. Well, son, I think he is making more money selling these amulets than what he was ever making as a third-rate diplomat.

After reading the letter, Mansoor thought about his mother's choice of wearing a hijab. Was his father right in questioning her decision? Here was a man who believed in personal choice, denying the same to his wife. But was Amma's decision really voluntary, or was it driven by external influences, such as Zakir Hassan or the increasing religiosity in the public sphere? Although he agreed with many of the points his father raised in that letter, why not just let Amma be happy in what she wore? If she saw it as a sign of modesty, let it be. The more he thought of his parents, the sadder he became.

Mansoor put away the letter when the air hostess announced that dinner was about to be served. With no alcohol to drown his agony, he asked for a ginger ale to go with his dinner. The new prohibition made him anxious about the Chivas Regal in his hand luggage. The possibility of the bottle getting confiscated and leading to a brush with the new law made him nervous. After he finished the biryani they served for dinner, Mansoor tried to sleep, but sleep had deserted him. He thought of Lisa. What was it that she had wanted to say? He was yet to confront his feelings for her. Mansoor remembered how she had wiped away her tears . . . Was it love? It was too painful to think about it.

*

When the plane stopped for refuelling at the Charles de Gaulle airport in Paris, Mansoor got out and went to the transit lounge to exchange some dollars for francs. The thought of the Chivas getting seized by Pakistani customs was still on his mind, so he strolled towards the duty-free shops to look for something else for his father. But what else could this son buy for his strange father? Not sure if Noor read books any more, he walked in and out of a bookshop without buying anything. Across the long terminal, he saw rows of elegant shops and restaurants flanking the corridors. He stopped in front of the display window of a men's wristwatch store. The watches looked too pricey. He decided to take his chances with the bottle in his bag. To hell with it! If the authorities tried to confiscate it, he would simply bribe them. It always worked.

The terminal bustled with life as Mansoor sauntered back towards his gate, idly watching passengers dash in every direction in their business suits and flowing dresses. He saw an airline crew walk past him, the air hostesses talking about an obnoxious traveller on a flight just concluded. Inside a bistro, a child yawned, a plate of half-eaten food on the table in front of him, while his mother pestered him to hurry up. Two more hours to kill, Mansoor thought. Near his gate, he saw an empty seat and quickly occupied it. Not knowing what else to do, he took out *Eros and Civilization* from his hand luggage, but his Eros was already tangled, and so, reading became a struggle. His mind kept turning to what awaited him at home—uncomfortable accusations, unbearable arguments, painful conversations—and he began dreading the thought of becoming a go-between for his old parents.

He wanted to call Lisa and open up his heart to her. But she would be in the library at this hour. Should he call Mehrun? Although she was aware of his parents' complicated relationship, Mansoor had never actually discussed it with her. Without thinking, he took out his pocket phonebook and automatically searched for her name under M, but there was no entry there. Then he looked under A. There it was: Mehrunnissa Alvi, her married name meticulously entered in his handwriting. The public payphone from across his seat beckoned him. Taking out the francs from his pocket, he went towards the booth. He had enough money for a thirty-minute call. But what if her husband picked up the phone? He would just hang up. After inserting the coins in the coin slot, he dialled her number. It was Mehrun who answered.

'Mansoor Babu! Where are you?'

Even after all these years, she addressed him as Mansoor Babu, a reaffirmation of the master–servant relationship that had existed between them.

He told her where he was and where he was going without telling her the reason for his trip back home.

'Oh, then I will see you in Karachi. I am also going home next week,' she said, and after a pause, she added, 'my husband is building us a house in Defence Housing Society.'

Mansoor remembered her shoebox-like house and wanted to joke about it, but he resisted. He knew that Defence Housing Society had become the poshest and most expensive area in Karachi, eclipsing all other neighbourhoods.

'Have you chosen a name for your house?' he asked, nervously unbuttoning and buttoning his jacket.

'I am going to call it the *Kashana-e-Jhoot*, the Abode of Lies.' She laughed.

Mansoor detected a hint of pain mingled in her laughter.

'Is your husband still travelling a lot these days? I see his name in the Pakistani newspapers all the time.'

Mehrun replied in the affirmative and then quickly changed the subject. 'So, how's Umreeka?' she asked.

Mansoor smiled at the way she pronounced America. He told her about his life in Iowa, about his studies and about Joseph being in America.

'Have you found a girlfriend?'

Mansoor hesitated before answering her question, and when he did, he lied. He was not ready to talk about Lisa with anyone, definitely not from a payphone in a busy airport.

'How are Noor Sahib and Begum Sahiba?'

'They are fine,' he lied again.

'I would like to come and pay my respects to them.'

'Yes, of course. Abba and Amma would be thrilled to see you.'

'Are you sure?'

No, he wasn't sure. He didn't even know what state they would be in. After he hung up, Mansoor felt a rising annoyance about the call, something disquieting, but he wasn't sure if it was guilt, shame, or pure idiocy. When he reboarded the plane, Mansoor's mind returned to his conversation with Mehrun. Why didn't he say anything about Lisa? Did he believe that the truth about his relationship with Lisa would affect his friendship with Mehrun? Was he sure that his parents would be thrilled to see Mehrun, now that she was a rich woman?

The telephone call depressed him; he didn't know why he expected that talking to Mehrun would somehow make him feel better. Mansoor's mind drifted to his father's agonising letter, and that added to his despair. The final leg of his long flight should have made him excited, but it didn't. Sitting cramped on such a long flight had made his legs ache. Mansoor got up to walk back and forth to stretch his muscles, but he sensed a heaviness in his steps. When he went back to his seat, Mansoor closed his eyes and tried to sleep. He needed to quieten his mind. He would have enough to deal with when he landed in Karachi.

Twenty-Three

Mansoor arrived in Karachi in the early hours of the morning—the pink clouds splashed their colour across the grey-blue dawn sky as if to prevent the sunlight from breaking through. Sikander came to pick him up. Although he must have known much about what was happening between Noor and Farhat, he said little. As the car approached the gates of the Kashana, Mansoor saw the wizened old Changez Gul sitting in an aluminium armchair, his legs stretched out, his eyes closed and his head tilted backward. Wasn't he sitting in exactly the same position when I left for America? Mansoor thought.

Sikander drove the car right up to the gate and then honked. That startled Changez Gul, and he jumped up. When he saw that it was Mansoor inside the car, he saluted him, and Mansoor rolled down the window to greet him. Changez opened the gates, and as the car pulled up near the front porch, Mansoor noticed the weeds growing along the driveway. Withering coneflowers, their once-bright colours faded, their leaves black and brown, accentuated the neglect that appeared to have spread through the Kashana.

'Does Jumman still work here?' Mansoor asked Sikander.

'Yes, Sahib, but only in name. He drinks heroine all the time.'

'You mean the drug? Heroin?'

'Yes, Sahib. Heroine.'

When Mansoor entered the house, he found his father waiting for him in the corridor. As soon as Noor saw him, he walked painfully towards him, grabbed him in a big hug and began to weep. It was not the father Mansoor had known all these years. The man had never cried like this. Separation from his wife had clearly crushed his dignity. His mottled scalp, the sagging wrinkles, the bent back, all told the sad tale of a shattered man.

'Where is Amma? Did you tell her that I was coming?'

'She is . . . at your . . . Aunt's house. I . . . didn't tell her . . .you were coming.'

Mansoor was disappointed. It was upsetting to come back to a desolate home. Without his mother, the house looked estranged. Thick layers of dust on the tables and cobwebs in the corners of the ceiling replicated the tale of shameful neglect from the front yard. Later, when Mansoor gave Noor the bottle of Chivas Regal, he smiled wistfully and told him, 'This is . . . is . . . the cause of . . . our sep . . . sep . . . aration, beta.' He held the bottle with both hands and sat staring at it for a while. Eventually, he said, 'My friend in need has be . . . come my enemy ind . . . eed.'

The convoluted tongue, the slurred speech unnerved Mansoor. 'Tell me from the beginning what happened,' he asked.

Noor put the bottle on the side table, sighed deeply and said: 'Wh . . . at is there to . . . to tell you! Ev . . . ev . . . everything gone. Nothing remains . . . not . . . thing remains. I am a man beaten by . . . by . . .'

Noor coughed and cleared his throat, wanting to say something but unsure about what to say. How could he tell his son about the distresses of his unhappy marriage of fifty years, that too with this jerky, hesitant tongue? Mansoor realized that there was something wrong with his father. It seemed impossible for him to talk coherently. He told his father to go back to sleep as it was still very early, and he promised that he would bring back his mother today.

After leaving his father, Mansoor went to the women's quarter, not entirely sure why. The room was a veritable shrine now.

On the marble floor, a beautiful and thick Turkish prayer rug greeted him, its corner folded, prayer beads spread out. In one corner of the room, on a wooden hand-carved Qur'an holder, lay a closed Qur'an. The paintings that had graced the walls of the zenana previously had all been swapped with holy verses printed on black velvet in heavy gold frames.

For Mansoor's mother, the worship of God was important; it was always there, but it was rarely noticed. She practiced her faith quietly, abided by it, but it was never unsettling for anyone else. The whole set-up that she had created in her son's childhood with Maulvi Nazir had been a weak attempt to inject faith, one drop at a time. Mansoor thought that the sacred and the sacrilegious, the rational and the absurd, and the all-important cultural artefacts of his life, had often sparred with each other, but they never came to a head, never threatened to obliterate each other. Even now, he would never trade one for the other. And what had happened to Uncle Zakir? The person who used to be so full of doubts, who believed in *bonum vitae*, the good life, how could he now suffer from the sense of religious and moral certitude? He had purposely become a man with insufficient imagination, refusing to enter any value system save his own. Obviously, he had played a role in bringing Mansoor's parents' troubled marriage to a breaking point.

*

The sun had finally come out, and hearing the calls of the vegetable vendors outside, Mansoor decided it was time to pay a visit to Nawab Khan Namaqul's house and bring his mother back home. Mansoor dropped Sikander home first and told him to take the rest of the day off. He then drove in the direction of his uncle's house. A balding Athanni, watering his flower beds, greeted Mansoor nervously. His flowing hennaed beard, sans a moustache, was a signifier of his new identity. Wearing a shalwar-kameez, he resembled the rotund Maulvi Nazir. Mansoor's unexpected appearance threw him off. They shook hands, and after exchanging a few clumsy trivialities, Mansoor asked him about his mother. Athanni's expression and tone changed immediately.

'She cannot go to that house.'

'That house? That house is her home. I am her son and I am going to take her back. Now get out of my way.'

This was the first time Mansoor had confronted his former extortionist, and it was the first time Athanni got scared of Mansoor. He quickly moved out of his way. Mansoor went inside the house and saw Farhat in a black hijab, sitting slumped in a chair at the dining table, reading the Qur'an. She looked at least twenty pounds lighter. As soon as she saw him, she froze, as if she had seen his ghost. Realizing that it was indeed her son, she came forward and squeezed him tightly. Tears streaked down her gaunt face and her lips trembled. Mansoor kissed her and hugged her back.

'Let's go home, Amma.'

And without a moment's hesitation, Farhat said, 'Yes, let's go.'

Just then Sarwat came charging in, followed by Athanni. 'Farhat, what are you thinking? How can you go back?'

But it was as if Farhat had been waiting for these magic words: 'Let's go home.' She went in and quickly changed her clothes, putting on a beige-coloured hijab, brought her suitcase and got ready to go. After she settled down in the rear seat of the car, Mansoor drove away. But dread filled her heart in the short journey back to her home, and Farhat began to quietly sob again.

When they reached the Kashana, the first thing Farhat did was to go straight to the kitchen and order Budhoo to prepare a hearty breakfast for her son. Then, as if absolutely nothing had happened, Farhat immersed herself in her household chores again. Noor, too, went on doing his things at the other end of the house. Without exchanging a word, without swapping apologies, they carried on with their disengaged routines. Like two sad people living a fractured life, separated by abstractions, they pretended to have patched up their differences in utter silence. Mansoor remained displeased, but what could he do? Under the circumstances, he could not have hoped for a better reconciliation. The cultural fact was that conflicts were resolved through silent affectations, not through exaggerated emotions. Here, silence, and not time, healed all wounds. Mansoor just hoped that their reconciliation would last and that people like Zakir wouldn't poison their relationship with their adjusted claims and amorphous promises. He also wished that his father would cut down on his drinking, but that was a forlorn hope; he did not remember a single day when his father had not had any alcohol. Noor had recently turned seventy, and to wish that he would change now was a vain hope.

*

Since its inception, political disorders and intrigues had plagued Pakistan like waterlogging and salinity. But each turmoil cracked the structural foundation of the country a tad more. The Supreme Court sanctioned every coup, justifying each upheaval as a regrettable requirement, calling it the Doctrine of Necessity. It was as if this was a divine idea, a reverential justice. But Noor was no longer interested in anything, not politics, not philosophy, not Pakistan.

One July morning in 1977, the wobbly democracy of Pakistan was dealt another blow. The chief of army staff, who had been carefully chosen by The People's Leader because he regarded him to be a simpleton with limited life interests like prayers and polo, dethroned his benefactor unceremoniously. Pakistan's history gyrated a full circle and gave the former prime minister a taste of his own despotism. But Noor remained silent. The genius schemer had fallen prey to a devious plotter. An opinion writer in the *Daily Hulchul* called the latest dictator General Behroopia, a person with many faces. Many people followed the lead and also began calling him that nickname in private. Tyranny continued unabated, albeit with a new look, and the age of religious machination started at full throttle. But Noor remained silent.

Both Mansoor and his father watched the latest dictator on live television. Displaying a packet of imported Dunhill cigarettes on his desk, the general talked about the corruption of his predecessor and made a promise to the people that he would restore the *real* Islamic democracy within ninety days. The G.O.D.s applauded his actions, and Zakir Hassan gave him the title of *Mard Momin*, the Man of Faith. Haider Rizvi wrote a glowing tribute as the managing editor of the *Gazette* the next day. But Noor remained silent.

The barrister had lost his mordant wit. The critic of Pakistani politics watched another coup brought on by another military dictator unfold in front of his eyes, and yet, he said nothing. Mansoor read Faiz's new poem to him, but nothing stirred him. The gridlock in his marriage and the breakdown of communication with his wife made Noor distant from his son as well. He stopped drinking altogether, but that did not impress Farhat at all. After begging Zakir's forgiveness, she had got back in his good graces and heard his lectures more intently now. Noor was duly informed about this, but he showed no reaction.

*

Mansoor and Lisa regularly wrote to each other. Several days before that night at the university pond, Mansoor and Lisa had gone to a party together. It was there that a mutual friend of theirs had taken their picture. It was a picture of love in all its simplicity. Lisa mailed a copy of that picture to Mansoor with her letter. When the airmail envelope arrived in the post, it made Farhat suspicious. As Mansoor opened it, the photograph fell out. Farhat quickly picked it up and began an intensive interrogation: 'Who is this girl? Why has your picture been taken with her? What exactly is your relationship with her?' Her rapid-fire questions made Mansoor stutter.

'She is . . . Lisa Reid . . . A friend of mine, Amma,' he replied with a bumbling hesitancy. 'The picture was taken at a university party that I went to. There is nothing more to it.'

'Don't you know it's a sin to be with girls who are not related to you?' she fulminated.

Realizing that the rod of fervency would now fall on him, he frowned. Mansoor regained his composure and replied, 'Amma, please don't start this with me now. I am not living in the fourteenth century. And I can't live in America without mixing with women.'

'Don't talk to me like your father! I have suffered enough from him, and I don't have the energy to suffer from you, too.'

'Amma, please,' he pleaded.

'Don't "Amma please" me. If you marry a non-Muslim girl, I will never forgive you. NEVER!' She then started to weep. 'My kismet is so bad; I am so unlucky.'

Mansoor knew that she had deployed her ultimate weapon, emotional blackmail, but not wanting to aggravate the situation any further, he remained quiet. He knew he would never forgive himself if he picked a fight with his mother before leaving for America.

With the high court closed for summer vacations, Noor quit going to work altogether, never telephoning his office and refusing to accept his clients' calls at home. All day he stayed in his bed and slept for long hours, waking up just to eat. His missing work like this worried Mansoor, but the two-day-old stubble on his father's face concerned him more, for Noor had never skipped shaving for as long as Mansoor could remember. The son offered to shave his father's stubble, or have the barber come home, but Noor refused. So with great trepidation, he asked, 'Abba, why have you taken a vow of silence?'

Instead of replying to the question, Noor gazed blankly at the window and then, after a long moment of silence, recited one of Ghalib's couplets:

Rahey na taqate guftar aur agar ho bhi
To kis umeed pey kahiye kay arzoo kya hai

(When the power of discourse is gone, but even if it hasn't
With what hope shall I say what desires I still possess)

Finally, he had said something without stuttering, without faltering. Every word of that beautiful couplet was enunciated distinctly; the pathos of Ghalib's deflated hope and the state of Noor's existence fading in perfect unity. For Mansoor, the return to normality in his father's speech was a good sign. Even though Noor had not picked up a book of poems in a long time, his ability to retrieve relevant couplets from memory, that too at will, still amazed him. After Sadiq's murder, poetry had lost all meaning for his father. There was no one with whom he could talk about Mir or Ghalib or Faiz any more. Was his father coming back from the dead now? He was not dead, but he did not seem alive either. Mansoor had read about the concept of death-in-life in literature. Eros is the desire for life; Thanatos, the wish to die. But when a man is neither alive nor dead, his being is a *zinda laash*, a living corpse. Was this the state his father was in now?

Mansoor remembered Sadiq Mirza once discussing Coleridge's 'The Rime of the Ancient Mariner' with his father, and how a part of one particular stanza summed up the conditions of Pakistan. His memory of the discussion was a bit hazy, but he did remember Sadiq giving him his copy of the book, nicely bound in cloth. Mansoor suddenly realized that he had never returned the book. Feeling guilty, he went to his room and rummaged through his disorganized bookshelf. And there it was: 'The Rime of the Ancient Mariner: In Seven Parts.' When he opened it, he saw the name M. Sadiq Mirza embossed on the title page. He wasn't sure which line or stanza Sadiq had been referring to that day, but as he read Part II, he came upon some lines and wondered if this was what his father and Sadiq had talked about:

Day after day, day after day,
We stuck, nor breath nor motion,
As idle as a painted ship
Upon a painted ocean.

He closed Sadiq's book, promising himself that he would treasure it for the rest of his life.

*

On that fateful day in August, when the hot wind, called the loo, dried out the vegetation and brought heat exhaustion to many, Noor stayed home again. It was his fifteenth day of absence from work. Like the previous days, he stayed in bed, doing nothing, looking vacuous and inert. Sometimes, he would cover his face with a muslin *dulai*, a summer quilt; sometimes, he would just gaze blankly through the window. Mansoor tried to cajole him to eat, but he refused. He attempted to regale him by reading from the *Morning Gazette* and the *Daily Jadal*, but Noor's mind wandered off into space, not even Coleridge's poem made him blink.

When Budhoo announced that lunch was ready, Mansoor dragged Noor out of his bedroom to the dining room. Farhat had already started eating since she was getting late for Zakir's lecture. As the three of them sat there at the dining table, Noor put the first morsel of food in his mouth, but then he forgot about it, chewing only when Mansoor prodded him. What was going on in his father's mind? Was he even thinking about anything? Mansoor's train of thought was interrupted by a woman's voice. Someone was talking to Budhoo in the kitchen. It was Mehrun. In a few minutes, she entered the dining room.

'Salaam Sahib, salaam Begum Sahiba, salaam Mansoor Babu.'

Noor stared at her blankly, while Mansoor and Farhat said wa-alaikum assalam in unison.

'What are you doing here?' Farhat asked, her voice stern and her mood belittling. It was the same chilly tone that she specifically reserved for Mehrun that returned to her without any hesitation now. Mansoor felt the distance in that tone. So much for 'Abba and Amma would be thrilled to see you.'

'My husband was going away on a business trip, so I decided to visit my father in Karachi.'

'Sit down, Mehrun, have some lunch with us.'

Farhat glowered at Mansoor when he said that. What was he thinking? *Bewaquf kahin ka*, what an idiot. Did he want to stir things up? Did he want to wake his abba from his distempered gloom?

Of course, Mansoor's words had absolutely no effect on Noor, even though they almost killed Farhat. So what if the girl had trapped a rich man and was now rich herself? Who was she to come here uninvited, Begum Banarsi saree? And that revolting diamond snare around her neck! So tacky! So garish! Her father was still a servant, and she was still a pukki churail, a true churail, or had she forgotten?

An awkward silence followed Mansoor's invitation, but Mehrun wisely eased the crisis by politely refusing the offer. 'Thank you, but I already had lunch. I just came to see my father and convey my salaam to you all,' she said.

'Where are you staying?' Mansoor asked.

'At the Palace Hotel.'

'Why don't you stay in our guest room?'

'Mansoor! Has your brain rotted? Is this what you studied in Umreeka?' Farhat remonstrated, looking thoroughly shocked.

'I think I'd better go,' Mehrun interjected.

Without saying goodbye, she left in a hurry, leaving the stuffiness of the dining room intact.

After she left, Farhat shouted at Mansoor. 'Remember your position and her position in life before inviting her for lunch or offering the guest room.'

'What do you mean, Amma?' Mansoor asked, chewing his roti. 'Mehrun is an important person now. She has money and she has status. What else do you want?'

Mansoor saw a faint smile on his father's face, or so he thought, as he challenged his mother.

'Don't you dare mock me! A churail will always remain a churail.' Her face inflamed with anger, she left the table without finishing her lunch. Mansoor could feel the boiling fury hissing through her body.

Noor remained reticent, oblivious to the tension, hardly eating and barely moving. And then abruptly, he too stood up. Without washing his hands or rinsing his mouth, as was his habit, he returned to his bed. Mansoor felt as if his parents had walked out on him. Had he made the situation worse? His stomach churned; he wished he had not provoked his mother. Setting aside his plate, he walked to the guest bathroom and washed his hands before following his father to his bedroom. Noor was stretched out on his back, his eyes closed, breathing heavily. Not sure what to do, Mansoor quietly settled himself on Noor's favourite chair and picked up Ghalib's book of poetry from his father's bedside table and began to leaf through it. Farhat came into the room wearing a turquoise hijab over a light blue shalwar-kameez.

'Khaleel is waiting for me outside; I am going to the dars,' she announced without looking at either.

Noor opened his eyes, tilted his head towards her and recited a couplet from a poem by the Nawab of Awadh, Wajid Ali Shah, himself an exile, written a few days before his death.

Dar-o-Deewaar pay hasrat se nazar kartey hain
Rukhsat ai ahl-e-watan hum tau safar kartey hain

(At the door and the walls, I gaze longingly
Farewell, my countrymen, for I leave for my journey)

As if he had mumbled something in Sanskrit, Farhat stared at him for a moment and then left the room without saying anything. Mansoor noticed a tear run down his father's cheek towards his ear. Noor closed his eyes again and began breathing heavily. After having lain like this for what seemed like an eternity, he unexpectedly got up and sat upright, as if priming himself to go somewhere. Noor then swivelled, shuffling to the edge of the bed, and gazed at the floor, as if thinking about what to do next. Mansoor asked him if he needed to go to the bathroom. Noor did not reply. Instead, he collapsed back on the bed, his feet still on the floor. Mansoor stood up. He could hear the wheezy air moving through his father's constricted airways. After a few moments, Noor became agitated. He got up and staggered towards the bedroom door, as if trying to catch Farhat, but before he could reach the door, he fell and banged his forehead on the marble floor. Mansoor ran, a fraction of a second too late, to grab him.

'Abba! Are you okay, did you slip?' he asked.

Noor did not reply. His face distorted, his breathing shallow, he struggled to get up, but could not. Mansoor helped him stand up and realized that the left side of his body was entirely lifeless. He knew then that his father had suffered a stroke. Summoning all his strength, Mansoor grunted, lifted his frail father up and carried him back to his bed. After putting him down on his bed, he bolted outside and hollered for the servants. His hysterical shouts brought Budhoo, Sikander and Changez inside the house.

'Abba fell down. We have to take him to the hospital,' he told them, and then addressing Budhoo said, 'Budhoo, you and Changez take him to the car.'

They each took an arm, placed them around their shoulders and half-carried Noor to the front porch towards the car. Blood ran down from Noor's nose. His breathing was sluggish and his contorted face displayed a cryptic fear. He tried to say something but only managed a guttural sound, his speech muzzled by the stroke.

'Don't worry, Abba. We'll take you to the hospital. You will be fine.'

Mansoor tried to elevate his father's sinking spirit even as panic assaulted his own. When they reached the car, Changez and Budhoo laid him down on the rear seat. Mansoor ran to the other side and squeezed in by his father. He raised his head and placed it on his lap. A feral cat ran out from under the car as Sikander turned on the ignition. Stepping on the accelerator, he swerved the vehicle towards Aga Khan Hospital. In a vain attempt, Mansoor tried to clean his father's bloodied nose and stem the flow of blood with his handkerchief, but it continued to ooze out. His trousers soaking in blood, his heart beating furiously, Mansoor cradled his father in his arms. He was still alive, still breathing, but any moment now he could cease to be. His existence was slowly dissolving. Noor struggled to breathe, barely clinging on to life. Mansoor hoped against all hopes that his father would use his will power to defy death, to frustrate the angel of death, Malak ul Maut, at least until they reached the hospital, but alas, that did not happen.

They were just ten minutes away from the hospital when Noor ul Haq breathed his last in Mansoor's arms. The sun had set on the eminent barrister. His life was done. With tears in his eyes, Mansoor said goodbye to his father, closed his lifeless eyes and caressed his non-existence.

A few months ago, while he was sitting in the university library, Mansoor had suddenly found himself thinking about his father's mortality. He had felt an immense sadness flowing through his arteries. Still, he had never imagined it would happen this way, and this quickly. The tungsten filament had finally snapped. His father's life would burn no longer.

*

In the aftermath of Noor's death, Farhat was an emotional wreck. Weeping and wailing, she begged her dead husband's forgiveness. After waging a bruising battle with him in their old age, she now felt contrite. In her mind, the purpose of her struggle was to show Noor the 'true light', the 'path to salvation', not to kill him. But now that he was gone, she just hoped that he had recited the kalimah before his soul departed. She began reminiscing about the last hours she had spent with him— the silly couplet, the last lunch and, of course, that wretched Mehrun who had appeared from nowhere just hours before, like the courier of death. And then she concluded that it was Mehrun who caused his death.

'That churail . . . that Mehrun . . . *She* struck him dead. She came and he died.'

Mansoor shook his head when he heard her whispering to Sarwat and Athanni.

Athanni's eyes gleamed. Embittered by Mehrun's change of fortune and her new prosperity, he found a perfect opportunity to join in and vilify his former co-worker. Mansoor noticed that he had his Yashica 35-mm camera hanging around his neck. The lurid journalist was hard at work, searching for the sensational even in death, he thought.

'Farhat Khaala, she is her mother's daughter, a pukki churail, an immoral woman. I used to work with her. I know her kind. She seduced Alvi Sahib, and I wouldn't be surprised if she cast a deadly spell on Uncle Noor,' he whispered back.

'Shame on you, Khaleel Khan, for smearing an innocent woman and spreading nasty rumours. Shame on you,' Mansoor whispered in his cousin's ear.

In Athanni's mind, Mehrun, Mansoor and the other 'low lives' collaborated and contributed to his miseries and failures, and his aunt's insinuations confirmed his convictions.

Feeling the heat from Mansoor's assault, Farhat came to her nephew's rescue. 'Don't try to defend that churail, Mansoor. She killed your father and you know it. And you stay away from her, too. Or she will put a spell on you as well!'

'Listen to your mother, Mansoor. Mehrun is evil; don't join her against your own family,' Sarwat added, trying to defend her son.

'And why do you have a camera?' Mansoor demanded. 'Don't you dare take any pictures of my dead father.'

'Farhat Khaala has asked me to take pictures,' Athanni replied with a smirk on his face.

Mansoor wanted to snatch his camera away from him, but if it was his mother's wish to participate in this ghoulish act, there was nothing he could do.

*

The news of Noor's death had reached every corner of Karachi. His clients, colleagues, relatives, friends and former friends began gathering at Kashana-e-Haq. Haider Rizvi came and hugged Mansoor warmly. His long absence from Noor's life had dried his tears for his friend.

Outside the house, the humid air and the gathering dark clouds threatened a downpour. In Mansoor's mind, a thought leavened: would his Abba have preferred a cremation rather than a burial—going out defiantly, just to spite those insufferable idiots? He remembered when Noor had told him that he wanted to donate his body to science. He did not want to be buried because he did not like the idea of becoming a meal for underground creatures, but then a cremation was not for him either, for he did not like being overcooked. His father liked the idea of donating his body to science, but not to Pakistani science which, according to him, was nothing but superstitions disguised as science. A soft smile appeared on Mansoor's face. He felt calmer, remembering his father's sense of humour.

When the rain came, all the men waiting outside rushed into the house, upsetting the carefully segregated gender gaps. In the crowd, Mansoor saw the bearded face of Zakir Hassan. How dare he make his grand entrance? And the gall, the utter gall to show his contemptible face at his father's funeral! *He* was responsible for his death, not Mehrun. Mansoor felt like pulling out a pair of scissors and cutting off that hennaed beard.

Acting as if he were the next of kin, Zakir took charge of the funeral rites, a self-appointed death director, obviously enjoying his power over the dead man. Who would question his divine authority? He ordered Athanni to take Farhat away to the other room since death broke all relationships between a husband and a wife. Her nikah was now invalid, terminated, khatam-shud.

'Viewing the body of her dead husband would be a sin,' Zakir told Athanni, but everyone in the room heard it, a stern decree that sent chills down the hall.

Farhat resisted. So Zakir weaved his way through the crowd, inserted himself next to her and said, 'Bhabi, you can't see his face now. Death has annulled your marriage with him. He is now a stranger to you.'

Mansoor, shocked by this new nonsense, tapped Zakir's shoulder and whispered in his ear, 'If she is no longer my father's wife, why are you still calling her bhabi? Why is this relationship still intact?'

Caught off guard, Zakir gently pushed him aside and then motioned Athanni to take Farhat away.

'Please let me look at his face one last time! I am still married to him,' Farhat pleaded.

'No, you shouldn't see his face, Farhat Khaala. It is a sin for a woman to see the face of her dead husband because after death he is no longer her husband,' Athanni parroted his mentor.

His face red with anger, Mansoor pushed his way towards his mother and announced, 'My mother will stay wherever she wants to. Leave her alone.

'Look son, if you want a proper religious funeral for your father, then you should abide by all the strictures. Don't argue. You can't pick and choose. It's better not to interfere in matters that you know nothing about,' Zakir argued with Mansoor, his tone stern, his face stony, still reeling from Mansoor's whispered sarcasm.

Realizing that she was creating a scene, Farhat turned her neck around to get one last glimpse of her dead husband and then told her son that she would leave the room. Her easy capitulation enraged Mansoor. Fifty years of marriage so hastily nullified, his father callously declared a stranger, all by Zakir Hassan's revelatory rubbish. Mansoor felt nauseated by all the unctuous pietism that elevated the minutiae. Suffocating rites, Athanni taking random snapshots and the torrential rains—silly subplots to make this the most dreadful day of his life.

His father's lifeless body lay wrapped in a white shroud in the middle of the drawing room. The odour of camphor and incense floated across the room, a pungent reminder that he was dead. Relatives offered prayers for his salvation, while uninvited mourners seeking bonus rewards in the afterlife sat there empty-eyed, reading sacred verses and performing their rhythmic acts as if participating in a choreographed performance. How his father would have suffered had he known about the excessive religious exertions displayed at his funeral. He had become irrelevant in life, and now it seemed he had become even more irrelevant in death.

Mansoor felt someone lightly tapping him on his shoulder; he turned around and saw Mehrun smiling sadly at him. Dressed in a cream-coloured silk saree, she was all elegance at that moment. He smiled back. They spoke without speaking; they felt without touching, and then he saw her walk towards his father's body. She stood there for a while and then walked away. As she passed him, she inserted a business card in his side pocket. From the corner of his eyes, Mansoor saw Athanni quickly snapping a picture of the two of them.

With all the pre-scripted sequences performed and the last-minute rites completed, Zakir ordered the people to lift the bier.

The rain had finally stopped and the clouds had disappeared, as if to let the sun catch the last glimpse of Noor's body. When the funeral procession reached the mosque for the final prayer, Mansoor stayed outside, not sure why he had come there. His father did not believe in any of this—God or the afterlife, heaven or hell. How ironic that they would be praying for what Noor, the materialist, had called his non-existent soul going to this non-existent place. How could Mansoor participate in something that neither he nor his father believed in? After the mourners came out of the mosque, Athanni noticed Mansoor standing outside and he quickly snapped another shot, as if he were creating a portfolio of Mansoor's offences.

*

Mansoor followed the procession to the Jannati Qabristan, walking with total strangers who, he thought, did not know him from Adam. At the graveyard, the rain started again. A man in a white beard said, 'He must have been a good man, for heaven is also crying over his death.' Mansoor saw Zakir and Athanni glance at each other. He noticed his grandfather's grave nearby and went to see what was written on his tombstone. As Noor's body was lowered into the grave, Zakir turned to Athanni and asked loud enough for everyone to hear, 'Where is Mansoor? It is the son's duty to turn his dead father's head towards Mecca.'

'I haven't seen him at all. I didn't even see him at the funeral prayer,' Athanni added.

'Well, Khaleel Khan, in Noor's son's absence, you should take over and perform this most important responsibility. You are the next of kin; you are the heir apparent.'

Athanni smiled and replied, 'Gladly, Uncle Zakir. I will gladly do that; what could be a greater reward than this?'

*

With the grave covered with dirt, Mansoor walked back. He knew that Athanni would be watching his every movement, taking a picture of every lapse in his actions. Snap. Snap. Snap. But Mansoor did not care. He walked, unaware of his surroundings, oblivious of the strangers around. He walked away from the funeral procession, in the opposite direction. Suddenly, Mansoor heard the honking of a car. When he turned around, he saw Mehrun in a taxi. She motioned him to get inside. Without thinking, Mansoor opened the door and sat next to her. The cab sped away towards the Palace Hotel.

Twenty-Four

Inside the luxurious room of the Mughal-style Palace Hotel, Mehrun and Mansoor went through a dizzying journey of impulsive sexual arousal. They made wild, frenzied love. After all, it was the union of a churail and a djinn, the most erotic union of all—self-revealing, transcendent, unequal in clarity and heedless to consequences. It was Agape and Eros melding together, their libidinal energies uninhibited. Mansoor and Mehrun had stumbled on freedom—anarchic and giddy at the same time.

Mansoor realized that if he were charged for a crime, it would be that he was making love to an outcast, to a woman despised, a woman whom his mother held responsible for his father's death, and that he was making love at the most sinful of times. But why was he there? Was he in love with Mehrun? Was he expiating for his mother's insolence? Was this his way of getting back at his community? He felt like screaming. He wanted to say to Athanni, 'Look, you idiot, you talk about staying away from her, but here I am, in a perfect union with her!'

Mansoor felt no guilt; he experienced no fear about having sex on the day his father died. Didn't Meursault, in Camus's *The Stranger*, have sex with Maria the same day? Or was it the next day? He shrugged that coincidence off quickly. Had Mehrun planned all this as a part of her revenge? No, that couldn't be it.

No, it had been spontaneous. One minute they were drinking, and the other minute they were kissing each other hungrily. She had always been close to him, but she had also always maintained a measured distance. That day, the gap became a singularity, and they broke all taboos and shed all inhibitions.

'You know, Mansoor ul Haq, as a child, you were forbidden to even play with me, and now, as a grown man, you have made love to me. You should not even be anywhere near me,' she told him with a sly smile on her face.

'Is that why you put the business card with your room number in my pocket?'

'Yes, I wanted to make love to the man who has always been forbidden to me.'

'Forbidden love is the best kind of love,' he replied. After a pause, he continued, 'At this time, I shouldn't be near anything except my father's freshly dug grave, exchanging banalities with perfect strangers and accepting their phoney sympathies.'

'Are you having regrets?'

'No, I am just wondering about the furore that must be raging because of my strange behaviour.'

As they talked, the phone rang. Mansoor picked it up and said hello, but no one answered, so he put it down and just shrugged his shoulders.

'Don't pick up the phone if it rings again,' Mehrun told him.

*

Athanni had a hunch that Mansoor was with Mehrun. He smiled deviously as a plot began to form in his mind. A plot of deep revenge, one that would settle all scores, restore his pride and show Mansoor never to mess with him, Khaleel Khan. Now, what would Mister Mansoor tell the world about why he behaved so badly at his father's funeral? Where was he when they had offered prayers of absolution for Uncle Noor? He was cavorting with that churail, that's where he was. When his father's head needed to be turned towards Mecca, what was the prodigal son doing? It was I, Khaleel Khan, who turned his head and threw the earth on my uncle's body. Not Mister America-return.

The first thing that Athanni did after he returned to the Kashana from the graveyard was to search for Mansoor. But when he did not find him, he went to look for Jumman instead. On spotting him, he asked, 'Where is Mehrun staying?'

'Payless Hotel, Babu. Why do you ask?' Jumman replied.

'Oh, nothing important, I just wanted to tell her something important about the bank,' he lied and then added, 'and her husband, Alvi Sahib, is he there too?'

'No, she came alone, Babu.'

'Do you know what her room number is?'

'I don't remember, Babu. But she wrote it for me on a piece of paper. I have it here in my pocket.' Jumman took out the hotel's business card and pointed to the room number written on it before handing it over to Athanni.

*

It was already quite late at night, but Athanni turned the key in the ignition of his rusted Hillman, caressed his Yashica camera and got the car started. He did not know what awaited him at the Palace Hotel, but he was sure that he was going to find something juicy. In a few minutes, he was on Drigh Road, speeding towards the hotel. The rainy night had emptied the streets, save for a few armoured vehicles that patrolled the city, reminding everyone that General Behroopia was in charge. Athanni's heart raced with excitement; his mind bubbled with anticipation as he approached the recently refurbished colonial-era hotel, hoping to destroy his arch-enemies. Parking the car in the parking lot, he made a mad dash inside and introduced himself to the night clerk as a lieutenant colonel from the army's intelligence unit, showing him a fake identity card. Athanni had acquired that card through his contacts at the *Daily Hulchul* to help him with his snooping. He always carried it in his wallet just in case he needed it.

'Did you see the woman in Room 210 going back to her room?' he asked in an authoritative tone.

'Begum Alvi? Yes, I saw her.'

'Was she with a man?'

'Yes!'

Athanni then described Mansoor to him, and the clerk confirmed the description. He then asked for the phone number to Mehrun's room. Hesitating a little, the clerk handed it out to him. Athanni went inside the clerk's office, sat on the chair, stretched his legs out on the table and dialled the number to Mehrun's room. When Mansoor picked up the phone and said, 'Hello,' Athanni's hunch was confirmed. Smiling wickedly, he put the phone down and went back to the clerk.

'Don't tell anyone about our conversation,' he warned the man. 'It is highly confidential. We are investigating these two. If you confide in anyone, we will know about it. And you will not only lose your job, but you will also be sent to jail for the rest of your life. Do you understand? This is a high-security matter.'

'Yes, sir. Yes, sir. Don't worry,' said the clerk, shaking with fear.

Spotting a hidden corner in the lobby, Athanni went towards it and sat on a wicker chair. Then, he attached a telephoto lens to his camera and waited impatiently for his targets to emerge. When Mansoor and Mehrun came down the stairs together a little later, holding hands and basking in the afterglow of lovemaking, Athanni took shot after shot until there was none left to snap.

His mission was complete—a thumping success. He had every proof that he needed to start the demolition derby.

*

General Behroopia announced the election date, but when the time approached, he cleverly called it off. His excuse—to make the previous regime accountable for its misdeeds and to rid the country's politics of all the 'corrupt elements'. A campaign calling for a new direction for the country began with the arrest of The People's Leader on trumped-up charges. All the parties that could have never secured a win in a free and fair election—such as the G.O.D.s—became part of this new charade, joining hands with the general, singing to his religious refrains.

Six months later, General Behroopia began his Islamization process by changing the penal code and exhorting the people to return to the *fundamental* values of religion. He instructed women to stop wearing the saree since it was the dress of the 'infidel Hindus'.

And what about the shalwar-kameez or the Western trousers and shirts that you wear? Mansoor thought. Are they not un-Islamic attires? What exactly is the Islamic attire anyway?

The religious thugs, armed with the new licence to propagate their nasty brand of a narrow creed, formed harassment units and began roaming the streets and markets, slapping women for their uncovered heads, slashing their arms with razor blades for wearing sleeveless tops. They beat up men who appeared westernized, humiliated young unmarried couples who ventured outside together and hounded anyone else who did not parade their religiosity. Married couples enjoying an evening stroll were also asked to produce their marriage certificates. The worst to suffer were the minorities, especially the Ahmadis, who were subjected to new rounds of persecution. Acquiring a passport became a torture for them. On the passport form, they had to sign a declaration that the founder of their religion was an imposter and a crook. State-backed intimidation and discrimination gained momentum and the G.O.D.s became the willing perpetrator.

*

General Behroopia's goal was to disorient his countrymen by imposing his constricted moral principles on them. And when his fellow travellers joined him of their own free will, their cacophonous hysteria left Mansoor cold. Protests, wars, elections and the loss of the eastern wing of the country had already made ordinary Pakistanis tired and cynical, their collective lethargy preventing them from protesting against this latest assault on liberty. Mansoor thought that the entire nation had gone into a cooperative communal coma. But what pulled them out of this stupor was Sher Khan, who had now become known far and wide as *Sher-e-Mazhab,* the Lion of the Faith, after he revealed his millenarian ardour. Announcing his retirement from test cricket, the thirty-seven-year-old wunderkind pledged to devote the rest of his life to his new cause, giving up his Italian suits for sets of loose kurta-pyjamas and a white skullcap, swapping whisky for Pakola and growing a long scraggly beard. Visits to the nightclubs were replaced by nightly calls to ordinary people's houses to guide them to the 'right path'. In ancient wisdom, he found new meanings; in traditional customs, he discovered his lost spirit. A regular speaker at Zakir Hassan's gatherings, he lashed out against the liberals and the secularists and berated women for embracing foreign feminism. The man who grew up in a Western atmosphere, who went to elite Western schools and who enjoyed rock and roll, now began calling the Western-educated Pakistanis 'desi coconuts'— brown on the outside, white on the inside, as if foreign coconuts were somehow different.

*

The day of Mansoor's departure for America arrived too soon. Hesitant to leave his mother alone in a huge house, he asked Sarwat to move in with her after he left. Not needing any persuasion, she agreed instantly. Mansoor had been accepted into the PhD programme at the University of Iowa, and he figured that in a year, he could complete his coursework, take the qualifying exam and return home to write his dissertation. At first, Farhat opposed his plan vigorously, using every tool in her motherly toolbox to make him change his mind. She did not want to live alone, and she definitely did not want him to return to America; but when Mansoor told her about her sister moving in, she reluctantly agreed. Sarwat did not even wait until he left. Putting her house on rent, she moved in with her entire family two days before Mansoor left. The alacrity with which the transition occurred enraged Mansoor; but there was nothing that he could do. After all, it had been his idea to invite her. Like vultures, they had attacked the remains of his house.

All this time, Mansoor remained ignorant of his conniving cousin's spy work. So far, Athanni had not made any threatening moves or questioned Mansoor either about his highly irregular behaviour at Noor's funeral or his presence at the Palace Hotel. On the contrary, he became civil and greeted Mansoor with a cloying smile each time their paths crossed in the Kashana. That day, at the airport, as Mansoor embraced his weeping mother and then bade farewell to her and to his aunt's family, Athanni quietly slipped a sealed envelope into his hand.

'What is it?' Mansoor asked.

'Just a parting gift! Open it on the plane.'

Surprised at Athanni's apparent thoughtfulness, his curiosity fully aroused, Mansoor put the envelope inside his hand luggage and went to the transit lounge. At that instant, how he missed his father, how he wished he was there. He remembered the day when he first left for America. His father, with buried emotions, had reminded him to write regularly to his mother. He remembered his farewell words and his tense face. Now he was gone. Mansoor's mind drifted to the day Noor died. He recalled the tears in his father's jaded eyes moments before he died, the couplet on his quivering lips, the blood haemorrhaging from his nose—it was an image that he found hard to shake off. As he took his seat on the plane, Mansoor realized that he had not mourned his father's death; he hadn't shed a single tear. But somehow, it did not feel strange.

After the plane took off, he reached for the overhead bin where he had put his hand luggage. Taking the envelope out from its pocket, he sat back and tore it open. Inside were two pictures. When he pulled the photos out, he realized that they must have been taken secretly—one was a photograph of him with Mehrun, both of them holding hands as they came down the stairs at the Palace Hotel, and the other was a doctored photo with his head twisted around, as if he was about to kiss Mehrun. On the back of the altered picture was an Urdu couplet with an accompanying English translation, just in case he didn't understand Urdu:

Ibtida-e-ishq hai rota hai kya
Aage aage dekhya hota hai kya

(Why cry, for this is the start of a love
Wait and see, what follows next)

At first, Mansoor was puzzled, but as the couplet's meaning sank in, he became infuriated. How dare he threaten me? And how did he get this picture with Mehrun at the hotel? That bastard, he thought. He's been spying! That's why the bugger had that silly grin on his face all throughout, that's why he was so polite!

But Mansoor could not understand Athanni's purpose in giving him the pictures at that particular point. If he wanted to blackmail him, he should have done that while he was still there in Karachi. Why now when he was on his way back to Iowa? He read the couplet on the back a couple of times, and then everything became clear. The eight-anna extortionist has now become a third-rate blackmailer, Mansoor thought. Realizing that the bastard was now comfortably ensconced in his house, he felt foolish. And as his stomach began churning, he muttered to himself, 'I have a serpent up my sleeve.' He promised himself that the day of his return from America would be Athanni's last day in his house, but then he didn't really know his devilish cousin.

*

Two weeks after that night with Mansoor, Mehrun returned to Dubai. Alvi received her at the airport, which was unusual. He had come alone in his black Mercedes, without the chauffeur. Surprised at this special treatment, Mehrun asked him the reason for his coming to pick her up as she sat in the car. He pulled out two photographs from his shirt pocket and handed them to her. 'Who is this person?' he asked.

A sudden paralysing fear struck Mehrun when she looked at the pictures. They were copies of the same prints that Athanni had given Mansoor. On the white border of one photograph was the inscription 'More to come.'

As Alvi started the engine and pulled the car out of the parking lot, Mehrun's throat tightened and her heart started to throb. She remained quiet, unable to answer her husband, stunned that someone would spy on her. Were there more incriminating photos of them?

'Who is this person?' Alvi thundered.

Recovering from the mind-searing silence, she replied, 'This is Mansoor ul Haq.'

'Should I know his name?'

'My mother used to work at his house. He is the son of Noor ul Haq, the late barrister.'

'Why were you holding his hand in public?' Alvi's voice rose as he continued his interrogation.

Annoyed by his queries, her fear changing into anger, she struck back with a question of her own, 'Have you hired detectives to follow me?'

'I didn't hire anyone. I received these photographs in the post.'

For a moment, she did not believe him, but the expression on his face was not that of a liar. 'Who is it from then?' Mehrun asked.

'How would I know? They didn't come with a note!' he snapped back.

They drove in complete silence for the rest of the way. The air-conditioned car with its tinted windows protected them from the baking heat outside. Mehrun, her heart pulsating in a nervous staccato, was unsure of how Alvi would react when they reached the privacy of their home. When they arrived at their grand bungalow, he steered the car into the compound through the wrought-iron gate, where a guard saluted them. And as soon as the car stopped at the front porch, he questioned her again.

'Did you sleep with him?' he addressed her very matter-of-factly.

When Mehrun did not answer his question, he shouted, 'I asked you a bloody question! And I want a bloody answer, and I want it NOW.'

Exasperated with her husband's interrogation and knowing full well the consequences of her silence, Mehrun took a deep breath and, summoning an ounce of courage, replied, 'You have had your affairs, and I have said nothing. All of a sudden why has mine become important to you!' And she continued, 'I don't ask about your affairs. Why do you ask about mine?'

'I am going to find out who this bastard is who sent this picture, and then I am going to kill him,' Alvi said in a menacing voice before getting out of the car and storming into the house.

*

Alvi sat in his dark study, brooding over this latest complication. He did not know how this 'new situation' would unfold. Would it affect his career? Would it affect his bank? Alvi was the chief architect of this financial empire that was headquartered in Dubai. He had not only helped create this international bank, but he had also contributed directly to its growth. While the bank had been expanding exponentially, his financiers were keen for it to grow even faster. In the short few years, he had almost single-handedly put them on a par with many of the old established financial giants; however, his backers remained impatient and impertinent. With a truly global workforce that was intelligent, hardworking and ambitious, Alvi had positioned his bank among the iconic banks of the world. To his financiers, however, that was immaterial. They wanted to rock Wall Street and shake Central London. Success had made them ravenous; growth had made them arrogant. With an enlarging appetite and diminishing patience, they ordered Alvi to show better results. They demanded a formidable transnational institution that functioned as an invisible government. In the beginning, Alvi thought that their goals were unrealistic, their demands impractical, but he eventually succumbed to their pressure.

'Just being a global bank is not enough for these bastards. They want me to fuck the world leaders,' he had told Mehrun.

He knew that to achieve gut-wrenching power, you have to stride through the corridors of corruption and wine and dine venal politicians, bloodthirsty arms dealers, rapacious drug lords and their cartels.

These photographs, a new threat to him, could potentially create a scandal and derail his career. He was too close to his goals, too deeply involved with the uber men and the underworld to let a petty blackmailer wreck his dreams. But with so many other things on his mind, he thought it better to deal with this one later.

He advised Mehrun to keep a low profile; she, in turn, decided to forewarn Mansoor about the photographs.

*

After Alvi left for work the next day, Mehrun searched for Mansoor's telephone number. Just then, her phone rang. She was sure she would hear Mansoor's voice on the other end, but much to her amazement, it was Joseph's booming voice that she heard.

'Hello, Mehrun Begum! This is Joseph, calling from Houston, Texas.'

'Joseph! How are you? I haven't talked to you in such a long time. How did you get my number?'

'Search and you will find God, they say, and you are a mere human, Mehrun Begum,' he quipped.

'I know you haven't found God, but tell me how you found my number.'

'I got it from Mansoor Babu.'

'Oh! Is he back in the States?' she asked.

'Yes, but I called you for an important reason.'

'What is it, Joseph?'

'I am interested in buying a Burger King franchise here in Houston. I have saved some money, but I will need quite a bit more. The banks here are unwilling to give me a loan because they say I don't have a green card or any "antenuptial experience", so I thought of asking you. Also, what is an antenuptial experience?'

'It is called entrepreneurial experience, you idiot. Is that why you called me? To ask me for money? Tell me, how much do you need?'

'The total cost is fifty thousand dollars, but my old boss is also helping me. I wanted to check if you can help with any shortfall.'

'That's a lot of money, but let me know the exact amount and when you'll need it by? Don't worry, I'll help you.'

Joseph could not believe his ears. Here was his personal banker, ready and willing to provide it with no questions asked. Joseph had heard about Mehrun's marriage to one of the top Pakistani bankers, from Mansoor, but little did he know that this banker had become one of the richest men in the world.

'Tell me exactly when do you need it?'

'I'll actually need it ASAP,' he said, proudly using this new American abbreviation he had learnt.

'Send me the details, and I'll try my best.'

'When I open my restaurant, Mehrun Begum, I will name a burger after you—the Mehrunnissa burger,' Joseph declared, and then laughed at his own joke. 'No seriously, Mehrun, I want you and your husband to come cut the ribbon.'

'I'll have to see about that.'

They talked for another half an hour or so, bringing each other up-to-date with what was happening in their lives. Joseph confided that he was 'after' a *gori mem*, a white woman, whom he intended to marry. Mehrun asked him about his mother, Pyaro. Joseph told Mehrun that his mother married his father's enemy, so she was dead to him. He then quickly changed the topic. It seemed that he had selectively severed all ties with his past, his mother, his relatives and Pakistan. The only histories that he still clung to were the ones that involved Mehrun and Mansoor, his childhood friends who had provided delicious escapades from his stark social reality. He told her he had no intention of going back to Pakistan, where he would still be a bhangi, no matter what. Mehrun laughed. At the end of the call, she took his telephone number and Mansoor's, and promised to call him back soon with news about the money.

Twenty-Five

After Mansoor returned to Iowa, he threw himself into his studies, spending most of his time in the library, away from all distractions. Only one thing troubled his mind—how to finish his doctoral course work, return home and kick his aunt's family out of his house, especially that scheming, treacherous blackmailer of a cousin. He owed that much to his father. Mansoor's only comfort and joy in Iowa was Lisa, who melted in his arms the minute she saw him. He realized how desperately he had missed her.

Bit by bit, he revealed his family saga to her, telling her about the real reason he had gone to Pakistan, his parents' contradictory tensions, their failed marriage and his father's death. As far as his relationship with Mehrun was concerned, she and Lisa remained non-existent to each other. Whenever the guilt of concealing their respective identities pestered him, he took a deep breath and shrugged it off. As long as their existence did not become a self-evident certainty, he decided he would remain quiet.

Lisa would sit there on the steps outside the library as Mansoor talked, listening attentively to his complicated family intrigues, a little confused by the undercurrents, but empathetic. She did not fully understand what he meant, but she saw the pain; she knew the stress; her own parents had recently gone through a messy divorce.

'Why didn't they get divorced?' Lisa asked.

'Divorce, in my culture . . .' Mansoor searched for the right word, and then continued, 'I don't know . . . it's . . . umm . . . complicated.'

'Divorce is complicated in any culture, Mansoor,' she replied.

'I guess . . .'

'After being married for forty years, my father dropped the bombshell on my mother. He told her that he wanted to get out of the marriage,' she said.

'Just like that?' Mansoor asked.

'Yeah, just like that. It happened just like that, out of the blue, on one absolutely ordinary day. Forty years and four children did not count for anything when it came right down to it. My dad just got bored with his life and with my mother.'

Lisa's mother, Sandra, had sacrificed her own ambitions so that she could marry the man she loved. Working two jobs to support him through graduate school, taking care of four young children all by herself when he was busy travelling for his firm, and then, forty years later, she had suddenly become too tiresome. In his sixty-second year of life, he realized that he did not love her any more. Living with her for the remainder of his life seemed like a burden of Sisyphean proportions; he wanted to reinvent himself.

So, when Mansoor talked about the strain between his own parents, Lisa knew exactly what he had gone through, but for his sake, she remained strong. She consoled him, comforted him and hurt with him. But back in her apartment, she let open the floodgates of emotions and cried like she had never cried before over how unfair life was.

*

That night, when Mansoor returned home after dropping Lisa off, he received a long-distance call from Mehrun. The repressed guilt returned unbidden. After the initial round of perfunctory conversation, Mehrun told him about the photographs that her husband had received.

'You too, huh? Do you know who sent it?' Mansoor asked.

'No, that *is* the mystery,' she replied.

'Well, it's from Athanni. He slipped an envelope with the two pictures into my hand at the airport, on the day of my departure. I think he was spying on us.'

'Athanni? I can't believe it!' Mehrun exclaimed. 'Did he say anything when he gave it to you?'

'No, he didn't. But there was a message on the back of one of the photographs, warning me that there was more to come. I bet he is planning something nasty.'

'Ameer Sahib was furious and said that he would kill the person who sent these if he ever found out his identity.'

'Let's keep quiet until Athanni makes his next move. You know, Mehrun, the most stupid thing I did was to invite his family to stay with my mother at the Kashana.'

'Why did you do that?'

'I don't know, I . . . I didn't want Amma to stay there all alone.'

'You shouldn't have done that. They'll never leave now.'

'I'll kick them out when I go back.'

'Mansoor Babu, that won't be easy.'

'We'll see . . .'

They talked for a bit longer about everyday things—his apartment, her friends and then Joseph's plan to buy the Burger King franchise and to have it's inauguration on New Year's Day, the perfect day to symbolically cut all his ties from his past. He had invited both Mehrun and Mansoor to the opening.

'Well, maybe I'll see you at the opening then?' Mansoor asked.

'I don't know, Mansoor, whether I'll be able to come or not. Ameer Sahib is being transferred to London to set up a new head office there . . . the timing might conflict.'

'So, how *is* he?'

'The same. He has asked me to keep a low profile. He doesn't want me to blemish his career.' She paused for a moment and then abruptly said, 'Well, I better hang up; he may be trying to call.'

Their night together at the Palace Hotel didn't come up even once in the entire conversation.

*

Mansoor felt a sense of insufficiency after his chat with Mehrun, like something crucial had been left unsaid, something unacknowledged. But did he really want to talk to her about that night at the Palace Hotel?

Standing near the living-room window, Mansoor gazed at the starry sky and thought about Mehrun and Lisa. Had he cheated on Lisa? And what about Mehrun? Had she seduced him? He didn't want to inflict pain on either of them. To keep quiet was probably the best choice, at least for now. Perhaps he would tell Lisa about Mehrun's existence at some point.

For now, he had to concentrate on finishing up in Iowa and hurrying back home. Athanni and the certainty of a showdown had to wait. But how would it affect his mother? She'd always had a tender spot for her sister—he knew that—but what tormented him the most was her emotional susceptibility to Athanni. With his smarmy voice and phoney attention, he had her wrapped around his fat fingers. She had become too close to Athanni, even suggesting in one of her letters that he had become like a son to her in Mansoor's absence. He thought about his beloved Uncle Zahid, and how much his mother would have needed him right now. But he died too young. He would have been able to handle the whole situation with Zakir Hassan, and especially with Athanni and his family. His mind drifted back to Zakir, how the man had changed. The urbane ex-diplomat had been totally replaced by this ultraconservative mullah, both in looks and in thoughts.

Religion, with its Sufistic spirituality, had always existed in his country as something private. But its new, literalist public face horrified Mansoor, and not without reason, making him fearful and angry at the revolt of the fanatics and their needless cruelties. He wasn't at all excited at the prospect of going back home. He shuddered at the thought of living in a repressive society where many intelligent, educated people now supported General Behroopia's moral imperatives. But what troubled Mansoor the most was just how arch-conservative the young people of his generation had become. They had lapsed into a pastiched nostalgia that never was. He wondered if Pakistan's short history was tragically repeating itself. He envied the West for having come out of the dark Middle Ages, their social problems notwithstanding; America had opened up Mansoor's eyes.

The thought about America turned his attention back to Lisa. Like the sweet, fragrant bela flowers back home, her bright and beautiful image appeared from the messy corner of his mind, and he smiled again. Saddened to hear about her parents' ugly divorce, he had felt for her when she told him their story. He was in love with her, that much he knew, but he kept warring with his feelings for Mehrun. Why had he slept with her? All these complications had muddled everything. He knew that Lisa, too, had developed deep feelings for him; he could see it in her eyes and he could feel it in her touch. But alas, theirs was a relationship that was doomed from the start. Too many dead-ends, too many winding roads lay ahead, or so he thought. He wasn't even sure where he would be two years from now.

Regardless of where Pakistan was headed, his future was there, and Lisa would be a misfit there. It would be unfair to ask her to give up everything for him and live in a distant land where everything was unstable. Besides, how could he make her comfortable in a country where he knew he would be miserable? Plagued by these misgivings, he shut his eyes, but the unrelenting thoughts stayed until sleep finally took over.

*

One shivery Iowa evening, Mansoor came back early to his apartment. It was only 4 p.m., but the darkness outside made it feel like the middle of the night. The temperature tumbled to record lows as the Arctic spell froze bodies and souls. Despite putting the thermostat to a toasty 75 degrees Fahrenheit, Mansoor could still feel the Midwest chill drilling into his bones. He turned on the television, took out the leftover chicken from the refrigerator and placed it in the oven to warm it up. The local weatherman was talking about the frigid weather and Mansoor almost died when he heard the man say that with the wind-chill factor, it was minus 60 degrees Fahrenheit outside.

With his dinner warmed, Mansoor sat down in front of the television to eat. It was during the middle of the NBC news report that Tom Brokaw, the anchorman, casually read a three-sentence statement that two former prime ministers, one from Iran and the other from Pakistan, had been summarily hanged early that morning. There were no other details. Stunned, Mansoor furiously flicked through different channels to hear more. But the executed leaders of these minor countries were too insignificant to compete with the exigency of a Pepto-Bismol commercial—a simple cure for unending heartburn eclipsing the dead leaders of Iran and Pakistan.

Enraged at the lack of coverage of such an important event, Mansoor telephoned Lisa to find out if she had heard anything; but she hadn't been watching the news. He then called the president of the Pakistani Students' Association.

'Did you watch the evening news?' Mansoor asked.

'No, why?'

'The general hanged The People's Leader.'

'Thank God! I am going to offer prayers of thanksgiving for the good riddance, my friend.'

Mansoor hung up in disgust. How could anyone rejoice as if there was justice in the hanging of these rulers—authoritarians, no doubt? Justice and execution, two moral imperatives that were at odds with each other. Wasn't that moral nihilism with all its connotations and grotesque plausibility? Did moral facts not exist? What about General Behroopia, who was becoming more repressive and draconian? Should he not be executed to correct his wrongs? The tragedy of Pakistan's history had risen again from the rubbles of its fleeting democracy.

Mansoor was no admirer of The People's Leader. On the contrary, he had despised him with equal ferocity. But he also believed that his execution was based on trumped-up charges. He had been murdered to pave the way for the mullahs and their brand of dictatorship. By killing him, he thought, General Behroopia will have wiped out all opposition. The People's Leader had built a cult around his own personality, and this very cult became his nemesis in the end. The next day, the local papers printed a short blurb about the two executed leaders. Mansoor crumpled the newspaper into a ball and threw it in the dustbin.

*

At the end of his course work, Mansoor took his qualifying exams and became a candidate for the PhD degree. Now, all he had to do was find a dissertation topic that would be relevant and soul-stirring, something related to the effect of corruption on Pakistan's economy. Once his research questions were approved, he could go back to Pakistan and do some original research.

After the last telephone call, Mansoor had not heard from Mehrun again and he presumed that she had moved to London. There were no more pictures or threatening letters from Athanni either, which made Mansoor wonder if he was still planning his next move. With his exams over, Mansoor suddenly felt empty. Lisa, who always went home to Connecticut for Christmas, decided to stay in Iowa City for the holidays. She was in no mood to face her divorced parents at the family celebration. So far, she had maintained her sanity, but Mansoor was worried that she might become depressed. To take her mind away from her parents' divorce, he suggested that they visit Joseph in Houston for the opening of his restaurant. At first, Lisa refused. But when Mansoor persisted, she reluctantly agreed on the condition that he would do the lion's share of driving. So, the next morning, they got into her 1972 Dodge Dart Swinger and headed towards Texas.

Driving past vast tracts of the snow-covered farmlands of Iowa, Kansas and Missouri, and then through the flat plains of Oklahoma, they finally entered the desolate stretch that was Texas some eighteen hours after leaving Iowa City. The diverse splendour of America was in full display even in winter. With Lisa by his side, the thousand-mile journey did not seem so tedious. Throughout the long hours on the road, they talked about every topic under the winter sky, every thing except their relationship and their future. They talked about American and Pakistani politics and the civil war in Lebanon. Lisa read aloud the poems of Auden and Yeats from her pocket edition of *Selected Poems*, her constant companions. She explained to him why jazz was considered a threat to America. And Mansoor introduced her to Ghalib's poetry and Manto's stories. He talked about the famous Pakistani ghazal singer Mehdi Hassan and his unique delivery.

And then, to lighten things up, he spoke at length about Joseph and his exploits, carefully omitting Mehrun from all the stories. Mansoor was deathly afraid that she might visit Joseph in Houston for his restaurant's opening. How would he be able to handle such an awkward situation? What would he do? Not wanting to think about Mehrun, his attention returned to Lisa. She had become emotional while talking about her younger sister, who died of leukaemia at the age of four. Her lips quivered and her eyes welled up as she talked about her little sister's last day. They had brought her home from the hospital to make sure that her last hours were peaceful. Mansoor put his right arm around her shoulder and squeezed her, and when she put her head on his shoulder, his eyes lit up.

It was December, but the Texas sun shone in all its brilliance. After Mansoor exited the interstate and drove into a suburb of Houston, he missed a turn and got a bit lost. But finally, around 5 p.m., he spotted Joseph's apartment complex. In a tony suburb, the gated complex stood like a retreat, shielded from the rest of the world. The contrast with Bhangi Para couldn't be starker. The memory of his visit there with Mehrun was still vivid. The railway line acting as the cordon sanitaire, demarcating the area from the rest of the city, the naked children, the old man who had misery written all over his wrinkled self, and the dead dog—still haunting him after all these years. Now Joseph had found a home that performed a reverse function for him. It cordoned off the city and prevented its sordidness from reaching his beautiful enclave. Mansoor could hardly believe his eyes. Destiny had finally opted to gleam on Joseph. He checked the address in his pocket phone book just to make sure that he was in the right place. Unmistakably opulent, distinctively plush, the Woodhaven Apartment Complex fanned out in all its splendour. The grass, still green, the terracotta walkways, the green tennis courts, the shimmering swimming pool—all vivid reminders of the affluence of the tenants.

*

Joseph greeted them enthusiastically, shaking their hands vigorously. America had transformed him. The Joseph that Mansoor grew up with, the one who roamed around in a loincloth and undershirt, was gone. In his place stood a tall, muscular young man, wearing a polo T-shirt and Levi's jeans, exuding ardour and displaying devotion. The only vestiges of his old self were his moustache, his Punjabi-accented Urdu and the familiar bidi sticking out from his mouth.

Mansoor asked, 'Where on earth did you find a bidi in Houston?'

'Oh, my friend, what is it that you cannot find in the Pakistani bazaars in Houston. Do you want some paan? I can get that too.'

Mansoor just laughed. Feeling happy about Joseph's achievements, he congratulated him on his success. Joseph, in his humbleness, attributed it to Mansoor for 'providing' his friendship and to his father for providing the money.

Although the two-bedroom apartment appeared luxurious, it boasted only a few pieces of furniture. A dark printed sofa, mismatched with two sturdy ladder-back chairs, clashed sharply with the beige-coloured wall-to-wall carpet, while a spacious coffee table stuck out in the centre. A set of sliding doors at one end of the room opened on to the balcony, where a black, round grill vented smoke and the aroma of barbecued kebabs. Although Joseph had been prepping for his restaurant's inaugural day, he had found the time to cook a lavish meal—two kinds of kebabs, chicken tikka and lamb biryani, along with ras malai for dessert. It was the big-hearted Joseph thanking Mansoor for his father's magnanimity, and both his guests ate ravenously. Mansoor was surprised by his cooking skills, and Lisa, who had eaten Pakistani food at Mansoor's apartment, felt that Joseph's cooking surpassed Mansoor's by more than a mile.

'Why are you buying a Burger King franchise? You should open a Pakistani restaurant,' she suggested.

'Lisa ji, someday I will do that, but first I will get rich, and then I will go into that ditch!' He laughed and Lisa raised her eyebrows.

After dinner, Joseph and Mansoor drank Heineken and reminisced about old times. Lisa stayed with them for a while, fighting the inevitable boredom with some wine, and then retired to the guest room.

After she left, Joseph went to his bedroom and came back with a cheque written in Mansoor's name, for twelve hundred dollars, and handed it to him.

'What is this?'

'Barrister Sahib had given this to me; it was a loan, even though he never said that.'

'Don't insult his memory, Joseph,' Mansoor replied, a bit hurt, and returned the cheque.

'I knew that you are like your father. He always gave and never took back. If you do not consider me a bhangi, let me hug you.'

'You were never a bhangi to me, Joseph.'

As he held his friend in a hug, Joseph began to cry like a child. Mansoor patted his back, trying to calm him down. Once he stopped crying, they drank late into the night. In his drunkenness, Joseph told Mansoor that he had also invited Zakir Hassan for the opening ceremony.

'Why did you have to invite him? He was the one responsible for my father's death.'

'Well, Mansoor Babu, he, too, was my benefactor. Had it not been for him, I wouldn't have got the visa.'

'He helped me get my visa, too, but I repaid him by praying with him!' Mansoor chortled, his laugh reminding him of how his father used to be in his intoxicated state.

'But I am not sure if Zakir Sahib will actually come. I spoke with him on the telephone some two months ago and he told me he was planning to go on a proselytizing tour with the Dheela Pyjama group,' Joseph added.

'How do *you* know about the Pyjama Dheela Topi Tight Party?'

'Haider Sahib zindabad!'

Mansoor laughed and then changed the subject, 'Is Mehrun coming?'

'No, she told me she was moving to London and would be too busy to come.'

Mansoor sighed, feeling relieved that a potential crisis had been averted. 'When was the last time you spoke to her?' he asked.

'About three weeks ago . . . I don't think she is happy, Mansoor Babu. I could sense it in her voice.'

Mansoor, surprised at Joseph's perspicacity and his ability to grasp the truth about Mehrun's marital situation, said nothing. They drank for a while longer and then retired, calling it a night.

*

The bright sun dappled its rays through the openings between the curtains in their bedroom, waking Mansoor and Lisa up the next morning. Realizing that it was late, Mansoor jumped out of bed and hit the shower while Lisa, her eyes closed, rested her exhausted self on the lumpy mattress. Joseph had already left to monitor the progress at his restaurant.

Outside, somebody fired up a lawnmower, startling Lisa with its raucous roar. She was now fully awake. A little tired and homesick, she began wondering if her family would celebrate Christmas the way they used to. Before they left for Houston, she had called her mother and made up some lame excuse for not coming home that year. But Lisa knew her mother didn't believe her.

She was still thinking about the state of things back home when the doorbell rang, its grating peal making her jump out of bed. She didn't want to answer it, but someone kept pressing it longer and harder, as if to annoy her. Had Joseph forgotten his keys? She got up, put on her nightgown and went to the front door. Through the peephole, Lisa saw a bearded man in a black tunic. Was he Joseph's relative? Her sigh almost audible, her fingers turning the knob with a frustrated pressure, she opened the door slightly.

The bearded man, taken aback at the sight of a woman in a nightgown, lowered his head and asked, 'Does Yousef Suleiman live here?'

'Who?'

'Yousef Suleiman!' he repeated.

'No,' she replied, but then hesitatingly asked, 'Are you talking about Joseph Solomon?'

'Yes, that was his Christian name; Yousef Suleiman is his Muslim name, which I gave him.'

'Oh.'

'Yes.' The man continued to look at the floor, his shifty manners puzzling Lisa.

'Well, Joseph has already left for work.'

'My name is Zakir Hassan and I have come from Pakistan,' the man said.

Lisa knew right away that it must be the same Zakir Hassan that Mansoor had mentioned when discussing his parents' marital problems. He had described his transformation in vivid detail. Making no eye contact with her, his behaviour off-balancing his manner, he made Lisa feel downright uneasy.

'Do you want to come in?'

'No, thank you. Are you Mrs Suleiman?'

'No, I am a friend of Mansoor ul Haq. We are just visiting Joseph.'

As soon as she uttered Mansoor's name, he lifted his head, his eyes passing over her face for one quick second before he averted his gaze and looked the other way. The man who had lived in the West and dated many women in his life now felt embarrassed at the mere sight of one. As he stood there dithering, Mansoor came out of the shower with a towel wrapped around his waist. Startled to see Zakir Hassan at the door, he stopped in his tracks and stared at him. A few seconds later, having regained his composure, he blurted, 'Assalam alai kum.'

'Wa-alaikum assalam,' Zakir replied.

Relieved to see Mansoor, Lisa scurried back into their room, leaving the gauche visitor to her boyfriend. Mansoor invited him in. Proceeding slowly, Zakir wiped his shoes on the doormat, entered the apartment and seated himself on a chair in the living room. Mansoor excused himself to get dressed.

Alone in the room, Zakir surveyed his surroundings. The coffee table, cluttered with empty beer cans, greeted him. His lips tightening at the *sinful* sight, he pulled his chair away from the *napaak*, unclean table. When Mansoor reappeared in his Iowa Hawkeyes sweatshirt and Levi's jeans, Zakir immediately ordered him to remove 'these vile things', pointing to the beer cans. Hiding his smile, Mansoor took the remains of the night to the kitchen. When he came back, he asked Zakir where he was staying.

'I am staying at the Hilton,' he replied.

'So how are things in Pakistan?'

'I don't know. I have been out of the country . . . I've been travelling for the last two months.' Then he bragged about his group of preachers and their success around the world.

Mansoor remembered the apt name Haider had given them, the Pyjama Dheela Topi Tight Party, and smiled. 'How is your family?' he asked.

'Alhamdolillah, praise be to Allah.'

The conversation limped along awkwardly, with Zakir replying only when Mansoor asked something. It was as if he was sitting in a Civil Service interview, making sure to provide to-the-point answers, nothing more nothing less. The silent interludes cumbered the air. Zakir's eyes kept shifting, as if he was searching for something in the room. He never asked Mansoor anything. With the conversation going nowhere, Mansoor invited him to stay for breakfast, but he refused. And when Lisa came back into the room, dressed in a white blouse and a black skirt, looking fresh and pretty, Zakir resolutely gazed at the floor again, ignoring her altogether. Mansoor thought of formally introducing her to him, but then Zakir looked at his wristwatch and abruptly decided to leave.

'Please tell Yousef that I am staying at the Hilton and that he should get in touch with me,' he said on his way out.

'What a rude man!' Lisa exclaimed after he left. 'All this time, he never made any eye contact with me!'

Mansoor explained to her, over a cup of black coffee and buttered toast, that the new Zakir considered making eye contact with women a grievous sin, while the old Zakir entertained them on his lap.

Twenty-Six

Joseph had invited all his benefactors out of a sense of duty, but he had excluded his mother, which seemed rather odd to Mansoor. The one who sacrificed so much to raise him, who scrubbed toilets in bungalows so that her son could eat two meals a day, was altogether forgotten, banished to Lethe. To Joseph, Pyaro had committed the indefensible sin of marrying his father's supposed enemy. And for this reason, she was not invited to what was surely the biggest day in his life. He never forgave her, and one day, in a state of double-distilled-drunkenness, he dispatched a telegram to his mother, using an assumed name, announcing his own death.

But then he felt compelled to invite Zakir, who viewed Joseph as *his* success story, for it was because of his prayers and blessings that the bhangi was experiencing prosperity in his life now. Zakir still believed that Joseph had actually converted to Islam. In his self-aggrandizing mind, it was he, Zakir Hassan, who had brought this man into the folds of Islam and given him his Muslim identity: Yousef Suleiman. Joseph, of course, played along, making Zakir feel like he had earned thousands of extra brownie points in heaven. When Mansoor told him about Zakir's visit that morning, Joseph became a bit agitated. He telephoned Zakir at the Hilton and invited the preacher-slash-ex-diplomat to come and stay with him in his apartment. But after an awkward silence, Zakir turned down his invitation, without any explanations whatsoever, and then hung up the phone.

*

Two days after Christmas, Mansoor and Lisa went to a shopping mall in the city, where he impulsively bought a bracelet with a heart charm for her while she was busy trying on some dresses in the fitting room. She hugged and kissed him when he surprised her with it in the car. Back at the apartment, Lisa was still admiring the bracelet when the doorbell rang. Mansoor went to the front door and looked through the peephole. The concave lens revealed Zakir's face. Mansoor frowned when he saw him. After he opened the door, he saw that Zakir was accompanied by an entire entourage of men, all dressed in shalwar-kameez. He knew right away that the entire born-again coalition had come to work on him, the 'aimless, lost Muslim'.

'We have come to talk with you, beta,' Zakir said.

'You didn't have to come all this way to talk to me, Uncle Zakir. You could have telephoned me, and I would have come to your hotel,' he replied, pretending ignorance about the purpose of their visit.

'No, I had this yearning to come and chat with you personally.'

'Okay, but about what?' Mansoor continued his pretence.

Without answering him, Zakir gently pushed him aside and walked into the apartment, the rest of the entourage barging in after him. Some found a chair, some sat cross-legged on the floor and some stood, leaving one chair for Mansoor. There were eight of them. Once seated, Mansoor spotted Sher Khan, the former cricketer. Clean-shaven again and dressed smartly in a cream-coloured shalwar-kameez, he looked a little out of place amidst those scraggly bearded men. After a brief pause, Mansoor asked if he could get drinks for them.

'No, son, thank you,' Zakir said. 'We are not going to waste too much of your time.' He paused and pursed his lips. Then, suddenly switching to his posh accented English, he said, 'Son, we get so busy in our lives, we get so embroiled in our mundane affairs that we forget our real purpose on this God-gifted earth.'

And I suppose you have come to remind me of that, Mansoor thought.

'We have been sent by God to this earth to serve Him. We are His servants and the way to serve Him is exquisitely prescribed in our holy book. If you read it carefully, the holy Qur'an has the answers to all our problems. Those who follow the dictates of our holy book will pass through the *Pull Sirat,* the bridge that leads to Paradise, without any difficulty. For this bridge is thin like a needle and sharp like a sword. The righteous will have no problem walking on it, but the sinners will fall like dead flies into the deepest hell. And—'

Before he could finish, Mansoor interrupted him, 'Excuse me, sir, with all due respect, you are not telling me anything new. I learnt about these things in the fourth grade.' He deliberately used the word 'sir', realizing the need to keep a healthy distance from him.

'Aah, yes! We all learn about our religion at an early age, but we soon forget it. Temptations, glamour and other worldly pleasures mislead us. My job as a Muslim is to remind you of your most important obligations and to guide you to the right path. When I was your age, I, too, was brash. I, too, thought that I would live forever, but my perspective changed when Allah showed me the true light.'

'Are you saying that I have been misled by these so-called worldly pleasures, and that you are on the right path?' Zakir's self-righteous speech had bristled Mansoor.

'No, please don't misunderstand me, beta. All of us have been misled. All of us are sinners. To be honest, I am one of the greatest sinners, but I try to atone for my sins by guiding people to the right path. Do not misconstrue what I say, beta; I am not saying that you are a sinner, for that is between you and the Almighty.'

'Let's hear what exactly you are saying then!' Mansoor said, his hackles rising.

'I am just asking you to expiate for your sins every day. And the best way to do so is by praying five times and reading the holy book every day. If you remember, I told you the same thing when you came to my house several years ago, and from what I remember, you promised to do that.'

'Well, if you are not saying that I am a sinner, then what should I expiate for?' Mansoor, much like his attorney father, cross-examined him.

'Let me ask you this: do you pray?' Zakir persisted.

'First of all, whether or not I pray is none of your business. But to answer your question, I worship my own god and in my own special way.'

Zakir had a look that said 'don't get cute with me,' but he took a deep breath and with perfect equanimity, continued, 'There is only one way to pray, my son.'

'And I suppose that way is *your* way?' Mansoor retorted.

'It is not my way or your way. It is the *Islamic* way.'

'Listen, Zakir Sahib, you don't have a patent on how to pray, and the Kingdom of God is not your personal fiefdom that you inherited from your forefathers,' Mansoor shot back. He remembered his dead father, and as far as he was concerned, Zakir had murdered him. And now the man had the gall to sit across from him and try to show him the righteous path.

Zakir kept his patience intact, but the others in his party fidgeted with anger. They had sat there tensely, listening to the conversation, but now they felt challenged by this neophyte. Nothing like this had ever happened to them, at least not in a Muslim household. And they regarded Mansoor as a Muslim and Joseph's apartment as a *Darul Muslimin*, the house of Muslims. They had never expected such a showdown. Sher Khan, openly displaying his disgust with Mansoor and the way the conversation had unfolded, stepped in on behalf of Zakir.

'Brother Mansoor, Brother Zakir is telling you what is good for you.'

'I think I know better than anybody else in this world what is good for me,' Mansoor's burning stare and his rising voice unnerved Sher Khan. Lisa, who had quarantined herself all this time in the bedroom, got concerned and came out to check what was happening.

'Is everything okay?' she asked, looking at Mansoor.

Mansoor just nodded his head. Sher Khan ogled Lisa intently, while all the others bowed their heads. She remained there for a few more seconds, in all probability trying to discomfit them, and then dashed out of the apartment 'to get some fresh air'.

'Look, Mansoor, I don't want to argue with you. I regard you just like my son. My only request to you is that you accompany us to the mosque and join us for the evening prayer, just for my sake.'

'Look, if I go to the mosque, it will be because I want to go and not because you want me to go, and it will definitely not be for your sake.'

'You forget, Mansoor, that you are in America because of me. If I had not arranged for your visa, you would still be languishing in Pakistan,' Zakir said this in his most clipped English.

'No, Zakir Sahib, I have not forgotten that. And I have also not forgotten that you murd . . . that you were the cause of discord between my father and my mother.'

That was the breaking point for Zakir. His eyes flashed with anger and he wrung his fingers as he thought about what to say next. But Mansoor had lost his patience by then. He got up abruptly and said, 'And now, gentlemen, I would like to end this conversation for it has gone far beyond its limits. Besides, I have better things to do.'

'Better things like fornicating?' the Lion Prince disgorged the last sentence in English. Like a word from his subconscious, it had sneaked out without his realizing it.

'Get out of here, all of you!' Mansoor ordered the men, as if it was his apartment they were all in.

'Well, this is not your apartment, you ungrateful son of a—' Without finishing his sentence, Zakir got up and stormed out. All the others glared at Mansoor as they walked out, while he frowned back at them, seething with anger.

*

When Joseph came back that evening, Mansoor told him everything. He felt ashamed about Zakir's behaviour and apologized profusely to Mansoor. As it turned out, it was Joseph who was inadvertently responsible for Zakir's showing up with his entire entourage. He had sounded so keen for Zakir to attend his restaurant's opening that the man had altered his proselytizing travel plan. Joseph's big wish was to have all those who had supported him in his life cut the ribbon together. When Mansoor heard about it, he protested vehemently and told Joseph that in no way was he going to share the stage with 'that self-righteous man and his sycophantic groupies'. To make it easy for Joseph, Mansoor decided to withdraw from the ribbon-cutting ceremony. Joseph obviously did not want that because he considered Mansoor the most important, but then he did not want to create a scene either.

*

Joseph threw a party on New Year's Eve at his apartment, inviting some of his friends and would-be employees. Mansoor and Lisa helped him buy the drinks and all the other party accoutrements that were needed. Considering that he had planned a busy inaugural for his restaurant the next morning, it was risky to have a booze and dance party that would inevitably go on well past midnight. But Joseph was no stranger to risk. Mansoor had seen him getting totally drunk the night before, only to hear him leave for his restaurant around seven in the morning.

With everything in place, Joseph put on Ghulam Farid Sabri's qawwali on his stereo at full volume.

'What kind of music is this?' Lisa asked him.

'This is Pakistani rock and roll,' Joseph replied.

'What? Are you kidding me?' she asked. Joseph just smiled in response, but Mansoor intervened and tried to explain the nuances of qawwali to her.

'A qawwali is a sort of Sufi devotional song that used to be sung at the tombs of Muslim saints in India during the Mughal period, but now they have also become very popular in Pakistani–Indian films.'

'Tonight is a big night for you guys because you get to meet my gori memsahib!' Joseph interjected, changing the topic.

Lisa looked at Mansoor, a bit puzzled by the unfamiliar word Joseph had inserted.

'What is her name?' Mansoor asked.

'Cheryl Hampton, but I call her my gori memsahib,' Joseph replied.

'What does that mean?' Lisa asked.

'It means my white lady!' Joseph winked mischievously at Mansoor, and Lisa smiled.

The guests started coming in by eight in the evening. As the music became louder and the guests more raffish, Mansoor shouted in Joseph's ear, 'I hope you didn't invite Zakir Hassan.'

'No, I didn't. But I did invite Sher Khan,' Joseph shouted back.

'Are you serious?'

'Oh, yes. I asked Sher Khan, what's a young man like you going to do on New Year's Eve?'

'And what did he say?'

'He said he was going to worship God at the mosque. So I told him that if he came to my party, I would introduce him to a few goddesses.'

Mansoor let out a big laugh. He hadn't laughed like that for a long time.

'Do you think he is going to come?' he asked.

Joseph asked Lisa to excuse them for a moment. Then he pulled Mansoor to the side and whispered in Urdu, 'If he still gets a hard-on, he will come.'

Mansoor laughed again, and Lisa knew Joseph had said something crude. Shaking her head, she went to the dining table and got herself a glass of pink champagne and for Mansoor, a Scotch on the rocks.

With every passing hour, the party only got livelier. It was close to ten by the time Cheryl Hampton, a tall, slender and stunning blonde, entered the apartment. As soon as she sashayed in, Mansoor knew who she was. Very proudly, Joseph introduced her to Lisa and Mansoor and got her some champagne.

'So, where did you two meet?' Mansoor asked Cheryl after they had all settled down with their drinks. Both Joseph and Cheryl began laughing.

'Oh god! It's a funny story! Joe, you tell him.'

Mansoor had never heard anyone call Joseph 'Joe' before. It must be something special. Cheryl's eyes revealed her feelings for him, but Mansoor did not notice much in Joseph's eyes, except that they were bloodshot and that they still had that impish twinkle.

'You see, Cheryl goes to the University of Houston, and I used to be the manager at the Burger King outlet nearby. I had seen her many times on my way to work. She always carried a bunch of really heavy books in her hand. You know . . . psychology books. I knew then that she was getting her degree in psychology. One day, I went to the mall, and there she was, shopping at the department store in a dark red dress. I discreetly made my way over to her, and when she was right next to me, I said to her, "You look like a sherry!" And with my accent and all, she thought I said, "You look like a Cheryl.'"

'I could've sworn he said that,' Cheryl jumped in. 'So I asked him how he knew my name. And he said, "I am a fortune teller." Now, I don't usually fall for that sort of bullshit, but since I thought he had just told me my name, I sort of ended up thinking that maybe he *was* a fortune teller. And the next thing he tells me is that I go to the University of Houston and that I am majoring in, how did you say it, Joe?' She turned to Joseph again.

'I said you were majoring in pisschialogy because that's how I used to pronounce 'psychology'. English pronunciations are stupid,' Joseph clarified.

Laughing, Cheryl continued with the story. 'The next thing I knew, he was holding my hand and telling me all sorts of things about myself, and surprisingly, eighty per cent of what he told me was right. Then he introduced himself, and the rest, as they say, is history.'

'No, actually, the rest is pisschialogy,' Joseph added, and everyone laughed.

The party was in full swing by now, with people laughing and drinking and dancing. Not everyone, however, was happy with Joseph's selection of music. Mansoor went to check if he had some dance music, but one look at his music collection and he was disgusted with Joseph's horrid taste. He turned on the radio and tuned into a station which was playing something that people could slow-dance to—Peaches and Cream's 'Reunited'. Mansoor held Lisa in his arms and began to dance. Everyone followed suit. Someone dimmed the lights, providing a perfect romantic atmosphere, but no sooner had that happened than the doorbell rang again. Mansoor saw Joseph going to get the door with a Heineken in his hand. When he opened the door, he saw Zakir Hassan and Sher Khan, dressed in their traditional shalwar-kameez, standing outside. Not knowing what to say or do, Joseph invited them to come in. But Zakir looked at the bottle in his hand, then at the scene within the apartment and turned livid. With his swelled-up carotid artery and his dilated nostrils, he erupted.

'I thought you had invited me to come and bless your restaurant! I thought you had converted to Islam! Shame on you for wasting my time. Curse be on you and your djinn friend Mansoor ul Haq.' And with that, he stormed away, Sher Khan following him.

'Fuck you too!' Joseph shouted. He saw Zakir turning back in anger, but Sher Khan whisked him away, perhaps realizing that getting into a brawl with Joseph would be the last thing they should do. Mansoor saw and heard everything, and when Joseph closed the door, he went up to him and asked, 'Do you think he will be there to inaugurate your restaurant tomorrow?'

'I sure hope so!' Joseph laughed. 'But if he's not there, you can substitute for him!'

And in the deepest recess of his mind, Mansoor heard the reverberating voice of Haider Rizvi chant:

Twelfth man . . . on the pitch . . . in he comes to serve;
Zero talent . . . zero knack, has a lot of . . . nerve

He then heard Zakir calling him: 'Mansoor ul Haq, the djinn! Mansoor ul Haq, the djinn!'

Mansoor wasn't sure if it was the alcohol muddling his brain or if he was hallucinating.

*

As the clock struck twelve, Joseph welcomed the new year, ululating. Arriving in the guise of drunken revelry, it heralded the end of his centuries-old untouchability. It broke the economic barriers, the social impediments and the psychological blockades of time immemorial. He knew that his progeny would never ever have to suffer the same contempt; his descendants would never again experience the humiliation of a hereditary bhangi-hood.

His quotidian existence was finally over, his mangled life was now straight. He had finally matriculated. Exuberant, he first hugged and kissed Mansoor, then Lisa and finally Cheryl. Then, calling all the revellers to attention, in a booming, emotional and intoxicated voice, he declared, 'My friends, I want to introduce to you my brother for life, Mansoor ul Haq. He and his late father, Noor ul Haq, the big barrister sahib, they gave me and my family sustenance when death took away my father. He and his late father gave me and my family a roof when floods swallowed our home. He and his late father gave me hope with their money when others shoved insults at me. And most of all, my brother Mansoor, I call him Mansoor Babu, he gave me the best gift of all—a lifelong friendship.'

With tears freely flowing down his cheeks, Joseph hugged his childhood friend again and again, shaking his hand. Despite the stoned atmosphere, Joseph's speech had touched many a heart. Mansoor, who had been unaware of the deep respect and loyalty that Joseph felt for his father, was overwhelmed by emotions too. Putting his arms around Lisa and Mansoor, an extremely drunk and emotional Joseph said to Lisa, 'Marry this man, because he will make you happy for life, just like he made me happy.'

Both Lisa and Mansoor were embarrassed at being put on the spot. But Mansoor had already been entertaining the thought of marrying Lisa, although he knew it would be impossible to convince his mother to bless their union. Mansoor remembered the awkward conversation that he had had with his father just before he left for America. Noor had told him that his mother would be deeply hurt if he married a white woman. Or was it an American woman? But then Lisa was half African American. He was sure her race would make it even more difficult for his mother to accept her. It did not matter that Aunt Sarwat was probably darker than Lisa. The word 'African' was all his mother would care about.

*

Around three in the morning all the guests left, and Joseph went to bed shortly afterwards, but Mansoor and Lisa stayed awake in the living room until the early hours of the morning. Snuggled on the sofa together, Lisa at last revved up enough courage to ask Mansoor what had been percolating in her mind for a long time.

'Mansoor, I have to know where I stand . . .' she said.

'What do you mean?' he asked. Although Mansoor was starting to feel the beginning of a massive hangover from all the mixed drinks he had guzzled, he knew very well what Lisa meant.

'I mean, where do I fit in your life? Where is our relationship going?'

'Do you have to know about it now?'

'Yes, because we never talk about these things. And I have to know so I can plan my life. I will finish my degree next May and I have to make some decisions.'

'Can't it wait till we are back home?'

'No, it can't. What you can tell me in four days, you can tell me now.' Lisa was determined to get some answers.

With shakiness of purpose, Mansoor said, 'I want to marry you, Lisa, but my life is too messed up at this stage for me to give you any certainties . . .'

Lisa didn't say anything. Mansoor had made love to her many times, but much to her dismay, he had never actually told her that he loved her. The social conditioning of his mind prevented him from saying the words out loud. He had grown up in a society where saying 'I love you' was thought to cheapen the pure sentiment of love. It was never announced, never displayed.

After a slight pause, Mansoor closed his eyes, gathered his thoughts and said haltingly, 'I . . . I love you, Lisa Reid, but . . . I have to go back . . . to sort things out with my mother and with my relatives.'

Mansoor had told Lisa about the ruckus his mother had created when she saw the picture of them from the party. After a slight pause, he continued, 'I also have to decide where I am going to live—in Pakistan or in America. My mother is all alone there, and I know . . . she . . . she wants me to return to Pakistan and live with her. I also know I will have a difficult time convincing her about me marrying you, so I have to break the news gradually.'

'Wait, wait, wait. Did you just say that you have to *convince* your mother about marrying me?'

'Yes . . .'

'But don't you think you have to ask *me* about marriage first? I mean, how can you be sure about whether I even want to marry you or not?' she asked.

'I don't want to ask you something that I may not be able to deliver. And I cannot force you to live in a place that you may hate.'

'I would sure like to try living in Pakistan. I know I can make adjustments,' Lisa said.

'Life in Pakistan is not so easy, Lisa. There are too many small annoyances. Too many restrictions. Too many things that you take for granted here are simply not available there.'

'I think you are trying to find excuses,' Lisa said with a degree of petulance.

'No, I am not!' Mansoor protested. His head swimming, he felt like he was going to throw up any minute.

'Mansoor, I know you've had too many drinks and that this is not the time to talk, but I would appreciate it if you could think things over and give me an answer in a couple of days.'

Lisa just could not understand why Mansoor alone could not make the decision regarding marriage. The need for his mother's permission to marry her was something that simply lay beyond her grasp. It was *his* life after all!

And then, with his eyes closed and his head throbbing with a headache, Mansoor asked her the question that he should have asked a long time ago, 'Will you marry me?'

'WHAT?' Lisa turned and looked at him, unsure that she had heard him correctly.

'Will you marry me?' he repeated.

'Mansoor, you don't have to ask me that question to end this discussion. I told you, you can think about it for a few days. I can wait.'

'I want to marry you, Lisa. And I will marry you today, on the first day of the new year, if you say yes.'

'Mansoor, wait. You just told me you needed your mother's permission, how can you say you want to marry me today? Are you sure you are not saying this because you feel pressured by me?'

'No, I am not asking you to marry me because of any pressure. So, what do you say?'

Before she could answer, they heard the telephone ringing in Joseph's room. After four rings, Joseph picked the phone up. Then they heard him shout into the phone.

'I think it's a long-distance call, probably from Pakistan,' Mansoor said, sitting up.

He heard Joseph say, 'Salaam, Haider Sahib. Yes, he is here with me. What? How did it happen? Sahib ji . . . Hello? Hello?' Then he heard Joseph clicking the cradle a few times and cursing the telephone system of Pakistan.

An unknown terror gripped Mansoor. His stomach tightened, his throat dried up and he had this terrifying feeling that something was wrong, and he knew it had to do with his mother.

Mansoor heard the door open and saw the silhouetted figure of Joseph appear from his bedroom. He was wearing a lungi, like he used to wear in Pakistan.

'What's wrong, Joseph?' Mansoor asked.

'Hey, you guys still up?' Joseph was startled to see them in his living room.

'Who was it on the phone?'

'Oh! No one! It was just a wrong number,' Joseph tried to lie, but his ashen face gave it all away.

'No, it wasn't. I heard you clearly. You were talking to Haider Rizvi. It was about my mother. Wasn't it? Is she dead?' Mansoor said all this in one breath. It was as if he had a sudden foreboding about his mother, or perhaps he had unconsciously prepared himself for the worst news. Joseph stood there motionless, his mouth open, his mind blank in utter disbelief.

'Yes.'

'Did he say when this happened?'

'No, the line got disconnected.'

'Can I use your phone to call home?'

'Yes, yes, of course,' Joseph replied.

For the next hour, Mansoor tried to call the Kashana, but the line appeared to be perpetually busy. Lisa could feel the hail of emotions that hit him. Frustrated with the telephone line, he got up and asked Lisa to wake him up around eight. She looked at the time. It was almost quarter to six.

Twenty-Seven

Farhat had a massive heart attack. With Athanni by her side, she was rushed to the hospital where, as she lay dying, she repeatedly called Mansoor's name and implored Athanni to phone him. He promised to call him but made no attempts to actually do so. To show the world that Mansoor was an utterly heartless person, he then spread the lie that he had placed the call and apprised Mansoor of the situation, making it amply clear to him that his mother was on her deathbed, but Mansoor did not want to come right away.

'Can you believe that he slept with that half-breed churail even before his father's soul ascended to heaven? And even though his dying mother wished to see him one last time, he simply chose to ignore her!'

Spreading gossip like this, first through his immediate family and then through all their relatives and neighbours, Athanni tried to turn everyone against his cousin; and all this, just to seize Kashana-e-Haq. It was a plan that he had concocted a while ago. To accomplish this goal, he had fake property papers prepared by a crooked attorney, transferring the legal ownership of the house in his name. The illiterate Farhat had signed the papers, thinking that she was only granting temporary power of attorney to her nephew to protect her son from the 'scheming churail' who had clearly ensnared him.

With time, Athanni had developed a nasty plenitude, a serpentine completeness. Extortion, thievery, bombing, animal killing, blackmailing—he had done it all. But his latest plot was a chapter taken right out of the book of nefarious accomplishments. Mansoor had never fully imagined the extent of his devilry. He had misread him, grossly underestimating the lengths that Khaleel Khan would go to in order to destroy him. He was unprepared to deal with the measures his cousin would take to satisfy his cretinous revenge fantasies. Khaleel Khan 'Athanni' was, in Mansoor's mind, always an idiot who needed to be taught the occasional lesson. He was dead wrong.

At Farhat's funeral, Haider asked Athanni if Mansoor knew about his mother's death. Athanni lied to him too, saying he had sent two telegrams and tried making trunk calls multiple times, but he could not locate him. Feeling a sense of lingering loyalty to Noor, Haider launched his own search for Mansoor. From Jumman, he got Mehrun's telephone number in London. It was she who informed him that Mansoor might be at Joseph's apartment and gave him the latter's telephone number. And that was how Haider was able to call Joseph and inform Mansoor about the tragedy.

*

Mansoor arrived in Pakistan five days after his mother's death. Although he had sent a telegram to his home address to inform the residents of his arrival date, no one came to receive him at the airport, making him feel like an alien in his own country. It was early morning when he landed in Karachi, and the January sun tried to sneak out through the clouds to heat up the cold air. Mansoor took a taxi and went straight to the Kashana. He expected to see Changez Gul at the gate, but the man had been replaced by a new chowkidar, who was reluctant to let him in. But when Mansoor told him that he was Sarwat's nephew, he relented. There was no sign of any of the other servants. The backyard garden where he,

Mehrun and Joseph used to play was utterly barren—the grass had died out, and the trees, once lush and green even in winter, stood in complete nakedness.

When he went inside, a fusillade of accusations, taunts and insults greeted him. With equal opportunities and matching eagerness, as if they had rehearsed it all, everyone in Nawab Khan Namaqul's family participated in this verbal assault. Sarwat accused Mansoor of causing her sister's death. Athanni and his father called him a shameless swine. Chowwani showed him the five fingers—the sign of shame. And before Mansoor had even realized what was happening, they ordered him to leave his own house. At first, Mansoor refused, and then he, in turn, ordered all of them to leave the house. But Athanni came back brandishing a copy of the title to the house.

'Your mother, my pious aunt, may Allah rest her soul in paradise, cut you off because of your kafir tendencies,' he shouted.

'Where were you the day your father died?' Sarwat asked.

Before Mansoor could answer, Athanni retorted, 'I will refresh your memory, you thankless son. You were whoring around with that churail. Weren't you?'

'And where were you when your mother died?' Chowwani jumped in, and then answered his own question, 'Whoring with some gori bitch!'

Insomnia and jet lag made Mansoor's head spin; the vicious, verbal shoving gave him a throbbing headache. Athanni and Chowwani loomed large like Munkar and Nakir, the twin angels of the grave, while Nawab Khan Namaqul and Sarwat fluttered their wings like Azrael, the angel of death. At that moment, Mansoor really wanted to become a djinn—exhaling smokeless fire and destroying these people with his blazing flames, incinerating them completely. Instead, he thundered, 'You are a bunch of vultures, and I will get back what is lawfully mine. I will see you all in court.'

'And we will see you in the sharia court,' Athanni replied.

*

As the mist inside his mind cleared, Mansoor found himself outside the Kashana. He heard strange whispers and murmurs; he saw Mehrun, Joseph and Chaos. And then, like the phantasm of a dreadful dream, the Kashana loomed up in front of him like a decrepit house, its paint peeling off, the flowers wilting and the huge jasmine vine dying out, the serenity of this beautiful bungalow that his father had so lovingly built usurped by this pack of bloodthirsty scavengers. Mansoor noticed a lizard on the boundary wall of the house, its tongue stuck out, not towards the sky, but towards him. It was as if the reptile had also joined the vulgarians in their derision.

Biting his lip, Mansoor turned around and dragged himself towards the house next door—the house that had always reminded him of a fortress. He wanted to use the neighbour's phone to call Haider Rizvi, the only person Mansoor trusted in this city of teeming millions. If his Uncle Zahid were alive, none of this would have happened. But Zahid seemed like a fabricated vision, a surreal character existing only in his mind.

He had never been inside the neighbour's compound, never played with their children, never even knew their names. Growing up, he was discouraged from playing outside the Kashana's walls, as if his parents wanted to protect him from the outside world. Mansoor rang the bell and waited, peering through the wrought-iron gate of his neighbour's house. When no one came out, he rang the bell again and was about to leave when he saw an elderly man, dressed in a kurta and pyjama, and with a prayer cap on his head, limply lugging himself towards him.

'What is it?' he asked as he opened the gate.

'I don't know if you know me, but I am your next-door neighbour, Mansoor ul Haq. Perhaps you knew my father, Noor ul Haq?

'I know you very well, you are that djinn,' the man replied. 'What do you want?'

'I am not a djinn, sir. I am a human being, and at this time, I just need to make one telephone call,' Mansoor replied.

'Get lost! I don't even want your evil shadow on my house.' He slammed shut the wrought-iron gate on Mansoor's face and walked away. The toxic falsehood spewed by Athanni had reached his door. Old rumours had been given a fresh lease of life.

Disappointed, his hopes dashed, Mansoor decided to take a taxi to the *Morning Gazette*.

*

When Haider heard about Mansoor's tribulations, he felt sorry for him. As a journalist, he had witnessed greed first-hand and had written about it. But for it to trek such a distance, and with such wickedness, seemed incredible even to him. Athanni's intrigues shocked him. Haider took Mansoor to his house and told him that he could stay there for as long as he wanted since his house was practically empty, now that his daughter was married and living in England. Haider's wife, a gem of a woman, made Mansoor feel at home. She had always been very fond of Mansoor and had secretly hoped that one day he might marry her daughter, Nikhat.

Since his return, each passing moment had felt like a non-stop low-voltage electric shock hitting his body. It took Mansoor a week to restore his sense of self as he slowly reflected on the recent events. As far as he could remember, he was sitting there with Lisa that night, asking her to marry him. The proposal had just come out on its own—no pressure, no push, no nothing—and then suddenly, the telephone had rung, shattering the serenity of the moment, sundering the life he was planning. He had taken an airplane directly from Houston to fly back to Karachi. Hoping to be comforted by his relatives, he had instead been jolted by their pre-emptive strike. But now it was time to get over the inertia, to regroup his thoughts, to plan out a strategy and to get back the Kashana-e-Haq, the Abode of Truth. To him, his house had become the Kashana-e-Jhoot, the Abode of Lies—a name Mehrun had said she would choose for her home in Defence Society.

That is what the Kashana was now—the Abode of Lies, the House of Hatred, the Refuge of Scoundrels. He had to cleanse his parents' home and also his family's name.

*

Once his sanity returned and he cooled off, he wrote a letter to Lisa. If he remembered correctly, he did propose to her in the wee hours of that morning in Joseph's apartment. In his letter, he explained the latest complication in his life. Sadly, he would be stuck in Pakistan for several months. He asked her to move his things from his apartment to hers. She wouldn't have too many things to shift since his had been a furnished apartment, and his most prized possessions were his stereo and his books. He still wanted to marry her and repeated his proposal. Once he was back in America, they could get married.

After a nerve-racking, month-long wait, he got a terse reply from Lisa. She had moved all his things to her apartment and was busy with her final semester. After she was done, she was probably going to settle in Connecticut, near her mother. As a postscript, she wrote, 'What can I say about your marriage proposal . . . Call me when you're back in the States.'

In Houston, she had indicated that she would like to try living in Pakistan. Would she still do that? A keen student of Pakistani politics, she knew that living in a country that was fast veering in a dangerous direction would be foolhardy. Settling near her mother in Connecticut made more sense.

*

With intemperate zeal, General Behroopia got busy inverting the clock of progress at a bewildering speed. After executing The People's Leader, he felt free to corrupt and mangle the Constitution. But with no legal grounds to govern and with no constituency of his own, he began bending the political and legal institutions to suit his own myopic view. Implementing an anger-filled version, he nurtured hate disguised as belief, focusing on the harshest sets of punishments for criminal offences. It was the handiest tool of deception, easily reconditioned and smoothly refurbished as the only true doctrine. In the past, the Doctrine of Necessity had been the ready excuse for military rule. But this general did not feel the necessity of this doctrine at all. He sideswiped the traditional courts and unleashed his terror through religious courts, the likes of which this unfortunate nation had never seen. With obsessive zeal, he focused his wrath on minorities, women and everyone else who did not follow his repugnant belief system.

The general introduced the Hudood Ordinance, sanctioning stoning for adultery, a hundred lashes for fornication, death for apostasy, eighty lashes for drinking and chopping off of the right hand for robbery. Thousands of women were imprisoned for honour crimes under this ordinance. Paving the way for his regressive brand of ideology, which was replete with bigotry and intolerance, he gave a free licence to his vigilantes to do as they wished. These thugs torched cinemas that showed 'immoral' movies, destroyed nightclubs that allowed 'lewd' dancing and attacked every public entertainment place that involved the mixing of sexes. The religious intelligentsia that replaced the 'corrupt Western intelligentsia', commended them and the general on their diligence. The *Daily Jadal* commented thus:

> We need punishments like these and a disciplinarian like him to show the corrupt the true path. The general is a soldier of the true faith and we need to strengthen his hands. General Behroopia is the first ruler who doesn't drink alcohol. He is the first ruler who prays every waking hour. He is a breath of fresh air. What is so sacred about democracy, anyway?

The English language papers put up a feeble defence using the Doctrine of Doubt. In our faith, they argued, the accused has the right to doubt. But who doubts the accused, and most of all, who read these useless English dailies? After all, they represented the colonial mindset.

Mansoor cringed when he read the shameless validations published in the newspapers. The Orwellian 'modern past' was something new. The idea that history is shaped by large, impersonal forces just got gutted by this grinning, grotesque theocratic figure, his name a cruel reminder of the dark reality that had swallowed the country.

When Haider returned from work that night, he invited Mansoor for a drink. Dimming the lights in the room, he took out a bottle of Johnnie Walker from his cabinet and made Mansoor a drink. As he handed him the whisky, he said, 'The last gift from your late father. I might as well share it with you before they flog us both to death.'

At that moment, Mansoor missed his father dearly, and Haider saw his Noor in Mansoor. After a few swigs, he asked him, 'So, what do you think of this bastard?'

Mansoor paused for a moment and repeated what his father had once told him, 'Uncle Haider, whenever you replace any concrete reality with an abstract idea of a homogenized people, you create a passive putty to be kneaded at will by the tyrants. This is the first step towards hell.'

'I miss your father so much, Mansoor.' Haider took off his spectacles and began to cry uncontrollably.

*

With his life suddenly interrupted, Mansoor now had to search for a new normal. Money was hardly a problem. His father had taken care of his financial well-being while he was alive. He had opened a joint account with Mansoor at Citibank. The considerable wealth that he inherited from his father was his to spend, but he also had substantial savings of his own in the High Finance Bank. So, after staying at Haider's house for two months, Mansoor shifted to one of the newer three-bedroom luxury apartments near Clifton Beach, one of the poshest places in Karachi.

He bought a used Honda Civic, and with Haider's influence, got a telephone line and a temporary job teaching economics at President's College. Once settled, he hired a young attorney, S.M. Abrar, a protégé of his father, and filed a lawsuit against Athanni and the rest of his family. Athanni had not expected Mansoor to give up his house so meekly, but he had not expected a trial so soon either. The speed with which Mansoor moved had taken him by surprise.

But Athanni had found a new purpose to his life, which did not include resting easy and letting Mansoor's lawsuit proceed smoothly. He hired his own lawyer, Mushtaq Ahmad, who filed a counter lawsuit in the sharia court, alleging, among other things, that Mansoor was unfit to own his parents' home because he was an atheist and a blasphemer.

'How are you going to prove that?' his lawyer asked, sceptical about the charges.

'Leave it to me, I will produce the evidence.'

Mansoor had a hunch that his lawsuit would bring about a counter lawsuit from Athanni. So, when he received the court papers for the countersuit, he braced himself for a long-drawn-out battle. Realizing that his stay in Pakistan would now be protracted, Mansoor wrote another letter to Lisa, explaining this added snag. A month later, he received a four-page missive from her. She had finished her PhD and got a job at the University of Hartford in Connecticut. After considering his proposal seriously, she had reached a painful conclusion and wrote, 'I cannot marry you and let you leave your heart behind in Pakistan. This is your Pakistan, and you need to retake it. I can't help you with that.'

Like a dagger, the words pierced his heart. Stunned by her words, he ached with an unnerving feeling inside his gut. He had not expected his relationship to end so abruptly, that too by way of a letter. She had laid out her reasons, elaborated her explanations and written her points down logically, but the pages now became blurred, and the details lost all their meaning. He put the letter on the table, closed his eyes and leaned back in his chair. Another heartache had invaded his life. All his loved ones gone, he stood there all alone. Amidst all the tragedy and turmoil, Lisa had stayed by his side like an angel of love. She had been his hope, his bliss, his reason for life, but now she had parted company too.

Twenty-Eight

It was General Behroopia who introduced terrorizing despotism in the country. He started every speech in the name of God, but he might as well have started it in the name of repression, for that was his true god. To establish a political base for himself, he fraternized with the new oligarchs, hobnobbed with the lota politicians and flirted with the fundamentalists, whom the people called 'the fundoos'. His most dangerous act was the toleration of the burgeoning Kalashnikov–heroin culture in the country. In his Pakistan, guns and heroin went hand in hand. Karachi, called the Gateway to the West, by The Great Leader, became the gateway for guns and drug traffickers.

Behroopia's allies became the animators of his cartoonish but treacherous regime. With their ill-gotten wealth and their rotten riches, they built profane palaces. They threw nauseating parties where they openly paraded their depravity and flouted every Hudood Ordinance with impunity, giving new meaning to the word 'untouchable'. The draconian laws were imposed only on the poor, the illiterate and the liberal enemies of the state. The obnoxiously wealthy had always had their separate set of rules, but now they stood way above the law of the land. They guarded their self-made rules and broke the decrees for their benefit at every turn. And when Mansoor saw all this, he just shook his head.

General Behroopia rejected intellectual pursuits and cultural values and discarded the rich Sufi tradition that had made the country more humane and tolerant. The display of wealth reached a new altitude, and the age of materialism approached a new normal. His brand of tyranny paled the autocracy of General Dundda.

*

To his surprise, Mansoor found teaching to be a satisfying experience, and he threw himself into it with all his energy and enthusiasm. He busied himself with his life in academia. This was the only way Mansoor could deal with his break-up with Lisa. Thanks to his informal style and the Socratic method of teaching, he became one of the most popular lecturers in the college. But popularity breeds jealousy. The older professors did not like his enthusiasm and his relaxed style. They questioned his coziness with his students. To them, that was a perversion of the student–teacher relationship. In their academic world, professors kept a cold distance from the students and never got involved with them at a personal level. Mansoor, as if to irritate them, did just the opposite and incurred their wrath. By introducing the students to topical materials and fun activities, he created a learning-friendly atmosphere in his classes, and that didn't go down well either. He called his students by their first names and asked them to do the same with him, thus bringing further derision and condemnation.

With a few like-minded colleagues and progressive students, Mansoor started the al-Ma'arrī Club, named after the eleventh-century blind, heretic poet of Islam. Some nine hundred years before John Lennon wrote his iconic song 'Imagine', al-Ma'arrī imagined a world without religion. The name of the club puzzled many in the college. Some thought that it was the Almari Club, the Urdu word 'almari' meaning a wooden closet for storing clothes.

Others joked that Mansoor was going to teach his students about refining their sartorial tastes. The homophobes dubbed it 'The Closet Club', a gathering place for homosexuals. But the club's mission was to promote intelligent conversations about forbidden topics and to encourage the students to think critically about politics, religion, philosophy and literature. If he had his druthers, Mansoor would have started a chapter of his club in every college in Pakistan.

Every week, the members of the club met in an empty classroom to discuss 'non-permitted' topics. With a roguish sense of humour and a caustic logic, Mansoor set out to upset the foundational trajectories of his country's life—the economy, the beliefs, the government, the class structures and the gender biases. He was at once daring and disarming, his enthusiasm prompted by his aspiration to create students who thought rationally and desired a caring society—one that General Behroopia was hell-bent on destroying.

Mansoor never took attendance and never asked a stranger as to why he or she was there. And so, when Athanni heard about the al Maʿarrī Club and its activities, he planted a mole, Farid Kidwai. A petty thief and a new convert to General Behroopia's cause, his job was to record anything incriminating on a videotape. Mansoor, in his naiveté, did not think much of that. The videotaping of lectures by students in America was not uncommon. For him, it was just another way to democratize education. So he welcomed Kidwai to make the recording.

But he pushed the objectives of his club a bit too far beyond the acceptable boundaries. For the college administrators, it was too much heresy; it was too much to take. His methods were upending the age-old system that had stood the test of time. Someone reported him to the principal of the college, who summoned him to his office and got right to the point.

'Mister Mansoor, you are not in Umreeka. You are not going to lead our students down the wrong path. Do you understand?'

'No, sir, I don't. All I am doing is trying to teach them how to think critically.'

'Don't give me your critical thinking bullshit. If someone reported you to the authorities, you would be charged with blasphemy. Do you know what the punishment for blasphemy is?'

'Yes, sir, but I have not committed any blasphemy,' Mansoor replied.

'Look, Mister Mansoor, I am good friends with Haider Rizvi; he has done me lots of favours, so I will pretend that this never happened.'

'But, sir—'

'And here's a piece of advice for you: don't walk on a path of no return. You may still have a future at this college.'

'Thank you for your advice. I will leave now.'

Mansoor got up and left the principal's office, the fancy trimmings of his idealism pared away by crude triviality.

*

After a hiatus of fifteen months, the hearing on Mansoor's lawsuit finally began. Much to his disappointment, however, it was held in the sharia court. Although it was supposed to be a case where Mansoor was the plaintiff, the judge, in all his wisdom, decided that the original suit and the countersuit were a waste of everyone's time. So, ignoring all judicial norms and precedence, he merged both the cases, despite his lawyer's vehement protestations. Mansoor had suffered a setback even before the arguments began.

On the first day of the hearing, Athanni arrived with his family, steadfast in his hate and resolute in his treachery, convinced that the sharia court would help them dry-clean his loot. To Mansoor, here was another proof that property trumped blood relationships. Ever since Farhat's death, Athanni made no attempts to hide his feelings towards his cousin. His festering childhood hatred had erupted like a full-blown malignancy. That Mansoor deserved to die because he was a blasphemer had become Athanni's drumbeat to anyone who would listen. Liberally using pious zeal to condemn Mansoor on every occasion, he lashed out at anyone who spoke favourably of his enemy.

S.M. Abrar launched a withering attack on Athanni and his family as he opened the defence. Most of the witnesses for Athanni wilted under his cross-examination. Athanni's lawyer, Mushtaq Ahmad, on the other hand, argued so weakly that even the judge began to fidget with boredom. His language, his mannerisms and his methods spoke volumes about the weakness of the case he was arguing. But then, in a surprise turn, Mushtaq called Mansoor on the witness stand. Although Mansoor could not be called in his own defence, the judge overruled Abrar's objections, rejecting all conventions and manufacturing rules on the spot.

The first question Mushtaq asked was, 'Are you a Muslim?'

'I was born into a Muslim family.'

'Do you consider yourself a Muslim?'

'I am a human being first, in essence, before I am a Muslim in existence.' Here, Mansoor flipped Sartre's existential philosophy dictum that existence precedes essence.

'Do you have a girlfriend in Umreeka?'

'No, I don't believe so.'

'Where did you go when your father died?'

'To the Aga Khan Hospital.'

Abrar objected to this line of questioning so much that the judge finally realized its irrelevance. He reprimanded Mushtaq and ordered the court recorder to erase all these questions from the text. When the court finally adjourned, Mushtaq went to Athanni and his family and told them that it had not been a good day for them.

The second day of the proceedings was even worse. Mushtaq introduced the video recording that Farid Kidwai was supposed to have made of Mansoor at the al-Ma'arrī Club. This was the evidence that was supposed to completely destroy Mansoor and establish him as an inveterate blasphemer. But to Mushtaq's humiliation, the tape had been recorded over a pre-recorded pornographic tape, and he had not even bothered to check the full recording before introducing it in the court. Somewhere, somehow, *Deep Throat* got fused with Aristotelian logic. The judge held Mushtaq in contempt of court and adjourned the court for two months.

*

When they went back to the house that they had looted, Nawab Khan Namaqul slapped Athanni hard, as if he were still a teenager, and yelled, 'You and your stupid attorney will send us all to jail.'

The badly humiliated Athanni took his anger to the streets of Karachi in search of Farid Kidwai. But Kidwai was back in jail, which meant that now Athanni had to come up with Plan B-2. When all plans from A to Z fail, there is always another Plan B-2.

*

Even though the al-Maʿarrī Club was officially disbanded, the obvious barbs and the cruel jibes persisted. So, with the winter vacation approaching, Mansoor decided to return to America for a few weeks to submit his PhD dissertation, which was now ready to be defended, and to tie up loose ends. He also longed to see Lisa in Connecticut. Her absence from his life had begun to torment him. After his thesis defence, he decided he would go to Connecticut to win her back.

Just as he was about to call his travel agent, the department secretary brought his day's mail in. On the top of the pile, a packet with the grinning picture of General Behroopia mocked Mansoor. It was the conference programme for the First-Ever International

Symposium on the Scientific Miracles of the Holy Scripture. Since the conference was sponsored by President's College, every faculty member was required to attend it.

Mansoor was ready to defy the ridiculous requirement, but his interest was comically piqued when he read the titles of the papers to be presented:

A Panel Discussion on Things Known Only to the Almighty
DNA of Angels According to Some of the Revealed Verses
The Revelation of the Big Bang Theory in the Holy Scripture
The Dis-Integral Calculus of Hypocrisy in Western Society
How to Solve Pakistan's Energy Problems: Harnessing Fiery Djinns as Nuclear Fusion

Without thinking, Mansoor drew two horns and a goatee on the picture of the general, and after crossing out the original title, wrote in his cursive handwriting, First-Ever International Symposium on Holy Crap. Just then Professor Abdul Basit, with whom he shared his office, entered the room. Noticing Mansoor's dismissive ridicule of the symposium and his caricature of the general as the devil, he took the insult personally.

Basit, a graduate of Princeton, had recently become a devotee of Zakir Hassan and had been planning to resign his professorship to join his organization. He had also become a fervent supporter of the general. Following in Zakir's footsteps, he too had become the most educated evangelist to his cause. To discover a 'Purer Version of Faith' in Pakistan, the zeal to proselytize had become acceptable and commonplace.

Snatching the programme from Mansoor's hand, he immediately thrust himself into an argument with him. Mansoor was getting tired of these quarrels. They all had a similar pattern—circular reasoning, a constant moving of the goalpost and ad hominem attacks. Always outnumbered and generally outgunned, he had begun to avoid confrontations with these true believers.

'You know, Mansoor, you always talk about rationality and enlightenment. You can have all that and still believe in God.'

'I never said that you can't.'

'Why do you make fun of someone's cherished beliefs?'

'I don't make fun of *anyone's* cherished beliefs, but cartoonish views are another matter.'

'And do you consider this scientific conference as cartoonish?'

'It doesn't sound like a scientific conference to me.'

'Is that why you wrote "holy crap" on the cover?'

Exasperated, Mansoor closed his eyes and took a long deep breath before continuing, 'Do you think these fake scholars with their pseudoscientific papers are doing any service to Islam? Do you think that any of these so-called papers are serious enough to get published in a peer-reviewed journal? You, a Princeton graduate, ought to know better.'

'Why? Don't you believe in miracles or in djinns? Do you even believe in religion?'

Mansoor paused for a moment, gathering his thoughts and trying to figure out a polite way to end this tedious conversation. A second later, he calmly responded, 'No, Basit Sahib, I am sorry to disappoint you, but I don't. Religion, in my view, is nothing more than the forced retrieval of an imaginary memory.'

'So you don't agree with General Sahib's policies of Islamization'

'No, I don't, especially not with the brand of religion that he is preaching! I think that he is using religion to serve himself!' Mansoor shouted with a pagan exhilaration.

'I know all about your al-Maʿarrī Club. Let me just tell you that it was a silly idea.'

'Life is incomplete without its bathos and sordor, Mister Basit. You ought to try them sometime,' Mansoor shot back.

'Try your sordor in America. We don't want it in Pakistan!' Basit's nostrils quivered as he shouted.

'Who are *we*? Does your *we* include *me*? Isn't this *my* country too? And why should this plural pronoun contain only you?' Mansoor demanded.

'I don't think that you like belonging here, Mister Mansoor. You don't seem to even believe in the most elemental reason for why Pakistan came into being. And if you don't believe in that, you forfeit the right to belong to this state.'

Realizing that the discussion was just dragging on, Mansoor extricated himself by saying, 'Mister Basit, I don't want to argue with you any more. You have your inherited beliefs, and I have my scepticisms. But let me tell you this: if I am allowed to teach, I will continue to ask uncomfortable questions.'

Without giving Basit the chance to re-engage, Mansoor stormed out of the office. He knew that this new altercation would soon become the talk of the college, but it was too late to care. He knew he would get into trouble for this, but it felt good.

And then, a few minutes after he left, Athanni knocked on the door of Mansoor's shared office and was let in by Abdul Basit.

Twenty-Nine

The day of the conference arrived quietly on a cold and sombre Friday in December. The sun shone with little warmth and no lustre. Mansoor drove his Honda Civic towards his college, taking the route that he always took. He had taken that route thousands of times before, but for the first time he became painfully aware of the teeming human bundles huddled together, sleeping on the cold, heartless, hard-edged footpaths of the city. It was a humanoid debris zone with raggedly clad bodies scattered across the walkways. For generations, these pavement dwellers had slept there, invisible to the early morning traffic, unmindful of the stumbling commuters and hidden to the city administrators. The government splurged millions of rupees organizing pseudo-conferences like the one Mansoor was required to attend, but it did not spend a single paisa on improving the looted lives of the poor. Mansoor felt tortured. He thought about the Kashana, the almost-palatial house that he had lived in growing up, and felt guilty. Perhaps when he got possession of the house again, he could convert it into a shelter for homeless people. What was the point of all this anyway? Mansoor agonized over his comfortable existence; he thought about the plastic people he'd met at a wedding party he had just attended, and he reflected on the bogus educational institutions organizing bogus conferences. General Behroopia had converted the entire country into a veritable charade, but what could Mansoor do? Falsehood, excuses and fraud—recycled each year, while the tragic human disorder on the streets remained irrevocable.

*

Mansoor was among the first ones to arrive at the auditorium where the conference was to be held. As he sat on an empty seat, doubts seeped into his mind and he began questioning his presence at the conference. By merely attending it, wasn't he legitimizing this faux exercise? Being in attendance meant he was a party to this profane transaction. It was no longer funny. The comical had bonded with the macabre. The changing laws, the shifting narrative, they were nothing to laugh about. As his heart thumped furiously, he felt he was about to go through a tragic, unnerving tour of zombie land.

A throng of people, masquerading piety, moving effortlessly, filled the auditorium as if this were the event of the century. Professor Basit came along with some of Mansoor's colleagues and his students from the al-Maʿarrī Club. They all ignored him. Mansoor closed his eyes, already tired. As the lights dimmed, Athanni sneaked in with a group of men and quickly slithered into a dark corner of the auditorium, away from Mansoor. He sat hidden from him, his eyes glued on Mansoor's back, seething with anger, the memory of the disgrace he'd experienced at the court still raw, the subsequent beating by his father still hurting.

The general arrived half an hour late, inaugurated the conference with his bland, smarmy speech, thanked the participants for their scholarly endeavours and left without even hearing the first presenter. Mansoor followed his example and left the auditorium soon after. Athanni walked behind him, keeping a healthy distance from him and holding a walkie-talkie in his hand.

*

Mansoor did not want to be caught up in the buffoonery of the so-called conference. It had utterly disgusted him. He could do with some fresh air. He needed to walk to unburden himself of this feeling of revulsion, to shake off the doubts that had hazed his mind. Leaving his car in the parking area, he wandered for hours through the crowded streets of Karachi, absorbed in his own thoughts, dodging the beggars, brushing shoulders with strangers, impervious to the cold air.

And Athanni trailed him from a distance. Was this the new Plan B-2? Was some madness lurking in ambush?

Mansoor remained unaware of his pursuer as he continued reflecting on his last years in Pakistan and the time he had frittered away. He thought of his future blankly closing down before him. At that moment, Mansoor felt a grave sense of gloom, like a lost child. The ties that bound him to his native land seemed undone; he felt homeless, uprooted and alone, with doors slammed shut, no place to call his own, the country, a picture of wretchedness. He should have gone back to America. He should have married Lisa. He should have cut all ties with his homeland. *His* country, as his father used to call it, had deserted him. Experiencing the pangs of being an exile in his own city, the city of his birth, he even began questioning his lawsuit. The entire country had become the Theatre of the Absurd.

'What is the point of all this?' he shouted, but no one paid any attention to him, except Athanni.

Mansoor suddenly realized that he was truly all alone in this world. He had no family, no friends; he was a fucking orphan. He wanted to give it all up to Athanni, who was probably still plotting revenge, always conspiring villainy.

To hell with the fucking lawsuit and the fucking house. What am I going to do with the house even if I win the case? I can't actually convert it into a homeless shelter! he thought.

He felt entropic. There was disorder in his country, but now it felt as if the disease was taking over his self. The world no longer made sense to him. What difference would it make if he got his house back tomorrow? What difference would it make if he returned to America, defended his dissertation and published a highly regarded book? Nothing mattered.

The cars were honking and people were laughing and talking, going on with their meaningless daily chores. Mansoor turned to Shaheed-e-Millat Road, Martyr of the Nation Road, named after the first prime minister who had been assassinated the day he, Mansoor, was born. He passed his old neighbourhood, insensate to everything except his brainwaves. His trance was broken when the muezzin called the faithful for the Friday prayers. In front of him stood his neighbourhood mosque, the same mosque where he used to go with his Uncle Zahid for Eid prayers, where he always felt like an abandoned orphan. Guarded by minarets on all sides, the mosque stuck out in its brilliant simplicity. Not one thing about it had changed. Mansoor stood there and gazed at the mosque for a long time. He noticed the same kerosene shop next to the mosque, still standing there defiantly despite the arrival of gas and electric stoves. The smell of kerosene still paralysed him, reminding him of that day in his distant past when Joseph and Mehrun had cremated that lizard. Joseph and Mehrun's ghosts appeared in front of him now, their hands joined together, singing that dreadful couplet.

Aadhi roti, aadha kebab
Girgit ko marna bara sawab
Aadhi roti, aadha kebab
Girgit ko marna bara sawab

As he continued standing there, he heard the chanting get louder and clearer.

Aadhi roti, aadha kebab
Kafir ko marna bara sawab

(One-half roti, one-half kebab
Killing an infidel is the highest reward)

Mansoor turned around and saw Athanni with a large, angry mob behind him. Some of the men were brandishing sticks and some were wielding knives and machetes. There was something fantastically ominous about these faceless people.

Pointing a minatory finger at Mansoor, Athanni shouted, 'Brothers, he is the blasphemer! He is the apostate! He has desecrated our religion and profaned our leader. He is an atheist like his father was. His punishment is death. BURN HIM! KILL HIM!'

Mansoor saw Athanni, with that chilling face, displaying the conference leaflet with his scribbles and drawing. Realizing that his cousin had incited the crowd against him, he turned around and began walking briskly, wanting to put as much distance as he could between himself and the sinister mob. And then, Mansoor heard people running behind him, chanting slogans. He turned back to check and realized that the crowd was closing in on him, preparing to attack. His heart froze and his feet jellied, but Mansoor mustered enough strength to run full speed ahead. As he picked up the pace, his breathing became laboured. He had scarcely cleared ten yards when he sensed his thighs becoming heavy and leaden. The chants of 'kill the blasphemer' pierced his ears. And then came the familiar couplet:

Aadhi roti, aadha kebab
Kafir ko marna bara sawab

As the angry pack closed in on him, the ground he scaled became a pointless space of confusion. Suddenly, Mansoor lost his balance, tripped over and fell flat on his face. Blood gushed out of his nose, and as he tried to get up, he was torpedoed by a stone. Mansoor fell back to the ground. When he tried to get up again, a metal rod hit his head. He heard his punishers ranting.

'Stone him to death!'

'No, behead him!' another person shouted.

He saw Athanni making his way forward from the back of the crowd with a kerosene canister in his hand.

'No, he is an evil djinn. He would like to be cremated in a smokeless fire. Let's honour his wishes!' Athanni roared.

One person pulled Mansoor up from the ground and another held him from behind. The smell of kerosene hung heavy in the air as Athanni, the predator, came face-to-face with him, all his demonic wretchedness written large and clear on his face. The person who had gripped Mansoor now released him, pushing him forward. Without saying another word, Athanni splashed the kerosene on Mansoor's clothes. And then, with pure venom in his eyes, he took out a cigarette lighter from his pocket, flicked open the flame and set Mansoor on fire. As the flames erupted, he chanted:

Aadhi roti, aadha kebab
Dahariya ko marna bara sawab

(One-half roti, One-half kebab
Killing an atheist is the highest reward)

Like a burning effigy, Mansoor became a fireball of flame—smokeless, odourless, invisible. For a moment, he stood there unruffled and unshaken, as if he cherished every moment of it, as if the fire had found the abode it was looking for, as if, much like Abraham's fire, it had become a peaceful garden that bore no harm.

And then the crowd saw another man set ablaze. It was Athanni. Mansoor had a stranglehold on Athanni. Trying unsuccessfully to liberate himself from the firm grip of the fiery djinn, Athanni screamed for help. But no one came to his rescue. They both grappled and scuffled and performed the Danse Macabre.

And the crowd watched, catatonic, two ignited bodies danced, flickered, struggled—a grand display of crackling pyrotechnics.

It was as though they were watching a wrestling match between the legendary Bholu Pahelwan and Dara Singh, with all the fireworks. The smokeless fire suddenly started emitting smoke. Athanni continued to struggle, his entire body engulfed in flames now. The crowd recoiled in horror as the djinn tightened his grip on Athanni and squeezed him until he became lifeless and fell to the ground. Still enflamed, the djinn stood there for a second, looking at the burning corpse on the ground, before walking away and dissolving into the rarefied air.

Witnesses later reported that after walking a few hundred yards, the djinn turned around and suddenly disappeared without leaving his ashes, without leaving a trace. Later, among the charred remains, the authorities could find only one body, only one set of bones, only one skull; Mansoor had vanished from the face of this earth, or so they said.

On the same day, somewhere over the Sindh province, there was another massive explosion mid-air. An army helicopter carrying General Behroopia and his top army commanders was mysteriously blown to smithereens. The blast annihilated everyone on board. The power-wielders were pulverized by an unknown assailant, the faithful brigade dissipated into the thin stratosphere. Nobody knew what happened; no one knew where their bodies went. The empty caskets draped with the national flag gave an illusion of a funeral. And to further the fantasy, the new government hastily erected a cenotaph to honour the 'Soldier of Islam'. Half the nation was shocked, the other half was relieved. Half of them mourned the general's death, and the other half offered prayers of thanksgiving.

Epilogue

Across the miserable landscape, sinister rumours spread about the baffling death of the generals. There were a thousand-and-one tales of conspiracy, each story more ominous than the other, and each theory more intriguing than the last one. A common theme in all these scenarios was that it was the 'enemies of Islam' who had killed the general. To those who spun these tales, 'they' killed him because he had devoted his life to Islam and its true revival. The nation quickly dubbed him a shaheed, a martyr. Ironically, they called his predecessor a shaheed, too. An Urdu poet lamented about the corruption of the word 'martyrdom':

> *Tum mujhe maar do to main hoon shaheed*
> *Main tumhey maar doon to tum ho shaheed*

(If you kill me, then I am a martyr
If I kill you, then you are a martyr)

It was a case of Martyrdom Gone Wild.

*

Rumours mystified the death of a lesser figure, Mansoor ul Haq, as well. There, too, were a hundred-and-one accounts of what happened near the mosque, each tale more tangled and each fib more disturbing. There was thrill, there was gore, and then there was the hyperbole. One 'eyewitness' saw Mansoor's blazing body ascending towards the sun, gravitating to where Jahannam, hell, is. Another 'eyewitness' saw him gliding up until his entire body crumbled into ashes and dust. Yet another bystander vouched that the whole thing was invisible. Yes, there was a fight, but only Athanni was involved. Like a madman, he fought with his own shadow and it was he who doused himself in kerosene.

But all the talebearers remained steadfast about one thing: there was a smokeless fire. There was a djinn, and Mansoor was that djinn, and in the end, Athanni was possessed by him too. Everything was so fanciful, so monstrous that one had to be there to believe it.

'The police found the charred body of my Khaleel but found no trace of that djinn; what else could explain that?' Sarwat told her remaining son, Chowwani. 'The day he was born, the Leader of the Nation was assassinated, and the day he died, the Leader of the Faithful was assassinated. I knew he was evil,' she railed.

Six months later, the sharia court gave the verdict against Nawab Khan Namaqul and his family. The court that was supposed to declare Mansoor ul Haq a blasphemer, posthumously vindicated him, evicting the Khan family from the Kashana. But where was Mansoor? What happened to his body? Who would be the rightful heir to his property? Nobody knew. Rumours and mystery continued to dog Mansoor's death, just as it had dogged his short life.

The court decided to auction off Kashana-e-Haq. Despite being derelict and in hopeless disrepair, the Kashana became a conquering obsession for Mehrun. She had to buy it, if not for herself, then for the memory of Mansoor. She had to buy it for her frail father, so that he could see his garden grow again. To ensure that no one else outbid her, she opened all her coffers and made the highest bid. She bought the house as if to finally avenge the murder of her friend, her lover. Her childhood dream house was now finally hers, and there she was, the new begum of the Kashana. Mehrun could have never imagined the circumstances under which she would become the mistress of this house. The wife of a multimillionaire banker, she could have bought any home, anywhere in the world, but she chose the Kashana in loving remembrance of Mansoor.

On the other side of the world, Joseph Solomon married Cheryl Hampton and bought a mansion in the exclusive Sugar Land suburb of Houston. With the profits he was raking in, he bought another Burger King franchise near Houston and created a scholarship fund in Mansoor ul Haq's memory at a local college. He, too, chose a name for his house: Bhangi Para.

Mansoor died, but the rumours about his death and about his being djinn did not—a resonant story, refusing to die. What was never witnessed by any eyes was spread by countless whispers. His death became the boast of the believers and the lament of the sceptics, remembered mostly by its messiness. He died a medieval death, choreographed by medieval minds.

Acknowledgements

This book is for my parents who are no longer here, who shared with me their ancestral stories in India, who made the journey to Pakistan during the turbulent days of the Partition and struggled in the new country's early days. They taught me the importance of honest work and persistence.

To Yasmin, who encouraged me throughout the writing of this novel. Without her constant support, her readings and rereadings, her thoughtful suggestions and her literary insights, my dream as a writer would have remained just that. There is no one I would rather spend my life with than her.

To Farhan and Nabeel, who, in their childhood, insisted that I create stories for them. Their questions about why, what, when and how helped me structure my stories to their satisfaction. To Saara, who became our daughter and brightened our lives.

To my *bhaiya*, Safder, who introduced me to literature and sent me novels and plays from London that were not available in Karachi. He encouraged me to write when I showed him my first effort at Urdu poetry.

To all my other family members who have impacted my life and supported me in so many ways.

To Jack Luzkow, my best friend, who read several early and later drafts patiently and gave me much-needed encouragement and valuable suggestions.

To my friend and brother Lokesh Chaturvedi, who read an early draft of this novel and whom I'll always miss.

To May Maxwood and Hatice Husnu, my first readers, who always thought that my book was very publishable. I am grateful for all their support.

To Venugopalan Menon, my dear friend and roommate at university, for his wisdom and hours of conversations about films and literature. His concerns about my studies were fully noted.

To my dear friend Shashi Lalvani, whose family was also uprooted from Sindh during the Partition and whose love of the province I share.

To Karachi, my birthplace, for the beautiful memories that pepper this story.

Finally, I want to thank my editorial team at Penguin Random House India: Tarini Uppal, who took a chance on me and was unstinting in her generous guidance and expertise. Her emails always came promptly and as a wonderful boost; and Aslesha Kadian, whose careful reading and excellent suggestions helped me greatly. I was fortunate to have such brilliant editors.